THE
SCARECROW
KILLER

An unputdownable crime thriller full of twists

MARGARET MURPHY

Detective Cassie Rowan Series Book 2

Joffe Books, London
www.joffebooks.com

First published in Great Britain in 2023

Cover art by Nick Castle

ISBN: 978-1-80405-775-9

For Murf

CHAPTER 1

Early October, 6.30 a.m.

A frost sparkled on the grass verges under a clear sky and the eastern embankment of the M62 was just beginning to flush with pale, pre-dawn light. Fighting drowsiness, Detective Constable Cassie Rowan cracked a window and tried to focus on the road. For the last five days, she had worked her regular two-ten shift, then an overnight on call. Tuesday night she'd crawled into bed at eleven and was shocked awake at 3 a.m. by the jangling ringtone of her phone — a call-out at the south end of Liverpool. Now she was heading home, already fantasizing about a few hours of undisturbed sleep.

Her headlights caught a flash of movement through the scrubby striplings on the embankment: bright, metallic, kingfisher colours; a lightning strike of blue fire.

Rowan braked, craning for another look. Another a fleeting glimpse — a youth in a hoody and jogging bottoms, arms flailing, running full pelt down the hill.

'Bloody idiot!' she muttered. 'He'll get himself killed!'

She glanced away to negotiate a pothole — only for a second — but when she looked again, he was gone. Nerves atingle, she pulled over, loose stones clunking and pinging against the car's undercarriage. Opening the window, she leaned out to get a better view; the blue shimmer of his track-suit top was partially hidden at this angle, but he was still there — hiding maybe — waiting for her to go. Turning on her hazards, she jogged a hundred yards eastwards, back the way she'd come.

The road was quiet, and she listened intently, hearing only the piercing call of a robin in the undergrowth and the croak of a passing crow. The air was sharp and fresh, and the frosted blades of grass crunched under her feet.

Catching hold of a whippy birch sapling for balance, she glanced around, but at this distance, the motorway lights had little effect and the dawn seemed to add a greyish tinge, which drifted like a mist, in and out, obscuring her view. She took a breath and let her eyes fall shut as she exhaled.

Relax . . . He's gone.

A lorry thundered past, blaring its horn, and Rowan startled, opening her eyes wide just as the sun crested the embankment.

There — another glimpse of movement and shimmer-ing colour beyond the tangle of grasses and saplings on the slope.

'Hey!' She waved her arms, trying to draw the youth's attention.

He didn't answer, but he seemed to sway, his move-ments weird — *off* — as though his legs were boneless.

Drunk? Drugged maybe?

Rowan started up the incline again, and for a second she saw the figure clearly through the scrubby copse. The hackles rose on the back of her neck: he wasn't swaying, he was swinging — hanging from a tree.

Oh, Jeez, no . . .

Her heart hammering, Rowan scrambled up the slope, branches snatching at her clothing and thorns scratching her skin. By the halfway point her phone was in her hand and she was ready to make the call to Emergency Services. Fifteen feet short, she stopped, trying to make sense of the scene. The sun's rays, dazzling off the hanging figure, created a halo of colours and she squinted, bringing a hand up to shade her eyes.

'What the . . . ?'

It wasn't a body after all. It was a hoody and tracksuit bottoms, hung on clothes-hangers and arranged to look like a body. The top half of the oddly assembled jumble turned slowly on a faint stir of wind and Rowan's heart jumped sideways. The face was a horrible mask, round and mud-red. Its eyes, green, bulging and bloodshot, glared above a squat nose. Its mouth was stretched in a malevolent grin crowded with sharp interlocking teeth.

Fighting a wave of nausea, Rowan bent forward, hands on her knees, taking a few breaths to steady herself. Anger overtook her relief: this was deliberate, someone's sick idea of a joke. Controlling the urge to tear the thing down, instead she took a few snaps on her smartphone before keying in the Emergency Services' number. They needed to get the damned thing moved before it distracted another motorist and caused carnage.

She set off down the slope, her phone to her ear, but at a sudden bustle of noise in the undergrowth she paused, glancing over her shoulder. An animal? Someone hiding? At that moment, flashing blue lights appeared further down the road: a police patrol still half a mile off, but approaching fast. Rowan groaned. She had hoped to make a quick call and go on her way. This meant introductions and explanations, further delays, keeping her from her bed and longed-for sleep. With a sigh, she disconnected the call and waited beside her Renault Clio.

The patrol car pulled in behind hers, and one of the cops climbed out, signalling her to stay on the slope and make her way to him along the embankment. Rowan knew most cops in the area by sight, but this one was new to her and she could see by the look on his face that he was preparing to launch into a stern warning about the dangers of stopping on the hard shoulder.

She slipped her phone into her pocket and pulled out her warrant card, announcing herself as police, and his expression changed to guarded curiosity. He took her ID and spoke into his shoulder mic, relaying her details to the cop inside the car. Rowan knew that her car number plate would have been read automatically and checked against several national databases; they would already know that she was the registered vehicle owner, and the Renault had not been flagged in any crime.

A moment later the cop handed back her card with a nod of acceptance and introduced himself.

'I'm guessing you're responding to a shout about a lad seen running down the embankment on the westbound carriageway between junctions six and five,' she said.

He seemed to debate for a moment how much he wanted to open up to her. Then she registered a micro-shrug as if to say, *What the hell.*

'Another motorist dialled triple-nine,' he said. 'We do get a few mad arses, taking a shortcut between Fernleigh and the new Turner Homes' development on the other side of the motorway.'

Fernleigh was a 1970s social-housing project. It was never her patch when she was on the beat, but everyone in the city knew it by reputation.

'Find anything?' he asked.

'Looks like a prank,' she said. 'Hoody and trackie bottoms hung in a tree about thirty metres that way.' She jerked her chin, indicating the direction.

The second cop joined them.

'Bloody kids . . .' he muttered. Screwing up his eyes against the glare of the sun, he began trudging off up the hill.

'Typical distraction tactic,' the first cop said. 'They know we'd have to check this out. Guaranteed — as we speak — there'll be two or three of the little shitheads knocking off a nice new Beamer on the new estate.'

'D'you want me to call it in?' Rowan said before she could stop the words coming out of her mouth. 'If you want

4

to check the Turner residents' cars are safely parked on their driveways . . .'

He shook his head, watching his partner scramble to the top of the ridge. 'My boss'd have my balls dangling from his rearview mirror by dinnertime if I walked away from this.' He winced. 'That was a bit graphic, wasn't it?'

Rowan disguised her relief at being exempted from the task with a laugh. 'I've heard worse,' she said.

He rubbed his chin. 'Thing is, some silly sod ended up as a bloody smear on this stretch of road a few months back, splattered thirty yards down the outside lane by a haulage lorry.'

This time, it was Rowan who winced, thinking, *Now that was graphic*. 'Traffic's building,' she said. 'I should leave you to it.'

'Need me to guide you back onto the carriageway?' he asked, like the good traffic cop he was.

'I'll manage,' she said, and he turned away to follow his colleague. The lettering of his high-vis vest reflected the early sunshine in a blinding flare of white light that triggered an image of the startling burst of orange, cyan and blue she'd glimpsed through the saplings on the motorway embankment and Rowan felt again the initial adrenaline-spike of shock.

CHAPTER 2

A week later

Thirty-seven minutes, thirty seconds.

Cassie Rowan pushed the button on her smartwatch to record her run and swung her backpack from her shoulder to retrieve her house keys, experiencing a warm glow that wasn't entirely down to the heat and sweat of the three-mile run home from a training session. She hadn't quite achieved her eleven-minute-mile goal, but it was within reach. It was 6.30 p.m., and dusk was closing in fast under cloudy skies. She listened at the bottom of the stairs for signs that Neil was home, but when she called her brother's name, there was no reply. She chugged a glass of water before heading upstairs; his bedroom door stood open and the bed was rumpled, but empty. It wasn't a good sign.

Shaking off the vague but persistent feeling of anxiety she'd been carrying around since last winter, she headed for the bathroom to shower, and ten minutes later she was listening to Radio Merseyside while she cooked prawns and angel-hair pasta for dinner.

The spell of dry weather was set to continue, it seemed, which was good for her training schedule. Rowan opened the back door to let the scent of the last summer roses drift into the kitchen. The garden itself was no wider than her narrow little house: just eight strides would take you from the back door to the gate that gave onto the alleyway, but last spring Rowan had planted half a dozen roses recommended by a nursery grower for their heady scent and low maintenance and it had become her place of tranquillity, solace and escape.

She dished up her evening meal as the news-report jingle marked the hour, and listened with half an ear, steeling herself for the phone call she would have to make if Neil didn't show up soon.

Global crises, wars, government infighting and gloomy financial predictions dealt with, the newsreader turned to local news: a fatal accident on the M62 between junctions five and six; a police appeal for witnesses. Rowan paused, set her fork down. The youth had been found on the motorway hard shoulder in the dead of night, the announcer expanded. The skin of Rowan's arms raised in goosebumps — this was the very same stretch of motorway where she'd seen the strange puppet-like drapery of clothing hanging in the trees a week before.

For days after that incident, any dazzle of white light had triggered a flashback to the bright flicker of colour she'd seen beside the motorway, and she would catch her breath, remembering her first thought that it was a teenager hurtling to his death down the incline.

She abandoned her half-eaten meal and snatched up her smartphone to google the story.

Seventeen-year-old Damian Novak, the *Liverpool Echo* online reported, was likely run down as he tried to cross the road. She skimmed past two video ads before she found the rest of the story: the vehicle involved did not stop at the scene, and there were no witnesses.

Below the text, a grinning photo of the lad astride his off-road scrambler bike — illegally *on* a road near his home, as it happened — and flipping two fingers at the photographer. But that wasn't what had Rowan scrolling through the photo gallery on her phone: Damian was wearing a hoody and tracksuit bottoms that shone in iridescent orange, cyan and blue.

Rowan skimmed through close-up shots of the roses in her backyard garden, images of sunsets over the Mersey docks and screenshots of cars for sale, finally coming to a halt at the 'body', hanging from a scrappy little mountain ash on the embankment.

The kingfisher blues and oranges were identical to Damian Novak's clothing in the newspaper photo.

She tapped in the number for Merseyside Police Contact Centre and asked to be put through to the traffic division. In the few seconds it took for someone to pick up, she had dredged up from memory the name of the officer she'd spoken to at the roadside, but when she was put through, the traffic cop told her that the clothing from the roadside prank had been binned.

She rang round three police stations trying to find out who was investigating the death before she gave up and paged the duty coroner instead. Her shoulders sagged when she heard that Roy Wicks was the lead detective. She rang St Anne Street station, where he was based. Wicks was off duty, but she persuaded the operator to patch her through to his mobile.

'Well, this is unexpected,' he said.

Rowan heard a clamour of voices in the background. He must be in a pub.

'What can I do *you* for?'

She heard the innuendo in his tone and tried hard not to let it bother her.

'Hit-and-run death on the M62,' she said. 'Can you talk me through it?'

'What's it got to do with you?' he demanded, instantly aggressive.

'I witnessed an incident the week before — same stretch of motorway — it might be related.'

'What kind of incident?'

8

She knew that as soon as she told him, he would dismiss her concerns. So she said, 'I asked first.'

The noise of pub chatter swelled and subsided around him for a few moments, but, finally, he sighed, sniffed, and then spoke.

'I'm not convinced it *was* a hit-and-run. The lad was dressed head to toe in black — whoever hit him probably didn't even see the silly sod.'

'How bad was it?' she asked, recalling the traffic cop's story about a youth who'd been mangled by a truck on the same stretch of road.

'We didn't have to scrape him up, if that's what you're asking,' Wicks said.

'So probably not a heavy goods vehicle, then.'

'Haven't a clue. What's your point?'

'If it was a lorry, you'd expect a lot of mess, but the driver could be unaware he'd hit someone. But if it was something smaller — say, a van or a car — you'd expect the driver to feel the impact. In which case, it more likely was a genuine hit-and-run.'

Leaving the scene of an accident was a criminal offence, taken very seriously in law enforcement. Rowan could almost *hear* the cogs turning as Wicks realised he'd missed details that would warrant further investigation and possible imprisonment for the driver who'd hit Novak. A few seconds later, she heard a forced exhalation at the other end of the line.

'What's your interest?'

It was a fair question; this was not her case, and, strictly speaking, Wicks didn't have to speak to her at all. So, she described the odd collection of clothing she'd found hanging in the trees near the same spot just seven days earlier.

'This was on the westbound carriageway,' she finished. Wicks was unforthcoming, so she added, 'Was the body found on the west, or eastbound carriageway?'

He didn't answer at first, and when he did, he was terse. 'West. So what?'

'So, it's a bit coincidental, isn't it, Roy?'

9

'Look,' he said. 'Damian Novak was a scally, probably just finished a night's thieving on the posh new housing development on the other side of the motorway.'

'Big assumption.'

He snorted. 'You wanna take a look at his arrest record. Oh, and did I mention he was dressed head to foot in black? That's practically "going equipped". Also, the paramedic who pronounced said he "*reeked* of weed". This would be the paramedic who had "pronounced" life extinct. Had a baggy in his jacket pocket an' all.'

'He rode a scrambler bike.' Rowan wanted to add, 'Did you even *look* for a bike?' But she'd learned a modicum of tact in the past year.

'You're talking about the *Echo* snapshot?' Another snort. 'That picture was years old, the bike was stolen goods, and *he* was banned. There was no vehicle involved.'

'Surely there must have been *one*?'

Rowan heard a rumble down the line that might have been the grinding of teeth.

'You're making this more complicated than it needs to be, girl.'

She sucked her teeth at the word 'girl', seeing it as Wicks expressing his frustration. He hated complicated cases because they invariably meant extra work.

'Why don't you simplify it for me, Roy?' she said.

Wicks was the kind of cop who didn't need to be asked twice to expound a half-baked theory in the absence of evidence, and he launched straight in. 'Damian finishes thieving for the night. He's blissed out on weed, can't be arsed walking down to the nearest footbridge, so he decides to take a shortcut across *six lanes* of traffic, misjudges the speed, comes a cropper.'

'You might want to wait for the post-mortem results before you write this one off as misadventure,' Rowan said.

'The PM's done.'

'That was fast.' She couldn't hide her surprise.

'The body was found in the early hours yesterday. We got lucky: the pathologist managed to squeeze him in.'

At that moment, the front door opened, a second later, a slam. Neil had finally come home. She really needed to speak to him, but he clumped straight upstairs without so much as a hello. If she finished the conversation with Wicks now, Rowan couldn't be sure she'd be able to persuade him to cooperate on a later call, so she postponed her talk with Neil and said, 'Cause of death?'

A huff of laughter. 'Stupidity.'

'Wicks—'

He sighed. 'Internal bleeding.'

'And the vehicle?'

'What about it? The driver didn't stop, and there's no witnesses.'

'Traffic cams—'

'There's nothing between junction six and five,' he interrupted. 'So that's a non-starter.'

'It can't be more than two miles from junction five to the end of the motorway,' Rowan countered. 'Exit four is the terminal junction.' A wide and intricate tangle of roadways converged at the terminus — something Wicks would know very well. 'There's got to be eight or ten sets of traffic lights. And *plenty* of cameras.'

'Yeah, but if the driver was canny, he could've come off at five, or sneaked off at the little slip road by The Rocket, jinked into the suburbs.'

Avoiding an unnecessary argument, Rowan didn't point out that there must be *some* cameras at junction five, but she couldn't resist saying, 'You seem to be coming around to the idea that the driver *did* know they'd hit someone.'

'How's that?'

'If he was oblivious, why would he go to all that trouble to come off the motorway early and avoid the cameras?'

'It might be his normal route home.' He sounded irritated that he'd talked himself into a corner.

'Worth checking, though . . .'

'We haven't got a definite time of death,' he said, his tone rising. 'It'd be virtually impossible to find the vehicle.'

11

She began to protest, but he spoke over her again. 'Look, Cassie, I've got this, so if your curiosity's satisfied . . .'

Implying that he didn't have time for idle chat and prurient interest.

Rowan bit back a sarcastic apology for having interrupted his drinking time and said, 'One final question.'

An impatient sigh.

'Did the crime scene unit find any evidence that the kid actually *had* been thieving? Goods, tools, cash?'

'He had a wad of tenners in his back pocket,' Wicks said.

'So maybe he was selling some of that cannabis he had on him, rather than engaging in a spot of burglary?'

'Maybe.' Wicks's tone implied *who cares?* 'Either way, he was up to no good,' he finished.

Rowan wanted to circle back to the coincidence of the weird effigy she'd discovered the previous week, but as she offered to send him the photos she'd taken, she realized he'd cut her off.

CHAPTER 3

Monday morning

Rowan got to work early and went looking for Ian Chan. Although she was still based at the old police station in St Anne Street, the recently opened headquarters nearby housed a sleek new forensic-science annex, and it was to this building that she made her way at 8 a.m. She needed insider info on the RTI that had killed Damian Novak, and, as a senior crime-scene investigator, Chan would be in the know. Better yet — as a friend who thrived on any whiff of scandal, he'd be more than willing to share.

Chan was seated at a desk in a large open-plan office that smelled faintly of new plastic and fresh paint. Rowan took a moment to marvel at the difference between this and the scuffed and grimy building she worked from.

'So, this is where the gods of cyberspace hang out,' she said from the doorway.

Chan was frowning at his computer screen and typing furiously. He responded slowly, like someone waking from a dream.

''S'up?' He turned his head a few degrees while his eyes remained glued to the monitor.

'I was hoping you might be able to spare a minute for a bit of goss,' she said. 'But I can see you're busy . . .'

She took a step back.

'Don't you dare leave!' he exclaimed. 'I'll be finished in . . .' he lowered his voice, eyes still on the monitor, fingers rattling over the keys, 'just . . . thirty . . . seconds . . .'

She grinned and stepped smartly inside, taking in the arrays of equipment, the cleanliness — even the extravagant availability of plug, phone, and charger sockets, with not a trailing wire in sight.

Twenty seconds later, Chan threw up his arms and punched the air. 'Done!'

'Wow — I wish my job was as exciting,' she said.

'You're kidding? That was paperwork.' He got to his feet and performed a series of stretches. 'Don't let them fool you with their lies — it doesn't get any easier just because it's digital.'

He looked over his shoulder, mid-stretch, and pasted a look of such tragedy on his face she wanted to laugh. Instead, knowing what he wanted to hear, she murmured sympathetically.

He cheered up instantly and hopped onto the nearest table, his short legs dangling inches from the floor, and she perched opposite.

'What do you know about the seventeen-year-old killed on the M62 yesterday?'

'That depends,' he said, instantly and uncharacteristically cagey. 'Who's asking?'

'*I* am, Ian — I'm sitting right here.'

He narrowed his eyes. 'Yeah, but who sent you?'

'My insatiable curiosity.'

He still looked suspicious.

'God, Ian, why are you acting so weird?' she demanded.

'*Because* we took a bit of stick from the lead investigator,' Chan said.

'And you think I've come to put the boot in on Roy Wicks' behalf? And anyway, when did you ever take stick from anyone?'

He snorted, giving her a look that said the question wasn't worthy of an answer.

Ian Chan was gay and out and often wildly flirtatious, to the horror of his deeply conservative Christian parents. Rowan suspected that he sometimes amped up the camp just to get a reaction, and although he was better at office politics than she'd ever be, Rowan had never seen him back down in an argument.

'I've heard his version, but I want to know what *really* happened,' she said. 'I take it you were at the scene?'

'I was — and the great buffoon told us — *told* us, mind — to "scoop up the mess and take a few photies". Practically tearing up pages ten to fifteen of the Best Practice Manual in the process. Cheeky bugger even had the nerve to misquote the bloomin' thing at me,' Chan went on. 'Bawling me out on "cost effectiveness".'

'I'm guessing you got your way, though.'

'I told him if he wasn't willing to agree a scene examination strategy, I'd go ahead and do it myself, and our approach would be cautious, thorough — and very, *very* slow.'

Rowan chuckled. 'That'd do the trick.'

'Not quite. He put in a complaint to our crime scene coordinator, who in turn put in a complaint to Wicks' line manager. Wicks was — what's the word?' He tilted his head back, looking up at the brand-new LEDs overhead for inspiration. 'Chastised. His excuse: he was concerned about public safety, people trying to get to work. Like he ever worried about work — or Joe Public, for that matter!'

'Maybe I'll send him a copy of the manual in the internal post. Marked urgent.'

Chan laughed. 'I dare you.'

As they'd been talking, people had started to drift in, and Rowan felt eyes on her.

Chan glanced around and with a dismissive wave of the hand, said, 'Don't mind them.'

'Um . . . this isn't exactly an official query,' she murmured, trying not to look furtive.

'Oh, Cassie. You should know by now — *un*official usually lands you in a very mucky creek.'

'Yeah,' she said, with a familiar sense of doom. '*And* without a paddle. But in the tiny mind of our . . . mutual friend, the case is already written up, boxed and filed. The "facts" as he sees them are so set in his mind it'd take a sledgehammer to shift him.'

'Well, you've got your passionate face on, so it's no use trying to talk you out of it.' Chan watched her for a few seconds. 'Go on, I'm listening.'

Rowan hesitated; she *really* didn't want to talk in front of his colleagues.

'I haven't got all day,' he urged, enjoying the attention. 'Are you going to tell me what's got you all fired up?'

She needed to give him just enough to make him want the details all for himself if she was to prise him from his spot centre stage, so after a moment's thought Rowan said, 'A puppet, dancing on the M62 embankment.'

Chan's eyes widened; he looked thrilled, as she'd hoped he would be.

'*That*, I was *not* expecting to hear.' He made a graceful dismount from his perch and jerked his head towards the door. 'Coffee?'

Two minutes later they were seated in a break room with miraculously clean tables and a passable cup of coffee each — vending machine, rather than filter — but you can't have everything, Rowan reflected.

'Okay,' Chan said, sitting opposite her. He leaned forward and looked her in the eye. 'A *puppet*?'

Rowan told him about the incident a week ago when she'd thought she had seen a youth hurtling down a hill at edge of the motorway to the east of the city. She described vividly the flash of colour and movement as he ran through the trees, arms pinwheeling, and her subsequent discovery of clothing carefully hung from a tree to look like a body.

Chan held out his hand. 'Pictures?'

She located the snaps she'd taken on her smartphone and watched as he swiped through them.

He exclaimed in disgust at the final two — both of the mask. 'Nasty,' he said with a shudder then, peering closer, he pinched and enlarged the image, sliding to the bottom of the frame.

Rowan angled her body, craning to get a look at the screen. 'D'you see something?'

'This Blakedale Marker.'

Rowan had included the marker — strictly called a 'driver location post' — at the bottom of the embankment. Spaced at regular intervals along major roadways, they identified the road, the carriageway and the location, so that the emergency services could be easily directed to an incident.

'Yup,' Chan said, reading the marker. 'That's *exactly* where we found the body.'

Rowan experienced a fizz of excitement.

'And our roly-poly friend doesn't see a connection?' Chan said.

'Coincidence, he says. According to him, the driver of the vehicle was unaware he'd hit anything.' Rowan kept her tone neutral.

'And he bases this theory on . . . ?'

'A combination of wild surmise and ergophobia,' she said, deadpan.

'Ergophobia — is that a *thing*?'

'An extreme and irrational fear of work,' she said. 'I looked it up.' She saw Chan commit that one to memory. 'Plus, the victim was a scally, *ergo* he got what was coming to him.'

He gave her a narrow look.

'Okay, that one, I did make up,' she admitted with a smile.

But Chan wasn't smiling. In fact, a small furrow had appeared between her friend's perfectly plucked brows. As someone who had been subjected to racial and sexual prejudice for most of his life, Ian Chan had a particular dislike for people who judged, categorized and dismissed others without a second thought.

'Ri-ight,' Chan said, like a man mentally taking off his gloves ready for combat. 'What d'you need to know?'

Rowan sifted through the questions she wanted to ask, knowing full well that, as this was not her investigation, she had no right to ask them.

'Wicks is convinced that the driver would not have been aware of the impact, but he *also* said that the cause of death was massive internal bleeding.' She raised her shoulders. 'I can't square the two.'

'That hill *is* steep, and if the kid *was* running, he might not have been able to stop at the bottom,' Chan said, as always dispassionate in scientific analysis. 'It's possible he ran into the *side* of a lorry and fell under the wheels — in which case, the driver might not have felt it.' He paused, gave a small shake of his head. 'But if that was the case, you'd expect to see more blood at the scene.'

'How much was there?' Rowan asked.

'Almost none — and considering the kid had multiple breaks of upper and lower limbs, and his nose was broken, you'd might've expected more. But there were no compound fractures, so . . .'

This meant no bones sticking through skin, and Rowan had seen enough broken bodies on roadways during her earlier years in uniform to know that RTIs weren't always bloody.

'He had slight abrasions to his forehead and left cheek,' Chan went on. 'He was lying face down when he was discovered, so the injuries might've happened as he fell. We retrieved particles of road grit from the wounds, but nothing to suggest he'd been dragged. Or, you know . . . squelched. Some lattice-patterned bruising on his left shoulder and chest — possibly from a van grille — but it's not well-defined and we haven't identified it.'

'Any glass or plastic from the vehicle?' Rowan was thinking headlamps or wing-mirror shards.

'None,' Chan said.

'Isn't that odd?'

He shrugged. 'Depends what part of the vehicle hit him.'

She exhaled, frustrated but determined to work through all the possibilities. 'Damian had weed in his pockets, and a wad of money; Wicks's theory is that he was on the rob over on the Turner Homes' estate.'

Chan grimaced. 'Nice theory, but there's bugger all to substantiate it. We picked up the usual roadside rubbish during evidence collection, but nothing of evidential value. And if the lad had been doing a spot of B and E, he wasn't tooled up for it when we got to him.'

'According to Wicks, wearing black is as good as.'

That earned her a scornful glance.

'I couldn't agree more,' she said. 'If he was out for a bit of burglary, he wasn't tooled up. According to Wicks, all he had on him was a small quantity of weed and a bundle of notes. But let's for the sake of argument say Novak was chased; he might've chucked his B and E gear.'

'It's *possible*,' Chan conceded. 'But if he did, it would have to've been on the exec estate — because, honey, we searched that carriageway *and* the embankment for a good hundred and fifty yards in either direction. And as for the money — he had a cool three hundred and fifty in his back pocket.'

Rowan stood. 'Okay, that does it.'

'What? Where are you off to?' Chan said, steadying her coffee cup, which was in danger of toppling.

'I'm gonna do what Wicks should be doing. I'm going to investigate.'

Chan held both hands up. 'Woah, woah, woah. You can't elbow him out of the way and take over his case — you'll get yourself suspended!'

'I *know* that, Ian. I'll take it to the boss, first.'

'Well, mind your manners. And — I'm saying this because I love you — *pur-lease*, Cassie, in the name of all that's holy, *think* before you engage that gob of yours.'

CHAPTER 4

Detective Chief Inspector Warman's door stood open, and Warman sat at her desk with three perfectly squared-off stacks of paper arrayed left, right, and dead centre of the scratched melamine top. She was typing something on a laptop, while referring to the stack of flimsies to her left.

Rowan took a deep breath, squared her shoulders, and knocked. This would be the hard part.

Warman looked up. 'Cassie.' No smile, no warmth of welcome in the older woman's voice.

Having worked with Warman for nearly a year, Rowan knew that it wasn't personal: this was her boss's default position. Her expression was habitually sour, her manner brusque and often forbidding, though Rowan had learned that she was capable of compassion. She believed procedure and good organization got results, and, for most purposes, it did, but she lacked imagination — and that had brought Rowan into conflict with her boss more than once.

'The seventeen-year-old killed in an RTC on the M62,' Rowan began.

Warman fixed her with her flat stare. 'What about him?'

'The investigating officer is convinced the driver of the vehicle was unaware,' Rowan said. 'But the victim had catastrophic internal injuries. It doesn't seem credible; the driver must have felt or heard the collision.'

Warman tilted her head. 'And why would this be any of your business?'

Rowan guessed her line about a puppet dancing on the M62 wouldn't intrigue DCI Warman in the way it had Ian Chan, so she gave her boss the cop-in-a-courtroom version of her encounter on the motorway the week before.

'I took a few shots.' She found an image in her phone gallery and placed her mobile on the desk in front of the chief inspector.

Warman closed her laptop and set it aside before looking at the image.

'Well, it is October, Halloween approaching. The mask suggests—'

'Yes, but the victim's body was found at *exactly* the same location.'

'Really? My understanding was the body was on the carriageway, and this photograph looks like it was taken on an embankment.'

Of course she would know — Warman made it her business to know the cogent details of every investigation under her purview. And she hated imprecision; Rowan was losing her.

'I didn't mean on that exact spot — but the geographical location is the same.' She swiped through the images on her phone to one taken from the verge. 'See the road marker? The body was found close to that specific road marker—'

Stop, Cassie. Stop. She'd already let slip that she'd made enquiries without permission. Adding a gabbled a self-justification would only alienate the DCI further. So, she took a breath and started again.

'Initially I thought it was a prank, too.' She retrieved her phone from Warman's desk and googled the article in the *Echo*, scrolling to the photograph of Damian Novak. 'Until I saw this.'

Warman took the phone from her and stared at the image of their hit-and-run victim, grinning, proud and defiant in the blues and oranges of his bird-bright sports gear. Watching her anxiously, Rowan saw her boss's eyebrows rise a millimetre and for first time in the last five minutes she looked less sceptical.

Switching between the photo in the news article and Rowan's scene image, she said, 'They look identical. Was he wearing this when he died?'

Rowan shook her head. 'He was kitted out for scally business.'

A muscle in Warman's cheek jumped, pulling tight the skin along the knife's edge of her jawline. She liked her facts clear and unadorned, with no possibility of confusion. 'I take it you mean black?'

'As sin.'

Apparently fascinated by the likeness, Warman continued swiping between the two images on her phone. 'It *is* an odd coincidence, isn't it?'

'That's pretty much what I said to Wicks.'

Warman glanced up sharply. 'You've already spoken to the investigating officer?'

'I thought he would want to see the pictures I took at the scene last week,' Rowan explained.

'And?'

'He hung up on me.'

Warman handed back the phone. 'You didn't report this incident at the time?'

Rowan bridled. Why did Warman always try to catch her out in some kind of wrongdoing?

'Traffic was on the scene before I even had chance to put a call through,' Rowan said, trying hard to keep the resentment out of her tone. 'And like I said, it looked like a prank. I didn't really think about it again till last night, when I saw Damian's photo in the *Echo*.'

Warman fixed her with her blue-grey eyes. 'Why did you bring this to me, Cassie?' she asked.

'Because Wicks isn't listening,' Rowan said. 'And I need to know if the clothing, the death, the location really *are* all coincidences.'

'You think somebody deliberately rigged the clothing to look like a real person?'

There was no question in her mind, but Rowan said, 'I think it should be investigated.'

That seemed to satisfy something in Warman's ordered psyche. 'Which would involve making inquiries . . .'

'A few.'

'People don't like having their cases snatched from under their noses.'

'I'm not aiming to,' Rowan said, irritated that Ian Chan and now her boss had assumed that was her intention. 'I just want to—'

'You and Wicks have a history,' Warman interrupted. 'And I'm not sure I could justify your poking around in what looks like a simple road accident.'

'Boss, I know it looks that way. Teenagers take stupid risks — it's practically written in their DNA — I accept that. But the fact is, Wicks isn't even bothering to gather evidence — and he's twisting what he *has* got to fit his own theory.'

'For example?'

'Cannabinoids showed up in Damian's tox screen,' she said. 'Wicks assumes that's why he ended up as roadkill.'

'It's a reasonable assessment.'

'Yeah, but he's conveniently forgetting that Damian also had three hundred and fifty quid in his pocket, and a bag of weed.'

'Indicating he might have been peddling the stuff,' Warman said. 'And from what I understand, he has form for it. But that doesn't change the fact that he did have drugs in his system. If he'd sampled the goods, he might well have made a dash to cross the motorway, realizing too late that he'd mistimed it.'

'So, why didn't the driver stop? And why isn't Wicks looking for the vehicle?'

'I will ask him that,' Warman said firmly.

Rowan was about to say, 'Knock yourself out — you know he'll ignore it.' But Chan's advice came back to her, and she felt her face flush to think he'd predicted that she would end up saying something she'd regret. *Engage the brain, Cassie*, she told herself.

'Thank you, boss.' She backed towards the door, then, as if the thought had only just occurred to her, asked, 'Would it be all right if I followed up on the clothing, though? That effigy was really weird.'

From the look on her face, Warman was about to say no, but Rowan forestalled her.

'I'll be discreet.'

Warman looked far from convinced, but after a moment of hesitation, she said, 'Just the clothing — you are *not* to meddle in Wicks's investigation. Clear?'

'Absolutely.'

'The emphasis is on "discreet", Cassie. Talk to a few contacts, ask a few questions. *Avoid* ruffling feathers.' She paused, her gaze fixed on Rowan for an uncomfortable few seconds. 'Tread carefully.'

'On tiptoe,' Rowan said. 'He won't even know I'm there.'

CHAPTER 5

Rowan called the coroner's office, asking to speak to the officer dealing with the Damian Novak inquest and was surprised to hear a voice she recognized.

'*Hoff?*' she exclaimed.

She had worked with Hoff — real name Peter Kirkhof — on her first big case. Although her initial role had involved her posing as a sex worker — minus the Hollywood glamour of *Pretty Woman* — she had ended up netting a serial rapist and killer, and she could not have done it without Hoff bending the rules to help her.

'What are you doing at the coroner's office?' she asked.

'Me job — what d'you think?' Hoff spoke in guttural tones inherited from his Dutch parents, enhanced by the catarrhal catch in the throat that made the Liverpool accent unique.

'Don't tell me you've retired?' Rowan felt a hole open up in the pit of her stomach: Hoff had been her backup on many of those freezing November nights, driving the unmarked police surveillance van, stocking it with blankets in case she needed a break to warm up, and making sure that there was always a flask of hot coffee to hand. He'd fussed over her like a dad.

'Why didn't you tell me?' she said. 'Did I miss the party?'

'Nah — I kept it quiet, didn't I? Didn't want no fuss,' he growled. 'Me pipes aren't what they used to be, and a nice cosy billet indoors is just what the doctor ordered.'

Hoff's 'pipes' as he called them, hadn't been what they used to be for a good ten years; he'd earned the moniker, 'Hoff the Koff', long before Rowan had met him, owing to his thirty-a-day smoking habit.

'I'm still on the payroll,' he said. 'Only the hours are better, and you take a lot less crap.'

'Less money, too,' Rowan said.

'Don't let my youthful good looks fool you.' He chuckled and the fluid in his chest gurgled like a drain. 'I've put in me thirty years, and then some. I heard there was a job going at the coroner's office, so I took the golden handshake and applied. They're practically chucking money at me these days.'

Rowan laughed.

'What d'you want to know about Damian Novak, then?' he asked. 'Checking up on soft lad?'

Hoff had no time for lazy police, and he'd been there when Rowan had been injured because of Wicks' sloppy work.

'No — I'm just following up on an incident that might or might not be related and I wanted to get your take on what happened to Damian.'

The pause at the other end of the line told her there was a story to tell. Finally, he said, 'This is just between us?'

'I'd prefer that . . .'

'Okay then. My *first* impression is, whoever gave this one to Roy Wicks wants his bumps feeling.'

Rowan said a silent 'Amen' to that.

'But you're prob'ly more interested in what the family had to say?'

The coroner's officer would be the first point of contact between the family and the coroner's court.

'You're a bloody mind reader, Hoff.'

'Flatterer.'

He paused and, hearing a faint wheeze, she wondered if Hoff had been retired on health grounds, but was too proud to admit it.

'It's just the mum and two surviving children,' he began. 'A boy and a girl. My feeling is that Mum has been struggling with this and that for a long while. In the short time I've been working here, I've seen three kinds of response from the bereaved: dignified and restrained; close-lipped and resentful, and then there's the type who pour out their hearts.'

'Which category does Mrs Novak fall into?'

'She kept me on the phone for half an hour.'

'Did she say anything useful?'

'Not really. Didn't know why her son might've been on the motorway at one in the morning. Apparently, Wicks had asked her why Damian had a roll of banknotes on him. She swore she'd racked her *brains* but couldn't explain it. Couldn't call to mind the names of his mates and she "honest to God" couldn't think of anyone who would want to hurt her boy . . .'

'Considering *her boy* had just finished a three-year stint at HMP Altcourse for manslaughter — he got released a year early on licence — I'm thinking she's either blind, deluded or lying.'

'My gut feeling?' Hoff said. 'She's "self-medicating".'

'Legally, or illegally?'

'I've only spoke to her over the phone,' he said. 'You'd have to judge that one for yourself, girl.'

She knew she shouldn't: Warman had sanctioned a few calls to contacts, discreet questions asked over a brew in the canteen or a pint in the pub; talking to the family would take her over the line. But she said it, anyway. 'You wouldn't happen to have their address handy?'

CHAPTER 6

An hour later, Rowan was sitting in a fifth-floor flat in Brackenhill Tower on the Fernleigh estate. Gina Novak was grey skinned, her face scarred by battles with a thousand troubles. The room was large but furnished with two outsize sofas, a leather recliner and a mismatched armchair, further encumbered by a TV, X-box, various gadgets, and at least a year's-worth of discarded free newspapers. Not a single window stood open, despite the heat blasting out from two radiators either end of the room.

Mrs Novak's two surviving children lounged unhappily on each of the sofas — the girl, Lily, with head bent and shoulders stooped, scrolled endlessly through social media on her mobile phone; the boy, Lukas, seemed tense. He chewed his nails compulsively, his eyes darting every now and then to the door into the hallway in transparent desperation.

Rowan sat in the armchair opposite Mrs Novak and nearest to the door, per police protocol for interviews with no backup. There was nothing she could do if Lukas decided to bolt out of the flat, but her presence so near to it would at least discourage him.

Mrs Novak's hand shook as she sipped from a mug and in a complaining voice she repeated to Rowan what she'd said to Hoff over the phone. Rowan listened sympathetically, slipping in a question here, an observation there. Mrs Novak's pink-rimmed eyes seeped the whole while and she wiped her nose with a paper tissue, which slowly disintegrated as she worked it like a stress ball in her fist. Rowan handed her a fresh one, glancing quickly at her two children, neither of whom had shown the least concern for their mother.

Lily, who had to be all of thirteen years, wore slashed jeans and a crop top revealing a tanned belly and a fair amount of puppy-fat. She must have spent the best part of the morning doing her make-up and hair: highlights, lowlights, volumizer, frizz-control — she looked like she'd had the lot. Lukas, a year or two younger, had the scally haircut of the moment: shaved at the sides, longer and layered on the top, brushed forward to create a fringe. He was dressed for action from his branded sportwear to his dayglo socks. A gleaming pair of white trainers — fresh out of the box it seemed — completed the look. He was quietly, and quite determinedly, paring away the flesh of his left thumb with the nail of his right.

'Did Damian tell either of you why he might be going out so late at night?' Rowan asked.

The boy froze, staring fixedly at his thumb, which was by now oozing blood.

'Lukas?' she prompted.

'Nah,' he said. 'I didn't even know he was out.' He stuck the bleeding thumb in his mouth, looking like the baby he really was. His sister smirked, eyeing him quickly over the top of her phone, and he hastily jammed his hand into his pants pocket.

'You've seen the picture of Damian on the *Liverpool Echo* website?' Rowan asked.

Mrs Novak nodded mutely, Lily gave an irritated shrug, but Lukas's face pinched for a fraction of a second, and she saw fear in his expression.

'Did he still have the hoody and sweatpants?'

Lily scoffed. 'That was *ages* ago.' She seemed to take it as a personal insult that her brother would be accused of wearing old clothes.

Rowan nodded. 'That's what I thought.' There had been a brief revival of the shiny nineties-style shell suit four or five years ago, which meant the *Echo* photo must have been taken around the time Damian was prosecuted for the death of the elderly woman. 'So, you didn't give the picture to the paper?'

Mrs Novak shook her head, perplexed.

Lily spoke up again. 'It was the one they used when he got done.'

'After the accident,' Rowan prompted.

Lily jerked her head in acknowledgement and went back to scrolling through her phone.

It seemed odd that the journalist hadn't asked for an up-to-date image. Rowan made a mental note to ask why.

'The reason I'm here,' she said, choosing her words carefully, 'is something . . . strange happened last week, when I was driving down that stretch of motorway.'

Mrs Novak seemed out of it, but the girl glanced up, curious, and although Lukas avoided her eye, he paled, and his right hand curled tightly.

Rowan described the assembled clothing she'd found on the motorway embankment and saw the first signs of real distress in Lily's face.

Rowan selected an image that didn't feature the grotesque mask and turned the screen towards them, watching each of them closely. Lily leaned forward and a moment later, grasped Rowan's hand and pulled her closer.

'Oh my God . . .' She turned to her mother. 'Mum, look,' she urged. 'It's our Damian's — his exact same kit.'

But Mrs Novak had sunk into apathy, and she waved the girl away.

Lukas, meanwhile, had crossed his arms and was staring at the toes of his running shoes.

He's fighting tears, Rowan realized.

'Lukas,' she said, gently, and he flinched as though she'd shouted.

He glanced in the general direction of the screen. 'Yeah,' he said. 'Creepy.'

'Do you have any idea what it might mean?'

He turned his dark blue eyes on her and she saw that he was terrified. He tried to cover it by tipping his head forward and combing his fingers through the longer hair on the crown of his head.

Hiding, Cassie thought. *He's hiding.* 'Lukas, if you know something—'

'Nah,' he said, at last. 'Don't know nothing.'

That was a lie, but she let it go for the moment; Lukas wasn't about to open up in front of his mother and sister.

'How about you, Lily?' she asked.

Lily shrugged.

'Could someone have been playing a practical joke on Damian?'

'Some joke,' the girl said.

'People can be cruel,' Rowan replied.

'Tell me about it.' Lily glanced at her phone, and a small crease appeared on her brow.

Rowan had seen some of the social media attacks on the family: mean jokes about sewer rats and roadkill; righteous comments to the effect that you reap what you sow; outright condemnation of the mother, and vile remarks and suggestions about her surviving children. Lily would be having a bad time of it.

'Was Damian being bullied?'

The girl snorted.

'Okay . . . Did he seem worried, or more anxious than usual?'

No answer.

'Come on, Lily . . .'

Lily huffed a sigh. 'He was freaking out about something the week before . . .'

'Any idea what?'

'We didn't talk that much,' Lily said. Rowan heard the slightest emphasis on 'we' and caught a fleeting glance at the younger brother.

'Oh?'

'He was out a lot, wasn't he?' the girl said, belligerent.

'And when he *was* home?'

'He spent most of the time in his bedroom.'

Rowan's tone had been unchallenging, but Lily was definitely on the defensive.

'Would it be all right if I take a peek at his room?'

The girl slid her mother a sly glance, and Mrs Novak seemed to rouse as if from sleep.

'No, it would *not*. Nobody give a *toss* about my boy till this happened,' she said. 'Suddenly you show up at my door, and it's all, "We're *soo-o* sorry, Mrs Novak." Well, *I'm* sorry an' all. That lad put bread on this table, and now he's gone.' She pointed at Rowan with one bony finger. 'If *you* wanna see inside his bedroom, I wanna see a warrant.'

Rowan blinked at the sudden switch from exhausted and drug-befuddled stupor to sharp-tongued harpy. 'I'm not trying to catch anyone out, Mrs Novak. I just want to find out what happened to your son.'

'Ah, that's nice of you, girl,' she said, her face hard. 'But you're still gonna need that warrant.'

'I'm sorry I upset you,' Rowan said, not wanting to stoke the woman's evident hostility.

'You know what?' Mrs Novak said. 'I've had enough of this. I want you out of here. Now.'

Rowan stood, taking a business card from her pocket. 'If you think of anything, my direct line number is on my card.' She held it out, but Mrs Novak kept her hands stubbornly in her lap, so she placed it on the arm of the sofa.

Lily had returned to her phone screen and young Lukas was picking at his thumb again, but, although they affected bored disinterest, they both looked tense — as if anticipating a mighty thunderclap.

32

Rowan addressed the girl directly. 'As I said, Lily, people can be cruel — their own unhappiness makes them bitter — and bitterness turns people nasty. They'll lash out at the easiest target — at people they feel they can hurt most. Right now, that's you and your brother, and your mum.'

'What would *you* know about it?' Lily stared at her with the same blue eyes as her brother.

'More than I'd like.' Rowan held her gaze. 'You should think about suspending your account for a week or two.'

The girl's face was such a picture of horror, you'd think Cassie had counselled her to gouge out her eyes with a spoon.

'People will vent their hate and tear strips off each other with or without you as a witness.' Rowan tried again. 'You don't have to watch them do it.'

Lily glanced back at her phone, then briefly — despairingly, it seemed — to her mother for corroboration. But Mrs Novak ignored the child, glaring instead at Rowan. Finally, she hauled herself to her feet as if her spare frame carried a terrible burden.

'Out,' she said. 'Now.'

Rowan had parked her car in one of the bays beneath the adjacent tower block. As she approached it, she saw three youths, maybe fourteen or fifteen years old, peering in at the windows; one was built like a barrel, the other two were skinny and shifty-eyed; all were dressed in sports casuals. The smaller of the skinny boys nudged the big lad, and they all straightened up, watching her approach, but holding their ground.

A few yards away, Rowan said, 'Make me an offer; I've been trying to get rid of this tin can since April.'

Barrel Boy dug his hands into his pockets; he was standing next to the driver's door. 'I could just take it.' He didn't give an inch when Rowan arrived next to him, and the other two watched avidly, waiting for his signal.

Rowan smiled. 'But then I'd have to arrest you.'

A shadow of uncertainty passed across the boy's irises.

'Thanks for looking after it, though,' she said, relaxing her stance, giving him the opportunity to stand down without losing face. The skin around his eyes tightened. Two bands of red appeared on his cheekbones, and she realized she'd offended him. Looking after cars for a quid a time was a kids' game, and this scouse scally saw himself as very much the man.

The boy drew himself to his full height and leaned towards her. 'How about you show me some ID?'

'That's not how it works,' Rowan said. 'But you're making me late for work and technically, that's obstructing a police officer in the course of her duty. If I arrest you — *that's* when you could legitimately ask to see my warrant card.'

His eyes flitted to the middle floors of the tower block, and she saw something spark in them. He knew why she was there.

'So, what's it to be?' she said.

At last, he gave way and she opened the door. But he was still standing too close, and she wasn't about to squeeze into the narrow gap he'd allowed, so she waited, staring into his eyes with a cold amusement she didn't feel, aware of the other two circling to her back. Finally, he stepped away, with a chivalrous wave of his hand.

Instead of heading out of the estate, Rowan drove a little deeper into it, parked her car, and returned to a vantage point at the corner of the area she'd just quitted, partly concealed by a support pillar under the awning of the next tower block. The three urban jackals had melted away; she didn't think she would have any more trouble from them — at least not today.

While she kept vigil, Rowan recapped her exchange with the bereaved family. Of the three, Lukas had seemed the most uneasy: picking at his thumbnail, avoiding her gaze — and he *really* hadn't wanted to look at the picture on her mobile phone. As if he knew what he would see, and he was in horror of it. Yes, Rowan thought, Lukas Novak knew a lot more than he'd owned up to.

She waited ten minutes, certain he wouldn't stay in the flat any longer than he had to, but there was no sign of the boy. She'd sneaked out on her lunch break; soon she would be missed at work. But just as she was about to give up, a small figure appeared from under the building's awning, and Lukas Novak appeared.

She drew deeper into the shadows, watching him cross the space diagonally, heading straight towards her. Rowan retreated to the shelter of a service doorway, stepping out only as he was about to pass.

Lukas leapt like a cat, swearing colourfully, and a second later was up on his toes, ready to run.

'Don't,' she warned. 'I'm sure you're fast, but I'm faster, and if I have to chase you, it'll piss me off, and I *will* take you in.'

He dropped the running stance and glowered at her.

'What's wrong, Lukas?'

'Nothin'.' He squirmed like his skin itched.

'You're hiding something.'

'I don't know what you're on about.' He jumped at a sudden clatter of noise to their right and threw a frightened glance over his shoulder. 'Look, I can't be seen talking to you, miss.' His voice was piping and loud with anxiety.

'You won't be seen if you stay in the shadows. And *keep your voice down.*'

He gulped.

'I want to help you, Lukas,' Rowan said. 'I *know* something is bothering you—' He began to shake his head, but she raised a finger to stay him. 'You were scared to even look at the picture.'

He puffed out his narrow chest. 'I'm not scared of nothin'.'

'Okay,' she held up her phone, 'if that's true, take a look at it now.' She clicked to the clothing hanging from a tree on the motorway embankment.

The boy flinched, closing his eyes for a second and pushing her hand away.

'*Everyone* is scared of *something*, Lukas,' Rowan said. 'It's normal — healthy even. As long as you don't let it own you.'

35

The smooth skin between his brows crinkled as he tried to make sense of what she'd said.

'Fear protects us from danger,' she explained. 'But it can also make us do stupid things.' She paused. 'Like you not telling me what you're so afraid of.'

He lowered his eyes and tucked his chin under.

'Did your brother tell you something? Was someone trying to frighten him with this?' She held up her phone again.

'I dunno.'

'Lukas—'

'I *don't*.' He looked into her face, earnest, offended that she didn't believe him. 'I'm not *lying*, miss. Damian never said *nothin'*.'

Rowan studied his face. 'I believe you,' she said, and meant it. But she was just as sure that he wasn't telling her everything. 'Okay, let's think about this a different way. Your sister said Damian was freaking out about something. Did you notice anything odd about his behaviour or his mood in the week before this happened?'

The boy thought about it for a second. 'Nah. He was just — you know — D.'

'And he didn't mention seeing his old shellie on the motorway embankment?'

'Nah, I don't think he even seen it.'

'What makes you say that?'

'Cos he would've said something — joked about it — something . . .' Lukas sighed, and his shoulders slumped. 'I wish he *would've* said—'

He cut himself off, as though he felt he'd said too much.

'You wish he *had* said something, because . . . ?'

The boy bit his lower lip.

Rowan had a sudden insight. 'Because you knew something, and you wish you could've told him?'

He nodded miserably, his lower lip protruding, and Rowan felt a sudden pang of sorrow for the little boy so carefully camouflaged beneath the designer sports gear, remembering how Neil idolized his own big brother.

'What would you have told Damian, Lukas?'

He wiped a hand across his mouth — his unconscious mind telling him to shut up — but he went on, anyway. 'I would've told him what I seen, and then maybe he would've been careful, and he wouldn't have . . .'

'What did you see, Lukas?' she asked, her voice an encouraging murmur.

He swallowed, wiped his eyes and nose with the cuff of his lightweight jacket.

'This mate of mine died a few months back — and he *knew* he was a marked man.'

'How did he know?' Rowan said, not wanting to put words in his mouth.

'It was the *dummy*, wasn't it?'

'Dummy?'

'The one done up to look like him.'

'You mean *dressed* like him?' she asked, with a cold, creeping certainty of what she would hear.

'Trackie bottoms, hoody, watch, ankle tag, tat — all of it.' He frowned, scrolling through the images on his mobile phone, till he found what he was looking for.

What Rowan saw sent shivers up her spine. Lukas was showing her a mannequin made from a creamy-white material, the face sewn on, scarecrow-style: button eyes, lips made from red felt; the hair, just visible under a beanie hat, was made from wool yarn, twisted and tied to look curly and brown. The figure was dressed in the uniform most of the lads wore in this part of town: tracksuit bottoms, hooded top with The North Face logo emblazoned across the chest. The three-quarter-length trousers revealed an ankle tag and — crudely inked in marker pen — the tattoo of a leg iron with a few links of chain.

But most chilling was what had been done to the effigy. Its wrists were slit, the edges of the 'wounds' melted to stop them fraying. From the gashes, red silk ribbons cascaded, streaming down the dummy's torso and legs and pooling on the ground.

'This looks like your mate?' she asked.

'The tattoo, the clothes — everything — the exact same as Justin.'

'And Justin is dead?'

He nodded earnestly, his eyes huge.

Rowan pinched and expanded the image. The dummy seemed to be slumped against an aluminium barrel and lying on grit or grey asphalt.

'Where was this?'

'It was dumped by the bins at the back of his block.'

'Who saw it?'

'Me and Justin.'

'What happened to it?'

'He told me to cut it up and dump it.'

'And did you?'

'Yeah,' he said, in a tone that said *duh!*

'It was good thinking, taking a snapshot.'

She saw a little boy's pride in being praised warring with his need to maintain his tough persona.

'Did you take any more? Different angles maybe?'

'Swipe left,' he said.

The next image showed more of the context, and at the bottom left of the picture, Rowan could see a smudge of muddy colour. She magnified the image and slid the smudge to the centre of the screen. It resolved into a mask identical to the one she'd found attached to the clothing on the embankment.

'This mask . . .' she said.

'Justin took it off.'

Again, she was careful to lead him. 'Took it off . . . ?'

'Off the *dummy!*'

'This mask was on the dummy?'

'That's what I said, didn't I? And when he took it off, *his* face was underneath.'

'Did you show this to anyone?'

He shrugged. 'A few of me mates.'

'The police?'

'I'm not a grass,' he snarled, outraged.

'So, why are you showing it to me, now?'

He hung his head.

'Lukas, it's okay, you can tell me . . .'

He cursed quietly under his breath, then gave a slight shrug. 'Justin said he'd kill whoever done the dummy. But he's the one who ended up dead.' He looked up, and Rowan saw in his eyes a terror that he could be next.

Rowan stared at the blood-red silk tumbling from the effigy's arms. 'How did Justin die, Lukas?'

'Like that.' He held out his hand for the phone but couldn't bring himself to look at it.

Rowan pinged the two images to her own phone before handing it back. 'Now you have my number. That's my personal mobile. You see anything, you need help, you even feel a bit nervous — call me.' She held on to the phone till he met her eye. 'I mean it, Lukas,' she said. 'Anytime.'

CHAPTER 7

Pat Warman had just hung up the phone when Rowan reached her office door.

Rowan raised her fist to knock, but Warman waved her in.

'Close it,' Warman said.

That tone meant trouble.

She did as she was told. 'Boss?'

'I've received a complaint.'

Mrs Novak, Rowan thought. Then, *Roy Wicks*. Then, *the coroner's office*. She racked her brains, thinking who else might have taken offence from her off-the-record inquiries, while her boss eyed her disapprovingly.

For once, she managed to outwait the silence.

'DC Wicks says you've been questioning his witnesses.'

'If he means the family of the victim, then it's more than he did.'

'You can't possibly know that.'

Rowan thought back to her interview with the family; Mrs Novak had said, 'Suddenly *you* show up at my door.' Not 'youse' or 'you lot', plural, but '*you*', singular.

'Sorry, boss,' she said. 'But I've got the feeling that I was the first detective they'd seen.'

'Let's keep "feelings" out of this, shall we?' Warman said.

That stung, and Rowan knew it was intended to; her improved relationship with Warman was like treading a narrow line on a treacherous path — keep one eye on the distance so you see what's coming — but you'd better watch out for the odd stone that could turn your ankle and throw you down a ravine.

Warman speared her with a look that said *you've let me down. Again.*

'What happened to being discreet?'

Rowan clenched her jaw tight against saying what she really thought about Wicks's attempt to rush the CSU into bodging evidence collection at the scene, and then ignoring the victim's family. He'd been obstructive — even negligent — yet it was Rowan who found herself on the defensive. In policing, it was fine to grumble about a colleague's short-comings among your peers but criminals were not unique in hating snitches.

Ian Chan would tell her that Warman was only inter-ested in facts, so that's where she began. 'I spoke to the cor-oner's officer and the CSM,' Rowan said, willing herself to remain calm. She didn't mention that Hoff was her contact at the coroner's office or that the crime scene manager was Ian Chan himself, because, although neither was relevant, she was sure that Warman would take them less seriously simply because they were her friends.

'There was nothing to suggest that Damian Novak had been on a burglary spree on the Turner Homes estate: no tools, no stolen goods — either on his body, or dropped in a one-fifty metre radius of the scene.'

'That doesn't justify your decision to overstep the mark and speak to the family,' Warman said. 'Wicks is within his rights to put in a formal complaint.'

'Has he threatened to?'

Warman arched an eyebrow; apparently, she didn't think Rowan had the right to ask.

'Did he mention Justin Lang when he came griping?'

Warman sucked her teeth at Rowan's insubordinate tone, but said, 'And who might that be?'

Rowan woke her phone and selected a file from her camera gallery before handing it over.

Warman stared at the stuffed effigy of Lang in confusion. 'What am I looking at?'

'If you slide right, you'll see a photo of the real Justin Lang. I got it from an *Echo* report about his suicide,' Rowan said.

Warman glanced up sharply at the word suicide, then turned her attention to the phone with greater interest.

The snap had been taken in a pub; Lang was holding a pint of lager and grinning at the camera as if toasting the photographer. He was wearing a grey North Face hoody and a beanie hat identical to the one used on the effigy. His hair was brown and curled from under the hat.

'You can't see his leg-tat in that photo,' Rowan said. 'But apparently, he had one just like the effigy — which appeared outside Justin's tower block a week before he died.'

Rowan watched as Warman pinched and magnified the ribbons of blood on the image.

'How did he die?'

'He was found in the bath at his flat with his wrists slashed.'

Warman stared at her. 'Where did you get this intelligence?'

'From Damian's kid brother,' Rowan said.

Warman blinked. 'And you think Damian was meant to see the shell suit on the embankment?'

'Yes. But the jury's out on whether he did. The sister says Damian was jittery the week before, but the kid brother says he was "normal"; he didn't think Damian was aware of it.'

'Do you believe him?'

Rowan took a breath before answering. 'I believe he's sincere — he feels guilty that he didn't tell his brother about Justin Lang. I couldn't find anything on the news sites or social media about Damian's effigy — and the responders who dealt with it took the thing down fast in case of rubber-neckers, so—'

'It's feasible Damian didn't know about it,' Warman finished for her. 'What about the younger brother — could he have seen it and not said anything?'

Rowan shook her head. 'He was really rattled, but I think it was because he saw the similarity between the photo I took on the motorway and the one he took of the Lang dummy. He said he would've warned his brother if he'd known.'

Warman swiped to the final image. 'Oh,' she exclaimed mildly. 'Is that a mask?'

'That's *the* mask,' Rowan said. 'Identical to the one I saw on the Damian effigy.'

'I think you might be getting ahead of yourself, there, Cassie.' Warman stared at the Lang effigy. 'Whoever made this placed it where Lang would see it; he *wanted* Lang to know it was meant to look like him.'

'Just like Damian,' Rowan insisted.

'I'm not so sure,' Warman said. 'Justin's mannequin, effigy — whatever you want to call it — had a lot of detail. As you described it, Damian's didn't.' Warman stopped, as though a thought had just struck her. 'Was there a face under the mask on the motorway embankment? Did you think to check?'

'I didn't touch *anything*,' Rowan said, curbing a flare of anger. 'Per scene protocol.'

'It wasn't an accusation, Cassie,' Warman said tartly. 'I'm just trying to establish the facts.'

Rowan felt her face flush; this was going badly. 'Well, I wish I had checked,' she admitted. ''Cos that clothing was binned, so now we'll never know.'

'In which case,' Warman said carefully, 'the effigy of Damian Novak — if indeed it was meant to be Damian — could be a coincidence.'

Rowan took a breath, ready to object, but Warman held up a finger to silence her.

'Someone went to a great deal of trouble to make a life-size mannequin that looked like Justin Lang — even to

43

predict the manner of his death. In comparison, all you have in Damian Novak's case is an assortment of clothing.'

That was Warman all over: just when you thought you'd persuaded her to your way of thinking, she'd do a U-turn and blindside you.

'Oh, it's *way* more,' Rowan said. 'It's the clothing Damian was wearing when he ran down an elderly woman and killed her.'

'You're sure of that?'

The disdain in Warman's voice only riled her more.

'One hundred per cent. The same image appeared in the paper after the accident that got Damian locked up. I checked back; the caption in the *Echo* reads, "Damian Novak, minutes before the tragic accident". I can send you the link if you like.'

That sounded sarcastic, and Warman hated sarcasm, so Rowan hurried on. 'Please, ma'am, hear me out. An effigy of Damian Novak appears on the M62 embankment, apparently hurtling down towards the traffic. Seven days later, Damian is mown down on the motorway in the very same spot. Okay, maybe that's a coincidence. But an effigy of Justin Lang — a former associate of Damian's — *also* appears a week before *he* died, and Justin's was an accurate mock-up of his suicide. Is *that* coincidence? Plus, both Damian and Justin's effigies were got up with the same monster mask.' She turned her hands palms up. 'Honestly, boss — when does coincidence become a pattern?'

Warman gave her a look that could sour milk, and Rowan was sure she was about to be booted out of her office. But her boss finally broke the silence with a question.

'When did Justin Lang die?'

'July,' Rowan said promptly.

'Very well. See if you can get hold of the post-mortem and coroner's reports. I want to see photos—'

'What about Damian?'

'I will deal with Damian Novak,' Warman said firmly.

'Okay,' Rowan said. 'But, one last thing?'

Warman looked close to losing her patience, so she kept it short.

'Why did the *Echo* use a four-year-old image of Damian?'

'I *suppose* they had it handy in their archive,' Warman said, exasperated.

'Sloppy reporting, though.'

'Newspapers are even more short-staffed than we are, these days, Cassie,' Warman said. 'Don't read too much into it — when budgets are slashed, corners are cut, you know that.'

'But the family swear *they* didn't send it in the first place, which makes you wonder who did.'

'If you're thinking of talking to the reporter, don't,' Warman said, clearly alarmed. 'We do *not* need a lot of press speculation about these deaths.' She handed back Rowan's phone.

'Understood.' For a second, Rowan considered saying more, but decided she'd already pushed her luck beyond normal tolerance limits. 'So, what's the plan?'

'Let me talk to the superintendent,' Warman said. '*Then* we can talk strategy.'

CHAPTER 8

Rowan was on her way out to the coroner's office when her personal mobile rang.

'Could I speak to Cassie Rowan?'

'Speaking. Who is this?' She'd recognized the voice, so she already knew it was Mr Singh, her brother's pastoral tutor, but Rowan was buying thinking time.

Having introduced himself, Singh said that he had 'concerns' about Neil's well-being.

'He's been withdrawn and moody, and has missed several sessions in the last ten days — were you aware?'

Loaded question. Rowan had fielded hundreds like it, caring for her younger brother over the seven years since the death of their parents.

'You will know that he was seriously injured last winter,' she said, avoiding a direct answer. 'Neil has ongoing issues with scarring to the tendons in his right arm.'

'Yes, I understand you were attacked in your home,' he said.

Her ears boomed with disorientating noise and Rowan saw a blur of shadow, felt a sudden pressure on her throat. She shook the vision away, angry that he'd tried to make this about her.

'How can I help you, Mr Singh?' she said in her most business-like cop voice.

She noted a slight pause.

'In the short term, we'd like to see Neil attending classes regularly,' he said. 'And as you are his primary carer, I think it would be helpful for you and Neil to have a sit-down with myself and the head of lower sixth.'

'I'm in the middle of something, right now,' Rowan said, feeling the old sense of panic at the possibility of social services interference. Neil was sixteen, but he had been under their supervision since he was nine and would have a designated social worker until his eighteenth birthday. That constant scrutiny had been a burden every day of the last seven years, making her feel that she was always on probation, and that someday she would be found lacking.

'The transition to sixth-form work can be tricky for some students, Ms Rowan,' he said. 'And Neil has had significant trauma to process in addition to the demands of his academic studies. The upheaval at the end of the last academic year could mean that he feels overwhelmed — which could be fuelling his loss of motivation.'

A drugs problem in their street had led to Rowan and her brother having to decamp to a safe house from May to July and he'd sat his exams in a school out of area. 'He'd virtually finished his courses, and he sat all of his exams,' Rowan said, careful to keep any hint of complaint out of her tone.

'And did very well,' Singh agreed. 'But his peer friendship groups were disrupted at a crucial stage, and in my experience a timely intervention can save a lot of problems further down the line.'

Friendship groups disrupted — *is he saying that Neil has no friends?*

'I'll talk to him,' she said.

'Excellent — I can set up an appointment now, if—'

'Let me speak to him, first — and I'll have to check my schedule before making an appointment.'

47

'Of course,' Singh said smoothly. 'You'll have this number on your mobile — you can reach me any time between eight thirty and five thirty, weekdays.'

She hung up with huge outrush of breath.

Her conversation with Neil had not gone well the previous night; it ended with him slamming his bedroom door in her face and refusing to come down for food or even a drink. She'd left a tray outside his door at eight and it had vanished into his room within minutes, but when she'd tapped at his door at ten o' clock he'd told her to leave him alone. Now that the school was involved, she would have to find a way to get him to talk; she just didn't know how.

CHAPTER 9

By the time Rowan returned to the CID office it was midday. A slender, fair-haired figure she thought she recognized was leaning over the desk next to hers, writing on a notelet. The sun was beginning to lower, casting a glare through the dirty windows, and she had to squint to be sure.

'Finch!' she exclaimed.

He came forward, smiling broadly, hand outstretched.

'It's been a while,' she said, shaking his hand.

'Yeah, I've been all over this year, covering absences, mostly,' he said with a grimace. 'Good to be working with you again.'

'Are you? Working with me, I mean.'

He nodded, grinning. 'DCI Warman asked for me,' he said with a flush of pride. 'I've been searching for other incidents involving dummies on the motorway.'

'Okay.' Rowan was surprised at her delight that he was on the team. 'What've you got?'

'I was leaving you a note — she wants to see us in meeting room three.'

Rowan knew that particular room would house no more than half a dozen staff, which didn't bode well for the size of the investigative team.

Ian Chan was already setting up the projector ready for the briefing. He slotted a memory stick into a USB port and flashed a smile at Finch, which made him blush.

Warman came in a moment later with a look of such severity on her face that Chan mouthed 'Yikes!' and scuttled to a seat at the table.

Taking her place next to the whiteboard, Warman began. 'We have permission to continue the inquiry. But as you can see, we are a small team,' she added with wry under-statement. 'Just the two of you, and myself. I'll do what I can to facilitate, and Ian Chan will assist with forensics.'

'What's the scope?' Rowan had already been repri-manded for poking her nose into Damian Novak's death and the effigies meant that overlap was inevitable.

'Novak, Lang, and any other death in which the unusual motif of models or effigies arise,' Warman said, as though reading from a task sheet.

Rowan glanced towards the door. 'Is Wicks not coming?'

'Wicks has been reassigned,' Warman said with a finality that did not invite further questions.

Rowan hadn't been looking forward to renewing her working relationship with Wicks, but the relief on Finch's face was palpable. He'd been a newly- hatched detective when they'd first met, fluffy and eager and, like an innocent chick, he'd imprinted on Roy Wicks, the very worst person he might have chosen to follow.

It was bad enough that Wicks was misogynistic and lazy, but Rowan had good reason to believe that he was also corrupt. It had taken a great deal of courage for Finch to distance himself from his former pal and would-be mentor, but he'd done it, and he had been commended for his part in catching a killer.

'Let's start with what we know already,' Warman said. 'Cassie — can you summarize your findings, so far?'

Rowan stepped up and logged in, accessing her parti-tion on the computer drive where she'd already uploaded the images. Seconds later, an image appeared on the whiteboard of Novak's mannequin, glittering like a rare bird among the saplings on the motorway embankment. She talked them through the sequence of events, including her interview with Novak's family, and her discovery that Justin Lang's death had been preceded by an effigy that had apparently foretold his suicide. She finished with side-by-side images of Lang's effigy and the snapshot of him in a pub.

'The coroner's officer said he'd send over Lang's report this afternoon along with the PM findings and images,' she said. 'But he showed me a few while I was there, and the similarities to the effigy are striking — the cuts to Lang's veins correspond to the position on the dummy.'

Warman nodded. 'I've requested the full coroner's report for Damian Novak, and I'll be talking to the team who investigated Lang's suicide later. I take it the Fernleigh estate youths cut across the motorway regularly?'

'As clockwork,' Rowan said. 'Traffic said there's been break-ins on the new exec development. But that doesn't explain why Damian had a significant quantity of cash and cannabis on him.'

'Then we need to canvass the residents,' Warman said. 'Unless young Lukas can tell us what his brother was up to? It might be worth bringing him in.'

'I think he'd clam up, boss,' Rowan said. 'He's terrified of being targeted as a grass. But he might open up on his own turf — I'd prefer to keep any questioning informal.'

'Very well,' Warman said. 'Ian, what can you tell us about the effigies?'

'I think we should look at that question from the other end,' Chan said. 'What can the effigies tell *us*?'

Warman gave an irritated twitch of one eyebrow, which Chan ignored, instead asking Rowan to go back to the first slide.

'The Damian Novak effigy,' he said. 'Shell suits aren't exactly scally haute couture, just now, so the person who assembled Cassie's "hanging man" might've bought the clothing second-hand online.'

'An online sale would be almost impossible to trace,' Warman said.

'But it might be worth checking local charity shops. See if they remember selling anything in that line — I mean, those colours are distinctive,' Chan added with a little moue of distaste. 'The Lang effigy's a whole other ballgame — being what you might call bespoke creepy.'

Rowan called up the image.

'You might ask is the fabric special in any way?' he said. 'What's the level of finish on the stitching?'

He looked at the other two, inviting suggestions.

Rowan frowned. 'The ankle tag might be traceable.'

'If we had the serial number,' Chan said.

'How do you even get hold of an electronic ankle tag?' Finch asked.

'You work in the judicial system: police, probation, or for one of the security firms that specialize in tagging,' Warman said.

'Or you're a scall yourself, and you steal it,' Rowan said.

'Or you could buy one off eBay,' Chan said.

'Seriously?' Rowan said. 'Is there *anything* you can't buy on the Web these days?'

'True happiness,' Chan shot back.

Rowan curbed a smile. 'The masks. I did a quick google search, didn't find it on the supermarket websites or Amazon, so I'm thinking we should look into local suppliers for them as well.'

Warman nodded. 'All worth following up.'

'The traffic cops who dealt with the shell suit said there'd been similar incidents,' Rowan said, recalling her conversation with them a week ago. 'Near-misses, mostly — but there was one fatality on that section of motorway several months ago.'

'They got that whole incident on a dashcam,' Finch said. 'It wasn't suspicious — the kid hopped over the fence at the top of an embankment and ran down to the motorway. He got as far as the central reservation, but he caught the lane barrier with one foot and fell into the path of a lorry. It was a genuine accident.'

'I want to see that dashcam footage,' Warman said.

'Sure.' Finch dutifully made a note. 'But there was another incident very like Cassie's: a lorry driver saw a body hanging from a motorway bridge — jackknifed his rig trying to avoid it.'

'When was this?' Warman demanded.

'Last autumn,' Finch said. 'The body turned out to be a scarecrow. The RTU thought it must be a Halloween stunt, recovered it, bagged it and binned it.'

'Did they keep samples, take photos?' Rowan asked.

'Nothing physical, but they've forwarded copies of the images.' Finch stood and Rowan took a seat to make room for him at the computer.

He cast the first image onto the screen. Taken on a foggy day, in late autumn, it showed the entire scene, presumably for context. The lorry cab faced in the direction of oncoming traffic. Its container load was slewed at a ninety-degree angle to the cab, blocking all three lanes of the westbound carriageway. Beyond it, emerging from the layers of mist, what looked like a hanged man.

Finch clicked through to closer images, one taken from directly below the dummy, and another at eye level with it, perhaps from the cherry-picker that must have been deployed to retrieve the effigy.

The team leaned forward as one. The 'body' wore the same demonic mask: a round, reddish-brown face, squashed-looking nose and a wide mouth, crowded with needle-sharp teeth.

'Dear Lord,' Warman murmured.

'This has been going on for a year — maybe more,' Rowan said, and for once her boss didn't tell her she was getting ahead of herself.

Rowan scoured the image for distinguishing features. Its hair, which had the shiny black gloss of a cheap nylon wig, was tucked under a black Liverpool FC baseball cap and both were beaded with condensation.

'Claw earring in his left ear,' Chan said.

'Is that a bracelet on its right wrist?' Rowan asked.

'No, it's a mangle,' Chan said.

She laughed, visualising an ancient laundry-wringer that had once stood rusting in their back yard. 'A *what*?'

'A man bangle,' Chan said haughtily.

'It's a stuffed doll, Ian — probably got up to look like a local scall,' Rowan said. 'And that's a plaited leather bracelet.'

'Whatever you want to call it, I could have guaranteed a ton of DNA evidence from it, if—'

'If wishes were horses, beggars would ride,' Rowan said, quoting her Scottish father. 'Speaking of which — did they get an image of what was under the mask, Finch?'

''Fraid not,' Finch said.

Chan peered at the mannequin. 'The rope is interesting,' he said. 'Can you magnify that section?'

Finch made an adjustment on the computer screen and the noose came into pin-sharp focus.

'Great,' Chan said. 'It's a high-res image.' He joined Finch next to the board. 'It looks like the rope is made from natural fibres — hemp or jute, maybe. And these flecks and slubs in the composition?' He pointed out some darker colouration in the brownish twist of rope, and a couple of uneven lighter-toned ovals in its make-up.

The rest of the team nodded collectively.

'They're unique to this rope,' he said. 'So, if there is a real-live counterpart to this effigy — by which I mean a real dead body — I *might* be able to visually match the rope from this image to the evidence collected from the body.'

'Well, that's something,' Warman said, although she didn't specify what. 'Finch, see what you can find at the coroner's office. We're looking for deaths by hanging around the end of October and beginning of November last year.'

'Just on the Fernleigh estate?' Finch asked.

'Let's say in the south Liverpool area for now.'

'If there is a pattern here, it's likely the death would have happened seven days after the dummy was spotted under the bridge,' Rowan said.

A quiver of uncertainty passed across Warman's blue-grey eyes; she would hate the notion of prejudging a case, but it looked like they already had a pattern, so, finally, she gave Finch the nod.

'I'll call round the charity shops, see if anyone recognizes the shell suit,' Rowan said. 'But we could use a team knocking on doors around the estate, see if they know anything about the effigies.'

'Out of the question,' Warman said. 'The superintendent will review staffing levels and budget only if we present him with evidence that the deaths are more than just bizarre coincidences.'

'There's an awful lot for just me and Finch to cover,' Rowan said.

'Then you'd better get cracking.' There was an icy splinter in Warman's voice, but she warmed up just enough to add, 'And as I said, I'll do what I can. There's also a PCSO on the Fernleigh estate who is keen to help — I'll give you her contact details when we've finished here.' She switched her attention to Chan. 'Anything on the body that might help us?'

'The primary investigation was a sh—' He bit his lip.

He was about to say 'shit-show', Rowan thought. *And he's always lecturing me about diplomacy.*

Then Chan scratched the corner of one eyebrow and began again. '*Requests* for evidence were minimal — basically what was in his pockets. But we collected a lot of detritus from the motorway, did some tape lifts at the scene, and Damian's clothing is bagged and tagged.'

'Analysis?' Warman said.

'We've had no requests for analysis, so it's all just sitting there.'

From the pinched look on her face, Warman had come to her own very negative opinion of the competence of the primary investigator. 'Let's start with trace analysis,' she said, her jaw clamped so tight that her lips barely moved.

Trace would give them fibres, paint flecks — perhaps an idea of the type of vehicle involved in the hit-and-run.

'What do you need from us?'

'Copies of all the images you have will be good for reference,' Chan said. 'And the full PM reports.'

'Of course,' Warman said. 'Is everyone clear which tasks they need to prioritize?' She glanced around at her small team. 'Good.' As the other two left, she said, 'Cassie — if you come to my office, I'll get you that community support officer's name. Oh, and before you set off for Fernleigh, I had a call from Elspeth Palmer.'

Alan Palmer was the psychotherapist who had helped Rowan crack her first big case and Elspeth was his estranged wife. Initially, Rowan had had him pegged as an arrogant tool bag who adhered slavishly to the rules of his profession. But she'd learned that there was a lot more to the man than that. He'd believed her when no one else had, risking his career and even his life working with her to bring an evil man to justice. They had become friends in the intervening months so, although she hadn't heard from Alan in a couple of weeks, she knew that he expected to finalize his divorce any day.

'She wants to speak to someone about Damian Novak.'

'Oh,' Rowan said.

Warman stopped, her eyes flat as a dead fish. 'Is that a problem?'

'No,' Cassie said, although that wasn't entirely true. 'We've never even met.'

Warman watched her closely, clearly not fooled by her answer.

Rowan faked a smile. 'She has an office in the city centre — I'll put in a call and see if she's available — go on to Fernleigh from there.'

CHAPTER 10

The offices of Elspeth Palmer's law firm were housed in a square, eight-storey building of mud-brown stone, surrounded on three sides by tall glass-and-steel tower blocks, one of which housed a riverfront hotel. Situated on the edge of the new business quarter with its wide streets and granite-flagged plazas, the area had an affluent feel. On a cold, clear October afternoon, the windows reflected images of nineteenth-century dock warehouses, refurbished and converted to apartments and restaurants. Glimpses of blue water on Princes Dock shimmered beyond them. A brisk wind blowing off the Irish Sea carried whiffs of seaweed and salt spume and above the thrum of traffic on the dock road she could hear the persistent cry of herring gulls.

A sudden updraught of air blew her hair across her face and Rowan almost missed Alan Palmer coming out of the lift as she headed inside. Palmer was tall, broad-shouldered and had the long, easy stride of a habitual walker. He carried his messenger bag slung across his body and Rowan couldn't help wondering if the divorce papers were filed in there alongside his consultation notes. They arrived at the reception desk at the same moment, he to drop off his visitor pass, she to inquire after Ms Palmer.

'Hello, Alan.'

Palmer turned, a preoccupied, almost worried look on his face, then recognizing her, he smiled.

'I wouldn't have expected to see you here,' Rowan said.

'I could say the same. Oh—' His brows drew down. 'This is about the boy killed on the motorway.'

'What do you know about that?' she asked; it was always good to get an objective viewpoint, and as Elspeth's soon-to-be ex, she reckoned that Palmer would not be too biased in her favour.

Palmer glanced at the receptionist and moved a few metres away, out of earshot.

'The firm does some pro-bono work; they defended Damian Novak after he was caught riding a stolen off-road on the footpaths around the estate. Elspeth was mentoring a junior lawyer, and her mentee got Novak a community order. He'd been home less than a day when he stole another bike, killed a grandmother and put her grandson in a wheel-chair.' He shook his head. 'Elspeth felt bad enough about that, but now Novak is dead, she feels doubly responsible.'

Astonishing how forgiving the man is after all Elspeth's put him through, Rowan thought.

'How are you doing?' she asked, realising that the silence had become uncomfortable.

'The decree absolute came through.' He must have seen the concern on her face because he added, 'I've come to terms with the divorce. We're trying to work out a way to make shared custody work.'

'Is she still set on employing a nanny?'

A slight contraction around Palmer's eyes told her he'd already lost that battle.

'I'm sorry, Alan.'

'It might help in the long run,' he said with a rueful smile. 'When Elspeth's away with work, she's agreed that I can have Lucy to stay with me.' He cleared his throat. 'How are you?' he asked. 'Is Neil doing better?'

'Honestly?' She exhaled, only appreciating at that second how much tension she'd been holding inside. 'I don't know,' she said. 'He was anxious and depressed for a couple of months after he was injured — I get that — I was anxious for him. But he seems convinced that the loss of feeling in his arm will end his chances of a career in sport. He's young, he was fit before he was injured, the doctors say that physically, he's healed well — and he was doing okay until spring.'

'What changed?'

She sighed. 'We had that trouble in the street.'

'The drug investigation?'

She nodded. 'As you know, we had to move out till the trial, for fear of reprisals. Since then, he's gone backwards: he's moody, despairing — seems to've given up. Even when we came home, he just couldn't settle. It was like he hated living there. He's so *angry*, Alan. I mean all the time.'

'Angry with whom?' he asked gently.

'Me, mostly,' she said.

'Do you know why?'

She looked up into the atrium of the building; its balconies and mezzanines provided clear sightlines to the offices at each level, and she wished her life was as simple and straightforward.

'I guess because I'm here,' she said. He waited, and she felt the pull of his interest, knowing, even as she decided to walk away that she would say more. It was astonishing how Palmer could break down her natural reserve with no apparent effort. Since taking on guardianship of Neil when she'd been barely out of her teens herself, she'd deflected intrusive questions from relations, teachers, social workers and employers, and given nothing away. Palmer, however, had managed on many occasions over the past year to draw her out with a mere look, or a murmur of interest.

'Mum and Dad are long dead, and Alex is so far away in New York—' She shrugged. Their brother was distant enough to be above the niggling day-to-day difficulties and arguments among siblings that came from sharing a house where there was no one to adjudicate. 'I suppose I'm the only member of the family left to kick against.'

'That's part of it,' Palmer said. 'But, Cassie, you've been Mum, Dad, sister and friend to Neil since he was a confused little boy of nine mourning the death of his parents. Then last winter something truly horrible happened to you — in your own home — and he had to face the reality that he could lose you, too.'

Rowan closed her eyes for a second. 'And just as he was beginning to feel safer, the drug thing happened . . .'

'And your home, your street — your entire *neighbourhood* — became a hostile place for him again,' Palmer said, finishing the thought.

Rowan took a breath. 'I get that he's scared,' she said, trying to be rational. 'But why's he so bloody *angry?*'

'He has a lot to be angry about,' Palmer said with gentle amusement. 'You might have died in that attack.'

'No wonder he hates me,' she groaned. 'It was my job that put us in harm's way.'

'It was bad men who did that,' he corrected. 'But while we're on the subject of blame, Neil might feel guilty that he didn't prevent you getting hurt.'

'He *did!* He stopped that bastard from choking the life out of me,' she blurted out, surprised how indignant she felt at the implied criticism of her brother, and by her own emotion at recalling the incident.

'We both know that,' Palmer said. 'But do you know what it does to a child, feeling powerless against a force much greater than his own. And worse — *much* worse — seeing his sister so close to death?'

Rowan bowed her head and Palmer dipped slightly to look into her eyes.

'And now Neil is left with a scar that could ruin his ambitions for a career in sport.'

'He doesn't *know* that — and anyway, sport isn't everything,' she said.

'Boys his age have a narrow view of the possibilities life holds,' Palmer countered. 'He'd set his heart on sports, and now that might not happen. He may feel like he's out of options.'

'He *isn't*,' Rowan insisted. 'But there's no use me telling him — he won't listen to me.'

Palmer nodded. 'He might hear it better from someone at school — a form teacher perhaps?'

'I had a call from Neil's pastoral tutor,' Rowan admitted. 'He's been sagging off. They want to see both of us; they're calling it an "intervention". I'm scared that—' She broke off. *Scared?* Her emotions were jumbled and hard to articulate, but now that she'd said it, she found that it was true — she was scared.

Palmer was watching her, his brow creased in concern. 'You need to get ahead of this, Cassie. It won't do Neil any good if social services decide he needs a residential placement.'

'God, d'you think they would?' She hadn't allowed her imagination to roam into the frightening realms of foster care.

'I'm not an educational psychologist, but, yes, I think it's a possibility,' he said.

'He'd hate me even more if that happened,' Rowan said. 'I *have* to get him to talk, but he won't even look at me, never mind communicate.'

'Who *will* he talk to?'

'Alex.' She didn't even have to think about it, and it shocked her to realize that it hadn't occurred to her to turn to her older brother for help. 'But like I said, Alex is in New York, and—'

'So set up a Zoom,' Palmer said. 'Or whatever you think is closest to a face-to-face chat.'

'I don't know,' Rowan said doubtfully. 'I'd have to tell Alex what's going on, and Neil might see it as a betrayal — he likes to give Alex the impression that he's really got it together.'

Palmer thought for a moment. 'From what you've said, Alex didn't handle the aftermath of the attack well.'

'He flew back to New York the day after Neil was discharged from the hospital.'

'So that's your approach. Alex needs to admit how difficult he found the aftermath of the attack. He needs to be honest about why he ducked and ran, just when Neil needed him most.'

'Oh, Alan, that's harsh—'

'Is it?' Palmer said, with a quirk of one eyebrow. 'He literally took flight.'

Rowan thought about it: Alex had pleaded pressure of work, and she'd been so concerned about making arrangements for Neil's care and making sure that he felt safe and comfortable that she hadn't the energy to challenge Alex's decision to leave. He hadn't even taken the time to come and see them over Christmas or New Year. She'd seen Neil's disappointment and hadn't been able find a way to console him. Neil had needed his big brother and, intentional or not, Alex had implied that he had greater priorities. 'No,' she said at last. 'You're right.'

'If Alex opens up to Neil about his fears and inadequacies, it will give Neil permission to share his own feelings,' Palmer said. 'And he does need to talk about his feelings — you can't reassure Neil when you don't know what he's scared of.'

Rowan nodded, slowly, seeing things clearly for the first time since the attack. 'I'll talk to Alex,' she said, resolute.

Sensing that she was under scrutiny, Rowan glanced to the bank of lifts across the foyer and saw Elspeth Palmer watching them.

Her cheeks burned and then she felt ridiculous for being embarrassed. She forced a smile. 'You should be charging for this,' she said, instantly cringing at the crassness of the remark.

'We're friends,' he said. 'It's what friends do.'

She nodded, humbled, and started walking towards Palmer's ex.

'And Cassie—'

She turned back to him.

'Neil doesn't hate you. It's just easier to be angry *at* you than scared *for* you.'

CHAPTER 11

The low-rise sections of the Fernleigh social-housing complex were laid out in curved rows of terraced and 'link' houses
built in the 1960s and early seventies. The tower where
Damian had lived was one of a cluster of three at the east-
erly edge, overlooking the grimy courtyards on one side, but
some of the flats must have views over the shallow-roofed
houses that sprawled beyond them, then southwest across the
motorway to flat, open countryside, petering off to marsh-
land then onward to the tidal banks of the River Mersey.

Rowan drove for fifteen minutes, trying to get a feel
for the wider estate, scoping out the land, riding over speed-
bumps, turning into cul-de-sacs, squeezing past cars with
half their width on pavements. Some of the houses were well
kept, their front gardens vivid with autumn colour: cherry
trees aflame with oranges and reds; blue hydrangeas beginning to burnish magenta at the leaf margins; glaucous sedums
turning rich aubergine as their seedheads ripened. Others
went for tightly-clipped lawns with annuals in regimented
lines along their borders, hanging baskets brimming with
petunias — red and white for Liverpool FC, blue and white
for Everton, reflecting the affiliations of the occupants. But
for every two or three of these, she saw a frontage with rusting

machinery on the oil-polluted ruin of a lawn. In these houses, blankets stood in for curtains at the windows.

She meandered, finishing up at the centre of the estate. On one side of the road, a short terrace, the roof of which was caved in at the centre. Smoke damage around the upper windows told the story of what had happened. Only the two end houses looked occupied. A strip of grass at the kerbside was badly scarred; deep gouges in the underlying clay, caused by cars perched askew at intervals half on and half off the verge.

Opposite the houses, a grey and dusty row of shops were protected from ram-raids by a series of concrete bollards at three feet intervals along the edge of the kerb. Most of the units were boarded or tightly shuttered, but a few stood open, their steel roller blinds only partially raised to let in a little daylight.

The only people she saw were an elderly woman with a shopper on wheels and a young mother pushing a double buggy.

Rowan parked up and ducked in through the nearest open door.

The shop was small, perhaps only fifteen feet wide, and much of the space was taken up by steel shelving; vegetables and fruit on one side and bread, rice, canned goods and bottles on the other. The grey floor tiles were cracked in places but spotlessly clean. The till was housed behind thick Perspex in a kind of booth that seemed to open to the rear of the building.

A short figure stood to one side of the space, her back to Rowan. Dressed in standard uniform black trousers, jacket and stab vest, she wore her black hair tied in a neat bun under her police-issue bowler-style hat. She was talking to a grandmother and child as they chose items from the shelves, but she turned and smiled as Rowan came through the door.

'PCSO Dawson?'

Dawson excused herself from the customers and stepped forward, hand outstretched. 'Jackie,' she said. 'You must be DC Rowan.'

'Cassie,' Rowan said.

'Welcome to our food co-op,' Dawson said, spreading her arms to encompass the narrow shop.

Rowan clocked the low prices along the racks and took in the toughened Perspex booth, which now held a tiny Asian woman of around fifty. Her hair, still sleek and black, was tied back in a ponytail and she wore a neat blouse with a Nehru collar in burgundy red.

'You need the security at these prices?' she asked, incredulous.

'We keep the tinned salmon behind the counter, as well,' Dawson said, with a grin.

'It is always better to be safe than to shut the stable door after the horse is gone,' the woman in the booth said.

'You're mixing your metaphors again, Ma.' Dawson chuckled and the woman raised one hand, waving away the correction as if it were a troublesome fly.

'Says the girl whose Hindi makes her grandparents curl their toes and cover their ears,' the older woman said.

Dawson laughed delightedly. 'What an image! Detective Constable Rowan, meet my mum.'

Rowan hadn't seen it before because Dawson was so light-skinned, but she had her mother's wide-spaced, dark eyes, and glossy black hair.

The only opening in the booth was a narrow arch cut at the lower edge of the screen, so a handshake seemed out of the question, and Rowan raised a hand in greeting instead. Dawson's mother favoured her with a disdainful tilt of her head.

'Is the food donated?' Rowan asked.

'Some,' Dawson said. 'But we have a community garden and summer to autumn the fruit and veg comes from that. Fancy a tour?'

Rowan smiled. 'I thought you'd never ask.'

At the end of the street, they looked back to the shops.

'You wouldn't believe it, but this used to be a thriving little hub,' Dawson said. 'We even had a pop-up library. The local authority would send a van once a month and bring a few new titles and orders for the library users.'

Gazing at the bank of grey shutters, it was hard to imagine. 'What happened?' Rowan asked.

'Vandalism, shoplifting. We even had a couple of incidents where gangs of kids steamed in and took what they wanted. The shopkeepers couldn't do a thing about it — there were just too many of them — and you can't insure against that kind of eventuality, not when it becomes a regular fixture. Then there's the rates.'

'The food co-op seems to be doing well,' Rowan said.

'We don't pay business rates because we're a charity,' Dawson said. 'But the retailers get hammered. They can't even rely on bin collections because the teams regularly blacklist the area. They've had abuse and threats, bricks lobbed at them — and it gets worse this time of year with fireworks literally thrown into the mix.'

'Have you had any support from Operational Command?' Rowan asked. The Merseyside Police Matrix Disruption Team was tasked with responding to gang-related disorder and they were based only ten minutes' drive away.

'They sent a Matrix van to sit across from the shopping parade for a few days.' Dawson shrugged. 'You know how it is: bigger fish to fry.'

Rowan gave a sympathetic nod. 'We had trouble with drug suppliers round our way last spring; my neighbour couldn't raise a response from the police via Crimestoppers and nearly got himself arrested trying to sort it himself.'

'But it did get sorted?' Dawson asked, her tone almost wistful.

'Eventually,' Rowan said. 'Long story — I'll bore you with it some time. Thing is, you do what you can — like you and your mum, organizing the food co-op.'

'Oh, no,' Dawson said, blushing. 'It's not like that. We've got a committee of five, and fifteen more volunteers staffing the shop — it's a community effort.'

Rowan glanced down at the little woman. 'You live here?'

'Born and raised,' Dawson said. 'Mum and Dad had a flat in one of the tower blocks in the eighties, when they were first married. Mum and I have a bungalow on the outer margins of the estate, now.'

'Just you and your mum?' Rowan said. 'What happened to your dad?'

Dawson shot her a sharp look and Rowan's cheeks burned.

'Uh, sorry,' she said. 'I run off at the mouth before my brain's engaged, sometimes. That was nosy — you don't need to answer.'

'No worries,' Dawson said, with a slight smile. 'Gave me a chill, that's all — it was like you were channelling Mum.' After a few moments, and another flustered apology from Rowan, she gave a little shrug and began speaking again.

'Dad fancied himself as a musician. He left when I was ten years old. Said he was off to find a "good gig" in London and he'd send for us when he was settled. That was fifteen years ago. It's been just me and Mum ever since.' After a pause, she said, 'How about you? Married? Single? Living with family or on your own? Hobbies? Religion?' Rowan laughed and she said, 'I'm serious — Mum's going to ask.'

'Single,' Rowan said. 'Some would say that's on account of my big gob.'

'I was joking — you don't have to say.' Dawson said laughing with her. She left a dramatic pause before adding, 'But Mum is going to ask . . .'

Normally Rowan would clam up at the first sign of someone showing an interest in her home situation, but Jackie Dawson had been open with her, and she sensed that it was safe to share confidences with the PCSO. 'It's just me and my sixteen-year-old brother at home,' she said. 'Mum and Dad died in a car accident when he was nine.'

'Oh, God, you're all on your own, then?' Dawson seemed stricken.

'We're fine. We have an older brother who lives in the States,' Rowan said, hearing again a defensiveness in her tone, thinking she sounded like a whiner. 'No religion, though I like a good Christmas carol,' she went on, injecting a little humour into her voice. 'And we do have a bunch of Scottish relatives in Edinburgh of the strict Presbyterian stripe, who we try very hard to keep at arm's length.'

Dawson rolled her eyes. 'I know *that* feeling.'

They continued walking companionably along the winding roadways Rowan had just driven, Dawson offering a nod and smile to nearly everyone they passed, introducing Rowan when she could persuade them to stop and chat.

Appraising her surreptitiously, Rowan thought PCSO Dawson's dark eyes gave a false impression of calm, as though she'd learned the trick of keeping a cop stillness of face. But her fingers told a different story: moving constantly, plucking at the seams of her uniform trousers or tapping out a rhythm on her thighs, they betrayed a more excitable nature beneath the veneer. The people Dawson dealt with might not notice — she had a way of holding a person's gaze, and the tiny, dancing movements of her fingers did not create an answering ripple in her shoulders — but Rowan saw those Judas taps and twitches.

For the most part, the locals seemed friendly and many clearly liked Dawson. Rowan was an unknown quantity, however, and they eyed her nervously — even with open distrust. Not one of them wanted to talk about Damian Novak.

'Don't take it personally,' Dawson said when they'd come full circle, ending back at the depressing parade of shops. 'Damian Novak was serious trouble. You won't see the neighbours gathered at the roadside to pay their respects when the funeral cortege goes by. You've been to his home, met his mum?'

Rowan nodded. 'I think she's grieving the loss of his earnings more than the loss of her son.'

'There's no denying he was a good earner,' Dawson said dryly. 'All of it ill-gotten.'

'Such as?'

'Drugs — weed, mostly, but I think he'd started peddling cocaine on the exec development on the other side of the motorway. And he had a perfect view of the approach roads into the estate from his bedroom window. When he wasn't out causing mayhem, he kept dixie for cops or any activity from rival gangs.'

'He was a lookout?' Rowan was thinking that he might have seen something he shouldn't have.

Dawson nodded.

'These rival gangs — are they from the estate, or—'

'We had a couple of attempts from a gang in Speke over the summer, but the Lang crew saw them off. The local lads keep to their own small patch of turf, and the majority of them would be in the Langs' pay, anyway.'

'Tell me about the accident that got Damian banged up.'

'Back then he was a runner and lookout,' Dawson said. 'If he wasn't on duty, he was razzing that damn bike up and down the footpaths and on the grass verges around the estate. We'd confiscated two off-roaders from him, but he just went off and stole another. That was the one he crashed into Mrs Bloor and her grandson at a pedestrian crossing. Mowed them down and never a flicker of remorse out of him. He was fourteen years old when he was locked up; back on the street at seventeen, and *still* a bloody menace.' She paused, then with a decisive nod, added, 'Yep, decent people heaved a sigh of relief hearing Damian Novak was dead.'

'The odd thing is, he was only carrying a small baggie of weed when he was killed.'

'He must've had a good night over on the new housing complex,' Jackie said. 'Sold out.'

Rowan lifted her chin in acknowledgement. 'He did have a wad of cash,' she said. Then, 'What d'you know about Justin Lang?'

'He's dead,' Dawson said, puzzlement creasing her brow.

'I know, but his name came up.'

'Lang was worse than Damian — a hardcore villain.' Jackie's eyes dulled, thinking about him. 'Twenty-seven, and he'd already done six years of prison time — four of those in a young offenders' unit. How did his name come up?'

'Damian's younger brother, Lukas.'

'Ah . . . I'm worried that Lukas is following in his big brother's footsteps,' Dawson said.

'Me, too,' Rowan agreed. 'He called Justin Lang "a mate".'

'And you're thinking a twenty-seven-year-old man shouldn't be mates with a kid not yet in his teens?' Dawson shook her head disgustedly. 'You'd be right. But the older lads are like Fagins. They flatter the kids, give them cash and a bit of bling to flash — grooming them really — reeling them into the life inch by inch.'

'D'you get no help with the social side?' Rowan asked.

Dawson scoffed. 'You know the story: cuts, budgetary restrictions — I was lucky to keep my job in the last round of "fiscal reviews".' The PCSO shook her head. 'Sorry, I don't mean to sound so down on everything and everyone. There's decent people, trying to live decent lives, here,' she went on. 'But they've learned to keep their heads down, lock their doors and draw their curtains at night.'

'Which might explain why no one saw the dummy got up to look like Justin Lang,' Rowan said.

'The what?'

Rowan showed her the images she'd pinged from Lukas's phone and explained that the effigy had appeared the week before Lang died.

Jackie looked from the phone to Rowan's face, her eyes wide. 'It does look a lot like Justin. You think his death is linked to Damian's?'

'We're looking into it,' Rowan said. 'Nothing concrete, yet.'

'Weird coincidence, though,' Jackie said, echoing Rowan's own feelings on the matter.

'No one mentioned anything to you about Lang's death?' Rowan asked. 'Something that, in hindsight, might seem significant?'

Dawson shook her head. 'If they had, I'd've passed it on up the line — maybe we could've helped. But that's another side-effect of the cuts: it's just me here; I'm supposed to be community *support*, but I end up policing. You can't build trust that way — people stop confiding in you.'

'Lukas said that Justin died like that,' Rowan said, swiping from the mask to the image of the effigy. She put it as a question, rather than as a statement of fact. They knew Lang's death had been ruled a suicide by the coroner, but they were still waiting on the full pathology and coroner's reports.

'Justin Lang slashed his wrists,' Dawson said. 'Bled out in his bath in his own flat.'

It seemed that Lukas hadn't been exaggerating.

'Thing is, I wouldn't have pegged Lang for a suicide,' Dawson continued. 'That lad was born without a conscience.'

Rowan nodded. 'I'll take that back to the team. You mentioned rivals. Could one of them have got to him?'

'It's *possible*, but, you know, the first sight of a stranger, the cry goes up like a whole tribe of howler monkeys.'

Rowan smiled in recognition. 'The scallies on the estate knew I was here before I'd knocked on the Novaks' door.'

'Yeah,' Dawson agreed. 'If someone was headed up to *Justin's* front door, I'd *guarantee* he would've known before they'd reached his landing. No one was getting through his front door unless he wanted them to. And anyway, there were no signs of a break-in or struggle.'

Everything seemed to confirm the coroner's inquest findings. But why? What could have made a mean-hearted, soulless bastard like Justin Lang so desperate that he would take his own life?

'I should talk to Lang's family,' Rowan said.

'You could *try* . . .'

'That doesn't sound hopeful.'

Dawson tilted her head apologetically. 'The Novaks kind of . . . fell into crime after the mum got addicted — they're amateurs compared with the Langs. Justin Lang's criminal credentials read like criminal royalty — he was part of a dynasty going back to before they even built this estate — emphasis on *nasty*.'

'Okay,' Rowan said. 'I'll hold off the Langs for now, but I still need answers.'

'You'd be better off talking to the women's groups,' Dawson said. 'We've got two: mothers and toddlers, and the Fernleigh Crafters.' She frowned, disappointed. 'But you've missed the crafters for this week.'

'It'd be useful to have the names and contact details of the groups' organizers,' Rowan said.

'Sure, I'll email you.'

'Can you think of anyone else who'd be willing to fill in the blanks about the family?'

Dawson thought about it, the fingers of her right hand nimbly touching to the thumb in sequence from her pinkie to her index finger: one, two, three, four; four, three, two, one, three times in quick succession.

'Jim North?' she said, as though testing the name to see if it would do.

Cassie raised her eyebrows in question, but Jackie's dark eyes seemed to look through her. The restless tapping of her fingers had stopped, and Jackie tap-tap-tapped her index finger to her right thumb, slowly.

At last, she nodded. 'Yes, Jim might do it.' She brightened visibly.

Rowan tilted her head, interested.

'Jim is ex-army,' Dawson said. 'Originally from the estate. He's a construction manager, now — working on a project in Liverpool at the moment. He runs martial-arts classes on the estate in the evenings.'

'Great,' Rowan said. 'When can I see him?'

'He'll be around later — his classes run from six thirty till eight, weekdays. Just meet me back at the co-op at around six twenty and I'll introduce you.'

CHAPTER 12

Rowan had a couple of hours spare before she was due back at base for a catch-up, so she decided to test DC Wicks' theory that on the night he died, Damian Novak had been thieving from the executive housing development on the other side of the motorway. She had already checked the database for reports of burglaries or thefts in the area and found none relating to that night. But people didn't always report suspicious activity, even if they'd scared off a would-be burglar. Whoever had strung the clothing up on the embankment must have known Damian, also that he'd used that section of motorway as a shortcut, and she hoped she might hear something that would give her a clearer insight into to why he'd been crossing the motorway at that hour.

To access the place, she had to join the motorway and head east three miles, then loop back at the next turnoff, travelling along minor roads almost all the way to where she'd started from. The journey, which was less than a mile as the crow flies, had taken her six miles out of her way, so either National Highways hadn't considered the new housing worthy of its own junction, or the developers at Turner Homes had seen the motorway as a geographical barrier to the troubled estate. It would also explain why youths from Fernleigh preferred to cross the motorway on foot.

She saw a Turner Homes route sign zip-tied to a signpost as she left the motorway, then more at regular intervals on traffic lights and lampposts, so she found the development easily enough. Flagpoles in the firm's orange-and-black colours marked the entrance to the estate, flapping and cracking in a chilly wind, and a twenty-feet-high roadside sign proclaimed that phase one was completely sold out and urged prospective buyers to put their names down for phase two before they, too, were snapped up.

She parked outside the show home at the entrance to the development. It was locked up, but a sign in the front widow directed prospective buyers to phone their headquarters or make an appointment via the website.

Rowan left her car and walked into the estate.

The builders had landscaped carefully, using mature trees and shrubs to create the illusion of a more established neighbourhood. The houses were a mix of semi-detached and detached properties on short roads and cul-de-sacs. Each home had a double garage painted in muted heritage colours — mostly pale greens and dove greys. The houses were planted on a small patch of lawn edged with low-growing evergreens, all neatly clipped, and each garage wall had its own electric charger point — apparently, Turner Homes prided itself on its green credentials. The pavements were so clean that Rowan could almost believe that no one walked them at all but glided along on clouds of affluence.

The first three doorbells she pressed rang out long and loud through empty houses, but the third was a smart doorbell. It gave a sudden squawk, then a distorted female voice asked, 'Can I help you?'

'Detective Constable Rowan, Merseyside Police. I'm canvassing the area about trouble from local youths?'

'You mean the Fernleigh lot.' It wasn't a question.

'Can you come to the door, please?' Rowan said.

'Hardly — I'm in Tenerife at the mo.' The woman laughed. 'Try number fifteen — she's probably got her eye on you as we speak.' With a squeak, the line cut.

Number fifteen was out, as were five others she tried. The house at the head of the T-junction was next; it must have a prime view of everyone who came or went from the estate. The houseowner answered the door, shivering in pyjama shorts and a tee shirt. He was red-eyed, his skin grey and sickly.

'Whatever you're selling, I don't want it.' He seemed slightly manic.

'Police, sir.' Rowan held up her warrant card and introduced herself.

His face crumpled. 'Oh, God — not the car again?' He flung the door wide and checked the driveway, showing obvious relief that his BMW sports car was safely parked where he'd left it.

'I understand you've been having trouble with car thefts in the area,' Rowan said.

'Mine was robbed off the drive *three days* after I moved in. But I'll catch the bastards at it next time.' He pointed to a dome camera just below the first-floor window.

'You wouldn't happen to have recordings for the last couple of weeks?' she asked.

The man snapped upright and paled from grey to ghost white. 'Why?'

'I'm looking into the death of a seventeen-year-old boy.' Rowan found an image on her phone of Damian Novak and showed it to the man. 'He was killed on the motorway.'

'The Fernleigh yob — I saw it online.'

'Damian Novak,' Rowan corrected. 'Do you know him?'

He blinked compulsively. 'Why would I know him?'

'I don't know, sir,' Rowan said, noting his defensive tone. 'But we think he did cross the motorway from the Fernleigh estate quite often, and this is the nearest housing this side of the road.' He'd barely looked at the image and she held it up again. 'Maybe you saw him around?'

The man raised both hands. 'No.'

'It's possible your security cam picked something up—'

'No!' he yelled.

Rowan took a step back, ready to defend herself if he kicked off and he seemed shocked.

'Sorry,' he said. 'I didn't mean — Jesus . . .' He rubbed a hand over his face. 'Rough night.'

I bet.

'Well, we all have those once in a while,' she said, softening her stance a little. 'Why don't I leave you my card, Mr . . . ?'

He didn't supply his name, and when she pressed for it, he said, 'Why d'you want my name? I don't have to give you my name.'

'No, sir, you don't. But it would save me having to look it up — I need to account for which houses I've canvassed, you see,' she added.

He remained obstinately silent. Clearly Mr Mysterious didn't think it was his job to make her life easy.

Rowan made a note of the house number.

'Look, I can see I caught you at a bad moment, but any help you can give might improve the situation,' she said. 'Fewer thefts, less anti-social behaviour, less worry about your property, fewer deaths on the roads.'

She handed him her card and he had the good grace to look abashed.

'If you remember anything, or if your neighbours mention something that might help, please call that number — and feel free to pass it along.'

He mumbled an insincere 'absolutely' and she heard the door close at her back as she walked down the drive. She didn't expect to hear a whisper from him, but she would be checking the name of the householder against the electoral register as soon as she got back to the office.

In the following half-hour, she found two more people at home before deciding that she'd try just one more. The last householder was a woman nursing a six-month-old baby. She put a finger to her lips and glanced down at the infant, beckoning Rowan inside when she'd checked her ID and leading her to the kitchen.

'Tea?' she murmured, wrangling the baby while she took mugs down from the shelf. 'No coffee, I'm afraid. Can't have it in the house while I'm breastfeeding — *zero* self-control. But I've all kinds of herbal.'

'Shall I?' Rowan asked, and the woman relinquished the task gratefully. 'I daren't put her down — little beggar seems to have a built-in alarm that goes off the second I put her in her cot.'

Her name was Lauren, and the baby was Olivia. Her husband was currently working on a project based in Leeds, but he came home for the weekends. She was taking extended leave from her job in graphic design but working from home three days a week. They chatted over tea for a while and Rowan got the feeling that Lauren was finding motherhood an isolating experience. 'It's a bit of a dormitory suburb this,' Lauren said. 'No community vibe.'

'You must be up nights, though,' Rowan said. 'Have you noticed any goings on?'

'This one's a good sleeper, believe it or not.' Lauren stroked the soft down on her baby's head. 'It's only during the daytime I get no peace. But that does mean that I often snatch a few hours to work late at night, and there's no question we have kids sneaking around.'

'Are these kids local?'

'Word is they're from the social housing across the motorway — isn't that where the boy who was killed came from?'

Rowan nodded.

'We had a lot of car thefts in the first six months — less since the people with the flashy cars started parking them in their garages. And you'll have noticed Harry with the Beamer has installed CCTV.'

'That's the man who lives in number twenty-three?' Rowan said, thinking Lauren must have been watching her going door-to-door. 'You wouldn't know his surname, would you?'

She grimaced. 'Sorry.'

'He wasn't very cooperative about sharing the security-cam footage . . .' Rowan puckered her forehead in disingenuous puzzlement.

Lauren chuckled. 'The problem with CCTV is it records *everything*, without prejudice.'

Rowan raised her eyebrows, half smiling, inviting the shared confidence.

'Harry's is definitely a party house. And those kids *bring* stuff as well as taking it away.'

'Such as?'

'Oh, you know — stuff to make the party really fizz.'

Well, that confirmed the drugs connection.

'So, what d'you do for company while your husband's away?'

Lauren blinked in surprise. 'You don't have kids, do you?'

Rowan shrugged, noncommittal.

'I don't have the *energy* for company.' Lauren said, jiggling the baby who had begun to stir. 'Although when Madam stops ruling my every waking minute, I have got my eye on a couple of groups in Birkenshore village.' Rowan had seen a sign for the village on her way in. 'That's if they'll have me,' Lauren went on. 'They're not fans of us Turner Homes exec types — think we've brought the tone of the neighbourhood down.' The baby was becoming cranky, but she paused, thinking, shushing her gently. 'Have you tried there?'

'Not yet,' Rowan said.

Lauren shifted the baby from her left to her right arm. 'You should. They've had just as much trouble as we have with lads from Fernleigh — and they've got a neighbourhood watch, so you might get more cooperation out of them.'

Rowan said her goodbyes as the wails of Lauren's baby rose like a siren behind her.

CHAPTER 13

The road to Birkenshore took Rowan in the direction of Birken Saltmarsh. Fresh river water and a hundred brooks and springs bubbling up through the overlying peat fed the marshes for most of the year, and the land was used for sheep grazing. Spring tides doused the lower reaches of the Mersey with salt water from the Irish Sea once a month, and occasional storm surges inundated the marshes all the way to Birkenshore, twelve miles along the river, keeping the land soggy and the marsh pools slightly on the brackish side.

The upper marsh was largely populated by birch trees clustered in small copses either side of a potholed, muddy lane. Rowan drove slowly, the ancient suspension of her car clanking and complaining all the way. At a T-junction, a cast-iron road sign in black and white gave directions to *The Shore* to the right and *Birkenshore* to the left. A modern blue sign alongside it warned, *Unsuitable for heavy vehicles — do not use sat nav*. Rowan took the left turn, and another sign a hundred yards on gave fair warning of a narrow bridge in half a mile. The road climbed thirty or so feet, passing exposed natural bedrock on either side, striped in layers of red-and-lemon-yellow sandstone. At the top of the rise, Rowan looked down on a cluster of sandstone houses, some of them thatched. A square tower marked the village church, and an imposing manor house stood aloof, a little further upriver. The lane drifted down the incline again but remained above the marshes, and Rowan supposed that the elevation would save Birkenshore from flooding during high tides. A precarious sort of existence, she reflected, yet the large houses on the edge of the village with their sandstone walls and sprawling gardens had a settled and comfortable look.

The bridge appeared after a kink in the road; a narrow humpbacked affair with no footpath and Rowan took it at a crawl. Glancing down, she saw fast-moving water fifteen feet below. Then, cresting the midpoint, she came eyeball-to-eyeball with an apparition of such malevolence that she braked, a surge of adrenaline sending little shockwaves tingling into her fingertips. The face had bulging green eyes, mud-red skin, and a mouth full of teeth like a pike. It was a perfect replica of the masks used to cover the faces of the Fernleigh effigies.

'Bloody hell . . .' She took a breath and wound down her window to examine the creature. This was much better crafted than the dummies they'd linked to the deaths of Damian Novak and Justin Lang on Fernleigh. The features were rendered in fabric, except for the eyes, which were large green beads with a vertical slit for the pupils. The goblin-like creature was anchored to the bridge by a wooden frame secured in the mud of the river. Its evil-looking black talons gripped the sandstone blocks of the arch as if it might launch itself over the top onto unsuspecting travellers. Rowan clicked off a few photographs and was about to drive on when a car horn blared behind her.

Startled, she glanced in her rearview. It was a massive brute of an SUV, its Chevy badge level with the midpoint of her rear screen, the monster grille an inch from her back bumper. The driver revved aggressively, and Rowan released the handbrake and drove on at a pedestrian pace, out of concern for her rear axle rather than to make a point. The vehicle swerved around her at the earliest opportunity with a final angry blast of its horn and a spurt of mud and gravel.

She found the SUV less than a minute later, parked at the roadside next to a café and bakery overlooking the village green. Drawing to a halt behind it, Rowan made a call on her work mobile to find out who the vehicle was registered to.

Taking in the buildings either side of the green, she saw at least two that looked Elizabethan set back off the road behind high walls. A crooked row of authentically Tudor-style half-timbered buildings housed the shops, and a solid block of Georgian properties and a few thatched cottages on the lane heading towards the manor house made up the remainder of the real estate.

Every property in the village must be listed, she thought.

The village hall abutted the church and a banner over its portal read, *KEEP BIRKENSHORE BEAUTIFUL!*. Another, draped over its boundary wall, exhorted visitors and residents to join their campaign on Facebook.

The bakery proudly announced its status as a British Baking Industry award-winner for its bread. Seated at a table by the door, was another effigy. This one was plump and pink-cheeked and wore a dazzling white apron and baker's cap. Peering inside through the mullioned shop window, Rowan saw that it bore a remarkable resemblance to the woman serving behind the counter. A moment later, a man strode out of the shop, stuffing half a meat pie into his mouth before he'd even reached the street. He glared at Rowan's clunker as if it offended him, and she was sure he'd surreptitiously checked the rear of his vehicle for damage.

'Mr Tetting?' Rowan asked.

'What do you want?' The man was six feet tall, well built, in his mid-forties, dark-haired and smooth-faced, as though he'd just come from a spa facial. He was dressed in boots and a wax jacket which shouted 'country gent', rather than 'farmer', although Rowan guessed that this man's carefully scuffed boots would be well beyond the means of most toilers on the land; his Burberry scarf alone probably cost more than her entire outfit.

'Mr *Julius* Tetting?'

Tetting had just pressed his fob key and was about to open the Chevy door, but her use of his given name seemed to give him pause and he eyed her narrowly.

'You really should be setting an example, sir,' Rowan chided. 'You being the organizer of Birkenshore Neighbourhood Watch.'

He squinted down his nose at her. 'What *are* you?' he asked. 'Press?'

Rowan presented her warrant card. 'Police.'

He sighed. 'For God's sake . . .'

'Speeding, overtaking without due care, tailgating—'

He flushed. 'Now *really*, Constable . . .'

'The speed limit in and around the village is twenty miles per hour,' she said, further discomfiting him.

He took a breath, held it, then released it in a burble of sheepish laughter. 'I'm afraid we rather got off on the wrong foot,' he said. 'Haven't eaten since six this morning, and I confess had a bit of a "hangry" moment.'

Rowan held his gaze and he dipped his head, eyeing her almost flirtatiously through long, dark lashes. 'How can I make it up to you?'

'Show me around,' she said. 'Answer a few questions.'

He seemed taken aback. 'Oh, well, if you're here about the neighbourhood watch, I'm sure I could draft in one of the ladies . . .' His gaze roved across the square as if he could click his fingers and summon one on sight.

But Rowan guessed that the best chance she had of gaining the locals' trust was an introduction from Tetting. 'You asked what you could do to make amends,' she said. 'This is it. You wouldn't want me to go away unhappy, would you, sir?'

He gave a surprised yelp of indignant laughter, then seemed to make his mind up to be charmed by her insistence. 'Very well, Constable,' he said. 'You shall have the VIP tour.'

He ditched the rest of his pie conscientiously in a black bin with what might have been the crest of the local manor embossed in gold on its glossy front, and they began at the village green. It had a pond and a massive tree, which was now burnished in autumnal bronze.

'Birkenshore is named for the birch woods surrounding it,' he informed her. 'And for centuries, the village had a birch on the green, but they're relatively short-lived — have to be replaced every hundred years or thereabouts. So now we have this fine old fellow,' he said, slapping the grey trunk of the old tree as if it was the flank of a horse. 'Hornbeam,' he said, as though she'd asked. 'Related to birch, but hard as nails — literally. Long-lived, too — this one was planted in seventeen-ninety.'

'The village goes back quite a way, then?'

'Birkenshore has an ancient heritage,' he said. 'Speke manor may be listed in the Domesday Book, but Birken Manor predates its more famous neighbour by a couple of hundred years.'

He meant the Tudor manor at Speke Hall a couple of miles up the road. It had been one of her parents' favourite places to visit as a family; Rowan couldn't help being impressed and Tetting seemed gratified by her reaction.

'This may seem a sleepy, sequestered little community to you,' he said in a confiding tone. 'But in its day, Birkenshore was a hotbed of subterfuge and insurrection. The Tettings were Popish Recusants during Elizabeth the first's reign, paying fines rather than submit to the heresy of attending Church of England services, protecting Catholic priests from certain death — Birken Manor has *two* priest holes and Speke Hall, as you may know, has only one.' He chuckled. 'They did, however, convert to Protestantism a hundred years later, which makes you wonder what was it all *for*?' He smiled fondly, shaking his head as if recalling the eccentricities of an elderly uncle.

Walking around the village, Tetting pointed out jolly effigies of local business owners including the pub landlord, a furniture restorer reupholstering a chair — the genuine article proudly displayed in her shop window at an eye-watering price; a convincing replica of the local blacksmith striking an anvil in front of his workshop; a bespectacled matron outside the volunteer library carrying a bundle of books, and the local dog walker — complete with her pack of exceptionally well-behaved canines.

'These are superbly crafted,' Rowan said, admiring a small gathering of child mannequins, set up as if playing 'ring-a-roses' on the green.

'We've been running the scarecrow festival for ten years, now; it's our biggest attraction,' Tetting said with a gracious nod. 'The tourists lap it up, especially when we get a mist from the marshes. So atmospheric.'

Rowan imagined the place would be picturesque in any season.

'We'll have some historical figures around the grounds of the manor later in the month, and a Halloween walking tour on the thirty-first,' Tetting went on. 'I might even make an appearance as a headless horseman.' He obviously relished the thought.

'But perhaps you think this is all rather twee.' He squinted down at her, his clear, smooth brow furrowing for a second, then he brightened. 'Come on.' He took off down a cobbled lane at the side of one of the Elizabethan houses. 'This used to be a farmhouse,' he said. 'There's a converted barn at the back I want to show you.'

He stopped suddenly, like a dog on point and looked up.

A hag with long arms, fearsome talons, a huge, hooked nose and greenish skin screamed out of the round window of the end gable astride a broomstick.

Rowan gasped.

'Magnificent, isn't she?' He beamed.

'She certainly isn't twee,' Rowan said. 'The goblin on the bridge—'

'Boggart,' Tetting corrected. 'A mischievous spirit of English folklore.'

'Is that what you call it? Is there anyone who could tell me more?' Rowan was hoping that they might be able to tell her where the masks had come from.

'Not my province. But I'm sure the village ladies could enlighten you. Some of them are really quite knowledgeable,' he added in a tone of astonishment. Then, after a moment's thought, 'Why don't I introduce you to my wife — she's on all the women's committees.'

He led the way back to the village green and his key fob appeared in his hand. 'Do you mind if we walk, sir?' Rowan said. 'It'll give me a better feel for the place.'

'A feel for *what*, though?' he asked. 'You're not really here about the neighbourhood watch, are you, Constable Rowan?'

'I never said I was.' She suppressed a smile at the fleeting petulance that crossed the man's face. 'I'm investigating a road death. It brought me to the new housing near the motorway, and from there to here.'

'Ah,' he said. 'That.'

'You've heard about the accident?'

'We hear rather more about incidents like this than we'd care to,' he said severely. 'I'm afraid the villagers feel under siege.'

'Why is that, sir?'

'Incomers,' he said with a baleful look.

'To the village?'

'Oh, no. We're a very settled community. It's that ghastly new development.'

'Attracted "undesirables", has it, sir?' Rowan asked.

He seemed to mistake her sarcasm for sympathy and carried on with a melancholy tilt of his head. 'In the past, it was a simple task to tell the, um, *rough element* from the locals.' Apparently, he'd forgotten that he'd placed Rowan firmly in the 'rough' category only twenty minutes ago. 'For the most part, it was a simple matter of letting that sort know that they weren't welcome; they took the hint and stayed away. But the Turner Homes' types are more difficult to categorize.'

Rowan was beginning to understand the animosity of the people she'd spoken to on the new development. 'How's that, sir?'

'Oh, *you* know — they have money, but no *taste*,' he said. 'All faux Tudor, Ikea furniture and plastic windows.'

'You can't see them from here,' Rowan observed, wondering if it was the architecture or the people he found most objectionable.

'You must think me the most dreadful snob,' he said.

Rowan didn't feel the need to reassure him.

'I'm really not. What you need to understand is those people have brought trouble into our midst,' he continued.

'How've they done that?'

'We never had any trouble from the denizens of Fernleigh until Turner Homes built those houses; it's their constant appetite for drugs that has emboldened the Fernleigh riff-raff.'

'Drugs?' Rowan asked. 'Where did you hear that?'

'One keeps one's ear to the ground,' he said vaguely.

'You must be worried that the builders are extending the development, then.'

'Hot air,' he said with a sneer.

'They're already advertising a second phase.'

Tetting shook his head. 'Hubris. I'm sure they'll *try*, but they'll never get it past council planning.'

'Because?'

They were standing next to the village hall, and he glanced at the banners.

'Community spirit,' he said. 'The people of Birkenshore will not stand for it. Turner has already been turned down once because of environmental impact concerns — risk of flooding, destruction of wildlife habitats — and so on and so forth. They'd have to dig drainage ponds and plant an *awful* lot of trees to satisfy the "green" criteria for a second phase.'

'The firm seems keen on environmental issues,' Rowan commented mildly.

He gazed at her in blatant disbelief. 'George Turner is a *builder*, Constable Rowan. He'll mouth platitudes, of course, but it's all talk. Anyway, he'd need two things to satisfy the barest minimum of mitigation requirements the council has stipulated.' He paused and Rowan raised an eyebrow in question. 'Access via my property, and more land.'

'Which you're not willing to give, and no one else is willing to sell.'

'Not at this time,' he said with a finality that sounded like 'over my dead body'.

They had come to a gate leading through stone posts into a gravelled drive. 'Birken Manor,' he announced. 'And I see Vivienne's finished my scarecrow at last.'

On a bench to one side of the gate, under an overhanging chestnut tree, a suave-looking effigy of Tetting sat, waxed jacket, riding boots and all.

'We Tettings built this manor,' he added, as if to prod Rowan into some expression of delight and gratitude that the squire of the manor should have spared her so much of his precious time, but she'd known exactly who Tetting was from the moment she'd checked his registration details, and had calculated that a vain man like Julius Tetting would be far more bumptious if she'd acknowledged his lofty status from the start.

The driveway was lined with trees, all a-flutter with falling leaves. Rowan relished the sound of birdsong, broken only by the distant roar of planes taking off or landing at the airport five miles away. As they neared the house, she was surprised to hear laughter and applause.

'We have a wedding on,' Tetting explained. 'They're in the marquee.'

'You've opened the manor to the public?'

Tetting smiled. 'I may be a snob, but I understand the need for change and progress — and as you can see, I've embraced it.'

'Yes, I noticed your stonking great Chevy is this year's model.'

He stopped, astonished, and perhaps a little offended, but, finally, he threw back his head and laughed. 'Your directness is a tonic, Constable.'

Normally, she would apologize for letting her mouth run off with her, but Rowan disciplined herself to silence. The man said he liked it, after all.

'We give wedding guests the run of the north wing,' he said. 'It's out of the way at the far end of the house, and they have a separate entrance for cars and so on. It's late Victorian, but no one has ever complained. You see—' He broke off, seeing a woman emerge through the front door.

She seemed startled and, for a second, Rowan thought she might dart back inside.

'Don't run away, darling!' Tetting bellowed. 'Come and meet Constable Rowan — she's an absolute hoot!'

Mrs Tetting regained her poise with an effort and stood placidly at the top of the steps, resting one hand on the carved stone handrail. She was tall and very slight, her bony shoulders poking like coat pegs through the fine cashmere of her sweater. Her hair, a russet gold, curled softly to her collarbones, and she wore a narrow skirt and flat shoes. Rowan was struck by a deep sense of melancholy in her expression.

Tetting sauntered up the steps and kissed his wife's offered cheek. 'You've really outdone yourself this time,' he said. 'My scarecrow is simply marvellous! Shouldn't wonder if Andy Pym weren't at the main gate sticking pins in it as we speak.'

He laughed uproariously at this, and Mrs Tetting responded with a wan smile.

'Constable Rowan, here, is fascinated by the boggart of Birken Bridge — d'you think you could enlighten her on a few details?'

The poor woman looked perplexed but good manners made her say, 'Of course, darling. I'll help in any way I can.'

At that moment, a car roared up to the house and skidded to a halt on the gravel driveway.

'Oh, Lord, speak of the devil,' Tetting murmured.

A wire-haired blond man in twill trousers and sports jacket leapt out of the car. 'You bloody hypocrite, Tetting!' he roared.

He was stocky, broad-shouldered, and puce with rage. Rowan hoped it didn't get physical; she wouldn't fancy her chances of wrestling Pym to the ground.

'Andy!' Tetting said, actually trotting down the steps to meet him. 'Meet Constable Rowan.'

Pym's gaze snapped to Rowan and he blanched.

'Come around to my study,' Tetting said, taking the man firmly by one elbow. 'Let's see if we can get this sorted out.' He led the unprotesting Mr Pym along a pathway and disappeared around the corner of the house.

Mrs Tetting looked helplessly at Rowan, but roused herself a moment later and said, 'What is it you wish to know about Birkenshore's resident boggart, Miss Rowan?'

CHAPTER 14

Rowan got back to St Anne Street station at four fifty-five with just enough time to grab a cup of horrible coffee from the machine before heading into the meeting room.

Finch kicked off with a report of his inquiries with the coroner.

'I asked if there'd been any suicides by hanging around the end of October, beginning of November last year, coinciding with the scarecrow on the motorway bridge,' he said. 'There was. Craig Breidon, aged eighteen. Found hanged in a stairwell of Hartsfern Tower, the block where he lived. He tied the rope to the top banister and jumped.'

'Did you get the images?' Warman asked. 'I gave the coroner's office a nudge after you called me.'

'Yes, boss.' He logged in at the computer and quickly clicked through to a file. A second later, an image appeared on-screen of the 'scarecrow' that Traffic Division had sent through from the motorway incident last October, alongside Craig Breidon, hanging from a rope inside a stairwell.

'Same cap, same mop of black hair, same leather bracelet,' he said.

'The claw earring's a match, too,' Rowan said.

'And there was no doubt about the verdict?' Warman asked.

'The family said he wasn't depressed, swore he wasn't the type to kill himself, but you know . . .' Finch shrugged, meaning *that's what families do*. 'The coroner was satisfied there were no defensive injuries or signs of a struggle. Not even scratch marks around the neck.'

Even determined suicides would often scrabble to loosen the ligature at their necks as the noose tightened, injuring themselves in the process.

'So he died instantaneously,' Rowan said.

Finch nodded. 'The pathologist reckoned the fall broke his neck.'

The suicide scene image was brightly lit, presumably by crime scene arc lamps, and Rowan asked, 'When did this happen?'

'Exactly seven days after the motorway incident,' Finch said. 'He was found at 5 a.m. by a shift worker on his way out to work, but lividity was fixed according to the pathologist, so he could've died four to six hours earlier. He was last seen alive and well by his sister at around ten fifteen the previous night, when he said he was going out to see someone. They never did find out who.'

Ian Chan appeared through the door at that instant. 'Perfect timing,' he chirped, unaffected by the frosty look DCI Warman gave him.

'Scooch up.'

Finch gave way and Chan took over the computer. 'Finch sent the evidence images to me earlier,' he said. 'And I've been doing some comparisons.' A new side-by-side image appeared on-screen: close-ups of the noose on the effigy and on Breidon.

He magnified the images, which were marked with arrows pointing out matching slubs and flecks in the fibres.

'Are we looking at a match, here?' Warman asked, staring at the screen.

'As near as I can tell.'

They sat in silence for a few moments. Now they had *three* deaths, all preceded by an effigy bearing the same weird mask about a week before the deaths. And all on one, small, 'problem' social-housing development.

'Clusters do happen,' Warman offered, cautious as ever.

'Not with effigies attached,' Rowan said, earning a scowl from her boss.

Chan had been scrolling through his phone, and now he spoke up. 'According to the Office for National Statistics, the number of deaths by suicide nationwide last year was just shy of eleven per hundred thousand. Typically, the rate is lower for the youngest age group. Based on what we've got here — two suicides, both in the tower blocks. You've got an average of four-fifty occupants per block. There're three blocks, let's say thirteen-fifty souls in all.' He did a quick calculation on his smartphone. 'Holy crap! That's equivalent to a *hundred and fifty* suicides per hundred thousand.'

Warman nodded. 'A significant spike, then.'

Goaded by Warman's monumental understatement Rowan said, 'Breidon died a year ago. What if there were more effigies, more deaths? What if they go back further than last October?'

'Then your deaths would be off the scale,' Chan said cheerfully.

'We'll look into that,' Warman said, adding with a sharp look in Rowan's direction, 'but let's not jump the gun.' She mused a moment. 'Still I do wonder why the deaths weren't flagged by the original investigators.'

Rowan scoffed. 'Well, if they're anything like Roy Wicks—'

Warman held up her hand. 'That will *do*, Cassie. The line manager in Justin Lang's suicide was DI Frinton; I'll have a chat with him.'

Rowan was about to offer her opinion of DI Frinton, but Ian Chan, still standing at the front, gave her a stern look and she subsided.

Warman turned to Finch. 'What do you know about Breidon?'

'Me? Nothing.' Finch sounded defensive, even panicked.

'Was there *nothing* in the coroner's report?'

'Oh, sorry, ma'am. I thought—' His colour was all over the place. 'Um, yes.' He flicked through the report. 'Breidon was affiliated to a gang operating out of the tower blocks on Fernleigh estate.'

'Just like Damian Novak and Justin Lang,' Rowan said. 'Damian got involved after a four-year stretch in a young offenders' unit.'

'The manslaughter conviction,' Warman said. 'What did Ms Palmer have to say for herself?'

Rowan went through her interview with the lawyer. Elspeth had confirmed that she had supervised a young lawyer at her firm who'd got Damian off with a community-service order after the first bike theft, with the result that the next one he stole ended in the grandmother's death and life-changing injuries to her grandson.

'So, a mea culpa,' Warman said dismissively. 'What a waste of time. Novak looked like he'd been trying to cross from the executive estate back to his home. So why was he there? To thieve? We know he was light-fingered, and there would be much richer pickings over on the executive development.'

'There was a spate of thefts of copper as the houses were being built,' Rowan said. 'And when the first buyers moved in, they had a few burglaries and car thefts. One of the residents said she'd seen youths sneaking around but I checked, and there've been no car thefts or break-ins for over a month.'

'That's an interesting turnaround.'

'Most of the houses have burglar alarms now,' Rowan said. 'And a lot of them have installed smart doorbells — some even have CCTV.'

Warman raised an eyebrow. 'Now, *that* could be helpful.'

'*Maybe* . . .' Rowan told them about Hungover Harry, and Lauren's sly comment that his was a 'party house'. 'The man nearly had a heart attack when I asked if we could see his security video.'

'You're suggesting that the Fernleigh youths switched from petty crime to drug dealing?' Warman asked.

'It would explain why they're still hanging around despite the drop-off in thefts,' Rowan said. 'And there's more money in drugs than petty pilfering.'

'Damian did have cannabis in his system,' Warman said, glancing at the PM report in front of her. 'And a small quantity on him when he was killed.'

'From what Lauren said about putting "fizz" into parties — and judging by the state Harry was in when I spoke to him, he was more than hungover; he was twitchy, sick-looking. My guess would be cocaine,' Rowan said.

Warman thought for a moment. 'All right. Lauren said there's no neighbourhood watch on the Turner Homes' development?'

'She implied it,' Rowan said. Warman was a stickler for details, and she'd been tripped up by a poorly chosen word too often in the past to fall into the trap now.

'You say some properties have CCTV?'

Rowan nodded. 'A few. More have smart doorbells. Harry said he'd take a look at his security cam. He's probably wiped anything useful off his drive by now.'

'Others might be willing to let us see what they've recorded, though,' Warman said.

'I'm wondering if the developers have any security cams, too,' Rowan added.

'I'll find out,' Warman said. 'How far did you get with the Fernleigh canvass?'

'Damian was known as a dealer — weed, mostly, but whatever he could get his hands on.'

'How reliable is that intel?'

'PCSO Dawson knows her turf.'

'Didn't you speak to residents yourself?'

It sounded like an accusation and Rowan felt her hackles raise, but Chan chose that moment to find a spot to sit, and that spot was right next to Rowan.

He 'accidentally' kicked her ankle as he sat. The look in his eye when she glared at him said, *be cool*.

'She tried to introduce me.' Rowan was pleased that she sounded calm and objective. 'But it's tough. I think people want to help, but they're scared — don't want to be seen talking to cops. From what Dawson said, Justin Lang was part of a criminal dynasty — that didn't collapse just because he died. She says he was bad to the core — grooming kids, using them as drug mules. He was training up Damian's younger brother before he died.'

'*No one* spoke to you?' It was as if Warman hadn't heard a word of what Rowan had said.

Rowan sucked her teeth, holding Warman's gaze until she felt in control of her temper. 'No one,' she echoed.

'You don't talk to the cops about the Lang family,' Finch said emphatically.

It sounded personal and Rowan said, 'You know these people?'

'The Lang crew is known from Knowsley to Childwall,' he said. 'They'll use every intimidation tactic in the book — and they're not afraid to get their hands bloody, either.'

Which was informative, but Rowan noted that he hadn't really answered her question.

'Jackie Dawson says she'll talk to the women's crafting group, see if she can persuade anyone to talk to me that way.'

'What did she have to say about the effigies?'

'She didn't know anything about them.'

'*Really?*'

'Young Lukas hadn't even told his brother about the Lang dummy — it wasn't common knowledge on the estate.'

It seemed grossly unfair to expect a single community support officer to do what the Matrix disruption team hadn't been able to achieve despite having dozens of highly trained officers and high-tech equipment.

Warman sighed. 'I'll talk to the coroner's office, ask them to extend the search for other suicides on the Fernleigh estate by a couple of years.'

'Jackie Dawson felt the suicide verdict on Lang didn't sit well,' Rowan said.

'He slashed his wrists, Cassie!' Warman exclaimed.

'I said I'd pass it along,' Rowan came back, not wanting a confrontation on someone else's behalf — she had enough of her own to keep her busy.

'You might ask the coroner's office to include deaths by misadventure as well,' Chan said. In response to a sharp look from DCI Warman, he added, 'Novak's death was ruled misadventure, but he still had his very own effigy.'

'Hm . . .' Warman tapped the table, her head bowed in thought. 'We need to know more about these effigies.'

'I might have a lead on that,' Rowan said. 'At least as far as the masks go.'

Warman tilted her head to show she was listening.

'There's a village just a mile or two down the road from the Turner Homes' development,' Rowan said. 'Birkenshore. It's an ancient settlement according to Julius Tetting — he's the local squire. Turner Homes wants to extend the new development, but the villagers blame them for a big jump in incidents of theft, vandalism and anti-social behaviour around the village. They say they never had any trouble from Fernleigh before Turner Homes started the build — they're waging a campaign against the second phase.'

'Successfully?' Warman asked.

'It's currently on hold,' Rowan said. 'Environmental issues, according to Tetting. I've yet to corroborate this, but he says the developer will need more land to make the changes the planning committee has demanded. And since most of the land around Birkenshore is owned by Tetting, and he's dead set against the expansion, he's confident the villagers will win.'

'So, there are tensions on both sides,' Warman said. 'But how does this fit with your lead on the masks?'

'The Scarecrow Festival is underway in Birkenshore at the moment, and there's something I wanted to show you. Can I—?' Rowan gestured towards the computer and Warman stepped aside.

Rowan connected her mobile to the computer via a USB cable and cast the image of the bridge ogre to the screen.

Finch sucked in air and Chan said, 'Yikes!'

'There is a distinct similarity,' Warman said, and Rowan consoled herself that while it wasn't a ringing endorsement, the word 'distinct' suggested that the DCI was at least willing to be persuaded.

So she took a breath and carried on. 'It's a boggart — a mischievous spirit of English folklore,' she added, quoting Tetting. 'This one is local to the district, according to Mrs Tetting, who helps to run the festival. She said they have at least one boggart scarecrow around the village each year. I ran out of time today, but I'll head back tomorrow; she's arranged for me to speak to a local historian first thing.'

'All right, but don't neglect the house-to-house.'

'A nighttime door-knock would probably yield a lot more from the Turner Homes' residents,' Rowan said. 'Most of them work during the day.'

'How would you feel about going back this evening?' Warman asked. 'I could probably squeeze some overtime out of the superintendent.'

'I've arranged to go meet PCSO Dawson back on Fernleigh at six twenty,' Rowan said, feeling ground down by the additional burden of work. 'She's going to introduce me to a voluntary youth worker named North — apparently, he runs self-defence classes for the kids on the estate. But I wouldn't say no to the overtime.'

Warman eyed her coolly, but a glimmer of amusement in her flat, grey eyes gave Rowan the courage to add, 'You know, we'd probably get a better result dropping flyers through letterboxes in Fernleigh, giving people the option to call Crimestoppers anonymously.'

'I'll give it some thought,' Warman said. 'It wouldn't hurt to have something to put in people's hands either way. And I'll see if I can get some special constables in to help with canvassing, too. Finch—'

'I'll draft the flyer,' he said.

Rowan stared at him in disbelief. *Draft the flyer? What had he been doing in the months since she'd last seen him? Organizing stationery cupboards for the big boys?*

'Good,' Warman said. 'We'll meet here for a briefing tomorrow morning, eight thirty sharp.'

A moment later, she was gone, and Rowan packed up, ready to follow, but she turned back to Finch. 'Hey, d'you want to head over to Fernleigh with me? I've got to nip home and check on Neil, but I can pick you up from here at six. It can't be much fun stuck in the office all day.'

Finch was fiddling with the computer, shutting the screen down. 'Thanks, Cass, but I've got to write up my notes.'

'You're sure? It'd be a chance to work on your interview technique.'

'Yeah. No, that'd be great — and I'd love to — but the thing is, I've promised Mum I'd take her out for a meal tonight.'

'Okay,' she said. 'No problem.' But it sounded like an excuse made up on the spur of the moment, and he was giving off an odd vibe. Where was the eager, enthusiastic Finch she'd spoken to this morning? She wanted to ask him, but he kept his head down, avoiding her eye, and finally she left him to it.

Ian Chan ambushed her on the stairwell. 'You need to zip that lip of yours, girl,' he said, voice echoing up the stairwell.

'What?' Rowan said, 'Why?'

'Were you really going to give your honest, unvarnished, *unasked-for* opinion of DI Frinton?'

Rowan shrugged, irritated. 'Frinton's a lazy, incompetent shiny-arse who creeps to the higher-ups by coming in under budget,' she said. 'Which means understaffing and under-resourcing his investigations.'

'Yeah, well, he's also about to be promoted, and you might have to work with him someday soon.' Chan said. 'Why burn your bridges before you've even come to them?'

'I didn't *say* it, did I? And what about you — "You might want to include deaths by misadventure". Did you see the look she gave you?'

'Someone had to say it.'

'You're thinking what I'm thinking, aren't you?' Rowan said.

Chan gave her a pert look. 'I dunno — what do you think I'm thinking?'

'That the suicides might have been faked. That Damian Novak, Justin Lang and Craig Breidon could be murder victims.'

CHAPTER 15

Later Monday evening

Rowan arrived back at Fernleigh's scruffy parade of shops five minutes early and there was no sign of Jackie Dawson. She waited in the car, not quite ready to take on the demands of her evening's work. It was almost dark, and the place looked even more depressing in the grey and fading dusk.

Neil had not been in the mood to talk about his school problems when she'd got home, but she'd forged ahead, telling him what Mr Singh had told her about his absences and poor performance.

'Bloody Singh — he's always on my back.'

'He's concerned about you, Neil,' she said. 'So am I.'

'I'm fine.'

'No, you're not. If you were fine, you'd be attending school, studying, getting the grades we both know you're capable of.'

'Yeah, well, it's all a bit pointless, isn't it?'

'Getting an education, pointless? No! If you want options in life, you need to study.'

'I'm out of options, in case you didn't notice.'

He held up his damaged arm as evidence, and Rowan saw that he was working himself into a temper.

'I have to go back to work,' she said evenly. 'But we'll talk about it tomorrow.'

'No. We won't.' He grabbed a loaf from the breadbin, a jar of peanut butter from the cupboard above it and slapped them on the worktop.

'We can't avoid it, Neil. Mr Singh wants us to have a meeting.'

'*Us*?' He stopped, dripping peanut butter gloop onto the counter.

'You and me, Mr Singh and the head of lower sixth.'

'I'm not a bloody *kid* — they want to talk to me, they should tell *me*, not you!'

Rowan knew from reading the sixth-form prospectus that the school encouraged students to accept responsibility for their learning. They had systems in place for unexplained absences, which emphasized their status as young adults. So the school would certainly have tried to contact him via their in-house messaging service, as well as sending WhatsApp messages. They may even have mailed a couple of letters home, addressed to Neil. She hadn't seen them, but Neil was usually home long before her day finished. He must have ignored all of these attempts before the school had resorted to phoning her.

She wanted to tell Neil all of this, but she could see the situation would spiral: Neil would storm off, slamming doors on the way, and when she returned home it would be to raging silence. So she took Ian Chan's advice and zipped her lip.

'I should be back before nine,' she said, scooping up her car keys and heading for the kitchen door.

'Who cares?' he mumbled through a mouthful of sandwich.

She felt her back muscles tense, but carried on walking, resisting a powerful urge to snap back. Alan Palmer was right: she needed help with this, and that meant involving the school and persuading Alex to take on the big brother role he'd so easily cast off nearly eight years ago.

A sudden rap at her window made her jerk violently. A fraction of a second later she realized it was Jackie Dawson and smiled reassurance as the PCSO held her hands up in apology, taking a step back from the car.

Rowan wound down the window. 'Sorry. Miles away. Where are we going?'

'We're already here,' Dawson said, grinning.

She nodded towards a building at the end of the row. A man stepped out of its steel-reinforced door and began rolling up the metal shutters using a window pole. He looked to be in his mid-forties; plump and round-shouldered, which took a few inches off his height, but Rowan estimated he was a good six feet tall. The lights were on, and a few older teens were already inside; it looked like they were setting up, ready for the evening session.

Rowan could see a screen at one end of the room, set up for a video game. 'I'd have thought this would attract trouble,' she commented.

'It has, now and then,' Dawson admitted. 'But Jim reckons that skulking in the shadows isn't a good way to gain trust — or interest, for that matter — kids initially drawn by the light and the promise of video games have become our most loyal club members. This is our shop window — it's all about visibility.'

It certainly seemed like it. As the last of the light faded, the place was lit like a lantern tower and as if they had been waiting in the shadows, boys and girls started to arrive like moths to the flame. Most of them looked around fourteen or fifteen, but a few were as young as twelve years old.

'It's the closest we have to a community centre around here,' Dawson explained as they crossed the road to the building.

'The premises are owned by Gareth Jessop — he's the guy you saw opening up. He ran the convenience store from this building for nearly ten years, barely scraping a living, but he saw it as a service to the community.'

'Why did he close the shop?' Rowan asked. Clearly the estate still needed a food store, and the food co-operative seemed to be doing well.

'It got broken into one time too many,' Dawson said with a sad shake of her head. 'That was a couple of years ago. Gareth's dad ran that shop from the day the estate opened till the day he died. The mortgage had been paid off years before, and Gareth owns the property outright, but he can't sell it — I mean who'd want it? He could've cut and run — no one would have blamed him — but he reopened the place as a community hub. The Fernleigh Crafters meet here, and the mums-and-toddlers' groups. Evenings are for the teenagers. Gareth's a voluntary community worker, effectively.'

Stepping over the threshold, Rowan saw that the place was a lot bigger than it appeared from outside. To the right of the shop window was what must have been a rear extension to the old store. Built of solid brick, it had been fitted out as a martial-arts dojo, a good ten metres long and eight wide. To the left, in view of the window, was a smaller area that housed a table-tennis table and a cluster of café tables with mismatched chairs. A six-feet run of retail shelving from the old shop had been converted for use as bookshelves, which were mainly stacked with battered paperbacks on the upper shelves and a hodgepodge of children's picture books lower down. A large urn, now switched off, sat on a counter in the corner, and Gareth Jessop was organizing two of the older children in pouring orange juice and arranging biscuits on a plate.

'I spoke to the crafters' group leader; she thinks we should call an extraordinary meeting, disguise it as a brain-storming session for their Christmas charity fundraiser. If Adela can't get them motivated, nobody can.'

'We need to move fast on this.' Rowan said, lowering her voice and turning away from the children. 'We've found another that has all the hallmarks,' she added, carefully avoiding the words 'death' and suicide'.

Dawson's eyes widened. 'Who? When?'

'Craig Breidon,' Rowan murmured. 'Last October.'

'Oh, God, yes. His poor mother . . . Craig wasn't a bad lad — not really — he was just too frightened to say no to the likes of,' she glanced over at the kids before finishing at a whisper, 'of those others we talked about. Was there a . . . ?' She seemed to be struggling for the word.

'Scarecrow?' Rowan nodded. 'It was hung from a bridge over the M62. Traffic cops thought it was a Halloween prank.'

'This has been going on for a year?' Dawson asked, distressed.

'We're just looking for similarities, right now,' Rowan cautioned. 'We've no proven link, yet.'

'Still . . .' Dawson took a breath and let it go. 'I'll call Adela when I get a minute, see if she can tempt the crafters in before the weekend.'

Gareth Jessop spotted them at that moment and came over, smiling. 'You must be Cassie,' he said. 'Thanks for what you're doing.'

Doing? Rowan was thrown. 'Um . . . Did Jackie explain why I'm here?'

He nodded, glancing across to the young volunteers. 'Showing an interest is what.' He lowered his voice. 'Best they get to know you a bit before we go into the nitty gritty of who you are.' His hair, cut close to his scalp was black and thick, and he had extraordinary green eyes, which sparkled with warmth. His voice was a pleasant baritone and she caught a slight Welsh lilt in it. 'You wouldn't think it to look at them, but some of these kids spook easily,' he confided.

Rowan turned, hearing a slight kerfuffle at the door.

'Sir, Jonty's here and you haven't put the ramps out, yet!' one of the young volunteers trilled.

For a few minutes there was a clamour of voices and a bustle of activity as a folding metal ramp was hauled out from under the window and put in place by Jessop, while one child held the door and another helped a slight boy who looked to be about fifteen manoeuvre an electric wheelchair inside. He was sallow-skinned, his chestnut-brown hair styled long and wavy on top and short at the back and sides. Rowan saw Dawson slip outside, her phone already in her hand.

It seemed that some of the older boys had been waiting for Jonty's arrival; now they crowded around him, one of them thrusting a games console into his hand.

Jonty stopped his chair and looked up at the club organizer. 'Wanna come over, learn a few hacks, boost yourself from level one, Gareth?' he called.

'I think I'm beyond redemption,' Gareth said, laughing, waving away the invitation. 'You know me, Jonty — all thumbs.'

'You do know that *should* be a good thing in gaming?' Jonty lifted the console, thumbs hovering over the controls.

Gareth replied with a double thumbs-up, which he quickly turned downwards.

The other boys were clamouring to make a start and Jonty zipped his chair over to the screen.

'He's a bloody inspiration, that lad,' Gareth said, glowing like a proud uncle. 'His nana was a regular when I still had the shop, and when she got a bit unsteady on her pins, she'd come and pick what she wanted — very particular about her fruit and veg, was Jonty's nana — and he'd pop in on his way home from school to carry them home to her.'

Rowan glanced at Gareth. 'This is the kid who—'

His face clouded. 'Run down on the bloody crossing, he was. His nana was killed outright. And you know what sickens me most? Damian Novak never gave it a second thought.' He shook his head. 'A lot of kids landed in a wheelchair like that would struggle to come to terms. But Jonty's never let it hold him back.'

Rowan watched Jonty from the other side of the social area, thinking about her brother, wondering how you built that kind of resilience into a child.

Some younger children started a mixed-doubles game of the table tennis, and over in the dojo area, kids from pre-teens to young adults were shedding coats and shoes. Already kitted out for the martial-arts session, they gathered at the edge of the mat.

'It must cost a bit to run this,' Rowan said. 'How d'you fund it?'

'Local government grants, donations and fundraisers. A couple of children's charities have chipped in, too — they paid for the matting — saved us fifteen hundred pounds.' His eyes glowed at the memory. 'The big superstore over in Speke retail park has been very generous, supplying drinks, biscuits and that — stuff approaching the sell-by date that has to be taken off the shelves, but there's nothing wrong with it.'

Rowan nodded, thinking about Lauren, stuck at home with a baby and no opportunity for social interaction. The Turner Homes' residents could do with some of Fernleigh's community spirit.

She couldn't help commenting, 'It's very forgiving of you to help the kids who put you out of business.'

'These kids had nothing to do with it.' He sounded offended. 'These boys and girls want more than what the gangs and grubby little drug dealers've got on offer. People look down on Fernleigh, but just cos it isn't a pretty suburb doesn't mean you can't have decency and kindness — you saw how those lads rushed to bring Jonty in here. Give kids a chance to do things differently — to be their better selves — they'll grab it with both hands. It's not much, this place, but it gives them an opportunity to grow. You can change a whole life track with a bit of guidance and support.'

'Sorry,' she said when he finally took a breath. 'That didn't come out right — and I'm not judging. I live on the borders of Everton and Walton, so I know a bit about social deprivation.'

A quizzical frown creased his forehead, and she felt him reassessing her. Then he broke into a laugh. 'There's me on my soapbox again. What I should've said is don't beatify me just yet: I got the insurance money, so I didn't *actually* lose out. Can't sell the place, but you know what? Since I closed the shop and started this project, I feel I've done more for this community than I ever did selling bad nutrition and cheap booze.'

Two of the teenage boys had got fractious over by the dojo and Gareth called across, 'Now, boys, settle down. You don't want Jim seeing you bickering.'

They ignored him. 'A word from me, they do what they like.' He laughed, though he was flushed with embarrassment.

At that moment, the door opened, bringing a rush of cold air, and a man strode in carrying a sports bag. He was tall, his mid-brown hair cut short, but softly spiked on top. He moved with confidence and grace, and the waiting children fell silent.

Then he said, '*Seiza!*' and all the children gathered around the mat dropped and shuffled into the correct kneeling posture.

'You can see why I leave the fisticuffs to Jim,' Gareth murmured, patting his gently mounded stomach. 'I've neither the physique nor the charisma for it.'

Peace restored, the other man returned to where Rowan was standing with Gareth.

'Sorry I'm late,' he said, then glanced at Rowan. 'You must be Cassie. I'm Jim North.'

Rowan offered her hand. He had a firm grip but made no attempt at a bone-crusher that would have marked him out as an over-compensator or, worse in her book, an intimidator.

'I'm not sure I can help you with this,' he said quietly. 'These kids are suspicious of police. Some of them are on a knife edge as far as committing to what we do, and I don't want to lose them.' He glanced at Jessop. 'Sorry, Gareth. Look, I've got to go and change — can I use your office?'

'Sure,' Gareth said. 'You know the combination.'

Irked by Jim North's summary dismissal, Rowan looked around for someone to chat to, but the crowd around Jonty's chair had grown, and shouts of excitement and approval went up over the sound of gunfire and explosions. The few club members not involved in the video game seemed engrossed in their own activities and she sensed that a rude interruption from a stranger would not be well received.

At that moment, a fight broke out between the two boys who were arguing as North had come in.

Gareth looked at her with alarm, and Rowan hurried over to them. 'Come on, lads,' she said.

The taller boy gave his opponent a hard shove, sending him cannoning towards Rowan. She side-stepped, catching the victim by the collar of his jacket, turning and gently lowering him to the mat. The taller boy stared at her.

'You need to sit down and think about why you're here,' she said quietly.

'You're not our sensei,' he said. 'You can't tell me what to do.'

'Every adult here is your sensei.' Jim North's voice boomed from across the room.

The boy flinched and turning, he came face to face with his class leader. 'Sir, I wasn't—'

'I don't want to hear it, Kyle. Take your place.' The boy hung his head, but gave no argument, and obediently knelt at the end of one of the lines. The smaller boy now came under his scrutiny. 'I want to speak to you and Kyle before you go home.'

The boy nodded miserably.

North beckoned one of the older girls and she stood. 'Could you take the class through a breathing exercise, please, Mylee?'

The girl bowed and walked to the centre of the mat as North guided Rowan to the far end of the dojo, out of earshot.

'Aikido?' North asked.

'A bit of this, bit of that,' she said. In fact, Rowan had attended several martial-arts classes, including aikido and kickboxing, since she'd been attacked last winter, but hadn't found one that suited her, yet.

'Well, you have to mix it up a bit in street situations.' He smiled and scratched his chin. 'Wanna show the kids some moves?'

Rowan shrugged off her jacket and kicked off her shoes before performing the martial salute, bowing, fist to palm, elated to have won his respect.

With a half-smile, North reciprocated, and they took up a fight stance.

CHAPTER 16

Tuesday morning briefing

The team had gathered five minutes ahead of DCI Warman's briefing deadline, giving Rowan time to introduce them to Jackie Dawson. Chan was welcoming, but Finch gave her a listless nod and continued scrolling through his phone.

'Cassie *really* impressed the kids when she went a round with Jim North,' Dawson said.

Ian Chan nearly choked on his morning coffee. 'I would've paid good money to see that.'

'Behave yourself.' Rowan felt her colour rising.

His eyes widened and she just knew he was going to say something she'd regret.

'I mean it,' she snapped, giving him the stink-eye.

Chan cocked his head. 'Oops, watch out, here comes trouble . . .'

Rowan felt her stomach tighten hearing the chief inspector striding up the corridor in her block heels. Warman's appearance was timed to the second; she arrived as the meeting room clock clicked to eight thirty. At this hour, on a drizzly October morning, it seemed obvious to Rowan that her boss would not be impressed to find a new team member in residence, but this self-evident truth had been beyond her grasp when she'd issued the invitation the previous night.

The fact was she'd been so buzzed after the martial-arts session that it had seemed the obvious course of action. After all, if she could gain the trust of fifteen kids from one of the toughest estates in Merseyside, surely she could talk DCI Warman round? But Rowan's optimism withered and died under the cold grey stare of her boss and she saw it for the adrenaline-induced bravado it had been.

Waves of disapproval seemed almost to physically assail Rowan in the slight pause before Warman entered the room. She made the last few steps to the front at a more leisurely pace, and Rowan had to force herself not to turn and try to gauge the degree of her boss's displeasure.

Warman placed her papers on the front table, then levelled her gaze at Rowan.

'Morning, boss.' Rowan's voice was a little too chirpy, and she consciously dropped her tone by half an octave. 'This is PCSO Jackie Dawson. Jackie, this is DCI Warman.'

Warman's gaze hardened and Rowan feared that there would be words after the briefing, but she kept talking. 'Jackie shared some interesting insights into Craig Breidon last night, and I thought she'd explain better than me, so—'

'So here you are . . .' Warman cut in. The air around seemed to crystallize with tiny needles of ice.

Jackie Dawson was immaculately turned out in uniform, her glossy black hair tied back and tightly wound into a bun. She began by giving some background on Craig: his dad had died when Craig was eleven, and his mum had struggled to bring up four kids on her own. She'd done her best to keep her eldest son away from the hard cases who lived in their block but working two jobs and caring for three more children under ten meant that she couldn't be around to supervise and Craig, regarded as a soft touch, had been bullied at school. Tragically, he'd fallen in with a crew calling themselves the Stoners in the hope that gang membership would give him protection. At seventeen, he'd tried to break away, had even started a catering course at college. When the gang leader found out, he'd squeezed Craig to take drugs into college — and when he was caught carrying, Craig was expelled immediately. Within a fortnight he was dead.

DCI Warman listened politely enough to Dawson's summation, although she made the PCSO give her account standing.

'What's the name of this gang leader?' Warman asked.

'Thomas Capstick — known locally as "Stickman". Craig's mum was convinced that Capstick murdered Craig.' Rowan heard a slight breathlessness in Dawson's delivery that reminded her uncomfortably of herself.

'Ever since Craig died, she's been going into schools in the area,' Dawson went on. 'Talking to kids about the dangers of getting involved in gangs.'

'So these deaths could be gang hits?' Finch said.

'Damian and Lang were both affiliated to the Lang crew, and Craig died after losing drugs belonging to Capstick, so it's possible, I suppose,' Dawson said. 'It never occurred to me till now that Craig's death was anything other than suicide.'

'I have Craig Breidon's PM report in front of me,' Warman said. 'There was no suggestion of foul play. No abrasions, bruising or ligature marks. He had taken a large dose of Ativan around the time of his death — he was taking it under prescription — and his blood alcohol was eighty-five micrograms.'

Over the driving limit, Rowan thought.

'You'd wonder how he managed to rig up the rope, then,' Chan said. 'Alcohol on top of an Ativan overdose? He'd be uncoordinated, confused, drowsy — maybe suffering extreme vertigo. And his blood pressure would be very low.'

'Yet he climbed ten floors to the top of the stairwell,' Rowan said.

'He may have used the lift,' Warman corrected.

'The lift was out of service,' Dawson supplied. 'I remember the CSIs had to lug their equipment up the steps.'

111

'Let's say for the sake of argument someone *did* do him in,' Chan said. 'They'd either have to carry him up ten floors or else walk him up on the pretext of helping him to get home. You'd need the strength of Hercules to carry a body that far, but with Ativan *and* alcohol in his system, Craig would be suggestible, compliant — even grateful—'

'So he cooperated with his killer,' Rowan chimed in.

'We need to be careful of looking for a pattern where none exists,' Warman said.

We've already got a pattern! Rowan wanted to shout. *The masks are the pattern. The effigies are the pattern!*

'But the masks and the effigies do support the theory that these deaths were more than simple suicide or misadventure,' Warman went on in her stolid, measured way, and Rowan blushed, realizing how narrowly she'd avoided a blunder.

'And there is another death we must consider,' Warman added.

Rowan shot a look at Ian Chan. He drew the corners of his mouth down in a gesture that meant *this is news to me*.

'Shortly after I received Breidon's report, the coroner's assistant rang me. She'd found a similar case to Lang's suicide. This happened eighteen months earlier — also on the Fernleigh estate — a young woman of twenty-two.'

Warman accessed a file and cast an image onto the screen. A fully clothed woman lay in a bath of water turned blood red. Her face was almost as white as the bath enamel.

'Lisa Blerring,' Dawson murmured. 'I was in college at the time, living away, but Mum told me about it.'

'Did you know her?' Warman asked.

'No, she was four or five years younger than me.'

Warman nodded. 'She was found in the bathroom of her parents' flat. She'd taken a massive dose of painkillers, rolled up her sleeves, and then slashed her wrists, cutting lengthwise through the veins from the crook of her elbow to the heels of her hands.'

Finch winced.

'Was there an effigy?' Rowan asked.

'I've made preliminary enquiries, but haven't found anything as yet,' Warman said. 'However, the similarities to Lang's death are striking: found in a bath of warm water, dosed with painkillers — in his case it was morphine, in hers, paracetamol. They were both dressed, sleeves rolled up, superficial veins of the lower arms slashed lengthwise.'

'Suicide note?' Rowan asked.

'Neither Lang nor Lisa Blerring left a note,' Warman said. 'But a short time before her death, Lisa had had a termination.'

Finch muttered, 'Oh, Jesus,' and Rowan glanced at him.

He was staring at the image, a grey, sick look on his face, a faint sheen of sweat on his brow.

'Are you all right, Finch?' she asked.

'N-no.' He shoved back his chair and stood.

Warman widened her eyes in surprise and disapproval.

'Sorry, boss.' He stumbled to the door. 'Think I'm gonna . . .'

There was an awkward silence as he blundered out and they listened to him run down the corridor. Then Warman tapped the front desk, recalling their attention.

'Based on this new evidence, the superintendent has agreed to draft in some special constables to help with the canvass. They'll be available from tomorrow morning. Cassie, did you get anything from the martial-arts teacher?'

Ian Chan nudged her with his knee and Rowan felt her face grow hot. 'He said he'd talk to the kids in his class. If they've seen or heard anything, he'll let me know.'

'The Fernleigh crafters are coming in 'specially tomorrow,' Dawson chimed in. 'If Cassie's available, we could talk to them together, ask if they know anything about the masks. And I was thinking, if I can persuade Craig Breidon's mum to come in and talk to them, we'd have a better chance of bringing them on board.'

Warman gave that look that Rowan thought of as: 'When a dog stands on his hind legs and starts to talk', and she cringed on Dawson's behalf. But after an uncomfortable silence, Warman said, 'Yes. Good idea.' She turned to Rowan. 'Cassie, you're talking to someone in Birkenshore about the masks this morning?'

'Yes, boss. I thought I might ask about the Fernleigh scarecrows, too.'

'Hold off on that,' Warman said. 'It's an aspect of these deaths I'd like to keep to ourselves for now.'

Finch came back into the room at that moment.

'Feeling better, Finch?' Warman said in a tone that held little empathy; maybe she thought he was hungover — though Rowan couldn't picture him getting pickled over a meal at Wetherspoons with his mum.

Always fair-skinned, now Finch was pale as paper. There was a slight pinkness around his eyes, too, and Rowan suspected he'd been crying.

'Sorry, boss,' he said. He sounded hoarse and he couldn't bring himself to look in the direction of the screen. 'The thing is, I knew Lis—' His voice cracked: the use of the victim's name was too emotional. He cleared his throat and tried again. 'I knew h-her. We were friends.'

'In college, or . . .' Warman said, her expression softening slightly.

'No. From school. We grew up together — on the estate — even hooked up for a bit, one summer, stayed friends till I moved away.'

Now Rowan understood Finch's reluctance to come with her to Fernleigh: it couldn't have been easy, becoming a cop on that estate. Finch didn't have Jackie Dawson's confidence and easy, sociable manner, and anyway a detective would be regarded very differently from a community support officer in the eyes of Fernleigh residents who might be on the fringes of criminality.

'Lisa was a good person,' Finch insisted. 'She wouldn't be involved in selling drugs.'

'Did you know she was pregnant?' Rowan asked.

He shook his head, pain creasing his face. 'We lost touch.' He seemed to struggle for a moment, then frowning fiercely, he said, 'Her best friend, Sophie, might be able to tell us more.'

'We'll pay her a visit this afternoon,' Rowan suggested.

He shook his head. 'If Lisa was mixed up with the Lang family in some way, it could be dangerous.' He looked frightened, and Rowan wondered just what the Lang family had done to Finch.

'All right,' Warman said. 'Cassie — you head off to your meeting with the historian in Birkenshore village. Finch — see if you can find out where Sophie works; if interviewing her there is a viable option, we'll go with that.' She stared gravely at Jackie Dawson for a few moments. 'After you've spoken to the crafters and Mrs Breidon, call in on Lisa Blerring's parents, see if you can get anything useful out of them.'

Warman wrapped up the briefing a few minutes later, and Rowan left with Jackie Dawson.

Neither said a word until they were out of the building.

'Well, I think we can safely say you made an impression,' Rowan said.

'She is so *scary*,' Dawson whispered, wiping imaginary sweat from her perfect brow.

'Tell me about it,' Rowan said, sliding her a cynical look through half-closed eyes.

'Why the hell didn't you *warn* me?' Dawson demanded, faking outrage, although the excitement in her voice gave her away. 'I honestly thought she was going to have me escorted off the premises.'

'If I'd warned *you*, you might not have come,' Rowan said. 'If I'd warned *her*, she would've had you escorted off the premises.'

Dawson stared at her. 'Oh, my God — you set me up!' She seemed torn between outrage and hilarity.

'Sometimes it's better to ask forgiveness than permission,' Rowan said. It was partly an admission and partly an apology.

'When she looked at me, it was like she could turn on her laser eyes at any moment and burn me to a crisp.'

'She could have, but she didn't . . .' Rowan narrowed her eyes. 'What is this strange power you hold over the warhorse — and how do I get some?'

Dawson laughed.

'I'm serious,' Rowan said, laughing too. 'I want it — now! I mean, did you *hear* what she said?'

'What, you mean, "Good idea"?' Dawson lifted one shoulder. 'It *was* a good idea.'

'D'you have *the slightest notion* how long it took before she said something like that to *me*?'

CHAPTER 17

The drizzle slowly abated as Rowan drove out of the city and by the time she turned off the motorway, a pale sun filtered through low-lying clouds over the Turner Homes' development. Driving on, she took the lane to Birkenshore and as she started the bumpy ride towards the village, shining wisps of mist drifted out like gossamer from the tops of the stands of birch. The sun shone through tiny droplets of moisture on every tree and sapling, gathering at the points of each drooping triangular leaf and refracting the light like a wealth of precious gems.

At the top of the sandstone escarpment, Rowan gasped in wonder. The sun shone brightly over a lake of pure white; it shifted in subtle eddies and whorls, gathering in pools of denser substance, lapping at the banked edges of the road and stretching in silky skeins over the patched canopy of scrubby trees below.

In the distance, the parapet of the church tower and the ornately decorated brickwork of Birken Manor's chimneys poked holes in the milky vapour, but the lower-lying marshes remained cloaked in its ever-shifting contours.

In her slow descent towards the village, the fog closed in, and she flicked on her headlights. Billions of tiny droplets reflected the light, merging the muddy grey road with soft swirls of condensate until they seemed to bond as one. Anxious that she might run off the track into a ditch, Rowan switched to her sidelights, tapping the horn at every bend in the road, praying that she wouldn't meet a car coming the other way.

Approaching the humpbacked bridge, she braced herself for the boggart. She wound down the window to listen for approaching traffic and gave the horn two sharp taps. A clatter of sound to her left made her jerk and grip the wheel more tightly. Birds, disturbed from their roost by the noise.

'Bugger!' she murmured. Taking a moment or two for her heart to settle, she took the narrow crossing at a snail's pace. The bridge's stonework drifted in and out in the dense mist; as for the boggart, she saw first a long, red, bony hand reaching over the parapet, its black talons gleaming and viciously sharp. The beast seemed to have shifted position, though that might be the murky conditions playing tricks on her.

The creature's arms were rendered in felt, but grotesque sinews and blood vessels had been stitched onto the fabric. The green woollen weave of its jerkin, patterned with intricate stitching, was pearled with moisture, as though it had just emerged from the stream below.

Where's the head? Had the effigy been vandalised?

Suddenly, the grinning face loomed out of the murk, its green eyes magnified by a watery coating, its sharp teeth centimetres from her and she cursed under her breath. The car's lights lit a drop of water hanging from the end of its pendulous nose. As she watched it, the beast seemed to slide in and out of the mist like a phantom. Unnerved, Rowan crunched the car into gear, and went on her way.

She parked outside the bakery. The fog was just as dense here, but she remembered that the volunteer library was directly opposite, on the other side of the green. Visibility was so poor that rather than chance toppling into the pond, she walked around the green, seeking out the effigy of a bespectacled matron outside a Tudor-style timber-framed building. The door was old oak, the ironwork painted black. She turned the knobbly iron doorhandle and felt the latch lift inside. The old building smelled of churches and decay.

Scanning the room for the matron represented by the effigy outside, Rowan saw several women browsing the shelves and another reading a story to a small group of rapt toddlers, accompanied by their carers. An elderly man sat peering at a computer and prodding the keys from time to time. Finally, she caught sight of a fifty-something woman shelving books. Her grey hair was cropped close at the sides and over the ears, while the top was styled in an elaborate peak tipped with soft raspberry tints.

Rowan introduced herself. 'I'm looking for Sal Fabian,' she added.

'You found her,' the librarian said, setting a bundle of books on a portable trolley and offering her hand. Her grip was firm and forthright.

'You don't look a bit like your effigy,' Rowan said, smiling.

'Oh, that old cliché!' the woman exclaimed. 'They put that hideous thing outside the library in revenge because I wouldn't let the crafters make one of me.' She lifted one hand and added in a stage whisper, 'They probably would have made me into a witch.'

Rowan saw heads turn and even the old man stopped tormenting the computer keyboard for a moment. 'Is there somewhere private we can talk?'

'Come through to my lair,' Ms Fabian said. 'I've just put a pot of coffee on to brew.' She showed Rowan through to an office tucked away at the far end of the main space. It was stacked four or five high with boxes. She shifted a couple from a chair and invited Rowan to sit.

'We had a big donation from one of the libraries the council's closing around Liverpool,' she explained, survey-ing the stacks of boxes. 'They've sent way too many, but I suppose they'd rather see books go to a library than to a charity shop. It'll take forever to sort them, and I'll probably end up sending a load to Bookbarn anyway.' She sighed. 'Heartbreaking, really.'

The coffee machine gurgled and spat and the nutty scent of freshly brewed coffee billowed up with the final burst of steam.

Rowan's stomach rumbled in anticipation.

Without a word, the librarian washed her hands at a small sink tucked in a corner of the room and reached for a cardboard box on top of one of the filing cabinets.

'You got here all right, then?' she asked. 'That road can be a nightmare in the fog.'

'It's certainly very different from my visit yesterday,' Rowan said. 'And they should have a health warning on that boggart. I nearly crashed the car — and *I* knew it was coming.'

Sal humphed. 'Julius thinks it's hilarious having that vile thing poised to strike on the bridge.'

'You don't see the joke?'

'It's a damned menace. One of these days someone *will* crash — or else have a heart attack. Then the joke'll be on him.' Sal pulled up another chair before lifting two cream scones out onto a plate and pouring coffee. 'So.' She nudged the plate to Rowan. 'You want to know more about our boggart. Can you tell me why?'

'No,' Rowan said, mindful of her boss's warning. 'Sorry.'

Sal tilted her head. 'Had to ask.' She took a sip of coffee, gathering her thoughts. 'They're malevolent spirits. In Lancashire mythology, boggarts live outdoors, causing mischief and frightening horses. They can be ordinary and human-like, but as you will have gathered from his effigy, our *particular* boggart is a monstrous flesh-eating water sprite.'

'A kind of bogeyman, then?' Rowan asked, taking a delicious bite of buttery scone and cloud-like cream.

'They're all variations on the bogeyman, boogieman, bogle theme,' Sal said. 'But they can be female, too. Jenny Greenteeth is a boggart infamous in Liverpool folklore — I remember my great aunt scaring me half to death with stories of Jenny luring children into the marshes or dragging them under pondweed in the canals hereabouts.'

'So there's an abduction element to what they do?' Rowan was thinking about Craig Breidon, drugged and possibly walked to his doom.

'Oh, yes,' Sal said. 'They're *often* partial to young children and elderly folk.'

'Could there be more than one Birken Bridge boggart?' Rowan asked. 'I found some stuff online about a whole clan of them that supposedly lie in wait under bridges at Boggart Hole Clough near Manchester.'

'No,' Sal said, talking around a mouthful of scone. 'Absolutely not. There's only one Birken Bridge Boggart. He lives under the bridge on the outskirts of the village and never ventures any nearer. Doesn't stop him terrorizing the folk hereabouts, though,' she added wickedly. 'And by the way, you should never name a boggart — naming them puts them in a foul, vengeful temper. Birkenshore folklore states, "A boggart that's named shall ne'er be tamed".'

'But he's called the Birken Bridge Boggart,' Rowan said, embarrassed that she was almost superstitious about saying it aloud.

'Oh, don't look so worried — that's not his true name,' Sal said, with a twitch of her mouth. 'And don't ask, cos I won't say it.'

'Okay . . . Who decided what he looked like?' Rowan asked. 'I mean, who designed the effigy?'

'It's been ingrained in local oral tradition since Anglo-Saxon times,' Sal said. 'He's described in a book on the history of the village, published in seventeen-oh-four — there's a copy in the Picton Library in Liverpool, and there's a carving of him in the stone of the manor gates. The effigy was designed by Mrs Tetting for the first scarecrow festival and as far as I know, she based it on the carving. They've used the same design ever since.'

'Does anyone sell memorabilia of the effigies in the village?'

Sal thought about this for a few seconds, mopping up a splurge of cream with the last of her scone. 'Used to,' she said thoughtfully. 'I can introduce you to Hermione, who owns the gift shop — she'll be able to tell you more.' She tilted her head. 'Is this linked to the trouble they've been having over on the new development?'

'Trouble?' Rowan asked.

'The thefts and anti-social behaviour.'

'Just following leads,' Rowan said blandly.

Sal gave her a shrewd look that said she didn't believe a word of it.

'Just give me a moment to get someone to keep an eye on the place and I'll take you to Hermione's,' she said, standing to rinse her hands at the sink.

The toddlers' story time had finished, and the children were being shepherded out of the door, and Rowan watched as Sal had a quiet word with the volunteer who'd conducted the reading. Then she guided Rowan around the village green to the row of shops.

The gift-shop window was decked out in orange and black, ready for Halloween. Evil-eyed pumpkins squatted on boxes and a miniature hay bale; a witch on a broomstick was silhouetted against a huge harvest moon set against a black felt backdrop; and ghosts hovered in the backlit windows of a cleverly constructed facsimile of the manor.

The shop owner, Hermione, had clearly fashioned herself on her Hogwarts' namesake, and she did bear a passing resemblance to the actress who played the young witch in the films. The shop had a fair number of Harry-Potter-themed gifts, too, and a notice by the till told visitors that Hermione would be available for photos and selfies at the manor on 31 October — at a price. The Birken Boggart was also present in the form of clay models of various sizes, mugs, and Halloween party invitation cards.

Rowan showed her an image on her phone of Damian's effigy cropped to show only the mask.

'Yes,' Hermione said. 'That *is* based on the Birken Boggart; I had them in stock here. A local printing company sponsored the festival a couple of years back; as part of the contract they were given permission to use the design for that year. He made five thousand, I believe — sold them to retailers in the area.'

'Can you remember when this was, exactly?' Rowan asked.

'Let me think . . .' Hermione gazed at the window of her shop onto the blank grey wall of fog beyond it. 'It must have been *three* years ago, because I was on the festival committee that year.'

'What's the name of this printing company?'

Hermione checked her contacts list and Rowan had the details a few seconds later.

As she stepped outside, she saw that the fog was beginning to lift a little and decided to check out the boggart at the manor house.

Finch rang as she walked down the track to the manor house and told her that he'd found out where to find Lisa Blerring's friend, Sophie. She was working the lunchtime rota at the restaurant in the city centre today and Rowan arranged to meet Finch there at midday.

The manor gates were adorned with Celtic knots and topped with medieval lion finials, but there was no boggart. Then she remembered that there was a tradesperson's entrance, which was now the designated way in for Birken Manor's fee-paying guests. Walking on a little further, she saw a second set of gates emerge from the mist. The boggart was set atop one of the gateposts, a grinning, pot-bellied imp with disproportionately long arms, crouching with knees bent and arms braced as if ready to spring down from its vantage point. It had been blurred and softened by a millennium of scouring winds, but it must have terrified generations of locals over its long history. At a time when superstition was rife and flesh-eating stories a reality, she guessed that the carving must have been as effective as a whole pack of guard dogs in protecting the manor.

SUVs and bijou gift shops aside, Birkenshore was like walking through a time slip into the last century. *Is that what the effigies are for?* Rowan wondered. A warning and a threat to anyone who dared disturb the peace of this strange community?

CHAPTER 18

Rowan was taking photos of the beast when a car rumbled up the lane and turned in through the gates. It was Mrs Tetting herself. She slowed and wound down her window.

'Were you looking for Julius?' she asked. 'He's out at the moment, I'm afraid.'

'No, I've been following up on the boggart,' Rowan said, knowing how bizarre that sounded. 'I understand that you designed the effigy on the bridge?'

'Yes . . .' This was the wary tone Rowan had noted in the woman's voice the day before — as if she was anxious that she might be criticized or blamed in some way. 'But it was Julius who insisted that it should be placed on the bridge.'

It seemed that Sal the librarian wasn't the only one who had complained about the alarming apparition at the gateway to the village.

'It's a striking design,' Rowan said. 'So intricately crafted.'

'Oh, well, the ladies make it these days,' she said. 'I only make Julius's scarecrow.'

'Ah, but it is your original design.' Rowan tried to flatter her. 'I don't suppose you have any sketches of it?'

The lady of the manor checked her watch. 'I have a meeting at eleven with an important client,' she said, suddenly brusque and business-like. 'But I suppose I can spare ten minutes. You'd better get in; it'll save time.'

At the door to the north wing — *Victorian, but no one has ever complained* — Mrs Tetting was greeted by a worried-looking member of staff in a grey suit with a gold clip naming him as *Events supervisor*.

'I'm afraid the kitchens are running behind schedule,' he said. 'The fish delivery was late, and Chef says it will delay the tasting by fifteen minutes.'

'Get hold of Julius,' Mrs Tetting said. 'Tell him he'll need to give the clients a tour — that will keep them happy until we're ready to take them through to the banqueting hall — I take it everything is in place there?'

'Yes, that's all set up.'

'I'll be along in a few minutes, after I've concluded my business with this lady.'

She showed Rowan through a maze of corridors tiled in black and white, across parquet-floored rooms, and finally through a locked oak door into the older part of the manor. The corridors here were laid to stone, but after a few more turns, they entered the main hallway, its wide-planked floor being coaxed to a mellow shine by a woman with a floor buffer. The reek of wax and lilies was almost overpowering. The woman smiled but continued with her work, and Mrs Tetting guided Rowan into a room off the hallway.

'This was a snug for decades,' she explained. 'For winter days when the morning room was a little too frosty.' The room was cosily furnished, and a large table next to the window was littered with cloth, clothing patterns and open folders containing swatches of textiles. 'It's my workroom, now,' she said, looking about her. Mrs Tetting's eyes were light hazel, Rowan noticed for the first time, and now they glowed with quiet satisfaction.

'You design the weddings?' Rowan asked, spotting what looked like a wedding-planner mood board.

'Oh, yes,' she said with obvious relish. 'I design, organize the furniture, the soft furnishings, flowers, decor and of course catering — whatever the client needs.' Mrs Tetting was opening and closing the shallow drawers of a cabinet under the table, but she paused a moment and said, 'Ah, *here* it is!'

She handed Rowan an A3-size, full-colour acrylic of the boggart mask. 'I'm almost afraid to touch it,' Rowan said, her scalp crawling with the memory of finding the mask on the effigy of Damian Novak. 'It's hideous, isn't it?'

'*Isn't* it?' Mrs Tetting said, accepting her words as the compliment it was intended to be. 'Give me a moment, and I'll run off a copy for you. Full size?'

'That'd be fantastic.' Rowan was impressed by the change in the woman.

Mrs Tetting swept the image to a large colour copier in a corner of the room and set about the task.

The front door opened and slammed and Rowan saw a shudder run through Mrs Tetting.

'What the hell's going on with the catering!' Tetting roared from the hallway. Then, 'Shut that bloody thing *off!*'

The hum of the floor buffer stopped abruptly and a moment later, Tetting bounded into the room, followed by two loud and excitable Labrador dogs. Their paws were muddy, their coats damp from their run on the marsh. Mrs Tetting's refuge seemed in very real danger and she exclaimed in dismay.

'OUT!' he thundered, and the dogs scooted, claws clicking and scratching the newly polished hall floor. Exasperated, he turned to his wife. 'For God's *sake*, Mrs T — there's a bloody disaster brewing and I find you entertaining the local constabulary with your *craft making!*'

'I'd rather you didn't call me that, Julius,' Mrs Tetting said coldly. 'It's vulgar.'

Tetting blinked and drew his chin in, as if she'd rapped him on the nose with a rolled-up newspaper, and Rowan thought the man really was rather like his dogs — rowdy and ill-disciplined, but responsive to chastisement.

'Well, I'm sorry if I've offended your dignity,' he said stiffly. 'But perhaps you'd like to explain to me how you plan to sort this mess?'

'We still have fifteen minutes before the clients arrive,' she said, glancing at her watch. 'If you'd like to make yourself ready to show them the chief points of the north wing, I think we can manage the delay quite nicely. Meanwhile, I will give Constable Rowan what she came for and have the tasting trays and champagne ready for our guests by the time you've finished.'

Tetting left the room muttering, and a moment later they heard him clumping up the stairs trailed by his exuberant dogs.

Rowan was beginning to think she'd underestimated Mrs Tetting; she had more steel in her than you would judge from first impressions. Even so, she noticed that the woman's hand trembled as she handed her the printout.

CHAPTER 19

By 11 a.m. Rowan had returned to the police station, spoken to the printing firm, extracting a promise that before close of business they would send her a list of retailers who'd placed orders for the mask, and then typed up her notes. Lunchtime traffic would be hell, so she left her car where it was and hoofed it to the restaurant, a fast ten-minute walk away.

The place was in the old business district of town, in a building the city council had sold off some years earlier. A section of the pavement had been cordoned off to allow for extra tables, and now that the sun had dispersed the morning drizzle, a few people were seated outside. Finch texted that he was trying to find somewhere to park, and Rowan amused herself in trying to identify Sophie. She stood a few yards away and watched through the plate glass window into the restaurant. Three women moved to and fro, taking orders, checking that guests had everything they needed, delivering food, taking away plates. One was a nervous eighteen-year-old, possibly a student, learning the ropes. *Too young.* Another, a woman of around thirty. *Too old.*

The third server had the Goldilocks factor — in her twenties, she was just right for Sophie. Dressed in black trousers and a crisp white shirt, she was chatting up an elderly couple and the old guy looked like he'd fallen in love. Rowan could understand it. The woman had an exuberance of blonde curls and although swept back from her face, a few loose strands caressed her lightly tanned skin; her pale blue eyes shone with health, and she held herself with grace.

Finch arrived slightly out of breath. 'That's her,' he said, jutting his chin towards the blonde.

Sophie was laughing at something the woman said. After making a note on her order pad, she was off, scooting down the length of the restaurant at speed, dodging and weaving through the tables with the ease of a dancer.

Rowan caught the look on Finch's face and realized the old man wasn't alone in being smitten. 'You ready?' she asked.

Finch gave a tight nod and they headed inside, where a greeter welcomed them. Rowan asked if they could speak to Sophie, and the greeter went off to the far end of the restaurant, where Sophie had just delivered the new order. The two women put their heads together for half a minute, Sophie casting glances towards Finch. At last, lip reading, Rowan saw her say 'fine', although it clearly wasn't, then Sophie stalked towards them.

She cut off Rowan's attempt to introduce herself. 'Not here,' she said, swerving past and stepping outside onto the street, moving just beyond the roped-off area. Traffic was a constant blare at this time of day, and nobody more than a few feet away would be able to hear what they said.

Arms folded, Sophie looked Finch up and down. 'If you're here to check up on Lisa, you're about three years too late.'

Finch winced. 'I just heard today,' he said. 'I'm awful sorry, Sophie — I know you two were close.'

The look she gave him felt like an arctic blast. 'Youse two were close once an' all.'

'You're angry — I don't blame you — but there's something weird going on over at Fernleigh, and we're trying to sort it out.'

'Like I said, too late.' The smiling, friendly waitress Rowan had observed unseen had vanished; this version of Sophie was hard-faced and hard of heart and Rowan sensed that Finch would make no headway with her.

'We found a link between Lisa's death and Justin Lang's,' she said, hoping to ignite her curiosity, if not her sympathy.

'Justin? What's it got to do with that bastard?'

'That's what we're trying to find out,' Rowan said.

'What, *now*? He topped himself *months* ago. And it's took you this long to—' Sophie broke off with scornful laugh. 'I always knew you were soft, Finch — I never thought you were slow on the uptake as well.'

'We've just been assigned to the case,' Rowan said, seeing that Finch was crumpling under Sophie's onslaught. 'Lisa committed suicide eighteen months ago, but you said we were *three years* too late. Is that because she was going out with Justin three years ago?'

'No. She *finished* with him three years ago — didn't want nothing to do with that twisted f—'

'And he wouldn't take no for an answer?'

'Oh, it was a bit more "hands-on" than that.' Sophie's mouth twisted in a kind of spasm, then she turned deliberately to Finch, glaring at him as though she could make him look at her by sheer force of will. 'He hounded her for months, sexually assaulted her, and youse lot did f—' Sophie broke off as two of her customers left the restaurant, passing close by.

Finch was staring at her now, his eyes red-rimmed.

'You could've *done* something, but you didn't do *nothing*,' she finished.

'She reported this to the police?' Rowan said.

Sophie stared at her as though she'd lost her mind. 'Are you from Planet Zog, or what?'

'I told you, Cassie,' Finch said, his voice rough with emotion. 'You don't mess with the Langs.'

Sophie eyed him with contempt. 'Yeah — you should listen to him — he's an expert on the subject.'

Rowan was developing a deep dislike of this woman. 'Thanks for the clarification,' she said. 'But since no one on this or any other planet told the police what happened to Lisa, maybe you can explain to me how he was supposed to do something, when he didn't know what was going on?'

Sophie sneered, defeated by the logic, but unwilling to admit it. 'He wasn't even interested. You *left*, didn't you, Finch?' She rippled the fingers of one hand. 'Flew away like a little bird and never come back.'

Sophie was telling him that he'd betrayed Lisa and the pain in his face said that Finch believed her.

Well, life isn't that simple. Finch still hadn't learned to stand up for himself in an argument, and Rowan had been a verbal scrapper all her life, so she spoke for him. 'You know Lisa had a termination just before she killed herself?'

She saw shock register on Sophie's face at the bluntness of the question, but she came back without hesitation. 'Course I knew. I was her friend.' Her eyes never wavered from Finch.

'Was Justin the father?'

'Couldn't have been no one else,' Sophie said. 'She'd've kept it if it was anyone else's. But Justin would've never let her go — she'd've been chained to him and his family for life.'

'He found out, didn't he?' Rowan said.

Sophie's shoulders sagged and she gave a brief nod. 'God knows how — maybe he guessed, and she couldn't lie.'

'The sexual assault,' Rowan began. 'Was that how—?'

'No, she got caught when he was still being nice to her, fooling her that he was human. That changed fast . . .' She drifted off for a second and Rowan could only guess how things had turned bad once Lang had turned off the superficial charm. 'It was when he found out about the abortion,' Sophie said. 'He wanted her to know he could take her anytime he felt like it.' She stared past them, fighting tears. 'He told her, "You wanna be free? You'll never be free of me."'

'You think that's why she took her own life?' It was an obvious question, but Rowan had learned never to assume what drove a desperate act.

132

Sophie gave a soft laugh. It turned to a sob and a tear spilled over her lower lid. She tilted her head back, knuckling the corners of her eyes to stop her mascara running. 'Nah, it was God and family put that blade in her hand.' She turned her gaze on Finch. 'You know what she was like,' she said, her voice coarsened by bitterness and rage. 'Good Catholic girl, holier than the Pope.'

Finch took a breath and Rowan saw that this was tearing him to shreds. 'The guilt got to her,' he said.

'You could say that,' Sophie said. 'She went to confession and the priest told her she'd committed a mortal sin. And as if that wasn't enough, Justin dropped in for a friendly chat with her mum and dad — told them what she done. You know the Blerrings, Finch — you can just picture how that went down. After they'd finished telling her what they thought of useless, baby-killing bitches who didn't have the self-respect to keep their legs together just cos some horny dog come sniffing around, she run herself a warm bath, lit some candles, slit her wrists.'

All of this was said to punish Finch, but it was plain that Sophie had tortured herself in the eighteen months since her friend's suicide.

Rowan was suddenly angry. They weren't here so that Sophie could assuage her guilt or take revenge on Finch for his imagined abandonment of her friend. They were here to find the truth about these deaths.

'She *told* you what her parents said?'

Sophie looked confused.

'The coroner's report said there was no suicide note,' Rowan said. 'So if she literally killed herself after her parents condemned her for the termination, she must have rung you — otherwise how would you know?'

'Who *rings* anyone these days?'

'Texted, then, or WhatsApped or—'

'Insta,' Sophie said. 'She posted on Instagram.'

Rowan dug in her back pocket for her mobile. 'What was her handle?'

'Don't bother. It's gone.'

'You need to explain,' Rowan said.

Sophie sighed impatiently. 'She posted a reel, but it vanished. Then her whole account got deleted, like *hours* after.'

'Do you know who deleted it?'

'Her mum and dad — who else?'

If Lisa had mentioned the rape, the Lang family might've done it, Rowan thought. 'Why would they do that?' she asked.

'She told the world everything they said to her. Wouldn't look good, would it, them being God-fearing Catholics — forgive the sinner and all that. I mean, Mary Magdalene was a prozzy, wasn't she, and Jesus loved *her*.'

'How would they get access to the account? They'd need her password.'

Sophie shrugged. 'Not my job, hon.'

Rowan could see she'd get nothing more on that subject, so she changed focus. 'You know she got into that bath fully clothed?'

'Like a good, holy Catholic girl. Wouldn't want her dad to see her in the nuddy.' Bitterness made this beautiful woman ugly.

'Did you know that Justin killed himself in the same way?' Rowan persisted.

For a fraction of a second, Sophie looked bewildered and, from the corner of her eye, Rowan saw Finch glance at her in question.

'Odd, isn't it?' Rowan went on. 'To my way of thinking, climbing into a bath fully dressed would be *really* uncomfortable, and your last moments on Earth, you'd want to be comfortable, wouldn't you — I mean, if it's in your control — and men like Justin Lang do like to feel in control.' She hardened her voice. 'I get that *Lisa* might feel embarrassed at being found naked, but I bet Justin thought he was God's gift.' She saw from Sophie's expression that she was right. 'You wouldn't think he'd be *shy* — I mean, it doesn't ring true, does it? Him being so modest — prissy, even.'

Sophie was trying to look like she couldn't care less, but Rowan could see that the sharp edges of her anger had been blunted by curiosity. She was seeing Lang's death differently.

'Like someone done it to him,' Sophie murmured, an almost dreamy tone to her voice and she glanced from Rowan to Finch, as if trying to gauge their thoughts. 'It did seem weird, him killing himself. I mean, I never seen Justin as the type to feel bad for anything he done.' She thought about it for a few seconds, then shook her head. 'Nah, it was suicide. Must've been — nobody round our way'd dare lay a finger on a Lang.' She took a breath, watching a bus rumble slowly past, then, as if it took courage to even think that Justin Lang's death might not have been suicide, she seemed to physically brace herself before saying, 'You think someone topped him — like that feller in *The Equalizer*?'

Rowan felt Finch shift nervously by her side, but he needn't have worried. In truth, she was more and more convinced that Lang's 'suicide' was a vigilante killing, but she wasn't about to put words in Sophie's mouth.

'I'm asking what *you* think, Sophie,' she said.

The waitress gazed at her blankly.

'Did you see Justin in the days before he died?'

'Couldn't bloody miss him on our block,' Sophie said. 'You'd think he owned the place.'

'Did he seem anxious or depressed?'

She seemed to find the notion funny, but her smile faded and a frown gathered at her brows. 'He was *angry*. Justin gave off this cool vibe, like nothing ever bothered him, but that week, he was pissed off like I never seen him before.'

'Did he mention any names?'

'Me and him weren't on what you call speaking terms,' Sophie said, with a pitying look at Rowan's naivety. 'But he was rattled.'

Rowan found a cropped image of the boggart mask and showed it to Sophie.

Sophie shoved her hand away with a disgusted, 'Ugh! What're you showing me that for?'

'You've never seen it before?'

'No.'

'And it doesn't mean anything to you?'

'Like what — Halloween?'

A woman appeared at the door of the restaurant, and Sophie said, 'That's my boss. I gotta go.'

Rowan handed her a business card. 'Please call me if anything else comes to mind.'

Sophie tucked the card inside her apron, making no promises. But she slipped her order pad from her pocket and scribbled a number on it, handing a scrap of paper to Rowan. 'You wanna talk to me again, text me first — I need this job.'

She left them standing on the pavement, and with an apologetic grimace, Finch offered Rowan a lift back to St Anne Street, but he was silent on the walk to the car.

Five minutes later, crawling through snarled traffic, Rowan said, 'You okay?'

'You didn't have to be so harsh.'

She shrugged. 'Well, she was pretty hard on you.'

'Lisa was her best mate.'

'Yeah, and *she* couldn't help her, so what d'you think *you* could've done?'

'I dunno,' he said miserably. 'Something.'

'You can't live people's lives for them, Finch. It wasn't like she called you and you couldn't be bothered to call her back.'

He shot her a guilty look. 'When we moved away, I didn't tell anyone where me and Mum were going,' he said. 'I ditched my phone, deleted my social media. She couldn't have called me if she tried.'

Oh, boy . . . 'Look,' Rowan said, 'You can't take the weight of the world's sorrows on your shoulders, and you can't change what happened to—'

'Do you think there's a vigilante on Fernleigh?' he interrupted.

'I didn't say that.'

'But you think there is, don't you?'

136

There was no point in denying it. 'Maybe. But to quote the boss, "Let's not theorize ahead of the evidence".'

'Maybe we should just let him get on with it,' he said.

She blinked. '*What*?'

'I mean, what good are we if we can't protect people?'

CHAPTER 20

Twenty minutes later, Rowan was in an unmarked fleet car, driving towards Fernleigh, Finch having returned to read the coroner's report on Lisa Blerring's death. If Lang's harassment had been mentioned as a possible factor in Lisa's suicide, there should have been some police follow-up. They also needed to know if the Blerrings had lied about the Instagram suicide reel, or had simply chosen not to mention it.

Once she was past the snarled traffic in town, she parked up to make a call to Jackie Dawson.

'Hey, Jackie,' she said. 'Have you spoken to Lisa Blerring's parents, yet?'

'They're next on my list,' Dawson said.

'Can you hold off on that? I'll come with you — Lisa's friend had some interesting info. I'll explain when I get there.'

Lisa's parents lived in one of the tower blocks, and Dawson advised Rowan to park her car by the shops.

'The local lads've got wind of your visit, and they keep a few bricks handy to drop on unwelcome visitors' cars.'

If she'd been driving her old clunker, it would have been tempting to take a chance on the local scalls trashing it so she could collect on the insurance, but a fifty-thousand-pound fleet car was an entirely different prospect, so they made the five-minute walk to one of the tower blocks. The afternoon had turned oddly warm and sultry, which only intensified the grey drabness of the estate.

Finch rang as they made their way and confirmed that Lang's name had not come up at the inquest, only that Lisa had been troubled since the termination, which went against her religious beliefs. The coroner had recorded that there was no suicide note, but it wasn't clear if the family had been asked directly about it. He'd left a message for the reporting coroner to call him.

They climbed to the fifth floor and Mrs Blerring took them into the sitting room, an arid cube of white walls and beige carpet, devoid of pictures, or even the adornment of a mirror. The electric fire, set into the wall, was scrupulously clean and polished, the glass coffee table set in front of a blue leather sofa was uncluttered and pristine. A small TV crouched in an alcove at one end of the room and the only ornament — a standing picture frame — held a photograph of Mr and Mrs Blerring, presumably on holiday because there was a backdrop of fields and sky and she was smiling. Rowan guessed she hadn't done much of that since the day the photo was taken: Mrs Blerring's mouth seemed permanently set in a thin line, as if she'd seen so much to disapprove of in her forty-something years of life that displeasure had been etched into her features. She regarded them under heavily lidded eyes and listened to the reason for their visit with cool indifference. She didn't invite them to sit.

'I didn't approve of the Lang boy,' she said flatly. 'I can't tell you anything about him.'

'We understand that Lisa broke off her relationship with him and that he harassed her for some months,' Rowan said.

'If he did, she didn't confide in me.'

Rowan could understand why. 'But it was Justin Lang who told you about Lisa's pregnancy,' she said.

Mrs Blerring's eyes darted away, then back to her face.

'She left a message online, just before she died.' Rowan watched the woman's face; her upper lip twitched in a sneer, which was quickly suppressed.

'Did she?'

'I think you know she did.'

'*Social media*,' the woman spat.

'Instagram,' Rowan said.

'The Catholic Church has provided guidance and absolution in the privacy and anonymity of the confessional for two millennia,' Mrs Blerring said. 'Yet she spurned the holy sacrament and blurted out her sins to an audience of strangers.'

'I understand that the video wasn't so much a confession, as a suicide note,' Rowan said bluntly. The woman opened her mouth to protest, but Rowan spoke over her. 'Why didn't you inform the coroner?'

'It was a private matter,' she said primly.

'It's a criminal offence to lie under oath at a coroner's court, Mrs Blerring,' Rowan said.

'I — I wasn't called to give evidence,' she said, sounding slightly less sure of herself.

'Then how did the coroner conclude that Lisa left no suicide note?'

'I . . . don't recall.'

'Perhaps your husband will have a clearer memory on the subject. Where is he now?'

'At work.' She looked positively shaken, now.

'He works in the education offices at the council,' Dawson supplied.

Mrs Blerring's eyes widened. 'You mustn't disturb him.'

Rowan ignored her. 'Your daughter's Instagram account was deleted shortly after she posted the video. What do you know about that?'

The woman's mouth opened and closed, opened and closed.

'Be careful how you answer, Mrs Blerring. From what I understand of the Catholic religion, lying to a police officer could be considered a mortal sin.'

The woman flushed angrily. 'How dare you! She wasn't in her right mind when she posted that dreadful thing. We were protecting her—'

'You deleted the account?'

Mrs Blerring looked like she was chewing on glass. 'Yes,' she managed after a struggle.

'How did you gain access? Did you have her password?'

'It was in her diary.'

'I'd like to see that,' Rowan said.

'You can't.' She clasped her hands in front of her. 'It's gone — burned.'

'You destroyed evidence?'

'I destroyed a *private diary* filled with a girl's self-indulgent, embarrassing ramblings.'

'Lisa was a *woman*,' Rowan said and couldn't help adding, 'I'm guessing what she had to say about you wasn't too flattering?'

Mrs Blerring took a breath and held it, clearly battling her temper. Rowan felt a profound sadness for Lisa — psychologically bullied in her own home, it was almost inevitable she would fall prey to bullies like Justin Lang outside of it.

'I'd like you to leave, now,' the woman said at last, her voice trembling with rage.

'Okay,' Rowan said. 'The coroner might want to follow up on that Instagram video, though.'

She felt Dawson's sideways glances at her as they walked all the way down the stairs in silence.

'I know,' Rowan said at last, when they were free of the building's shadow. 'I probably could have handled that better.'

'She's not an easy person,' Dawson said with charitable understatement. 'To be honest, I was relieved when you said you'd come with me.'

'She's a lying, sanctimonious hypocrite,' Rowan said. 'Did you see a single photo of Lisa in the place?'

Dawson tilted her head. 'Well . . .'

'No. Neither did I.'

A noncommittal, 'Mm,' from the PCSO made Rowan's mind fly to DCI Warman and she groaned.

'What?'

141

'Pat Warman,' Rowan said. 'She's Roman Catholic. What's the bet that by the time I get back to St Anne Street, word will have reached her about the rude, disrespectful "girl" who came to ask questions about her poor dead, sinful daughter.'

Another silence followed, then Dawson said, 'If you want, *I* could talk to Mr Blerring . . .'

Rowan laughed. 'God, Jackie, you're a tonic. I'm going to drop in to have a chat with Jim North before I stop by Mr Blerring's office. I promise I will be the very picture of charm and diplomacy by the time I see him.'

* * *

Jim North worked as construction manager at a new residential and retail development in the Baltic Quarter of the city. Formerly an industrial area, it now housed a curious mishmash of new-build, mixed-use properties, refurbed warehouses, and semi-derelict buildings divided into studios for creatives and techies. During the daytime it had a lively buzz, with indie cafés and restaurants doing good trade but at night, clubs housed in defunct warehouses pounded out bass beats till well after midnight and bars spilled raucous and argumentative crowds onto the streets. Then the cool vibe morphed into something much edgier — even dangerous.

The building site was fenced off behind a fifty-metre-long section of boarding and Jim had arranged to meet her in a narrow, cobblestoned back alley, explaining that she wouldn't be allowed on site. He emerged through a small door as she turned the corner. He took off his hard hat and ruffled his hair and Rowan felt a sudden tug of attraction.

'All right?' he said, raising his voice over the din of drilling, the clank-clank-clank of a pile driver and the rumble of machinery. 'Mind if we head to the Baltic? I need some scran — me stomach thinks me throat's been cut.'

Just five minutes' walk away, Liverpool's street-food market was at the apex of the Baltic Triangle. A large portion of it was housed in a vast red-brick Victorian building, which had once been home to Liverpool's oldest brewery. In the last few years, its million square feet of obsolete real estate had slowly begun to fill with indie traders, supplying food specialities from around the world.

'I won't hear anything back from the kids till I see them at the dojo,' he said as they walked.

'That's not why I'm here,' Rowan said.

Man on a mission, North strode purposefully past pubs and cocktail bars without a second glance, and Rowan had a job to keep up with him.

'So?' he said, slowing a little.

'First things first,' she said with a half-smile. 'You obviously need to get fed.'

Huge murals created a vibrant contrast to the drab greys and mud-red brick facades of nineteen-sixties light industry units, some operational, some long derelict. A fantasy creature, rising from the Mersey river's turbulent water filled one factory's gable end, while a photorealistic rendering of Stephen Hawking gave good advice about positivity. Footballers — always a staple of Liverpool's urban lore — rubbed shoulders with dancing Mexicans, and an interactive depiction of an angel's wings created an eclectic mix of the real and surreal.

Rowan settled for a Greek salad from a Mediterranean food bar and went in search of a table, while North disappeared off for a few minutes, returning with a bottle of water and two massive wraps filled with spiced turkey and salad.

'All the scran a hungry Scouser could ever need,' Rowan said, eyeballing the tortilla in his fist.

'Well, you put me through my paces last night.' He took a bite and sighed contentedly. 'Have you thought of fighting competitively?' he asked before taking another.

'No — it's just self-preservation I'm interested in.'

He twitched one shoulder. 'You're fast though. Lemme know if you change your mind.'

She waited till he was halfway through the second roll before telling him why she'd asked to speak to him. 'I wanted to find out what you know about Lisa Blerring and Justin Lang.'

'Lisa helped out at Gareth's community hub now and then.' His frown said that he knew her sad story.

He seemed to be debating whether to say more.

'I could really use your help with this, Jim,' she said. 'Her mother stonewalled me and I doubt her dad will be any better.'

He set the roll down and wiped his face with a napkin. 'What d'you want to know?' He had blue eyes, and when he looked into hers, she saw a challenge in them; he wasn't going to make this easy.

'Did the kids talk about Lisa's suicide?'

'Some.'

'Such as?' She couldn't understand his reticence.

'It was all brought out at the coroner's inquest,' he said. 'It'll be in his report.'

Interesting that he'd attended the inquest.

'Some things were held back,' she said.

His face darkened. 'There was a video, then?'

'What do you know about that?'

'Only rumours. I never saw it myself.'

'Do you know why she killed herself?'

'The termination was cited at the inquest. And her parents — well, you can guess what they were like.'

'What about Lang?'

He lifted one shoulder. 'Drug dealer, supplier, local bully boy — born of a long line of bully boys. But you'd already know that.' He shot her a another searching look. 'Where's this going?'

'It just doesn't feel right that he committed suicide.' The manner of Lang's death was in the public domain, but Rowan still needed to be careful not to ask leading questions or give too much away about their investigation.

'You never know what'll make a man crack,' he said. 'And in my experience, a bully like Lang is often just one knock away from a cowering wreck. It's the low self-esteem,' he added, an unforgiving gleam in his eyes. 'Torments them.'

'Did he give you any trouble at Gareth's place?'

'I had a few run-ins with him in the early days, but he stayed away after we had a man-to-man chat.'

Rowan didn't intend to ask for details of how that went down.

'You think that's why he killed himself — someone gave him the knock that sent him over a cliff edge?'

He took a swallow of water from the bottle before answering. 'Another bottom-feeder they call Stickman took credit for it — said Lang couldn't hack going toe to toe with him.'

'He slashed his wrists.'

'Yeah, well, karma's a bitch.' He stood. 'I need to get back to work. Is there anything else?'

'No — just let me know if you hear anything from the kids.'

'Sure.' He walked away without looking back, leaving Rowan to wonder at the hum of hostility she'd felt as soon as she'd mentioned Lisa and Justin. He hadn't really answered her question about why he thought Lang killed himself, either, and it occurred to her that this was the second time in hours that the Stickman's name had come up in relation to the deaths.

CHAPTER 21

Thomas Capstick, known as 'Stickman' for his skinny build, parked his car in one of the bays next to Hartsfern Tower. He had no worries about vandalism. He could leave it for five minutes or five days, knowing that when he came back it would be exactly as he left it — which, today, was shone up nice. He'd just come back from the hand carwash over on a retail park out Garston way. Two miserable, shivering illegals had been set to work by a big guy who obviously took no shit from the hired help. Neither one of them could speak proper English, but like good little minions they ducked their heads and nodded and did what he told them to.

Stickman stayed and kept an eye on them, cos them two looked half-starved and he wasn't gonna trust two scabby bastards who'd probably nick the boiled sweets from your glove box if you so much as blinked. He'd checked his ride before he paid (cash only — big surprise) and tried not to laugh at the minions' worried side-glances, waiting for him to call them out on shoddy work.

Some might've considered him hanging about a waste of half an hour, but his Dacia Duster was gleaming and he'd just scored himself a boss pair of Air Jordan trabs in red and

white to go with his Fila Santana trackies (black and red).
Yeah, Stickman was feeling good.

The Lang tribe thought they were untouchable cos they
humped like rabbits and had brothers and sisters, uncles and
aunties and cousins and half-brothers in every block. And
if that wasn't enough, they stuck their weasel-faced inbred
throwback second cousins and step-whatevers on every street
corner from here to Speke Boulevard. For six years, Stickman
had been the only serious rival to the Lang crew on Fernleigh.
They'd had to do a bit of a rethink when Justin supposedly
topped himself.

They'd tried to double down after that, beefing up their
protection, putting knives in the hands of little boys. He
shook his head at the immorality of it. If the rest of that
pathetic band of bellends thought that a few kids with
blades would be protection against Thomas Capstick, they'd
learned different. The Stickman had his own crew — and not
munchkins with a bad attitude, neither — Capstick's crew
were grown-ups — proper hard men.

The Stickman's own rep gave him an X-Men-style personal force field — bastards couldn't touch him, wouldn't
dare even if they got the chance. Which was more than could
be said for the Langs, seeing how they'd lost two of their
crew in four months. True, Damian Novak wasn't family
or nothing, but he was one of the Langs' blue-eyed boys; if
they gave out prizes in this business, Damian would've won
the golden coke spoon for salesman of the year. Got himself
a sweet deal supplying on the other side of the M62. Funny
that he got found splattered on the motorway — karma,
Stickman called it.

The lift had a message stuck on it. *Out of service. PLEASE
USE STAIRS*. Like you had any choice. Wasn't like he could
fly up to the eighth floor, was it? But he was in a good mood,
so he hitched his trackie bottoms and diverted, strolling to
the concrete stairwell and mounting the steps two at a time
with his long stride. At the turn of the stairs, he stopped.

Some dickhead was sprawled by the fire door, one skinny leg stuck out across the step. If this was a druggy after a little pick-me-up, he'd got the wrong feller. Everyone round here knew Stickman didn't deal himself — Stickman had his own minions for that.

'Ey,' Stickman shouted. 'Knob 'ead. You're in me way.'

The crusty didn't move.

Hood up, head slumped forward, one hand limp between his bony thighs, he was stoned out of his brains, no doubt about it.

'I asked nice. Now you're gonna get your head kicked in, mate.' Stickman followed up with a swift kick to the dosser's skinny arse. He felt the muscle give, but there was no response, so he grabbed one arm and yanked.

Something was wrong: the flesh gave too easily, and he could feel the bones shift beneath. He tightened his grip, planning to chuck the cheeky get down the stairs.

A loud *crack*, and something snapped under the pressure of his fingers. He winced, but this smackhead was so out of it he didn't feel a thing. Curiosity made Stickman go on. He dragged the hood down.

'Fuck!' He released the thing. Staggering back he came up hard against the concrete of the stairwell wall, cracked the back of his head. *The face . . .*

Red, with green eyes, and pointed teeth that could strip you to the bone, like the tank of piranhas his dad used to keep to scare him when he was a kid. But Thomas Capstick wasn't a kid no more — he wasn't scared of nothing.

If his heart was rapping hard at his ribcage it was because of the knock to his head when he'd stumbled. Tripped over the stupid dummy on the stairs, that's what he done. Just tripped. He might have concussion or something cos he was seeing stars and he felt a bit sick. He planted his hands flat against the wall to steady himself and booted the thing hard in the midsection.

It *rattled* — like a bag of bones might rattle. Stickman kicked it again, heard the shinbone snap. But it didn't make him feel better; he felt sicker. A cold sweat broke out on his neck and his back.

The druggy fell backwards, catching the mask against the brickwork. He snatched at it and the elastic broke, revealing another face under it.

Stickman's guts flooded with cold, and his legs felt suddenly weak.

He was looking at *himself. His* face moulded out of cloth and wool. *His* jutting forehead, *his* shaved dome, a shadow of regrowth inked in by a thousand tiny dots. It even had his Stickman tattoo inked on the left side of its neck.

Someone had spent good money to dress the dummy up in a Fila tracksuit in red and black and a pair of Air Jordan trainers, just like his. Cold fear melted away and his skin felt hot enough to burn. Someone was gonna be very sorry for shitting on the Stickman's doorstep.

He roared, raising his foot and bringing it down hard on the face, the neck, the torso, the limbs, pounding the nasty thing till every 'bone' broke.

CHAPTER 22

Tuesday evening

Rowan made her way to her desk feeling slightly disorientated. Her late lunch with Jim North had unsettled her, and from there she'd gone on to a frustrating meeting with Mr Blerring. He was complacent and patronising, explaining that she couldn't possibly understand the trials of helping a teenage child to negotiate the difficulties and temptations of growing up in a socially deprived area.

That had set her teeth on edge right from the start: the dread of facing her brother that evening — trying to persuade him to agree to meet with his teachers — had been pulsing in and out of her thoughts all day like a throbbing headache. But Mr Blerring wasn't finished.

Parental responsibilities, he pontificated, meant sometimes you had to shoulder the burden yourself, making the right choices for a child who was in danger of being dragged down into the quagmire of moral turpitude.

'Turpitude,' Rowan repeated.

But Lisa's father had missed the sarcastic tone and began to explain the concept to her.

'I know what it is, Mr Blerring,' she cut in. 'I see it every day in my job. But when a grown woman asserts control over her own body, I hate to hear that called "moral turpitude". See, I know you deleted her final words from Instagram; I know you destroyed her diaries. We could argue about the morality of that, if you'd like? *You* might call it "making choices" on Lisa's behalf, but I call it coercive control—'

He didn't even flinch. Just smiled, holding up his hand to interrupt. 'You can't *know* anything, Constable Rowan. The account, the diaries — they're gone.'

Rowan was choking on rage that wasn't entirely about Lisa or the Blerrings. She made an effort to calm herself but didn't completely succeed. 'I know what Lisa said, and I know what *you* said to her.' She shook her head. 'I just don't know how you can live with yourself.'

Warman had called her into her office on her return, and Rowan had been braced for a roasting, but the DCI was surprisingly calm, despite Mrs Blerring's complaint, which had been quickly followed by her husband's.

'The coroner asked the family if Lisa had left a note,' Warman said. 'They say they weren't asked if there had been a posting on social media.'

'What's the difference?' Rowan demanded. 'Lisa told anyone who would listen why she felt there was no other way out, and they covered it up.'

'The difference,' Warman said in her precise, infuriating manner, 'is that they weren't asked directly. They can hide behind the semantics and convince themselves they didn't commit a sin because they didn't actually lie.'

Warman seemed to be wrestling with anger — Rowan just couldn't tell if it was aimed at her.

'But in the Catholic faith there are sins of *omission* as well as *commission* — and those sins will surely find them out.'

Rowan tried not to fidget under her boss's solemn gaze. Warman had never spoken about her religious beliefs before, and she was at a loss for something sensible to say.

In the end she mumbled, 'Yes, boss,' and then tried not to cringe at the banality of her response.

Warman nodded, dismissing her, but had Rowan caught a twinkle of amusement in her boss's eye as she turned to leave?

* * *

Looking down at her desk, Rowan was still in a kind of daze.

Finch was at his desk nearby. He looked up and murmured a greeting.

Rowan nodded, staring at a jiffy bag that had been placed on top of her computer keyboard. Addressed for her attention in black biro in a spidery scrawl, the top left corner was marked *DELIVERED BY HAND* and under it, *URGENT*. The evening debrief was due to start in less than ten minutes; she had time to grab an awful coffee or open the jiffy bag. Remembering the two cream slices she'd bought at the Birkenshore bakery for herself and Neil — a bribe for this evening's tough talk — she decided to skip the coffee and brew a decent cup when she got home.

Picking up the package, she broke the seal and reached inside, encountering something pliable and unpleasant to the touch. Soft and yielding, slightly cool . . .

Like dead flesh. The idea had popped into her head unbidden, and Rowan experienced a queasy misgiving. Holding the edges of the bag, she pressed the sides gently to widen the opening and peek inside. Two green eyes glared out from an angry red face.

A boggart mask. Her stomach curdled.

Maybe she'd made a sound — she couldn't recall — but something made Finch glance across.

'Woah,' he said. 'What's up?'

Ian swept into the office at that moment. 'I've come straight from a crack house in Kenny, where I have been since ten this morning.' He dumped his scene-kit case on the floor and flopped into a chair. 'Seven hours, processing the mankiest scene I've attended in a long time after the untimely demise of a dedicated crack fiend. So if I smell like cat's piss with a top note of acetone, don't judge me.'

He looked from Rowan to Finch, clearly offended that neither of them had uttered a word of sympathy.

'Um, Ian . . .' Rowan said.

Alerted by the strain in her voice, Chan took in what was happening, and clicked to professional mode. 'Put it on the table,' he said, retrieving his case.

Rowan complied, her heart thudding, and Chan snapped on a pair of nitrile gloves, then, using two pairs of tweezers, he eased the package open to get a good look inside.

'Were you expecting a delivery from Fine Print?' he asked, squinting into the padded envelope.

'They said they'd email me,' she said.

'Well, there's a letter in here from a . . .' Chan withdrew a ten-by-seven centimetre quality comp slip with the tweezers. 'Rico Alvez.'

'"Thought you might want to see the real thing in all its gory",' he read, adding, 'Those are his words, not mine. "Have emailed the list of buyers."'

'Bloody hell,' Rowan said on a rush of outbreath. 'Sorry, guys, I thought—' She stopped. 'Never mind what I thought — it's from the firm who made the masks for a Halloween festival a couple of years ago.'

She extracted the thing from the padded envelope, still strangely affected by the nastiness of the depiction.

'Well, I wish they were all this helpful.' Chan yawned and stretched, caught a whiff of something from his clothing and grimaced. 'Let's get this briefing done so I can take a shower and burn these clothes.'

They moved to the meeting room. It was after five by now, but there was no sign of Warman.

By ten minutes past, they were talking about the day's work, and Rowan told the story of the Blerrings' destruction of evidence and her oddly supportive exchange with Warman.

'I don't know why you think it's odd,' Chan said.

'She was *on my side*, Ian.' Rowan flipped her hands palm up, resisting — just — the urge to add, 'Duh!'

Chan rolled his eyes. 'Oh, you mean she *backed you up*? What did you expect?'

'Honestly?' she said. 'A bollocking.'

He laughed. 'You've got to shake that persecution complex, girl!'

Rowan began to protest, but Ian Chan, still chuckling, reached for her pinkie finger and gave it a friendly shake.

'*You* were in the right, *they* were in the wrong. Lisa was a casualty of religious zealotry. The fact that the zealots happened to be Lisa's parents made it worse.' He glanced over his shoulder to make sure the DCI hadn't crept in behind him. 'I bet the old warhorse would've have cheered you on if she'd been there.'

'You think?'

'God, you can be dense sometimes!' Chan slapped his forehead dramatically. 'Don't forget she was one of the first women to make her mark as a senior detective in Merseyside Police — she's had more than her fair share of misogynists trying to tell her what she could or couldn't do. And as a devout, church-going Catholic, she would not like the idea of Lisa being driven to despair by her own religion.'

Rowan looked at him askance. 'What made you so damn wise all of a sudden?'

'What d'you mean "all of a sudden"?' Chan shot back.

Finch hadn't said a word all this time, and Rowan said, 'What's up, Finch?'

'I know we're not supposed to speculate,' he began reluctantly. 'But we've got four, now. Lisa, eighteen months ago, Craig Breidon last year, Justin Lang four months ago, and now Damian Novak. Isn't it in all our minds? Shouldn't we be talking about a, well . . .' He seemed almost embarrassed to say it. 'A *serial*, targeting drug gangs?'

Rowan couldn't deny it, but she felt obliged to say, 'You'd have to discount Lisa — she posted that video, even if we can't find physical evidence of it. And it's unlikely she was involved in drug trafficking — she'd broken up with Lang a year before she died.'

'What about the masks?' he said. 'The effigies? Craig, Justin and Damian all had effigies — which all had the same mask. And Ian said Craig Breidon couldn't have hung himself; he had too much Ativan in his system.'

'I'm not arguing with you, Finch — I just think we need to be careful before we say something that could cause panic,' Rowan said.

'And there are limits to what we can do in linking the deaths to the effigies,' Chan added. 'We don't have the physical evidence, and without it, all we've got is speculation.'

'But the suicides are so similar,' Finch insisted.

Chan shrugged. 'You could write those up as suicide contagion.'

Rowan nodded in agreement. 'Copycat behaviour after suicide deaths.' It was especially prevalent in young people from their teens up to mid-twenties. 'But Lang was twenty-seven, which doesn't fit the demographic. And he was a leader, not a follower — I don't see him copying his ex-girlfriend's suicide.'

'Me neither,' Chan agreed. 'But *where's the evidence*?'

'Our best chance is to focus on Damian Novak,' Rowan said. 'He's the most recent, and if we haven't got evidence yet, it's still out there, waiting for us to find it.'

'The boss requested all the triple-nine calls made to Emergency Services about his effigy on the M62 embankment,' Finch said. 'Went through them herself. One caller reported seeing two figures — one in dark clothing. Presumably that was whoever set up the effigy.'

'God love her!' Chan exclaimed. 'She's mucking in like a trouper!'

'That narrows down the time frame, doesn't it?' Finch said. 'We can start searching ANPR, appeal for drivers to check their dashcams — we might even get CCTV footage of whoever put it there.'

Rowan nodded. 'Yep. You should definitely suggest that when she gets here. And talking of time frames: DC Wicks said it was hard to establish Damian's time of death — why was that?'

She called up the pathologist's report on her laptop and skimmed it. 'Novak's stomach contents included partly digested burger and fries and there were large pieces of burger, bread and fries still in his stomach, indicating that he died shortly after his Big Mac.'

'Witnesses saw Novak at a McDonald's in Speke six hours before he was found,' Finch confirmed from his own notes.

'So he bolts his food, gets knocked down in a fatal collision soon after, and lies undiscovered on a busy stretch of motorway for nearly *six hours*?' Rowan turned to Chan for his opinion.

'Everyone's digestive system is unique,' he began. 'Damian's digestion *might* have been slower than average, so he might have been on the road for a shorter time. But it would be extremely unlikely for a young, healthy male to still have large chunks of undigested food in his stomach six hours after he'd eaten.'

'So he probably *did* die shortly after he ate,' Rowan said. 'Isn't it weird that he wasn't found sooner?'

'Actually, yes,' Chan said. 'Factoid: the average lifespan of someone standing on the hard shoulder of a motorway is fifteen minutes — yep, a quarter of an hour, folks. Extrapolating from that, that if you're knocked down at the side of the motorway, you will be *seen* by multiple drivers — if not run over by them. Logic dictates that Damian wasn't on the road for very long.'

'It's also odd that he was found in the same location as the effigy.' Rowan flipped through her own notes on her laptop, her excitement mounting. 'Craig's was hung from a motorway bridge and Lang's was left next to a wheelie bin at the foot of his block. But Craig was found in the stairwell of his tower block, and Lang in his own bath.'

'What are you saying, Cassie?' Chan said.

Rowan took a breath. 'Isn't it possible that Damian was killed elsewhere, and his body *dumped* on the motorway?'

Chan nodded slowly, his eyes lit with an elation akin to hers. 'More than possible. And because we lab geeks insisted on a thorough collection of evidence at the scene despite Wicks' protests, we might just be able to prove it.'

Rowan stared at him avidly.

'Give me a minute.' Sliding his phone from his back pocket, Chan headed out of the room.

Rowan swivelled to look at Finch. He looked as thrilled as she felt. But her optimism was trampled underfoot a second later by the arrival of Warman.

She looked like thunder, and, if Rowan had been of a fanciful nature, she would have said that a dark cloud seemed to hang just over her gathered brows.

Warman placed a buff folder on the table at the front of the meeting room and lifted out a sheet of A4 paper. Holding it by the top two corners as if it was radioactive, she revealed a full-colour image of the Birkenshore Boggart mask.

'This,' she said, 'has been shared on a whole raft of social media platforms.' Her voice was clipped and precise — which was a bad sign. 'There is a story in the *Liverpool Echo* online about a "voodoo curse" on residents of Fernleigh.'

She glared at Rowan as if she'd caught her, bloody knife in hand, performing a ritual with burnt feathers and chicken blood.

She dropped the sheet and held up another. It was the image of Justin Lang's effigy, which Rowan had snatched from Lukas Novak's mobile phone. 'One youth, who chooses to remain anonymous, is quoted as saying, "You see one of them dolls, you're as good as dead." Dolls,' she repeated, still fixing Rowan with the evil eye. 'By which I assume he means "effigies". And I specifically asked you to keep the effigies within the investigative team.'

'I did,' Rowan said.

'Then you must have *implied*—'

'I was careful, boss,' Rowan interrupted. 'I didn't give any hint about the importance of the mask when I spoke to the Birkenshore villagers. And I won't even meet with the Fernleigh Crafters till tomorrow, so if *they* know, they either got it by telepathy, or from someone other than me. Damian's kid brother made the connection before we'd even officially started this investigation — that's why he showed me the effigy of Justin Lang in the first place. Those images probably came from his phone. He admitted at the time that he shared it with some mates when he found it.' Warman's lips tightened in a thin line and Rowan went on. 'It was bound to come out eventually — and after I spent yesterday evening with kids at the community hub, I guess they talked, swapped stories and—'

'And images?' Warman arched an eyebrow.

'Well, that's the nature of social media,' Rowan said tartly, her face hot with anger at the injustice of the implied accusation. 'A picture paints a thousand words and all that.' She glared at Warman, knowing she sounded insubordinate. But what did she have to do to gain this woman's trust?

'Bombshell!' Chan shouted the word so loudly that both Rowan and Warman broke off from their war of nerves and looked at him.

'What *is* it, Ian?' Warman rasped.

He bounded into the room carrying a laptop aloft like an Olympic torch. 'Cassie remembered that there was some trouble establishing Damian Novak's TOD.' Ian Chan was tiny — barely five feet four — but he successfully crowded the statuesque DCI out of her premium spot in front of the projector screen with a wiggle of his hips, and Rowan had to stifle a laugh at the astonished look on her boss's face.

'Damian had eaten at McDonald's six hours before he was found,' Chan went on, setting up the laptop. 'But he'd barely started digesting his Happy Meal, so . . . our Shirley Holmes here reckoned he must've been killed very soon after.'

'Well, that's hardly a revelation,' Warman said testily. 'I've seen the report — it's all in there.'

'It is,' Chan said, raising one finger, as if she'd made an astute observation. 'So how come his body wasn't found sooner?'

Warman paused to think. 'You have a theory?' As always, she was resisting the invitation to speculate.

'Cassie has. She thinks the fatal collision happened elsewhere at some location yet to be discovered. The motorway was the deposition site.'

Warman gave Rowan a frosty look. 'Oh, is that what she thinks?'

'And I concur.' Before Warman could get another word in, he launched into an explanation. 'I've been out on a fun-filled crack-house day trip since early this morning, so I really haven't had time to check in with my colleagues. Prompted by Cassie, I remedied the situation and checked on the scene analysis. And . . .'

'Get *on* with it, Ian,' Warman said, losing whatever patience she had left in her meagre reserves.

With a flourish, Chan cast two images on the projector screen, side by side.

'The image on the left is a sample of grit taken from the motorway, where Damian's body was recovered,' he said. 'The one on the *right* is taken from abrasions to Damian's face.'

'They're different,' Finch murmured.

'*Completely*,' Chan said, beaming. The sample on the right was composed of jagged, light-grey particles, which looked almost crystalline. The motorway sample was much darker and had a mixture of large and small grains, which were rounded and more regular.

'Motorways take a hammering, so the aggregate used in their construction has rounded or cuboidal grains, which are hard-wearing and stable when mixed in hot asphalt,' Chan said, pointing out the features. 'But the gritty particles recovered from Damian's facial abrasions are longer and more angular. They also tend to flake, which means they wear more quickly — so this grit might have come from a minor road, or a car park — even a pavement.'

'This is definite?' Warman's voice had lost all trace of irritation, and if Rowan were to describe it now she would say there was a kind of awe in her boss's tone.

'I'd go so far as to say definitive,' Chan said. 'The grit from Damian's wounds does not match the motorway grit. Another point to consider is the fact that Damian was found flat on his face on the motorway with a broken nose. As we'd established in an earlier discussion, someone falls flat on their face, breaks their nose, you'd expect to see a lot more blood.' He paused. 'Which means the motorway is the deposition site, not the primary scene. Damian was killed somewhere else.'

After a stunned silence lasting a long ten seconds, Rowan spoke up.

'Okay. He was killed on a side street, and then moved to the motorway — but why was Damian's the only body found close to his effigy?'

He shrugged. 'Not my job — but have fun finding out.' He glanced down at his laptop and his fingers rustled over the keys. 'I've sent the details to your inboxes. And now, I'm off to shower the stench of degradation off me till I'm pink and perfumed as a newborn.'

A moment later, he was gone, leaving Warman open-mouthed.

CHAPTER 23

Rowan found Ian Chan half an hour later, talent-spotting at the bar of his favourite watering hole on the Albert Dock.

He'd changed clothes and his hair looked freshly washed and styled. Given the jacket in lightweight olive suede and perfectly pressed chinos he was wearing, Rowan wondered if he had an extra locker in the new police HQ, just for his wardrobe. The suede looked fresh out of the box, despite the rain they'd had that morning, and he'd definitely been wearing black jeans and scuffed trainers at the evening debrief. Now, he was shod in black leather Chelsea boots, with enough of a heel to give him extra height, but not so much that it screamed insecurity.

She sat next to him. 'Seen anything you like?'

He shot her a side-glance. 'It's all about sex with you, isn't it?'

She laughed. 'I wish.'

'You want a drink?'

'I'm not staying — I've a heart-to-heart with my little brother planned for this evening.'

He grimaced. 'Good luck with that.'

Rowan huffed; she was going to need it. 'I wanted to thank you for bigging me up in there.'

He tilted his head at forty-five degrees, acknowledging her thanks but implying it wasn't a big deal.

'You did lay it on with a trowel, though.' He wrinkled his forehead and she said, '"Shirley Holmes" was way OTT.'

'Poetic licence,' he said. 'And I had to do *something* — I mean, I leave you alone for five seconds and by the time I get back, you're in a staring match with the woman who holds your career prospects in her bony hands.'

'Oh, don't exaggerate—'

'Who's exaggerating? It was like *Gunfight at the O.K. Corral.*'

'I wasn't in a staring match.' Rowan's effort to feign indignation was ruined by an irrepressible grin at the image he'd conjured up. 'And we don't carry guns.'

'Just as well! I mean if looks could kill . . .'

'Be serious for a minute, will you? I need to ask you something.'

His eye had snagged on a man at the other side of the bar and she could see he wasn't listening, so she waved a hand in front of his face and, chastened, he dragged his attention back to her.

'Lisa's friend, Sophie, didn't recognize the mask and I'm thinking if there *was* an effigy of Lisa, she'd have told Sophie.'

Chan nodded.

'Anyway, I can't see Lisa being involved in criminality — she broke off with Justin Lang at great risk to herself. Plus, her parents deleted her posting on Instagram telling the world just how unhappy she was.'

Another nod.

The bar was beginning to fill up, and she lowered her voice. 'Lisa's death was a genuine suicide. She's not one of our victims.'

His eyes popped wide. 'You're calling them victims, now?'

'Well, Damian didn't pick himself up from the Fernleigh estate, wait a few hours, then carry himself a few miles up the road to the motorway.'

'Sarcasm is such a low form of humour,' he said, with a flicker of a smile. 'But just cos he was moved, it doesn't mean his death wasn't an accident.'

'That's stretching a point. But even if it was, whoever ran him down has a lot of questions to answer.'

'I'll give you that.'

'So, here's my question: did you find any evidence that might help us to identify the vehicle?'

He rolled his eyes. 'Like I said, we collected tons of evidence.'

'So . . .' She knew she didn't need to explain what she was asking him to do.

He rubbed his forehead and had the good grace to look a bit shamefaced. 'I suppose I did dash off a bit fast after my evidential bombshell, but, honestly, Cass, the stench of that crack house was giving me a headache.' He took a breath. 'Okay. Yes, we did collect small flecks of white paint from Damian's clothing, which may have come from a vehicle. And I'll suggest that we do microscopic and mass spec analysis on samples at tomorrow's briefing. Okay?'

'Okay.' She gave his arm a friendly knuckling and flicked a surreptitious glance across the bar towards the man Ian had been ogling. 'Now go and convince that poor guy we're not "together"— he looks disconsolate.'

She was on her way out of the bar when her phone rang; it was Alan Palmer.

'Are you available for a chat? It's about the deaths on the Fernleigh estate.'

Rowan checked her watch; it was almost 6 p.m. 'Can we meet in town? I have to be home by seven.' If she got back any later, she might miss Neil, and she had a plan to execute.

'Sure. My office? It won't take long.'

'I'm at the Albert Dock — I can be there in five minutes.'

* * *

In addition to his work as a psychoanalytic psychotherapist for the NHS, Alan Palmer had a private practice, and his city-centre consulting room was in Quorum House, a newish glass-and-steel structure almost opposite the Albert Dock. Rowan crossed the marble foyer to the reception desk to pick up a visitor's pass and headed straight to the elevator.

She knocked at the outer door and he shouted through for her to let herself in. The place smelled ravishingly of Palmer's favourite Colombian roast and absurdly, she felt the closest to happy she'd been in weeks.

He edged through the door of his little kitchenette with two steaming mugs in hand.

'What?' he said, and Rowan realized she was smiling.

'Nothing — just anticipation of a decent cup of coffee I didn't have to make myself.'

He chuckled. 'Well, don't let me keep you from your moment of contentment.'

She took the offered mug and sniffed the nutty aroma before taking her first sip. He didn't rush her, and she didn't feel awkward taking a moment: Alan Palmer had a knack for making you feel comfortable.

When they were both seated, he placed his coffee cup on the table in front of him and said, 'I know you're pressed for time, so I'll get straight to it. There's been speculation online about strange effigies, linked to deaths of young men from the Fernleigh estate.'

Rowan nodded. She'd skimmed through the social media postings of Justin Lang's effigy. Set alongside pictures of him in life, the menace inherent in the dolls had convinced her more than ever that they were meant as a direct threat to Craig, Justin, and Damian.

'Was there an effigy of Damian Novak?' he asked, plucking the thought from her head.

She paused mid-sip. 'Why d'you ask?'

'I'm sorry,' he said. 'I know you can't discuss the details, but there are more effigies.'

'"See one of them voodoo dolls, you're as good as dead"?' Rowan said, quoting one of the comments on the *Liverpool Echo* article.

'That's why I wanted to speak to you. I'm not sure "voodoo doll" is really what the effigies represent.'

'Oh?'

'You know what a doppelganger is?'

'A double,' she said. 'Not twins — more like a haunting.'

He nodded. 'They're often portrayed as doing exactly that in literature — haunting, stalking, even trying to take over their double's life. Usually, they work in one of two ways: first, as the identical second self who acts as conscience, like the double of William Wilson in the story by Edgar Allan Poe. Then there's the divided polar opposite — think Dr Jekyll and Mr Hyde.'

'Is this a "thing" in psychoanalysis, or just an interest of yours?' she asked.

He didn't answer straight away, and Rowan realized that her tone had been dismissive; Alan Palmer's subtle pauses did that to you — gave you time to reflect on what you'd said. It wasn't always a pleasant experience.

'Sorry,' she said. 'That didn't come out right.'

'Sense of self *is* important in psychoanalytic psychotherapy,' he said, answering her question as if it had been asked in the spirit of genuine curiosity. 'Similarity and difference, Self and Other. It's also relevant in terms of neurological conditions. The experience of seeing one's double is a disturbing reality for some: encephalitis, schizophrenia and PTSD sufferers can all have episodes of seeing their doppelgangers. In the final stages of neurosyphilis the French writer Guy de Maupassant would bow to his doppelganger and offer his hand, and Linneaus, the great botanist and taxonomist — a chronic migraine sufferer — had a double who would accompany him on his walks in the garden.'

The idea made Rowan shiver.

'As for the literary references — it's always secretly a relief when some of the thinking has already been done for you, so, yes, psychoanalytic analysis of great literature is a "thing" with us,' he went on with a self-mocking smile. 'Dostoevsky is probably the most analysed of the lot.'

Here, Rowan felt on firmer ground. 'We read *Crime and Punishment* for English Lit when I was sixteen,' she said.

'Dostoevsky was quite the social psychologist,' Palmer said. 'In eighteen forty-six — ten years before Freud was even born — he published a story called *The Double*, about a man whose life was clawed from him, one small step at a time, by a doppelganger who had all the social skills he lacked.'

Rowan nodded. 'One of my sociology lecturers at university recommended that. I couldn't really get into it.'

'Because . . .'

'I dunno.' Rowan took a breath; she owed him a little indulgence after her earlier rudeness. 'Okay . . . The guy in the story — the clerk — was such a wuss I just wanted to give him a good shake.'

'He is a bit buttoned up,' Palmer agreed. 'Eager to please, more than a little inept. And although he hates to admit it, Golyadkin knows these things about himself, which makes him nervous and even more inclined to make mistakes.'

Rowan's thoughts flashed to her own brashness, and from there to Finch's timidity, and she immediately felt embarrassed for herself and ashamed to be so quick to judge her colleague.

'But Golyadkin is not a bad person,' Palmer went on. 'And what happens to him is awful — unjust.'

Rowan felt her cheeks grow hot. 'That doesn't apply, here,' she said with an irritated shrug. 'Justin Lang was king-pin of a gang, a violent bully and possibly a rapist.'

'And the others?'

'Others?' He was blatantly fishing, now, and she wasn't having it.

'The other effigies,' he said. 'The other deaths.'

She blanked him.

'Craig Breidon,' he said. 'Damian.'

A cold wave swept over Rowan. News must have got out in a big way — and all in the forty minutes since their briefing had ended.

'Show me,' she said.

He handed her his phone and her shoulders sagged. Every newspaper in the North West, from the *Liverpool Echo* to the *Manchester Evening News* had some version of the story — with photographs. Thankfully, the hanging puppet of Damian in his kingfisher shell suit wasn't there, but the image of him on a stolen off-road bike was, and it was only a matter of time before someone dug out their dashcam and found a matching image on the motorway embankment.

'The "voodoo doll" hashtag is trending on Twitter and Instagram, too,' he said.

Rowan handed back his phone. 'According to Fernleigh's Police Community Support Officer, Lang and Damian Novak terrorized the estate, selling drugs, threatening anyone who tried to stop them, grooming kids, drawing them into crime,' she said. 'Damian encouraged his own eleven-year-old brother to join the Lang crew.'

'You didn't mention Craig Breidon.'

She sniffed. 'Jury's out on him. But you can't seriously think they were targeted to try to make them *better people*?'

'No,' Palmer said, calm and unruffled as always. 'But I do think there's a symbolism at work here. Someone went to a lot of trouble to make effigies that display key characteristics of those who died. And I certainly think they were meant to frighten the targets — can you imagine the horror of being confronted by yourself?'

She recalled Lukas Novak tormenting himself that he hadn't told his brother about the Lang effigy. 'Maybe he would've been careful,' he'd said.

'So you think the effigies were a warning?'

'That, and a threat.'

'Yeah.'

'I understand that the effigies appeared seven days before the deaths?' She hesitated and he added, 'At least, that's what the papers are saying.'

'Seven days,' she confirmed.

'Did you know that there's a widely-held superstition that seeing your double is an omen of death?' Palmer asked.

See one of them dolls, you're as good as dead echoed in Rowan's thoughts. 'I do now.'

'All three were suicides?'

'According to the coroners' verdicts,' she said, choosing her words carefully.

'Interesting. If there *had* been any doubt about the deaths,' he said, holding her gaze, 'I would've said that whoever made the effigies wanted his targets to suffer.'

'Punishment?' Rowan said. 'Revenge?'

'You'll only find that out if you catch him. But whatever his motivation, he wanted them to be afraid, not just at the moment they died, but for the seven days leading up to their deaths. He wanted them to know that death was coming, and that it would be awful.'

CHAPTER 24

Wednesday morning

Rowan sat in her car with her eyes closed for a few seconds. In the course of two hours, she'd spoken to the Fernleigh Crafters. They were as baffled by the effigies as the police. But Craig Breidon's mother had made an impassioned speech, and they'd all agreed to keep their eyes and ears open and do anything they could to help. From there, she'd paid a visit to Jonty's mum with PCSO Jackie Dawson.

It was only out of respect for Dawson that Gaynor Bloor had allowed them through the front door of her little bungalow. Jonty and her mother had been on a crossing when Damian mowed them down. 'A *pedestrian crossing*,' she'd repeated. 'But he blamed them for being too slow. Seeing Jonty struggling in a wheelchair hadn't bothered him in the slightest when he'd got out from his "holiday camp" youth-offenders' unit.' Mrs Bloor told Rowan she was 'over the bloody moon' that Damian Novak was dead; it was almost enough to convince her there was a God. The pain behind the woman's bitterness stirred up some ghosts for Rowan and she was alarmed to find herself tearing up. She thanked Mrs Bloor for her time and stood to leave.

The mother's parting words as she saw them out: 'Jonty still has nightmares. At least that bastard Novak got a taste of what that was like. Shame it was over so quick.'

'Cassie?'

Rowan opened her eyes. Six special constables carrying clipboards were strung out along the street, handing out pamphlets and asking a set of pre-agreed questions of every resident they could persuade to open their doors. These were the promised extra personnel to help with canvassing. Finch was stuck at the office, scouring CCTV for vehicles travelling on the westbound carriageway of the M62 in the thirty minutes before the first triple-nine call had been made about Damian's effigy. He would contact any vehicle owner who'd used that stretch of motorway in that time frame. A police constable had been drafted in to do the same for the night Damian's body was found. Merseyside's RPU had also tweeted and placed signs close to the deposition site appealing for dashcam footage. They hoped to catch an image of the 'two figures' reported on the embankment a week before Damian had died; better yet, a vehicle stopped on the hard shoulder around the time his body had been dumped.

Rowan couldn't help thinking they were wasting their time.

'Okay?' Dawson asked.

'Yeah.' She heard a tremor in her voice. 'Just — the driver who killed Mum and Dad . . .' Her chest tightened and she took a couple of calming breaths. 'He was drunk. Kept telling the cops they'd come out of nowhere, driving like lunatics.' She took another breath. 'He was clocked by a traffic cam going fifty miles an hour the wrong way down a dual carriageway.'

'Oh, Cassie . . .' She touched her arm lightly. 'Look, d'you want to take a break?'

'No,' Rowan said. 'But can you take me to where it happened?'

'Where Nana Bloor was killed?'

Dawson wasn't happy about it, but she directed Rowan to a pedestrian crossing about half a mile away. It was on the kidney-shaped road that ran through the estate, with streets and cul-de-sacs running off it. They parked up near a low-slung red-brick building.

'They were on their way to chapel,' Jackie said, lifting her chin to indicate the building.

The chapel sat squat behind a grey aluminium fence. It was not much different from the other housing except for the car park out front and windows set high in its walls, tucked tight under the eaves of the roof.

Rowan got out and walked back to the crossing. Traffic lights, pedestrian barrier — dented but intact — zigzag markings, straight stretch of road, no overhanging vegetation. Not one single extenuating circumstance that might have explained why Damian hadn't seen Jonty Bloor and his grandmother.

Dawson had followed her.

'Day or night?' Rowan asked.

'Day. He tore out of that side street on the stolen bike.' Dawson pointed in the direction of a narrow road about twenty yards away. 'Mounted the pavement, scattering chapelgoers, bumped back onto the road and accelerated. Jonty and his nana had waited for the lights to cross because Nana Bloor was a bit unsteady on her feet. Ploughed straight into them, got up and ran off.'

Rowan bowed her head, picturing the scene. Imagining the horror Jonty and his nana had felt as the bike bore down on them.

The road surface was pitted and particles of grey grit gathered at the edges of shallow potholes. 'What was the road like back then?' she asked, stirring the grit with the tip of her shoe.

'Actually, not bad. They'd done some repairs after that bad winter we had — the accident was about six or seven months after.'

Something glinted on the road a few feet away and Rowan stepped out, then crouched to get a better look.

'Woah!' Jackie followed her. Arm up, palm out, to halt an approaching car. 'Cassie, watch the traffic!'

'Look at this,' Rowan said.

Keeping her arm up, Dawson twisted to look over her shoulder. 'What is it?'

'Perspex, possibly from a headlamp.' She took a picture with her mobile phone, pinched and magnified it. Her heart thumped hard in her chest. 'I think there's blood on it.'

'Cass, that doesn't mean—'

Rowan stood, pivoting on the ball of one foot, examining the area around. The dented barrier was of the old type: hollow steel frame with lattice infill. A still calm settled on her as she made eye contact with the increasingly irritated driver of the car. She lifted one finger, telling him to wait, giving him a hard look in case he didn't get the message.

Two minutes later, as Rowan snapped off more images, he pipped the horn and spread his hands in exasperation.

'Tell him he needs to turn around,' Rowan said, switching to her list of contacts. 'We need to get this section of road closed and the immediate area taped off.'

'Cassie, you can't think—'

'Hold the traffic,' Rowan said. The DCI's phone went straight to voicemail, so she left a brief message and placed a call to the control room for assistance.

Holding both hands up now and alternately glowering first at one lane of traffic, then the other, the flustered PCSO said, '*Think* about it, Cass. Damian was killed over a week ago—'

Rowan ignored her, jogging instead to her car, explaining the situation to the operator and emphasizing the urgency, before taking out a roll of blue-and-white police-incident tape.

By the time she had the area taped off, a white CSU van had pulled up fifty yards down the road and a marked police car had arrived. They took over, redirecting traffic as Rowan drew Jackie aside.

'The road grit is similar to the stuff they picked out of the lacerations on Damian's face,' Rowan said quietly. She held up her phone, swiping through the images as she explained. 'The barrier — obviously dented.' She enlarged a section of the lattice-work infill. 'Remember the PM findings — bruising to Damian's shoulder and chest? They thought it might be caused by impact with a van grille, but they couldn't identify it.' She swiped through three more images of the lattice: distance shot, close-up and macro. 'See the white flecks? The CSIs recovered specks of white paint from his clothing.'

Dawson's lips moved soundlessly and Rowan made out *Oh my God . . .*

Rowan's hand was trembling, and Dawson held it steady while she swiped back through all of the images. Finally, she raised her eyes to Rowan's face. 'Bloody hell, Cassie. You've found the primary crime scene.'

'Maybe,' Rowan said. 'We can't talk about this to anyone — not to our guys or —' She glanced around at the crowd gathering at the cordon. 'Anyone.'

CHAPTER 25

Lukas Novak was running for his life. He vaulted a fence into a back garden and dragged out his phone. Hiding behind the garden shed, he found the woman detective's number and hit call.

'Lukas?' she said.

'Miss, he's after me,' he gasped out. 'He's gonna kill me.'

'Where are you?'

Panicked, he tried to remember where he'd come from, how far he'd run. 'I dunno.'

'*Think*, Lukas.'

He squeezed his eyes shut for a second and it came to him. 'Snowdrop Street, behind the shops.'

'Can you hide?'

'I am, but—'

'Stay put — I'll be there in two minutes. Who's following you?'

Lukas yelped. The back door of the house had opened. A man appeared, holding the collar of a big bull-nosed staffie.

'Get out of it, you little bastard!' the man yelled. 'I'll set the dog on you!'

The staffie lunged, snarling, his teeth bared.

'No, mister, don't. Please, I—'

The dog flew at him and Lukas scrambled for the fence, screaming. He got his right leg over the top, but lost contact with his trailing foot and the dog snagged the cuff of his trackie bottoms. He felt his trousers pulling down and with a high-pitched squeal, he yanked at his waistband. The material tore and the dog fell back.

Screaming, begging the man to call the dog off, Lukas swung his left leg up.

Too slow!

The beast righted itself and leapt, snapping wildly. Lukas felt a terrible pressure on his heel. The staffie had a grip on the back of his trainer. The shoe slipped and was held only by Lukas's instep, but the dog hung on.

'Get off me!' Lukas screamed. His heart beat so hard it hurt.

The dog's eyes bulged, showing the whites; its lips, curled back, exposed a row of pointed teeth, wet with drool. Lukas shook his leg backwards and forwards, desperate, panting, trying to dislodge the animal. Finally, his shoe came off and the dog fell again, baying, worrying at the shoe like he might worry a rat.

Frozen in terror, Lukas could only watch, horrified.

The man came out of the house with a long-handled broom and ran at him, cursing. With a yelp, Lukas got moving again. He dropped to the ground, but fell awkwardly, twisting his ankle. He limped off, gaining pace, sobbing, wiping snot onto his new Nike hoody.

Footsteps behind him.

Lukas put on a spurt of speed, shedding a watch, cigarettes, a mobile phone — all stolen goods — running till his chest burned and his injured foot went numb with pain.

The man following him knew the alleyways and quiet backwaters of Fernleigh better than he did, anticipating his switchbacks, cutting him off at corners, appearing suddenly from between link-houses, matching him turn for turn, hounding Lukas till he'd run out of escape routes.

Trapped in a blind alley, Lukas turned, cornered, ready to fight. Tears blurred his vision, and for a moment the face of his pursuer was a blank mask with dark holes for eyes. Expecting to see the wide, evil grin of the red mask, he was almost grateful that this hunter had no mouth.

Cowering against the wall, watching helplessly as his pursuer came closer, Lukas wiped the blinding tears from his eyes and saw that it was the martial-arts guy, North. The big man reached down to him, and Lukas lashed out with his shod foot.

North deflected and slapped the side of his head hard, setting Lukas's ears ringing.

Dragged to his feet by the hood of his jacket, Lukas struggled, trying to wriggle free, but North dangled him till he stopped.

'Now walk.'

Lukas made the mistake of putting his full weight on his left foot. Pain shot through him like a steel rod from his heel to the base of his skull and he cried out.

'You're lucky it didn't take your foot,' North growled. 'Now stop whining and walk.'

He limped on tiptoe, the hard concrete cold through his sock, North shoving and pushing him every step of the way.

He'd lost track of where they were, and it wasn't till they turned the corner that he realized they were at the edge of the estate, in the shadow of the tower block where he lived.

He's brung me home to finish the job!

Sobbing, begging forgiveness, convinced he was about to die, he limped ahead of the ex-soldier.

At the entrance to the stairwell, North said, 'Inside.'

Lukas spun round, sinking to his knees. 'No, no, please, mister. Mum and Lily's home,' he cried. 'They never done nothing — please don't hurt them. I'll never rob nothing again. I'll stop dealing — I swear.'

He was clinging to the man's arm, and North shook him off.

'I know where you live,' North said. 'And next time, I might not be in such a generous mood. Do not say a word about this.' He thrust his face inches from Lukas's, baring his teeth. 'If you do, I'll know.'

Lukas whimpered, then babbled more promises, hardly knowing what he said. He curled into a ball, covering his head with his arms, expecting a rain of blows to fall on him. When he dared look up again, North was gone.

The sound of running footsteps brought him to his feet. Struggling with the stairwell door he glanced wildly over his shoulder. It was the policewoman.

'Jeez, Lukas, what happened to you?'

'Nothin.' He couldn't hold the door and it slammed against him. He cried out, and she held it, putting an arm around him and half-lifting him.

'Who did this to you?' she demanded.

'No one. I fell.'

'You fell and lost your new trainer?'

Tears started to his eyes, and he dashed them away with the back of his hand.

'Tell me where you lost it, I'll go and get it for you.'

Yeah, and get done for robbing that house. 'It's gone,' he lied. 'Fell down a grid.'

'Lukas.' She laughed, like it was funny. 'You're a terrible liar.'

'I'm not. Gonna sue the council. I coulda killed myself.'

'Okay.'

They walked the next few flights in silence, Lukas leaning heavily on the policewoman. He felt cold, almost fainting with the pain, now.

'Did a man help you to get home?' Rowan asked.

'No. Nobody did.'

'I saw a man.'

He tried to shrug, but with her arm tight around him, he couldn't get much movement. 'Nothing to do with me.'

They reached the door of his flat and he turned the latch key. His mum yanked the door open and grabbed him by the arm. Her thin fingers dug into the flesh and he winced but didn't complain.

She stared, hard-eyed, at the detective.

'What've you done to this lad?' Her voice was a hard rasp.

'No, Mum, she didn't do nothin',' he protested. 'She just helped me.'

'He needs to get that foot checked,' Rowan said.

'He's *my* son — I'll decide what he needs.' As Lukas limped inside, his mum blocked the woman, then slammed the door.

His mother's face was twisted with rage, but she spoke softly, as the detective was still outside. 'Talking to bizzies now, are you? Making friends, sticking up for them? If you bring the Langs down on us, I'll—' She raised her hand and he flinched but she didn't follow through. 'Get in your room. I'm sick of the sight of you,' she hissed.

CHAPTER 26

Rowan returned to the road crossing, where CSIs, clad head to foot in white Tyvek suits, were creeping slowly over the taped-off area, picking up tiny fragments of plastic and other detritus like giant, highly fastidious grubs. As she'd expected, Ian Chan was absent. Although it was over a week since he'd helped to process the deposition site on the motorway, she knew he wouldn't want to risk even the slightest chance of cross-contamination.

Police constables watched the edges of the cordon and directed cars back the way they'd come. The streets on this part of the estate came off the bean-shaped access road, which meant that drivers wanting the streets near to the chapel might have to go all the way around in the opposite direction, just to get fifty metres from where they'd been seven minutes earlier. Some people weren't happy about it, which accounted for the grim looks on the uniformed officers' faces. Kids on bikes were circling, shouting comments, and when a news crew arrived and unpacked microphones and recording equipment from the boot of their car, the kids began to gather there, asking questions, looking for an opportunity to lift something valuable.

It was a school day; these kids should be in school, but truancy rates were a third higher than the national average in this borough, and clearly the 'Every Day Counts' strategy wasn't working on Fernleigh.

Dawson was on the other side of the tape, mingling and chatting easily with the friendlier onlookers. Rowan didn't doubt for a moment that she would be gleaning as much information as she could from the residents while the excitement of so much police activity had brought down their guard.

Reaching the outer cordon, she got a call from Chan — they'd had the go-ahead to fast track any DNA from the scene and, as soon as the CSU had finished, they would be doing a series of comparisons between the white flecks they'd collected from the motorway, and whatever they retrieved at this new potential scene on Fernleigh estate.

She disconnected, feeling a warm glow of vindication in her chest and her eye snagged on Jim North standing apart from the melee on the far side of the tape.

She wandered over. 'Didn't expect to see you here.' He gave her a quizzical look and she added, 'I thought you'd be at work — that big development must be a huge responsibility.'

'Lunch break,' he said, apparently immune to her clumsy attempt at flattery.

'Odd way to spend your lunch break,' she said, taking a more direct approach. 'It must be a fifty-minute round trip from Liverpool to Fernleigh.'

He ignored the comment, looking past her into the onlookers.

Scanning it, she thought. Like a cop might scan a hostile crowd to identify the troublemakers. He would have had his share of that kind of surveillance as a British soldier in Afghanistan.

He narrowed his gaze on the youths circling the news reporters like jackals. 'Is this Damian?' he asked.

She looked up at him. 'I don't follow.'

'Sure you do,' he said. 'Damian was found on the motorway a few miles away, but all the police inquiries seem to be focused on Fernleigh. Next thing, you show up at the exact location of a four-year-old road fatality and call in Forensics.'

'Maybe there was an accident here today,' she said.

He shot her a sideways glance. 'Whatever happened here, it wasn't today,' he said, examining the scene critically. 'And if this *is* about Damian, it was no accident.'

'You know that this is where Mrs Bloor was killed?'

'Everyone who lives here knows it.'

That might be, but she would like to know why he was here on his lunch break and just happened upon what she was convinced was the primary scene in Damian's death. What was it Jackie had said? 'First sight of a stranger, the cry goes up like a whole tribe of howler monkeys.' The Langs had their lookouts, perhaps Jim North did, too.

'If you have information that could help this case,' she began, but he waved her away.

'I don't know who did this,' he murmured.

'Did what?'

He shifted stance, looking at her properly for the first time. 'Oh, come on . . .'

She didn't budge, and she didn't look away, and after a few moments he sighed. 'Hashtag "voodoo dolls" is trending on social media,' he said. 'So is hashtag "hex".'

'You believe in curses?'

He straightened up, a frown creasing his forehead; he seemed to be giving the question serious consideration.

'The dolls are real,' he said. 'As for the rest — at the very least, whoever made them is scaring the crap out of lowlifes who thought they were immune — until now.'

'And that's a good thing?'

'Well, it can't be *bad*.'

She shot him an incredulous look and he said, 'You can't expect me to believe you never felt the urge to make things right.'

'That's why I'm here,' she said levelly.

He scoffed. 'You think you can make things right by asking questions, talking to kids, enlisting the crafting circle as your neighbourhood watch?'

181

'You say it as though there's something wrong with that,' Rowan said. 'Isn't it good to give the community ways to monitor itself, help with policing it?'

'Good intel is worthless if you do nothing with it,' he said.

He had a point. If all the law-abiding residents of this strife-torn estate got out of intel-gathering was an occasional high-vis police presence, it would do no more than make the criminals a little more cautious about how they conducted business. And when, inevitably, the police withdrew, their brave efforts to develop community solidarity would only reinforce the reality of their helplessness.

'You're right,' she said simply. 'We have to do better. But I'm police, and it's my job to uphold the law.'

He searched her face, a hint of exasperated amusement playing around his eyes. 'You're not being honest; I know you're willing to go off-piste to get a result.' She hesitated and he said, 'Don't bother denying it, Cassie.'

He was talking about the killer she'd helped to bring down last winter. Rowan had to admit she did colour outside the lines on that one, but she wasn't going to give in to his argument that easily. Instead, she exclaimed, 'You googled me!' Then, 'Well, that's not creepy *at all*.'

He scratched his neck with the back of his hand, catching the levity in her tone. 'Due diligence.' In his favour, he did have the good grace to look a little shamefaced. 'Someone comes around asking my kids questions, I need to know who they are.'

'*My* kids?' she repeated, emphasising the possessive.

'The kids I feel responsible for.'

'Do you feel responsible?'

He sighed, ran a hand over his brow. 'I know it sounds corny, but I just want them to have a fighting chance in life.'

She softened a little. 'Not corny.' She felt the same way herself, but she'd rather suffer having her toenails pulled out with pliers than admit to it to him.

'It's only fair you should know — I looked you up, too,' she said quietly. 'And you *don't* live here anymore. You own an apartment in Allerton; you left here fifteen years ago.'

He shook his head, his jaw tight. 'I couldn't live here again — I'm not brave enough.'

If he hadn't looked so serious, she'd have laughed at the idea.

'I mean it,' he insisted. 'This place was hell fifteen years ago. It's worse now.'

'Then why'd you come back? Why spend three or four nights a week here? You built a good career in the army, rose to Staff Sergeant. You could've gone on to bigger things.'

'After we withdrew our training forces from Afghanistan in twenty-one, I guess I lost faith,' he said. 'So many people had given so much — risked *everything* and—' He broke off.

'It was wasted,' she said.

He gave her a quick glance, as if the comment had surprised him. 'It was. All that talent. All the energy, vision, enthusiasm to make their lives better, wasted.'

'So you came home, to this?' She glanced around, taking in the lads goading the police, play-fighting, causing annoyance, knowing that those same kids would be hawking drugs when the sun went down.

'I wasn't much different when I was their age,' he said. 'Bit of a scall. Not averse to carrying "product" for whoever would slip me a few quid for the favour. But I was lucky: I had a teacher who was Army Reserve, got a few of us interested in the cadet force. Best thing that ever happened to me.'

'Until Afghanistan.'

'Until we *left* Afghanistan,' he corrected.

'So you came home. Does that mean you still have family here?'

'Not anymore.'

She tilted her head.

'I had a kid brother,' North said, in an emotionless monotone, as if he was just keen to get it over with. 'Ben. He was a lot like me — hard case, scall, nowhere near as tough as he thought he was.'

'What happened?'

'He got into drug-peddling, overdosed on his own product.'

'Jim . . .' Her breath caught. 'I'm so sorry.'

'He was sixteen years old,' he added, and she felt a chill run through her, thinking of Neil.

'When did this happen?'

'Three years ago. I came home for his funeral. Went back, but when the UN pulled out of Afghanistan for good, I quit.'

'D'you know who Ben was involved with — I mean, which crew?'

'Doesn't really matter. If it hadn't been one, it would be another.' He shook his head. 'The point is, I didn't do enough for him.'

'It always feels that way, but you can only do what you can.'

'Nice platitude.'

Rowan was drawn to North, felt she had a lot in common with him: the loss of family, the guilt, the younger brother she felt she should have protected better, so that hurt.

She sucked her teeth. 'Okay. Good talking to you.' She walked to her car, stopping to check in with the crime scene manager on the way, and to let Dawson know she'd be in touch later.

'You're leaving?' Dawson said.

'There's nothing useful I can do here, and now word is out about the effigies, I thought I'd have another chat with the people in Birkenshore. Will I see you at the debrief this evening?'

Dawson grinned. 'Try and stop me!'

Feeling North's eyes on her, Rowan told herself she was imagining things. Even so, she couldn't help twitching her shoulders against the burning itch between her shoulder blades. And as she got into her car, she saw that he was watching her, his face a mask, but anger came off him in waves, and the intensity of his stare felt like a physical weight.

CHAPTER 27

Rowan felt lighter driving off the estate, putting distance between herself and the oppressive mood of the place. Was this how Neil felt, coming home, dreading what might happen next in their street? Feeling unsafe as so many people on Fernleigh felt unsafe?

The cream cakes she'd brought home from Birkenshore's prize-winning bakery had broken the ice the night before, and Neil had provisionally agreed to meet with his teachers. She was to be allowed to attend, on condition she 'didn't try to act like she was Mum'.

Rowan only wished she knew how: Mum would have known how to get him to talk. Dad would have passed on the wisdom he'd gathered from twenty-plus years of driving a taxi. Ferrying passengers at closing time who'd had a skinful, commiserating with football fans dragging home after matches where the result hadn't gone in their favour, he'd somehow manage to remain friendly and open, and, more often than not, had turned angry drunks from their intended violence. She couldn't be Mum, and she certainly couldn't be Dad — and she knew for sure that it was male counsel her brother needed right now.

Which was why she stopped before taking the narrow lane to Birkenshore, finding a quiet lay-by where she could make the phone call that would activate phase two of her plan.

Her first two attempts went straight to voicemail, so she dropped a text.

Alex, pick up the damn phone!

The next time she dialled, he picked up. 'Hi Cass. Look, I'm on my way to work. Can this wait?'

'No, it can't.'

She didn't say any more, and he spoke into the silence. 'Is it Neil?'

'Right on the nose, big brother.'

'Well, don't torment me — what's happened?'

She got a perverse satisfaction from hearing the tension in his voice. 'He's missing classes, failing assignments — failing even to *attempt* assignments — he's moody, difficult—'

'He's a *teenager.*'

'Thank you for mansplaining that to me. In case you've forgotten, I'm the one who saw him through puberty, so I know a thing or two about teenage mood swings. This is different.'

Maybe he'd heard the tension in *her* voice, because when he spoke again, his tone was sober. 'Different how?'

'He's depressed — constantly doomscrolling about his injury, yet he won't do the physio exercises he was given. He's out till late most evenings, won't tell me where he's been, won't talk to me—'

'He's a mess, I get it,' Alex said.

'Do you? You call once a fortnight if we're lucky. We haven't seen you since before Christmas — and don't give me any guff about pressure of work — I know you've been to your London office.'

It was a guess, but his silence told her she was right, and the confirmation hit her harder than she expected.

'Jesus, Alex! You couldn't spare *one day* to come and see your kid brother?'

'I would have, but—'

'But you didn't.'

'He said he was fine.'

'Of course he did, you pillock!'

'Okay, Cassie — calm down.'

'I'll be calm when you talk to him.'

'I did.'

'Three weeks ago.' He started to object, but she interrupted. 'Check your diary. I'm guessing you said you were fine, he said he was fine, then you talked about football for a bit — Liverpool's chances, maybe a thing or two about what you're both binge-watching on Netflix — and that was about it.'

'You make it sound banal. But it's just what guys *do*.'

'He's not a *guy*, he's a boy — your little brother. He pretends it's no big deal that he's not getting better because he *wants* to be a man so you'll be proud of him.'

'I *am* proud—'

'Did you tell him that?'

'Not in so many—'

'So how's he gonna know it? You're not *here*, Alex. Male telepathy doesn't travel over thousands of miles. You can't give him a warm look, a manly hug, that punch in the arm that says *so much more*—'

'Enough with the sarcasm,' he hissed. 'This isn't easy for me, either.'

'I'm sorry,' she said, swallowing an answer that would only end with him hanging up. 'I get sarcastic when I'm upset. But you need to understand that Neil says he's fine because he thinks that's what you want to hear. *You* say you're fine, and it's probably true. But that's because you don't have to see him shutting himself off, depressed and frightened, and alone. You're protecting yourself — I get that. But this isn't about you — it's about your kid brother. Neil is hurting. He's trying to be brave, but he really is just a kid.'

'Okay, what d'you need?'

It sounded like the kind of thing he would say to a client. Did he think his brother's pain was something to be managed, like bad press? Put the right spin on it and he'd turn that frown upside down?

She almost said it and put a hand over her mouth in an unconscious gesture. *Take a breath*, she told herself. *This isn't about you, either, Cassie Rowan.*

'Cass — are you there?'

'I'm thinking,' she said, carefully organizing her thoughts into bullet points. 'He needs his big brother to tell him that it's okay to be scared. He needs to know that it's okay to ask for help. He needs you to tell him the physio will only help if he sticks with it. He needs permission to say—'

'He's not fine?' he said. 'All right, I hear you, sis. And you're right. You know, if you ever get bored with policing, there's a high-paying job with your name on it in PR.'

'So you'll call him?'

'I will.'

'Tonight,' she said.

'Well, I—'

'No excuses, Alex. I'm going to ring him now, tell him I'm ordering in a banquet from his favourite Chinese to give him a reason to be home. So *you* need to ring at 7 p.m. our time.'

'Cassie, that's two in the *afternoon*, here!'

'Take a late lunch,' she growled. 'This is important, Alex.'

He huffed. 'Look — why don't I ring him now?'

'*No* — I want to be around if there's any fallout.'

'Jeez, it's that bad?'

'You can*not* imagine . . .'

'Okay,' he said, sighing, 'Okay . . . I guess I can move some things around.'

She resisted a sarcastic snipe about his hectic schedule. 'Be honest with him, Alex. Tell him why you've been avoiding him—'

'Oh, come *on* . . .'

'Well, what else would you call it?'

'God, when did you get to be such a hard-ass?' He was sounding more American every day.

'Do *not* be late,' she said. '*Listen* to him properly — and tell him it's okay to ask for help.'

'Why don't you just send me a script?'

'I'm serious, Alex. Mess this up and I swear I'll come over there and drag you home to say it in person.'

'*Okay*, sis!' But now he was laughing. She heard a ping. 'There, it's in my phone, on my calendar, and I've set a reminder. Now, can I get to work?'

CHAPTER 28

Wednesday afternoon

Now that word was out, Rowan wanted to show around images of the victims' effigies to as many people as possible. The Fernleigh Crafters had been at a loss, but the use of boggart masks suggested that there was a link between Fernleigh and Birkenshore. If Mrs Tetting could be persuaded to call in the local crafters, maybe they would shed some light on who might have made the effigies.

It was after one o'clock by this time, and Rowan parked at the edge of the village green, hoping to catch the volunteer librarian who had been so helpful on her first visit. Before she tackled Mrs Tetting, she wanted an unvarnished opinion of her as well as the crafters she organized; she hadn't forgotten Sal Fabian's tart remark that the crafters would portray her as a witch. Why? Because she was unconventional? Were the Birkenshore women really so small-minded?

Ms Fabian was issuing books to a young mother with a fractious three-year-old boy. The child replied to every gentle suggestion the mother made, with a voluble, 'No!'

The librarian caught Rowan's eye as the mother bent to pet the child and Rowan could see that the interaction was wearing on her. Sal's raspberry-tinted quiff seemed to have wilted under the constant barrage of noise, which echoed to the barn-like rafters of the building, and Rowan could practically hear her teeth grinding.

Waiting at the desk was out of the question, so Rowan occupied herself by scanning the noticeboard. Opening hours were listed and almost every inch of space was covered with flyers: school visiting times, an appeal for volunteers to help in the library; introductory courses for computers and smartphones; a book group; Mums-and-Toddlers' Story Time; finally, a large A3 poster promoting the campaign against Turner's building development. Nothing about the village crafters.

The oak door opened, letting in cold air and a litter of soggy leaves; an older man dithered on the threshold, seemingly undecided whether to come in or flee the bellowing child. A dismayed shout went up at the issue desk as the boy saw his chance and made a dash for it.

Rowan scooped up the child with a laugh. 'Not so fast, Houdini!'

The boy gazed at her, astonished, then started screaming, turning bright red and flinging himself backwards in his fury at having been thwarted. The mother dashed across and prised the child from Rowan's arms as if she'd tried to abduct him.

'It's all right, darling. I'm sure the lady didn't *mean* to upset you,' she said, with a stony look that suggested she had the measure of Rowan's type. 'Shall we go and see the scarecrows playing ring-a-roses?'

The child roared, 'Nooooooo!' and as the door swung closed after them, his cries could be heard gradually fading as the doting mother carried him away.

The remaining readers seemed to heave a collective sigh, and Rowan made her way to the desk.

'Good to see I haven't lost my touch,' Rowan said, prompting an amused snort from Sal Fabian.

'What can I do for you today, Ms Rowan?'

'Cassie. I was hoping to speak to the local crafting group; who would I need to see about that?'

'That would be the *present* Mrs Tetting.'

Odd phrase. Rowan could almost hear ears flapping, so she didn't ask for an explanation. 'Where do they meet? I couldn't see anything on the noticeboard.'

'They're called the Shore Crafters — it's a play on words, apparently.' Sal rolled her eyes at the lameness of the pun. 'They meet in the village hall, or in Mrs Tetting's inner sanctum at the manor. Didn't she tell you this yesterday?'

Village gossip, Rowan thought. *Everyone knows everyone else's business.* Rowan ignored the question, but noted that although Mrs Tetting *had* mentioned the crafters, she hadn't said that she ran the group. 'I don't suppose they have a meeting today?' she asked.

The librarian half-closed one eye, thinking. 'Tuesday, I believe. But with the open day coming up, they may be doing a few impromptu sessions. Is this about the voodoo dolls?'

Rowan heard a distinct rustle behind her as people leaned in to listen. 'A friend of mine thinks they're more like doppelgangers.'

'Ooh, I like that,' Sal said, her eyes widening.

'He said I should read *The Double*.'

'Dostoevsky?' Sal grimaced. 'Did you give it a go?'

Rowan dipped her head, embarrassed. 'I couldn't get past the third chapter.'

'I'm not at all surprised,' Sal said. 'Golyadkin's an annoying little whiner. For me, Poe's *William Wilson* is far superior. Or if you don't mind being plagued by nightmares for a week or two, you could try Stephen King's *The Dark Half* — the sadistic alter ego of a literary writer begins to take over his life.'

'So these doppelgangers always try to steal the real person's life?'

'Always. And there's a showdown at the end, where one or the other dies.' Sal tilted her head. 'Sometimes both.'

Rowan nodded, wondering if the symbolic meaning of the effigies was important to the person who made them, and if it was, what was the symbolism of the masks? Could the maker of the effigies be a Birkenshore villager with a grudge? She wanted to ask, but not with an audience.

Sal seemed to sense her hesitation and with a flourish, opened the door into the crowded office. It was stacked even higher with boxed books. And Sal apologized, clearing a space for Rowan to sit.

'They sent another carful this morning. We've had to ask them to stop.'

'I might know a community group who'd take some off your hands,' Rowan said, recalling the old and battered paperbacks on the shelves in Jessop's converted shop.

'Tell me it's Fernleigh,' Sal said with a wicked grin. 'Tetting would have a hissy fit.'

'About that. What did you mean by the "present" Mrs Tetting?'

'That's how he introduces her at village fetes and the Christmas booze-up they host for the locals up at the manor. Everyone laughs and *she's* supposed to find it *hilarious*. She doesn't, although *he* certainly does.' Sal hmphed. 'I never could like a man who laughs at his own jokes. Why she lets him get away with it, I'll never understand.'

'I think she's one of nature's peacekeepers,' Rowan suggested.

'She's so self-effacing she's almost transparent,' Sal scoffed. 'There's a saying in the village that the manor's haunted, but it isn't by a Tudor lady or headless knight — it's the present Mrs Tetting.'

'I was wondering about the animosity between Birkenshore and Fernleigh,' Rowan said, feeling sorry for the lady of the manor and wanting to deflect Sal from her character assassination. 'Can you see anyone going so far as to make these effigies to intimidate troublemakers from the estate?'

Sal had been busying herself with coffee, but she paused a moment. 'Feelings do run high, but in reality we don't see much of them down here on the marsh,' she said. 'Yes, there was a graffiti problem, but that was Andy Pym's doing. He threw open the tennis-club bar to non-members and offered a cocktail hour in a bid to bring in new custom. The place got trashed — cost him a fortune making it usable again and we had some unpleasant incidents around the village for a few weeks after.'

Andy Pym, Rowan thought. He was the man who'd had words with Julius Tetting on Monday.

'Is there any reason why Pym might've fallen out with Tetting?' she asked.

'Not *really* — Julius is a bastard, but he does send custom Andy's way when he can. Of course, he's blocking the development, and a nice new crop of execs could have brought in a lot of new members to the tennis club . . .'

'Tetting does seem heavily invested in the village and its history.'

'Oh, he invested all right!' Sal exclaimed.

Rowan crinkled her brow.

Sal folded her arms and looked down at Rowan. 'I bet he told you that the Tettings founded the manor in the early eleventh century.'

'Well, yes.'

'What he no doubt *neglected* to say is they sold up and moved to London in the fifteenth century. The feudal system was on the wane by then, and the peasants began to gain a few rights — some even established themselves as farmers and landowners. The Tettings didn't like the oiks getting above themselves, so they sold out to Thomas, Viscount Hockenhull. The Hockenhull family held the land and the manor for centuries — in fact, until nineteen seventy-five.'

'So how did Tetting get his feet back under the manorial table?' Rowan asked.

Sal handed her a mug of coffee. 'No cakes this time, I'm afraid.' She sat at her desk, shoving papers and a stack of books to one side so they could make eye contact.

'The Tettings went on to amass a fortune in sugar and cotton imports,' she explained. 'But in the nineteenth century Julius's branch of the family diversified into the hospitality industry. By the mid-twentieth, two world wars, the Great Depression, successive death taxes, and hyperinflation meant that old families were having to sell up or watch their houses fall down around them. Julius's dad made a killing buying up old country houses for a tenth of their real value and upgrading them to exclusive hotels and retreats.

'Then Julius's father heard that the Hockenhulls were selling up. He made them a generous offer — even gave the viscount and viscountess a corner of the old pile as a kind of grace-and-favour apartment.'

'I suppose there's nothing like having real-life minor aristocracy in residence as window dressing to bring in the paying customers,' Rowan said, and Sal tugged her raspberry quiff in lieu of a forelock. 'But where does Julius's wife fit in all this?'

'She was the Hockenhulls' miracle baby, born late in her mother's life. Julius was a good ten years older than her, so he didn't really notice little Viv. The viscount wouldn't risk the future of the Honourable Vivienne to a state education, so she was packed off to boarding school from the age of twelve. Ah, but when Viv came home for her eighteenth birthday party Julius was besotted. His father was dead by then, so he was mighty rich. He wooed her, pursued her — some say hounded her — until she agreed to marry him.'

'And yet he shows her no respect.'

'He respects the *history*. Loves Vivienne's "Honourable" title — I don't think he ever really loved *her*.' Sal laughed. 'You know, officially, the title died when her father popped his clogs, but Julius insists on having it on their stationery. He even petitioned to have their son "recreated" a viscount.'

'How did that go?'

'Monumental failure,' Sal crowed. 'They did away with most of that tosh in the nineteen-sixties.'

'There's a son?'

Sal's face clouded. 'Richard. Nice kid — big reader. Julius shipped him off to Harrow at the stroke of midnight on his thirteenth birthday, of course. A boy with his antecedents needs the "right" connections in life, after all.' She uttered a cry of disgust. 'The man's a despicable snob.'

And that's not all, Rowan thought. Julius Tetting had implied that his family were the ancient incumbents of Birken Manor, when it was his wife's family; that he personally had set up the manor as a wedding venue, when his father had done the work; that he was the manager and organizer of the business, when it seemed his wife shouldered most of that burden. What else was he lying about?

CHAPTER 29

Coming out of the library, Rowan found Julius Tetting eyeing her old banger like a traffic warden itching to slap a ticket on it.

'Ah,' he said as she approached. 'I thought I recognized this. Here asking more questions, I suppose?'

'You've an eye for the vintage,' she said, convinced that her patched-up clunker was as much an offence to the local squire as her intrusive questions. 'And asking questions is kind of in the job description.'

He sniffed, apparently not so amused by her directness as he had been the last time they'd met.

'Well, your little visits aren't helping the campaign,' he grumbled. 'Not good for the impending Halloween festival, either, Constable. Not good at all,' he muttered darkly.

Rowan was tempted to point out that she was not his PR, but as she was about to visit the manor, she didn't want to risk being barred from its grounds. Instead, she said mildly that she was investigating a number of deaths.

'Yes, I saw that stuff about dummies left lying about Fernleigh. But you can't possibly think that just because the prankster made use of Birken Boggart masks, that they must be from Birkenshore? Why on *earth* would anyone from here want to venture into that godforsaken place?' he demanded.

Rowan didn't venture an explanation.

'I'm tempted to get Vivienne and her ladies busy making heads so we can mount them on pikestaffs around the village. It'd be more effective than you lot at keeping the dross out!'

He'd started his diatribe in a sardonic tone but, by now, he'd turned red in the face. Rowan waited for a moment or two, watching him and counting in her head so that she didn't make the mistake of saying what she thought: that he was a blustering bully, and his wife might be better served mounting *his* head on a pikestaff.

'I was hoping to catch you, sir,' she said calmly enough. 'That argument you had on Monday with Andy Pym — what was that about?'

'Argument?' he said, a picture of bewilderment.

Rowan waited.

'There *was* no argument,' he said with an air of great affront.

'He seemed pretty het up, sir.'

'Well, of *course* he was — Andy's been mooning about the place for over a year, blaming everyone but himself for his failing business. He upset a *lot* of people when he spoke out against the campaign to stop the development and like the business genius he is, succeeded in losing even more custom. Since I instigated and now lead the campaign to keep Birkenshore beautiful, *naturally* his biggest grievance is against me.' He glared at her. 'Is that a satisfactory explanation, Constable?'

Rowan wouldn't be satisfied until she'd got Mr Pym's version of the story, but she thanked him politely. 'I'll let you know if I have any more questions.'

He stamped off to his SUV and roared out of the village.

Rowan waited until he was out of sight before turning towards the lane to the manor house. The sky was grey, the clouds low and heavy, and the blur of purple sea asters had mostly faded, replaced by tufts of downy seed heads. Flocks of small birds flitted from one clump to the next, continually on the move, feasting on the late autumn bounty.

She paused for a moment to enjoy it. On Fernleigh, the background hum of motorway traffic was a constant, like white noise, but here, near the marshes, the wind in the reeds was a calming *shush*, broken now only by the lonely bubbling call of a curlew. Birkenshore even smelled different: leaf mould and the fresh, salt tang of sea air, in contrast with Fernleigh's sharp chemical cocktail of nitrogen dioxide and ozone.

Mrs Tetting, she was told, was busy organizing another event and couldn't possibly spare the time, but as Rowan prepared to push for an audience, the door to the workroom opened and the lady of the manor appeared, looking a little flushed.

'Constable Rowan,' she said, as though she'd been expecting her, and was pleased she'd come. 'Do come in.'

The room was a-foam with white linen and silk apricot bows, over which three women laboured with heads bent.

'I'm sorry,' Rowan said. 'You're obviously really busy.'

'We have a large wedding in the Old Hall tomorrow,' Mrs Tetting explained, her cheeks pink and her eyes lit with inner fervour. 'The bride decided at the last minute that the linen needed cheering up with a bit of colour. So, here we are — and we're coming along splendidly, aren't we, ladies?'

'We're the "A" team, Vivienne, we'll do just fine,' said the oldest woman, smiling, and the others nodded. From the accent, Rowan guessed that the seamstress wasn't from the upper echelons of Birkenshore, yet the warmth and informality of the exchange suggested that Mrs Tetting was not as bound by class divisions as her husband.

'If you can spare the time, I'd appreciate it,' Rowan said.

'Of course,' Mrs Tetting said, with one of her fleeting, anxious glances.

'I'd like your opinion of this.' Rowan showed her the Justin Lang doppelganger.

Mrs Tetting said, 'May I?' and Rowan handed her the phone.

She pinched and enlarged, moved the image around to get a better look at the stitching and the fabrics.

'It's not terribly well crafted,' she said, her tone pragmatic and unemotional, given the rivers of blood represented in the image. But Birkenshore had some fairly disturbing effigies of its own, Rowan reflected.

'It *is* inventive, however,' Mrs Tetting added. 'We use unbleached calico for our scarecrows — one hundred per cent cotton fabric — quite tough and durable. But this looks like a polyester–cotton mix; it's cheaper, smoother, also easier to manage than calico, which can be rather stiff and unyielding.' She collapsed the image to its original size. 'I don't recognize the style—' She broke off and addressed the senior member of the group. 'Gemma, do you have any ideas?'

The seamstress took the phone, shook her head and handed it back.

Rowan swiped to Craig Breidon's effigy, hanging from a motorway bridge, and offered it to her.

'Goodness, he's macabre, your prankster, isn't he?'

Rowan didn't answer, and, looking into her face, Mrs Tetting paled. 'Is this how he—?'

'We're not jumping to any conclusions, ma'am,' Rowan said. 'We're exploring possibilities, that's all.'

Mrs Tetting searched her face and seemed unconvinced. Finally, she gave a nod as if to say she understood. 'You have to be discreet,' she said.

'It doesn't ring any bells?'

'I'm afraid not,' the woman said regretfully.

'Last one.' Rowan swiped to her own image of Damian Novak's effigy, taken on the motorway embankment. She wanted to see Mrs Tetting's reaction; what she saw was astonishment.

'What is it?'

'The clothing Damian Novak was wearing four years ago, when he ran down an elderly woman and her grandson.'

Astonishment turned to horror. 'How are they — I–I mean, did they survive?'

'The grandmother died; her grandson now uses a wheelchair. But he's doing okay.'

The woman handed back the phone. 'How terribly sad,' she murmured.

The collection of clothing meant nothing to the other women, but the youngest of the three said she'd seen the image of Damian on the stolen bike on social media and had read that he'd been found dead on the M62.

Mrs Tetting had seemed lost in thought, but now she spoke again. 'It reminds me of Harlequin — you know the character?' she asked, continuing smoothly into a description when it was obvious Rowan did not. 'A nimble, acrobatic, wily servant in the *commedia dell'arte* of the sixteenth century. Always short of food and money, and generally covetous of what others had.'

It was a fair sketch of Damian.

'His clothes were highly coloured, like your photograph, and considerably patched,' Mrs Tetting went on. 'But this effigy's really nothing like the others — it's only half made. What makes you think—?' She caught her breath, and her shoulders drooped. 'Oh, I see — it's the mask — it links them all.'

She saw Rowan out and as they crossed the hall, she burst out, 'Oh, I wish we'd never agreed to have those dreadful masks made!'

'Mr Tetting thinks you should mount the boggart's head on pikestaffs to scare off troublemakers.'

'Well, that was in very poor taste,' Mrs Tetting said primly. 'Death is not a joking matter.' She flushed, perhaps thinking that she was being disloyal. 'Of course, Julius has a genius for business, and the sales did raise revenue — as well as awareness of the festival.'

She opened the front door as a gust of wind teased the trees either side of the driveway, bringing a drift of orange and buttery yellow leaves down all around them.

Rowan gasped at the beauty of it and Mrs Tetting laughed in unselfconscious pleasure, spreading her arms wide as if to catch the leaf fall and gather it to her.

'You have a truly lovely home, Mrs Tetting,' Rowan said.

'Thank you — I know I'm truly privileged,' she replied. 'And please, call me Vivienne. But you know, we nearly lost it all — I mean we, the Hockenhulls.' She quirked her eyebrows. 'I'm sure the village gossips have filled you in on the background.'

'I understand that Julius's father bought the house,' Rowan said diplomatically. 'That must have been a relief.'

A fleeting pain crossed the woman's face. 'It was bittersweet. Father in particular felt that he'd let the place down: the village, the tenants, Mother, and me.' She must have caught something in Rowan's expression because she added, 'I'm sure that sounds old-fashioned, patriarchal — even feudal — but actually, my parents were very modern in their way.'

Rowan had her doubts, but she murmured encouragement, wanting to know more about the dynamics in this household.

'I suppose you'd call my parents new-age hippies. They cared about the land in a way that's on-trend now, but was considered the province of weird tree-huggers back in the eighties and nineties. And they were clueless as far as business went — farmed organically, but never got the certification; planted hedges when everyone else was grubbing them up; didn't apply for half the subsidies they were entitled to. The biggest landowners benefitted most from EU subsidies, and Birken Manor sits on over *two thousand* acres — ten times larger than the average farm. Mummy and Daddy probably missed out on millions.' She sighed. 'And they were gentle, kind souls — so of course they were fleeced by every tradesperson they engaged.'

'They had a strong bond with the land,' Rowan offered.

'They were rooted in it like the old beech tree on the village green,' Mrs Tetting said. 'I think it would have killed them to leave.'

'You married Julius to save the house,' Rowan breathed.

Mrs Tetting glanced at her sharply. 'My husband was wrong about you when he said you're "a hoot". You're not

— you're shrewd — and if I may say, a little unguarded in what you say.'

'Mouth like the Mersey Tunnel, I know. Sorry,' Rowan said, her face burning.

By now, they had reached the end of the drive. Mrs Tetting turned to look at the house and her eyes were moist as she said, 'Anyway, the house was already saved by the time I married him. Seeing it restored saved my parents. They loved their last years here, and it achieved their lifetime ambition when I accepted Julius's offer.'

Rowan glanced at her askance — she seemed to be saying that she'd married her oaf of a husband to ensure continuity of the Hockenhull line at Birken Manor.

CHAPTER 30

Wednesday evening debrief

Ian Chan led with his report on the new crime scene. They'd moved to the largest meeting room as the team had swelled since the last briefing, and Chan was loving the attention.

'We're lucky it hasn't rained much in the last ten days,' he said. 'Most of the trace evidence would've gone down the drain otherwise. As it is, we retrieved blood and human tissue from the pedestrian barrier, along with clothing fibres and flecks of white paint similar to those found on Damian. We'll do a mass spec and microscopic comparison of the motorway and Fernleigh samples in tandem — results by end of play tomorrow. For now, we've established that the white flecks are from a vehicle that was originally blue. The white is an overpaint. If you can find the vehicle, we might just be able to physically match the flakes to damaged areas of paint on it.' He looked across at Finch. 'How's it going with the traffic cam records?'

Finch cleared his throat. 'Nothing's turned up, yet. Something might come out of the dashcam appeal. The RPU is reporting a good response to their tweet and as soon as I have the footage from them, I'll get cracking.'

Chan took up the thread again. 'We had thought that the criss-cross pattern of damage to Damian's chest and shoulder might have been caused by impact with a vehicle radiator grille, but we couldn't find an equivalent in our databases. However . . .'

He cast an image to the screen of the pedestrian barrier's diamond pattern alongside a close-up image from Damian's post-mortem showing bruising in the same distinctive pattern. A cardboard scale in each image demonstrated that they were equal in size.

A murmur rippled through the room.

'We've also determined that the grit taken from the road is identical to that found in grazes on Damian's face and clothing. DNA profiles for the blood and tissue samples could be ready for tomorrow morning's briefing if they're fast tracked?' He glanced at Warman for her approval of the extra strain on the budget.

'Absolutely,' she said. 'We need to move fast on this.'

'If it's a link to the two scenes you want, I'm way ahead of you,' Chan said. 'Even without blood and DNA, I *can* confirm — with a high degree of confidence — that the pedestrian crossing at Fernleigh is the primary scene in Damian Novak's death.'

Another wave of enthusiasm and someone said, 'Nice one, mate.'

Warman focused on Rowan. 'Good work, identifying the scene, Cassie.'

Rowan sat a little straighter and tried not to look self-conscious.

'What made you think to look there?'

Rowan wasn't about to admit that the parallel between her parents' deaths and Nana Bloor's had sparked a morbid interest in where she'd died, so she mumbled, 'Just a hunch.'

'Well, it was a good one. This establishes absolutely that Damian Novak was murdered — and that the effigy placed on the motorway embankment a week before he was killed was purposefully linked to his death.'

Coming from someone who didn't approve of hunches in general, and was pathologically averse to voicing her approval, this was high praise indeed.

Rowan knew that Warman's displays of warmth were apt to cool fast, so she took her opportunity while she could. 'Damian was mown down at the precise spot where old Mrs Bloor died — that's got to be significant, hasn't it?'

'It may be . . .' Warman said, already tightening up.

'And Damian was found in the same location as the effigy, *and* he was moved from the primary scene — does it mean that his death has some special meaning to the killer?' The words were tumbling out, but she didn't dare stop for fear of Warman calling a halt before she'd been heard. 'Also, his mannequin is different from the others — "half formed" — was how Mrs Tetting described it. Why? What makes him special?'

Warman seemed to assume that the questions were aimed directly at her. 'As far as we know, Damian's worst offence was causing the elder Mrs Bloor's death and life-changing injuries to her grandson,' she said. 'It's possible whoever ran Damian down is related to the boy.'

Rowan shook her head. 'It's unlikely. Jackie and I spoke to Jonty's mother. It's just her and Jonty, now. Her husband died years ago, and she doesn't have any family in the area.'

Warman looked at the PCSO. 'Jackie?'

'Mrs Bloor is bitter,' Dawson said. 'But right now all her energies are poured into giving Jonty the best life she can — and he's doing great — in fact, he's a role model for some of the kids.'

Warman paused, a deep frown-line etched between her eyebrows. 'Finch, I'll assign a detective to help you with the CCTV and dashcam reviews. Make it your priority tomorrow morning to contact Damian's social worker and probation officer, see if they have any insights.'

While Finch made a note, Warman looked towards Rowan again. 'You mentioned Mrs Tetting's comment on the effigies. Were the Fernleigh Crafters any help?'

Rowan shook her head. 'Not really, but they are willing to cooperate, watching out for suspicious activity and reporting it to Crimestoppers or direct to our helpline. There isn't much sympathy for the likes of Justin Lang and Damian Novak, but Craig Breidon's mum was very persuasive.'

'I take it you showed the effigies to Mrs Tetting?'

'And three of her staff. They didn't recognize the style, but Mrs Tetting said the maker used a cheap polycotton alternative to calico, and the maker isn't a skilful crafter.'

'Anything else?'

'Yeah,' Rowan said. 'Damian's brother was involved in some kind of tussle today. He rang me in a panic, said he was being chased. I was at the primary scene, but I eventually caught up with him as he was going into his block of flats; he'd lost a shoe and he was limping.'

'Did he explain how he'd been injured?'

'He clammed up,' Rowan said. 'Claimed he'd fallen. I helped him up to his flat, and his mother slammed the door in my face.'

'Try again,' Warman said.

'On my to-do list.' Rowan didn't add that she thought there may have been someone with Lukas as she'd turned the corner. She'd been at the furthest edge of the courtyard, a good twenty-five metres away, and had only caught a fleeting glimpse. It might have been a neighbour, and Warman had no patience with 'might haves'.

Perhaps Warman noted her hesitation because she said, 'Is that it?'

Rowan nodded.

'I had another phone complaint about you today.' Warman said.

Does she have to be so abrasive?

Rowan caught a warning glance from Ian Chan and took a breath, waiting for the other shoe to fall.

'Julius Tetting has complained about your "impertinent" questions.'

'He was tetchy,' Rowan said.

'You're being too kind,' Warman said with a rare gleam of humour in her blue-grey eyes.

Encouraged, Rowan added, 'He's also a fraud.'

Warman raised an eyebrow. 'How so?'

'He's lied to me consistently about his family history and his business. Andy Pym who owns the tennis club stormed up to the manor house while I was there on Monday, shouting the odds. Tetting whisked him away to his office, and I was focused on other things, then, but thinking about it, Pym shut up fast when Tetting introduced me as police. I asked Tetting about it today. He says it's resentment because of his campaign to prevent the building development.'

'What does Pym say?'

'I called at the tennis club, but he was unavailable,' Rowan said. 'In Chester for a Tennis Association day-conference.'

'Does he have form?'

Rowan shook her head. 'A four hundred pound fine for D and D as a student; other than that, he appears to be a model citizen. I left messages on his firm's landline and with a member of staff for him to call me — I'll follow up tomorrow.'

They moved swiftly on to other matters, but, even so, the debrief ran late: representatives of the teams canvassing both Fernleigh and the Turner Homes' development gave their feedback, confirming that thefts on the Turner Homes' estate had gone down in the last six to eight weeks, but there had been an increase in the number of youths spotted loitering in the area. Fernleigh residents had been less forthcoming. Tasks were allocated for Friday, and Warman wound up by saying she might be able to get a few more trained staff — both clerical and detectives — to spread the workload.

It was approaching six twenty, and Rowan could not be late for Alex's phone call at seven, so she slipped out as the rest of the team gathered their stuff and exchanged a few pleasantries. She thought she heard someone calling her name, but dashed through the door onto the fire-escape stairs and ran down the first few flights until she was sure she was well ahead of the crowd. She was about to climb into her car when she heard Dawson shouting her name.

She waved, and slid behind the wheel, but Dawson ran towards her, holding both hands up, palms out, and she didn't have it in her to drive off.

She wound down the window as Dawson jogged across the car park, panting.

'Flipping 'eck, you're fast!'

'I'm late for something, Jackie,' Rowan said. 'Can this wait?'

'Just — Jim North rang — he's at the reception desk, wants a word.'

'About?'

She hesitated. 'I think he wants to apologize.'

'For what? Jackie, have you been talking to him about me?'

'No!' Dawson blushed. 'I didn't . . . I just noticed at the scene — and he . . .' She gulped.

Rowan fumed. If he had intel relating to the case, she would have to see him, but if he wanted to make some half-arsed apology, because Jackie was trying to mend bridges—

'It'll have to wait,' she said. 'Urgent family business.'

She drove off, leaving Dawson a forlorn-looking figure in her rear mirror.

CHAPTER 31

Rowan flipped through the TV channels nervously, unable to settle on anything. She dreaded that this transcontinental pep talk between her brothers would end in Neil locking his bedroom door in sullen withdrawal from the world and especially her, or worse, with him pounding down the stairs and storming out of the house in a passion. She hadn't hung around when Neil called from his room to tell her Alex wanted to say hi — just a quick hello, then she'd excused herself, leaving them to chat.

For the past half-hour, she'd crept into the hall every ten minutes to listen at the foot of the stairs. Since they'd been in conversation for this long, things looked promising. Unless Alex had chickened out.

That thought sent her out into the hallway again, uncertain whether to be angry or upset. At that moment, Neil's bedroom door opened. She hurried back into the sitting room and focused on the TV until she sensed Neil's presence in the doorway.

'Hey,' she said. 'What's the noos from Noo Yawk?'

It was an old joke. As a little boy, Neil had been fascinated by the differences in pronunciation, and had even compiled a list with phonetic spellings. His mouth twitched, but he didn't seem able to look at her.

Her heart sank. 'Is Alex okay?' she tried, knowing from long experience that any direct inquiry into Neil's state of mind would be met with hostility.

'He's good,' Neil said, and immediately frowned.

Rowan switched off the TV and turned fully in her seat.

He lifted one shoulder, let it drop. 'You know what? That's bollocks.' He glanced sheepishly her way, waiting for the scolding at his use of bad language. When it didn't come, he went on. 'You know why he hasn't been to see us this year?'

Rowan knew very well, but Neil needed to put it in his own words.

'He didn't know what to say to me about this.' He held up his damaged arm. 'And he thinks he should've been the one to stop that bastard who attacked you.'

'Oh.' She hadn't been expecting that.

He gave her a shy look. 'He said he was *proud* of me.'

'So he should be — I am, too.'

He shook his head, breaking eye contact as if it was all too much.

'Ever since it happened, he's been saying he's *fine*, when he's really been all twisted up inside with guilt. And I'm thinking I can't tell him what I really feel cos he'll think I'm a wimp.' His frown deepened, and then he glared at her. 'I mean, what the actual *eff*? Why couldn't he just *say* something?'

Rowan pressed her lips together. If she was talking to Alex, she might have said sarcastically, 'He couldn't admit he was scared, cos men aren't *like* that — men have nerves of steel.' But this had been a huge revelation for Neil, and she was terrified of saying something snarky that would make him clam up. Seconds of silence stretched to half a minute, and she became worried he would shut down anyway.

'Did you tell him how you really feel?' she asked tentatively.

He shoved his hands in his pockets. 'Unsafe,' he said. 'I feel unsafe.'

'At school?' She felt a burning heat in her chest. 'Neil, are you being bullied?'

He gave her a lofty look. 'I can handle myself at school. It's here I don't feel safe. At home.' His left hand went to the scar on his right arm, an unconscious, protective action.

'Oh, Neil . . . That was a one-off—'

He laughed. 'Listen to yourself, Cass! It's already happened twice. When that guy broke into our house. Then last spring — a whole bunch of people could have *died*.'

A drug dealer had moved into a house across the street from them, and the consequences of that still haunted her — Neil wasn't exaggerating when he said people could have died; the entire street had been evacuated because of the risk of a devastating explosion. And it hadn't ended there: for some months afterwards, she and Neil had been forced to lay low in a safe house under witness protection.

'It was terrifying,' Rowan said, remembering how her heart had contracted painfully when she'd first known that Neil was in danger. 'But nobody died. And you were so brave, looking after Amoya when she was being hassled, being there for me—'

He scoffed. 'Like you ever needed anyone.'

'The *only* reason I don't ask for your help is because it's not your job to look after me — and, yes, there's a lot I don't tell you. But I couldn't have got through what happened to Mum and Dad without you.'

He slid her a sideways look.

'Truly,' she said.

He tilted his head and twitched his shoulders, which she took to mean that he believed her.

'I want you to be happy, Neil,' she said. 'You don't want to live here anymore, is that it?'

'Sometimes,' he said.

'Have you talked to anyone about it? Your friends, maybe?'

'They wouldn't have a clue what I'm on about.'

'How do you know?'

He shrugged. 'They've never been through anything like this.'

'Are you sure of that?'

He tucked his chin in and squinted at her like she was being deliberately dense.

'Why would they? They have normal lives.'

Rowan smiled sadly. 'I've been in this job long enough to know there's no such thing as normal.'

'Whatever.'

He was shutting down; best to change the subject entirely, come back to this another time. 'Okay,' she said. 'You want me to admit when I need help? The food'll be here in five minutes — and we're going to need forks.' She gazed at him helplessly. 'But they're in the kitchen . . .'

'Ha-ha-ha,' he said, making it sound like a slow hand-clap, but he disappeared in the right direction and without slamming any doors.

The doorbell rang and Rowan leaped to answer it.

As she set the cartons out on the coffee table in front of the TV, Neil came in with two forks and an open bottle of beer.

'Relax,' he said. 'It's for you.' He handed her the bottle and reached for a can of Coke from the bag of goodies.

They argued for a few minutes over which action movie they'd watch but as they settled in, he nudged her, still staring at the screen.

'Just so you know, Alex thinks you're a hero.'

Rowan glanced at him, incredulous: she'd always been 'Saint Cassie' or 'Little Miss Perfect' in her barbed conversations with Alex. 'He said those actual words?'

'No. He used the F-word. Now shut up and pass me the crispy duck, I'm starving.'

CHAPTER 32

Thursday morning briefing

The meeting room was jammed. DNA results were in from Fernleigh. The blood and tissue samples from the pedestrian barrier were a definite match to Damian Novak. The flakes of white paint on Damian's body and clothing also matched the flakes adhering to the damaged barrier. Ian Chan explained that the colours, layer sequence and thicknesses were the same at both sites, and infra-red microscopy had confirmed the chemical composition, too. There was no question that their primary scene was Fernleigh, and the motorway was the secondary.

'The Press Office is preparing a statement for immediate release,' Warman said. 'The official line is that in the light of new evidence, Damian Novak's death is being treated as suspicious. Anyone with information should contact the team via the hotline or anonymously via Crimestoppers.'

A few people made a note in their phones or on notepads.

'Do we know the make or model of vehicle we're looking for?' Finch asked.

Chan nodded. 'As I said last night, the white layer was overpainted onto the original blue finish — it's uneven, so

214

probably a DIY job. The blue paint types it to a Ford Transit panel van in ocean blue. The bad news is they've been making these since twenty-oh-seven — there must be hundreds of thousands of them on the road.'

'Worth checking local ownership with the DVLA,' Warman said. 'We'll withhold information on the vehicle until that's done. Teams will continue canvassing, asking about the effigies: who saw them, was anyone seen placing them, did anyone have images—'

'And are there any we don't know about?' Rowan suggested.

'That's an odd question,' Warman said.

'I think it's worth asking around, boss,' Rowan said. 'I mean, we don't know when this started — the effigies might have been a thing on the estate since even before Craig Breidon.'

Warman thought about it for a second, then, with a brief nod, gave her permission to continue.

'I was talking to Jim North at the primary scene yesterday afternoon,' Rowan said. 'Jim runs a martial-arts club on Fernleigh for the kids,' she explained for the new members of the team.

'That's all we need,' someone muttered. 'Scalls with karate moves.'

'It keeps a lot of trouble off the streets, gives the kids discipline, confidence—'

'We'll take that as a given,' Warman said, with a warning scowl to the detective who'd complained.

'Jim's younger brother got mixed up in drug dealing. He died of an overdose. Can we look into that?'

'You think North could be involved in these deaths?'

'No — I didn't mean that.' The idea was ludicrous.

'Then what *did* you mean?' This was Warman at her most haughty; she must be taking a lot of stick from the higher-ups and she was always coldest in high-stress situations.

'Officially Ben North died of an accidental overdose, but given the pattern that's emerging here—'

'Pattern?' Warman sounded so brittle that Rowan could almost hear the distant sound of breaking glass.

'Of suspicious deaths,' Rowan said. 'We know that Craig Breidon was too drugged up to have rigged the noose that killed him. And we have *proof* that Damian was mown down and then moved to the deposition site.'

'The *coroner's* conclusion was that Breidon committed *suicide*,' Warman said firmly.

Rowan opened her mouth to protest, but Warman raised a finger. 'I haven't finished. I have requested a full review of the evidence in the Breidon verdict. But until we have the results of that review, the accidental death verdict will remain in place.' She widened her gaze, releasing Rowan for the moment, and taking in the rest of the team. 'There is a lot of press speculation, to say nothing of the bloggers and mythologizers who've tapped into this "voodoo doll" nonsense. We do not want to feed the hysteria by drawing conclusions before the facts.' She paused, taking them all in. 'So I'll reiterate: the official line regarding Damian's death is that we are treating it as "suspicious". Does anyone have any problem with that?'

She waited until she'd seen people shake their heads. Under her fierce gaze, a few even murmured 'No, boss.'

'You will not engage in speculation with journalists or gossipmongers,' she went on. 'You will *not* "no comment" on any speculation. You will instead refer them to the Press Office or to me. Are we clear?'

Another ragged chorus, more voluble this time, went up. Everyone, it seemed, was crystal clear.

Warman focused again on Rowan, and she braced herself for the crushing blow.

'However, it does make good investigative sense to ask if there are effigies we don't know about.'

Rowan experienced a cool wash of relief; her skin had begun to itch under her boss's glare.

'I want the Langs and Craig Breidon's mother reinterviewed as well,' Warman went on. 'Did the deceased receive actual threats — verbal or otherwise — in the weeks before they died? Who would have a motive to target them?'

It wasn't for Rowan to say that they would be wasting their time. She already had her task allocations for the day, so she suppressed a shrug and waited for Warman to allocate the tasks to others on the team.

The chief inspector wrapped up with a promise from the chief constable that there would be increased patrols on Fernleigh. Rowan resisted a glance towards Jackie Dawson, but she did wonder how the PCSO felt about another short-term promise of high police visibility that would evaporate as soon as press attention drifted to other, fresher news.

CHAPTER 33

It was another misty day on the marsh and Rowan kept the wipers on all the way from the main road. From the vantage point of the escarpment the village seemed draped in grey, aside from Birken Manor, which rose like a mournful spectre out of the murk. On the gentle slope down, it felt as if she was descending into a different world and time.

She'd been feeling upbeat since Neil had come clean about his anxieties the night before, and had even begun to tap into her mental map of the Liverpool areas she'd visited and liked since becoming a cop. Now, feeling the marsh close in on her, she realized that she and Neil would be looking for different things in a house move and it wouldn't be easy to find a compromise that suited them both. Neil would want to be close enough to the city centre to be able to meet up with mates and get to and from school without having to spend half his day travelling. But as someone had pointed out not so long ago, her kid brother was growing up fast; soon he'd be wanting his independence. Would he go to university? He was bright enough, but the events of the last eight months had taken their toll, and if he didn't get straightened out at school Neil's chances of higher education would be slim to none. What if he decided he wanted to move away, relocate entirely to a different city — even follow his brother to the United States? The family home was his as much as hers, and wherever he went she would want Neil to have somewhere to call home, but if he wanted to set up on his own, she would have to sell and split the money, and that would limit both their choices.

As the gloom drew in around her, Rowan's mood darkened.

When she'd first driven down this lane, she had almost imagined herself living here, had seen it as a rural idyll — until she'd realized that Sal felt ostracised by many of the villagers. Why? Rowan herself had never really been good at fitting in; being a surrogate mother to her pre-teen brother when she was only a teenager herself hadn't helped. She wondered how Birkenshore's easily shocked and highly conventional residents would respond to Fernleigh's young single mothers — she doubted that they would have set up a food co-op and community hub, supporting and encouraging them in the way that Gareth Jessop, Jackie Dawson and Jim North had done. Here, privileged though they were, even the landowners seemed ill at ease and self-absorbed.

By the time she'd reached the T-junction, the mist had turned to fog, and Rowan began to feel almost suffocated by the sombre mood of the place. She turned right, following the sign to the shore, hoping to finally catch Andy Pym at the tennis club. The low hedge on her left faded to invisibility again and again, and with no lane markers on this narrow stretch of road, she had to stop twice for fear of veering off into a ditch. Bays at intervals along its length served as passing points, though she didn't meet a single car; this lane seemed to serve a cluster of houses, all with high walls towered over by ancient oaks and beeches dripping condensate and leaves. The road was a dead end, finishing with a small car park for visitors to the shore and she knew from her previous visit that the turnoff to the tennis club came just before, but in the dense fog she almost missed it.

Julius Tetting's summary of Pym's business yesterday, disparaging as it had been, made her view the club with a fresh eye. The driveway off the lane was more potholed than anywhere else around the village and the wood of its window frames looked weathered to a soggy pulp. The brickwork had been painted Wimbledon green, but any similarity to the All England Lawn Tennis Club ended there. The building, perhaps dating back to the 1960s, was of a square-built, ugly, utilitarian design with a flat roof; the planter near the entrance contained a few geraniums and silver cineraria, now brown and rotting; the car park held only two cars, at least one of which must belong to staff.

In the foyer, the damp, slightly musty smell she'd noticed the day before had intensified, adding to the generally dismal atmosphere. Rowan tapped the bell to the side of a hatch that served as a reception desk, and a minute or two later, a snub-nosed brunette in her mid-twenties came down the pine-clad corridor to her left. It was the same woman Rowan had spoken to on her last visit, but Rowan couldn't recall her name.

'He's still not here, I'm afraid,' the woman said.

'You gave him my message?' Rowan asked, still grasping for the name: a Norse goddess; she remembered thinking the woman's short stature, dark hair and brown eyes were at odds with Rowan's image of blonde, statuesque Viking women.

'I spoke to him last night — he said he'd give you a call.' The woman spoke with a West Country burr, and Rowan wondered what had brought her to this quiet enclave within the Merseyside boundaries, yet not of it.

'Yeah, well, he didn't call.' The name suddenly came back to her. 'Can you get him on the line now, Freya?'

'He might be in a presentation . . .' Freya said, sounding oddly uncertain, now that she'd been properly addressed.

'I thought he was at a one-day conference?'

The receptionist's eyes shifted left, then back to Rowan's face. 'He was . . . ?'

Her inflection irritated Rowan; either he was at a conference or he wasn't. 'A straight answer would be good right now.'

'He's been stressed,' Freya said.

'About?' Rowan cocked her head, waiting for an explanation, avoiding putting words in the woman's mouth.

'Well, what d'you want me to say?' Freya demanded, on the defensive.

'Whatever happens to be the truth,' Rowan said. 'I need to speak urgently with Mr Pym. You say he *was* at a conference; where is he now?'

'Look, I'm only an employee,' Freya huffed. 'He doesn't tell me everything.'

'Not *everything*, but . . . ?'

Flustered, she reddened, and Rowan waited for her resolve to crumble under her stare; finally, it did.

Throwing her hands up, Freya muttered a curse. 'Not that it's any of your business, he went to see about a loan. He wants to do the place up, make something of it — it's not easy, keeping a business like this afloat — especially after all that's happened these last few years.' She immediately pressed her lips together as if to stop herself from saying more.

Rowan played her advantage. 'Mr Pym was furious with Julius Tetting on Monday; do you know what that was about?'

The receptionist folded her arms, refusing eye contact.

'Tetting said it was sour grapes; Mr Pym alienates people—'

Her deliberate goading worked.

'Well, he's one to talk,' Freya snorted, her eyes flashing angrily. She struggled for a moment, perhaps undecided whether she should say more, but having come to a decision, she looked squarely at Rowan. 'Tetting isn't all he's cracked up to be,' she said. 'I don't know the details, but I *do* know that Mr High-and-Mighty promised Andy he'd be okay — that he'd *make sure* he was okay — but all he's done is driven clientele away. That housing development up the road should've brought in a wave of new members, but thanks to Tetting's meddling, the club's worse off than before they built it. It's not *right* — that bastard turned everyone against him!'

'Did Mr Pym tell you this, or is it something you overheard?'

Twin streaks of red appeared across Freya's cheekbones, then she rallied. 'When those two start yelling, it's hard *not* to overhear.'

Actually, Rowan preferred an overheard conversation to hearsay — evidentially speaking. 'When is Mr Pym expected back?'

Freya glanced away. 'I'm not sure.'

'Freya . . .'

She sighed. 'Oh, all *right* . . . He said he'd be back by now.' She glanced nervously at the clock hanging from a nail over the door.

'Does he always check in with you?'

Freya gazed at her blankly.

'Could he be around, and you just haven't seen him?'

'Um, I suppose . . .'

'Okay, I'm going to knock on a few doors, wander around the courts — okay?'

'Uh, yeah, sure.'

The acknowledgement was exactly what Rowan wanted to hear — in reality, Freya was within her rights to escort her off the premises but having permission to poke around the place meant she wasn't likely to fall foul of the law. She couldn't say why she felt compelled to track Andy Pym down; she just had an uneasy feeling that the undercurrent of restlessness and dissent in Birkenshore was in some way related to Pym's argument with Tetting.

The function room, and two drab meeting rooms were empty. The entrance door to the beer cellar was behind the bar. It was secured with a Yale cylinder and a Chubb mortice lock. Two additional hasps and padlocks on the top and bottom of the door convinced her that Pym wasn't below stairs.

The tennis club sat on a large plot overlooking the marsh and the courts were only accessible through the building. Rowan stepped out into a dense bank of fog. It was freezing cold, and totally silent. High chain-link fences bordered each of the six courts on offer, all standing empty this morning. She walked back through the building to reach the car park. The garage to the side was locked, too; she cupped her hand to one grimy windowpane and peered inside; it held a white van. She experienced a spurt of excitement, but the fog had seeped inside, and the windows let in very little light, so she couldn't see if it was damaged.

She popped her head inside the foyer, where Freya was waiting anxiously. 'I don't suppose you have a key to the garage?'

'No.' There was that odd, questioning inflection again.

Convinced that the receptionist was lying, Rowan said, 'Is there a way in from inside the building, then?'

'No.' More firmly, this time.

'The two cars parked outside — whose are they?'

'Mine, and Andy's. He drove the Merc today — said he wanted to make an impression.'

Rowan had no right to take it any further so she repeated her request for Mr Pym to contact her urgently and left.

Warman wanted her to push Tetting harder, so she headed over to his place. If she couldn't get him talking, maybe Mrs Tetting would be up for a chat.

Driving through the gates to the main house, Rowan saw with a stab of alarm that Tetting's scarecrow, perched at the end of the bench under the chestnut tree, had acquired a boggart mask like the ones used on their suspicious deaths.

She slammed on the brakes and wound down the window. The creature leered at her, its teeth dripping with moisture. The fog had created a silvery sheen over the eyes, too, giving them a creepily lifelike gleam that seemed to glow from within. Was this meant as a threat to Tetting?

She parked and walked back for a closer look. The verge was wet and trampled; there might be liftable shoeprints, and Ian Chan would never forgive her if she messed up any potential evidence. So she stood at the roadside and dialled his mobile number.

'Is this work?' He sounded tense.

'It is. Can you talk?'

'Two minutes,' he said. 'Sorry, darling, there's been a shooting in the city centre and I'm up to my eyes in gore.'

Ian was one of very few men allowed to call Rowan by anything other than her name, or rank.

She quickly outlined the situation. 'You'll want fingerprints and trace?' he said.

'Plus footwear impressions, if you can find any.'

'I'll be on this for a few hours,' he said. 'I'd send someone else, but we've got two teams on this, and another at a secondary scene in Norris Green.' He paused. 'Could you tape it, make sure nobody touches it? I'll get there as soon as I can.'

'I'll do that,' Rowan said.

She walked back down the drive with a roll of blue-and-white tape in hand and began marking out a perimeter. Wedding guests arriving in cars peered through their windows, smiling, no doubt charmed to think that this was all just part of the Birken Manor experience. She did her best to keep her back to them in case of social media junkies, attaching the tape to the gatepost and a couple of bollards on the verge, then walking back to the wall and finishing at the railings.

Job done, she phoned Warman to let her know.

'Have you spoken to Tetting, yet?' Warman asked.

'I'm on my way down the drive to the house now,' Rowan said.

'All right. Let me know what he says.'

Rowan felt eyes on her as she parked the car and saw Mrs Tetting at one of the ground-floor windows. She darted away when she saw Rowan, and a second later the front door flew open.

'Have you seen Julius?' she said.

'I was coming to see him now,' Rowan said.

She was pale, her breathing shallow.

Rowan guided her inside. 'What's happened?'

'I don't *know*.' Mrs Tetting wrung her hands and glanced about the hall as if she might find the answer there, but the gloom of the day seemed to have penetrated the house and the entrance hall was swathed in shadow. Rowan could taste the metallic tang of the fog at the back of her mouth.

'Have you tried his phone?' she asked.

'He's not answering.'

A sudden baying went up from behind a door further down the hall and Mrs Tetting shuddered violently. 'Oh, I'm so sorry,' she said, as if suddenly appalled at her lack of manners. 'Do come through.' She led Rowan into a sitting room at the front of the house and paced nervously.

'He said he was going to walk the dogs on the shore and he'd be back in time to welcome the wedding guests. But they started to arrive at ten and there was no sign of him. That's just not *like* him, Constable.' She clasped her hands and squeezed so hard that the knuckles went white. 'Then the dogs showed up at the house.' She gestured vaguely in the direction of the continued howls and barking, then brought her hand back to her waist as though she wasn't quite sure who it belonged to.

'Mrs Tetting,' Rowan said. '*Vivienne.*'

The woman blinked.

'It's probably nothing — he got delayed or diverted.' Rowan tried to sound reassuring, but she was troubled by the coincidental absence of Andy Pym from where he should have been.

'But if he had a fall, or got into some other trouble, it might help if you'll allow me to take the dogs.'

Mrs Tetting was shaking her head.

'They might lead me straight to him.'

'No,' she said. 'No. They're already traumatized; Julius would never forgive me if . . .' She clamped her hand to her mouth. 'Oh, dear God, where *is* he?'

Rowan took both her hands in hers — *so cold!* — and led Mrs Tetting to one of the sofas.

'I'm going to ring my boss,' she said. 'Is there anyone you can call to sit with you?'

Mrs Tetting checked her watch. 'Gemma will be here in ten minutes — she's helping out with the wedding.'

'Okay,' Rowan said, saddened to think that there were no friends or family Mrs Tetting felt she could call on. 'I'll sit here until she arrives. In the meantime, is there someone who could organize a search party?'

'Yes! Quinn, our estate manager — he deals with the farms and grazing rights and so on.' She seemed so excited at the prospect of being able to do something positive that she began to rise from her seat.

Rowan gently pressed her to sit again. 'Ring him,' she said. 'Get him to come here.' She left Mrs Tetting on the sofa and moved to the window to call DCI Warman.

'We may have a problem,' she said softly. 'It's Julius Tetting; he's missing.'

CHAPTER 34

'For how long?' Warman demanded.

'About an hour.'

'An *hour*? For heaven's sake, Cassie — that's hardly an emergency.'

'He was supposed to be welcoming guests at ten fifteen. He didn't show up, which I'm told is uncharacteristic. He's not answering his phone, and the mask suddenly appearing on the scarecrow right outside the manor house just seems—'

Her boss interrupted her with an irritable sigh.

Warman responds to the concrete, Rowan thought. *Facts, direct observations, evidence. Okay* . . . 'Then his two dogs came home in a distressed state. Added to which, Andy Pym has gone AWOL, too.'

'This is the club owner who has a grudge against Tetting?' Warman sounded less irritated.

'Yep.'

'Do we know where these two were last seen?'

'Tetting was heading for the shore, in the direction of Pym's club; Pym was somewhere in Liverpool, trying to secure a loan. But he should have been back a while ago. I can talk to his receptionist, find out exactly where he went, have a word with the loan company, in case he's been delayed.'

'A delay is the most likely explanation,' Warman said. 'And of course, the same could be true of Tetting.'

'Except for the dogs, and the mask.'

'Quite,' Warman said crisply. But she added in a conciliatory, almost confiding tone, 'The shooting in the city centre means we're really stretched; I can't justify a search team at this early juncture.'

'His wife is organizing a search party, but I'm supposed to be standing guard over this mask till the CSU can get here to process it,' Rowan said. 'And I can't do that *and* knock on doors.'

'All right. I'll ask for a two-crew unit. You can have one of them remain with the scarecrow — or effigy — if that's what it is. The other can accompany the search team and offer advice. You might ask Mrs Tetting to search inside the house as well.'

'Will do — thanks, boss.'

A man drove up in a Land Rover at that moment.

'That's Quinn.' Mrs Tetting hurried to the door. She made a great effort to remain calm as she introduced Rowan and explained the situation.

Quinn — it turned out this was his given name — was a man of about forty-five, lean, vigorous, tawny-haired and as brown as a nut. He listened calmly, showing no more emotion than a furrow of concern between his brows. Minutes later, he'd sent a group message out.

'I've told them to meet at the shore car park and we'll walk Mr Tetting's usual route. We'll be thorough, Vivienne.' He didn't offer any platitudes or false reassurances, but he held Mrs Tetting in his quiet gaze for a second and something passed between them. She reached out and squeezed his arm, her face pale, but she seemed to draw strength from his stoic control and appeared more self-possessed.

Rowan walked Quinn to his car, explaining that an officer in uniform would accompany him and advise. Just then a marked police car pulled into the drive.

'I hope he's brought wellies,' he said, with a sly glance at her low-heeled boots. 'It's clarty on t' marsh today.'

His accent was more Lancashire than Liverpool, and Rowan guessed 'clarty' meant muddy.

'I'm sure they'll manage,' she said. 'At least the fog seems to be lifting.' The sun was just visible as a milky disc through the mist.

Instructions given, one constable remained outside the scene tape while Rowan returned inside. Mrs Tetting was giving her own instructions to the events supervisor Rowan had seen on Tuesday. It seemed the lady of the manor was anxious that the wedding guests should not be troubled by what was going on in the household.

She must have registered Rowan's surprise because after the man had left, she said, 'This is a very special day for this couple. Their families have spent a substantial sum on it, hoping for the perfect wedding.' Tears sprang to her eyes. 'I can't spoil it for them — I simply can't.'

Gemma arrived soon afterwards and Rowan asked her to bring in some help to search the house.

'If he hit his head, or fell suddenly ill, he might have gone somewhere to sleep it off,' Rowan said in a murmur.

The seamstress understood immediately. 'He's got high blood pressure,' Gemma said quietly. 'I'll make sure every room, cupboard and WC is searched.'

Rowan left the organization in Gemma's competent hands and returned to the tennis club.

Pym had finally returned. He was sitting at the bar with a large whisky in one hand, and he was not cooperative.

'You must have noticed people out on the marsh as you came in,' she said.

He shrugged. 'So?'

'They're searching for Julius Tetting — he's missing.'

Something flashed momentarily in his eyes, alarm perhaps. 'I don't see what that has to do with me.'

'You were supposed to be back from your appointment over an hour ago, which means you were missing at the same time.'

He turned to face her, sliding one elbow along the bar, still holding the whisky glass. 'Are you serious?'

'Can you tell me where you were, Mr Pym?'

He flushed angrily. 'It's none of your damned business!'

'Have you spoken to Mr Tetting today?'

'Same answer.' He took a swallow of his drink.

'You know how this looks, don't you?' she said.

He sneered. 'Like you're clutching at straws. I'll expect a full apology when he turns up half stoned, scratching at his wife's bedroom door, begging forgiveness.' Judging by the slur in Pym's speech, Tetting wouldn't be the only one under the influence.

'Are you saying this as a fact?' she asked. 'That he's done this before — or are you making up stories?'

'I leave that kind of pettiness to the village gossips.'

He really seemed to think himself above the rest, Rowan thought, astonished. Well, she was about to demonstrate to him that he was not.

'You are known to have a longstanding argument with Mr Tetting,' she said. 'I saw you having a go at him myself — and now you're refusing to answer simple questions regarding your whereabouts after the man has vanished. If you're withholding information that might put him in danger, it won't be an apology you'll be looking for — it'll be a lawyer.'

He sighed petulantly. 'No, I haven't seen him. Which is probably just as well — I might have punched his smug face if I had.'

'I take it the meeting didn't go well,' she said.

'You can leave now, Constable Rowan,' he said, his voice raw with anger.

She drove back to the village and asked around, but nobody had seen Tetting that morning, and he hadn't been into the bakery, which apparently was unusual. Sal wasn't on duty at the library, but Rowan saw her outside the greengrocer-cum-deli and trotted across the green to speak to her.

'Probably chasing some skirt,' Sal said.

'You're the second person to suggest he'd be off doing something he shouldn't,' Rowan observed.

Sal laughed. 'Julius is notorious for his little peccadillos. Let me guess what your other "informant" suggested—' She sniffed and wiped her nose ostentatiously, then leaned in and whispered, 'I'm right, aren't I? Expensive tastes in stimulants, but decidedly cheap taste in women — I do *not* refer to the long-suffering Mrs T.'

'Is she aware?'

Sal snorted. 'I think Vivienne's just grateful he doesn't come pawing *her* anymore.'

God, these people are vile! Rowan thought. 'You wouldn't happen to know where he might go when he's off on a spree?'

Sal shrugged. 'Beats me. It's just what I've heard.'

By three o'clock, Rowan had visited every business in Birkenshore and spoken to any locals she'd happened to see on the street. She rang Quinn; he said they'd keep going till sunset. Resolving to take the line with Mrs Tetting that no news was good news, Rowan made her way back to Birken Manor. It was sunny now, and warm, and she stood chatting to the officer who'd been given the unenviable task of guarding the effigy. One of the staff had been thoughtful enough to bring out a sandwich and a cuppa for lunch and they'd told him that the house search had turned up nothing.

He waved his hand in front of his face, swatting away midges, and Rowan guessed he'd have a face full of bites by the evening.

'You couldn't stand watch for a minute, could you?' he asked. 'I'm busting for a pi—' He blushed. 'I mean—'

'Dying for a slash?' Rowan said. 'Don't worry about it, I grew up with two brothers.' The crease of worry on his forehead vanished and Rowan said, 'Go on, but don't keep me waiting — I might think you're taking the piss.'

He laughed, pointing a finger at her. 'I see what you did there.'

The lane was silent for a few minutes, the wedding party no doubt halfway through eating their improbably expensive meal. A jet taking off from the airport shattered the peace for a minute and as it faded into the distance, Rowan listened to the piping of birds on the marsh, hoping to hear the call of the curlew. She became aware of a low insect drone and looked around for the source. The hedgerow flowers had already turned brown and set seed, and there were no climbing roses at this end of the drive. Something flew across her line of sight and she raised a hand to chase it away, startling half a dozen more in the process and lazily, they rose as one from the bench inside the perimeter.

Her skin prickled and her mouth felt suddenly dry. They weren't on the bench — they were on the *effigy*.

Raising the tape with two fingers, Rowan ducked under and took three careful steps, her heart beating fast. The flies were gathering at the rear of the effigy. She stood still, bending forward to peer at the back of the head, and saw that the flat cap was soaked in what looked like blood.

She took one more step, then she eased the mask up a fraction. A wave of nausea swept over her, and she had to close her eyes for a second to control the terrible urge to vomit.

It was Julius Tetting.

She forced herself to breathe shallowly — the coppery, slightly sweet smell of blood and the eager buzz of insects made her stomach roil. Even so, she needed to check for a pulse. Steeling herself, she placed two fingers against the carotid artery. He was dead.

CHAPTER 35

Thursday evening debrief

Rowan listened to the team with half an ear, still turning over the events of the day in her mind. Within an hour of discovering Tetting's body, she'd been hauled back to base. A DCI had been brought in to head the Tetting murder inquiry, she was told. DCI Kwame Weller had a strong reputation, and Rowan knew that the murder had to be investigated by a different crew, but it galled her that she was not to be part of it. To make things worse, she'd heard that Roy Wicks had been drafted onto Weller's team.

She'd updated her report on her interactions in Birkenshore and sent copies to Warman and Weller, fuming at the injustice.

The house-to-house team leader summarized the results of the canvas so far; it seemed to be a big fat zero, Rowan brooded.

She couldn't get the image of Julius Tetting out of her mind, posed like one of his beloved scarecrows, right on his own doorstep, where his wife might have found him. How much hate did it take for someone to do such a horrible, cruel thing?

Had he been murdered while he was walking the dogs on the shore, then moved, like Damian, to the deposition site? Locked out of the investigation, she didn't have access to that information. She hadn't noticed anyone on the drive to or from the tennis club, but the fog had been so dense then that she might have missed Tetting, or even his killer, walking on the other side of the road. Tetting would no doubt have waved her down, wanting to know her business, but for anyone trying to remain unseen, the conditions had been perfect.

Could Tetting have been killed on the lane by the house? It seemed unlikely — the wedding guests had started arriving by mid-morning, so a violent altercation would almost certainly have been seen — heard, too, since sound carried far in these flatlands.

No, the shore was the likeliest place, at the farthest reaches of the village, sparsely populated, and since the tennis club had no customers at that time there would be nobody to hear any argument. Unless the argument had happened in the club itself, in which case, they would have a potential witness in Pym's loyal receptionist. The problem of how the body might have been transported from the shore to the manor still remained but if the killer had used a van, most people seeing it would have assumed that they'd been delivering goods to the manor house. And a van could easily have shielded the bench from view, allowing the removal of Mrs Tetting's scarecrow and its replacement with Julius's body.

Rowan would dearly love to take a squint at Andy Pym's van. She'd passed all of the information she'd gathered to DCI Weller as SIO, but would he follow up? She glanced at Warman; did she dare ask her boss to find out?

A scowl from Warman was sufficient warning that her inattention had been noted. The DCI called on Finch to report back on his chat with Damian Novak's social worker and Rowan tried to focus on what he was saying.

'Damian Novak was out on licence,' he said. 'And he had a year to run on that. His social worker and probation officer were scheduled to meet. He'd been warned about failure to turn up for community service on multiple occasions — apparently he'd been late for meetings with his probation officer, and failed to show when his PO arranged a home visit.'

'So he was sailing very close to the wind,' Warman said.

Finch nodded. 'They were going to request a recall for breach of licence.'

'Who would know about this on Fernleigh?' Warman asked.

Dawson spoke up. 'Word gets around. Even if his supervisors hadn't delivered the bad news yet, Damian must have known that they wouldn't let him go on flouting the rules.'

Finch nodded in agreement. 'And they were aware that he was dealing drugs again — they wanted him off the streets, safely locked up.'

'That makes sense as far as the effigy is concerned,' Rowan chipped in. 'It's been bugging me that Damian's wasn't an effigy at all in the real sense of the word. If he *had* been recalled to finish his prison sentence, he'd have been out of reach for at least another year. Maybe the killer felt rushed.'

'It's possible,' Warman said. 'But what does that tell us?'

'I don't know — that Damian was important to the killer?'

'In what way?' Warman sounded genuinely curious.

Rowan didn't have an answer and was almost grateful when Warman moved on.

'Where are we on the CCTV?'

'There's no sign of a vehicle stopping on the motorway to ditch the body,' Finch said smartly.

'How d'you work that one out?' someone piped up from the back. 'There's no camera near the deposition site,'

'That's right,' Finch said. 'But we estimated the time it would take to travel between the nearest traffic cam at junction five and the next camera at junction four. It's two minutes, tops, at that time of day. We scoured the traffic cams for two hours either side of when Damian's body was found, timing *every* vehicle using that stretch of motorway.

Not one of them took more than two minutes from junction five to junction four.'

'They could've just slowed down and kicked him out,' the same detective offered.

'Not possible,' Chan put in.

Heads turned. He must have slid in at the back part-way through the meeting.

'The only motorway grit we found on Damian was on the ventral surface,' Chan explained, miming — actually camping it up — *face, chest, knees*, like an air steward taking passengers through emergency procedures. 'Front of the body,' he added for the slower-thinking members of the team. 'If Damian had been kicked out of even a slow-moving car, you would expect to see transfer from the road surface elsewhere on his body: side of the face, arms, hair. All over, if he'd rolled. We didn't.'

'Which means the killer must have hauled the body down from the embankment?' Rowan asked.

'It's the most likely scenario,' Chan said.

Rowan sat back and folded her arms. 'He'd have to be incredibly strong.'

Chan tilted his head. '*Maybe . . .*'

'Why "maybe"? There were no drag marks on the embankment.'

'No, but we did find tracks — possibly a quad bike . . . ?' he mused. 'They weren't good enough to get impressions.'

Warman addressed Finch. 'It might be worth checking roads that pass near the top of the embankment to see if they have traffic cams.'

Finch sagged a little, but he braced and, making a note, said, 'The dashcam stuff has started coming in, so we could use an extra pair of eyes on that, too.'

Warman wrapped up soon after, and Rowan squeezed through the press to catch Ian Chan before he disappeared.

'Was Tetting's body moved?' she asked.

He gave her a pitying look. 'You know I can't tell you that.'

'You've nicked my best pair of Chelsea boots — it's the very least you can do.'

Ian had seized them for comparison with footwear impressions at Birkenshore with a blithe, and rather tactless, 'Sorry, darling, you're all over the scene.' His insincere apology hadn't softened the blow one bit.

'Come on, Ian.'

'My lips are sealed,' he said.

People flowed past them, making for the nearest exit and a few desperately needed hours of rest.

'I believe the body *was* moved,' Rowan said, lowering her voice and watching him carefully. 'Am I wrong?'

He remained stubbornly mute.

'I'm right!' she exclaimed with a triumphant grin.

'How d'you reckon?'

'Easy,' she said with a twitch of one shoulder. 'If I was wrong, you couldn't have resisted letting me know.'

His eyelids fluttered. 'I can't even begin to unravel the perversity of that reasoning.'

She headed straight towards Warman's office.

'Hey, wait,' Chan called after her, alarmed. 'Where are you going?'

'To exercise my persuasive powers.'

'Ha!' he exclaimed. 'Good luck with that.' Then, more anxiously, 'Do not drag me into this — I mean it, Cass.'

Rowan raised one hand without looking back and dismissed him with a wave.

Warman's door was open, and she was deep in paperwork, but she glanced up from her desk as if she'd been expecting the interruption. 'Cassie. I understand it's difficult to let go of Birkenshore, but you know the protocols.'

'Of course.' Rowan tried not to sound chippy. 'But I know the villagers — I've got the background on the place — I could liaise.'

Warman raised her eyebrows. 'What you *know* is the work of a few days.'

That felt like a slap in the face.

'I'm not denying it's good work,' Warman added, softening the blow. 'It *is* — you've managed a lot with admittedly meagre resources — and your report is comprehensive.' Another sop to her vanity. 'I'm sure DCI Weller's team will catch up.'

Yeah, cos Roy Wicks is such an asset. Rowan didn't say it, even though it choked her to keep the words back.

'We need you on Fernleigh, Cassie,' Warman said. 'You've done excellent work there, too. Now you need to consolidate it.'

Rowan tried to hear all the positives — Warman didn't give praise lightly — but she couldn't get past the huge roadblock Warman had put in her way.

'Can we at least *consider* the possibility that Julius Tetting's murder is linked to the Fernleigh deaths?' she burst out.

Warman stiffened slightly. 'I'm confident that DCI Weller will consider all possibilities. But you must see that the circumstances in Birkenshore are very different to those on Fernleigh.'

Rowan had to agree: DCI Weller's investigation had a core team of twenty-three, with a detective inspector and a detective sergeant to assist him. And Weller's lot were setting up an incident room in the new police headquarters, with its sleek facilities and even better resources. It couldn't be more obvious if they'd put up a billboard — Tetting's death was 'important'.

'The killer used a mask—'

'To *disguise* the body,' Warman interrupted. 'Not as a warning or a kind of foreshadowing of what was to happen. And as far as we know the only effigy of Mr Tetting was lovingly handcrafted by his own wife.'

'I know,' Rowan said. 'But I've had hints that he was a drug user.'

'The cocaine.' Warman sounded impatient now. 'Yes, I've read your report.'

'And the body was moved — as if whoever killed him wanted to intimidate Mrs Tetting — or hurt her. I mean, it's sadistic, leaving the body in that precise location, isn't it?'

'How do you know the body was moved?' Warman snapped. 'Who have you been talking to?'

Rowan had prepared for this, and she was anxious to keep Ian's name out of it. 'There were no signs of a struggle on or near the bench,' she said. 'And Tetting's cap was soaked in blood, but there was no blood on the bench or on the ground under it.' In fact, Rowan hadn't looked under the bench, but Warman had just confirmed her guess, so it was a fair bet there would be very little blood at the secondary scene.

Warman eyed her silently for a few moments and Rowan knew she wasn't going to win a staring contest with the DCI, so she asked another question.

'Do we know how Tetting died?'

'That is not in your purview.' Sparks crackled in Warman's eyes.

'If we're not allowed to consider the exact circumstances of his death, how can we be sure whether Tetting's murder is linked to Fernleigh or not?' Rowan argued.

She waited as thunder gathered at Warman's brows and the air seemed to hum with tension.

'It's a reasonable point,' Warman conceded at last. The air in the room seemed to expand and Rowan swallowed a gasp of surprise.

'You've already deduced most of what I'm about to tell you,' Warman began, her tone clipped and as formal as Rowan had ever heard it. 'But this must remain between you and me.'

'Yeah — I mean, yes, ma'am.' *Was Warman about to take her into her confidence?*

'Close the door,' Warman said. When she was satisfied they wouldn't be overheard, she began.

'As you observed, Tetting had sustained a massive blunt force injury to the back of his head. The pathologist isn't willing to speculate on COD until the post-mortem, but he has confirmed that there would have been significant blood loss from the head wound. He also had a small nick to his left cheek, made by a sharp object, yet to be determined. This looks like a heat-of-the-moment attack,' Warman finished.

'Pym was very angry when I spoke to him earlier,' Rowan offered.

'Per your report . . .' Warman said pointedly.

'They *really* need to check his van—'

'And I'm sure they will,' the DCI cut across with a warning look.

'What about the mask — trace evidence?'

'As you documented, the village was foggy most of the day,' Warman said. 'The forensic team did find smudged fingerprints on the mask, but they are not usable.'

'I'm sure Pym's receptionist knows more than she's saying — if I could have a chat with DCI Weller—'

Warman raised her voice. 'Cassie, you need to let this go.'

Rowan drew herself to attention.

'I will liaise with DCI Weller's team. If you have any ideas or thoughts, you can bring them to me — my door is open.'

Warman waited for Rowan's, 'Yes, ma'am,' before breaking eye contact and returning to her paperwork. Rowan was dismissed.

CHAPTER 36

The evening was full of surprises.

Rowan was adding the final touches to a pan of scouse, squinting at a recipe on her mobile phone to check she hadn't missed a staple ingredient, when the front door slammed, announcing that Neil had finally come home. She took a couple of breaths, suppressing the strong impulse to bawl him out for being late. It was nearly eight o'clock, and he'd ignored the text she'd sent an hour ago.

She'd half expected him to go straight upstairs, but she felt a draft of cold air at her back as he opened the kitchen door.

'Sorry I'm late,' he said. 'Is that scouse?'

'Looks like it — I just hope it tastes like it,' she said. 'Mum always made it seem easy — like you just bunged everything in and it cooked itself.'

He hung over her shoulder, breathing in the aroma, and she realized with a shock that he must have grown a couple of inches in a month.

'It's ready,' she said. 'Just wash your hands and set the table, will you?'

He shrugged off his coat and went to the sink to do as she'd asked without argument — the second surprise of the evening — and Rowan began to harbour fantasies that his big brother's pep talk had brought about a sea change in Neil.

'There's beetroot in the cupboard.' She jerked her head towards the wall unit to her left. For a Liverpudlian, scouse without beetroot was like a boiled egg without salt. A couple of minutes later, they each had a steaming plate full of the thick lamb stew.

Neil managed to clear a third of his plate before she'd added a couple of beetroot slices to her own.

'What's brought this on?' he asked.

'What?' she said. 'I cook all the time.'

'Not scouse, you don't. Scouse is your comfort food.'

That was surprise number three; her little brother was more observant than she'd given him credit for.

She was ready to brush off the insight, when she realized that if she demanded honesty from Neil, she had to meet him at least part-way.

'I got kicked off the Birkenshore village inquiries today,' she admitted.

'I'm not the only one in trouble, then,' he said, smirking as he shoved half a potato in his mouth.

'I'm *not* in trouble,' she protested. 'In fact, my boss said I'd done excellent work.'

Neil made slurping noises that had nothing to do with food.

'Don't be childish,' Rowan said crossly. 'It's just that someone was murdered there, and they have to set up a new investigation.'

'And you're not on it.'

She saw the gleam in his eye — he was pushing her buttons — but there was a playfulness behind the slightly malicious edge, and it was good to see Neil looking cheerful after months of moodiness and depression.

The appointment with his pastoral tutor and head of sixth form was arranged for 2 p.m. the following day — she would have to ask for permission to take a couple of hours off.

She took a breath, ready to give Neil a tentative reminder when her phone beeped — a text notification.

Neil tut-tutted. 'Phones at the table, Cassie?'

She turned it over to read the screen, and her expression seemed to bring him up short. It was from Lukas Novak.

'I'll be right back,' she said, taking it through to the sitting room.

She dialled and when he answered her call, his voice sounded so muffled that she wondered if he was hiding under his duvet.

'That feller on the news,' he said softly.

'What feller?' Rowan kept her tone calm, though her scalp tingled.

'That posh nob from Birkenshore, owns the big house. Our Damian used to supply him.'

'With what?' Rowan asked.

'Coke, mostly.'

'Regularly?'

'Whenever he had some big party thing — confronts, or something.'

'Conference?' she said.

'Yeah, that's what I said, confrunce. It was a *lot* of blow.'

'This is really helpful, Lukas,' Rowan said.

'Uh, well . . . anyway, gotta go.'

'Lukas,' Rowan said. 'Are you all right?'

'Me foot hurts, but . . .'

'The man I saw you with—'

Rowan heard a yelp of anxiety, and then a muffled banging.

'That's me mam. I *really* gotta go.'

The line went dead.

When she got back to the kitchen, Neil had covered her meal with a plate to keep it warm.

'Nothing worse than cold scouse,' he muttered as if the thoughtful gesture shamed him.

'Fact,' she said, blinking away a tear fast, and he rewarded her with another smirk.

He piled another mound of food onto his plate and wolfed that down, before standing up.

'Neil,' Rowan said. 'About tomorrow—'

'Don't worry,' he said. 'I won't forget.' Including Lukas's call, this had to be surprise number five. 'You using the telly?' he asked.

She shook her head; she needed to think through what Lukas had just told her.

'I'm gonna do some gaming then.'

'Sure,' Rowan said. 'Just keep the sound down.'

He rolled his eyes, extracting a set of earbuds from his coat pocket and inserting them into his ears.

'All right,' she said. 'I get the message.'

He shrugged, palms up, mouthing *I can't hear you*.

She shooed him out of the door with a grin and fell to thinking. If Julius Tetting *had* been brokering deals to supply cocaine for corporate events at the manor, it put a whole new complexion on his murder. And if Damian Novak was his supplier, it proved a substantial link between Birkenshore and Fernleigh. Could the animosity between Andy Pym and Tetting have been about his drug dealing? And if so, did Pym want in on the deal, or was he disgusted by the squire's hypocrisy — in fact, hadn't he called Tetting a "bloody hypocrite" just days ago at the manor house?

She picked up the plates and was scraping them into the bin when another thought stopped her dead. Did Vivienne Tetting know about the drugs? She wanted to ask.

The phone was in her hand before she'd given herself time to think, but she stalled immediately: she'd given out business cards but hadn't taken phone numbers. She tapped the side of the screen, thinking that there was one she could look up.

The answerphone kicked in, and Rowan was on the point of hanging up, but changed her mind and decided to leave a message. Two minutes later, she got a call back.

'Hi, this is Sal at Birkenshore library. Is that you, Cassie?'

'Sorry, Sal, I know it's late — I didn't really think there'd be anyone at the library at this hour.'

'I couldn't settle at home with all that's been going on here,' Sal said. 'Julius Tetting — my God!' She sounded excited rather than horrified.

'Yeah,' Rowan said.

'D'you know who—' She stopped herself. 'I suppose you're not allowed to say.'

Rowan choked back a laugh. 'Not even if I knew.'

'So why did you ring?' She sounded put out.

Rowan hesitated. She should take this to the new DCI, but she wanted some answers first, and for that she needed an excuse to be in Birkenshore that wouldn't end in her suspension from duty.

'I was hoping I could introduce you to Gareth Jessop tomorrow morning,' she said. 'He's the guy who runs the community hub in Fernleigh.'

'Ah — great minds! I've been sorting books out to box up for him. He can take some away tomorrow, if he wants, and we'll have a chat about what's on his wish list.'

'Sal, that's fantastic — he'll be so grateful,' Rowan said.

'Stuff that,' Sal scoffed. 'He's more right to library stock than this bunch of Tories. What time?'

Rowan calculated how long the morning briefing might last and added on an hour in case she was delayed. 'Would ten o'clock suit?'

'Perfect. Bring cake.' Sal hung up.

Smiling, Rowan scrolled through her contacts and found Gareth Jessop's number.

CHAPTER 37

Friday morning

There was already a visible police presence in Birkenshore village by the time Rowan arrived. She'd snagged a Peugeot 308 fleet car, which would blend in better than her old clunker, and she parked on the side of the green furthest from the manor house lane, hoping to keep a low profile.

Five minutes later she headed into the library bearing pastries and cakes from the village bakery.

The sound of a squeaky wheel made her glance back. It was Gareth Jessop with an ancient roll cage that must have been a legacy from his grocery business. It was folded flat for the moment, and he seemed to be fighting its tendency to buck and jam; she didn't envy him moving the thing loaded.

He smiled sheepishly. 'I was hoping to make a slide in unnoticed,' he said. 'No chance with this flaming thing!'

Rowan turned the great iron doorknob and swung the door open for him.

Sal was at the other end of the library, lifting a box from the office to add to a stack of three by the door. She greeted them with a wide smile, pouncing on the box of pastries in Rowan's hand and removing it to the safety of her office.

Returning a moment later, she offered her hand to Jessop. 'You must be Gareth.'

Rowan introduced her, and Sal feigned embarrassment. 'Apologies for that unseemly show of greed,' she said. 'I do solemnly promise to share once we've got these boxes loaded.'

Jessop laughed in his pleasant musical tenor, earning a few scowls from the early bird readers, and Sal made a point of raising her voice and introducing him to them as a local hero from Fernleigh, adding, 'He's tackling social and cultural poverty, one book at a time.'

Blushing, Jessop shot Rowan a wild look of alarm.

'Leave the poor man alone, Sal,' Rowan said. 'He's not here as a living PowerPoint for you to illustrate how community socialism works.'

Sal apologized a second time, though she didn't look at all contrite, and Jessop started to load the books onto the sagging cage.

She disappeared into the office and toted a fifth box, flipping it open to show him the quality of the books.

His eyes widened. 'Oh, my goodness — they're practically new!'

'Brilliant council planning, as usual,' Sal said with a sneer. 'Bought in a load of new stock, then shut the damn libraries down. There's plenty more if you want them,' she added. 'If you want to get that lot off to your car, you can have a rootle when you get back, see what else takes your fancy.'

She dumped the open box on the floor and added one of the labelled items to his trolley; it creaked in complaint. As she reached for a fourth, Jessop held his hands up nervously.

'Um, I think I'd better limit it to three at a time,' he said. 'This old thing's not up to much, these days, and I've had to leave the car on the other side of the green. With all these police around, I didn't want to risk a parking ticket.'

'Bring it around to the side of the library,' Sal said. 'There's an alleyway; it belongs to us, so you won't be hassled.'

'I'll bring the trolley to the door,' Rowan said, hoping to avoid a grilling from Sal.

Jessop looked anxious. 'It's a bit temperamental.'

'I'll give Cassie a hand,' Sal said, adding with an amused glance at Rowan, 'We'll be gentle.'

He hurried out the door, shoes squelching across the parquet, keys already in hand, and Sal mouthed, 'Bless!'

Rowan gently deflected Sal's questions as they moved the wonky and bucking roll cage and excused herself as soon as they'd shifted the donated books to the door.

'No problem,' Sal said. 'You must be incredibly busy. But you'll come back later for the cake?'

Rowan smiled. 'Try and stop me.'

As she stepped outside, Jessop arrived back at the library in a grey, rust-spotted Volvo. He seemed nervous of the narrow alley, so Rowan guided him in and by the time he'd squeezed out of the driver's seat he was puffing slightly and red in the face.

'I can't thank you enough for arranging this.' He started to tear up. 'People are really so kind . . .'

'I think you saved Sal from being buried under an avalanche of books,' Rowan said. 'It was good of you to come over at such short notice.'

'*You're* doing *me* the favour!' he exclaimed, his laughter a little watery. 'Anyway, it's good to get out and about — I used to love the warehouse runs for the shop.' He took a breath and let it out with a woosh, then mopped his brow and surreptitiously wiped his eyes with a large, very white, handkerchief.

'This *is* a lovely place, isn't it?' he said with determined cheeriness, beaming out at the lush grass of the green, now carpeted in autumnal bronze.

'Yeah, well, appearances can deceive,' Rowan said, dismayed to glimpse DC Roy Wicks swaggering towards them. She slunk over to her car and zipped off in the direction of the tennis club.

* * *

By some miracle, Pym was available and sober, though still hungover from the day before.

'Oh, God,' he moaned. 'You again. Look, I told that other detective — I was in a meeting with a business loan specialist from between nine and nine thirty yesterday morning.'

'You were expected back here soon after that meeting.'

'Don't you people *talk* to each other?' He'd raised his voice, and he winced.

That hangover must be a doozy, Rowan thought.

He took a breath and let it go slowly before going on, 'I went for a coffee afterwards, took my time — I needed to decompress.'

It wasn't Rowan's job to chase down that alibi, and she felt reassured that Pym had been interviewed — especially as he seemed intensely irritated by their inquiries. So she asked the question she'd come here for.

'The argument you had with Julius Tetting,' she began.

'Business,' he exclaimed. 'Just business!'

'What kind of business?'

He glanced around the shabby foyer of his club. 'Isn't it obvious?'

'No,' she said.

He eyed her with contempt. 'Then let me make it simple for you. He promised me that he'd send business my way from the manor house bookings. He didn't. And I lost existing members after he turned the entire village against me.'

'Okay. But that's been ongoing for years. When you came speeding up the manor-house drive, you were ready to knock him flat on his back. Like you'd just discovered something that made you raging, stinking mad.'

He seemed to lose focus; his gaze slid away, and Rowan knew she was on the right track.

'I understand the end-of-conference parties at the manor were fuelled by more than alcohol,' she went on, treading carefully — she might have to report this interview back to DCI Weller. 'Is that why you called Tetting a hypocrite?'

He slowly rolled his head back to gaze at the water-stained ceiling. He even smiled a little. 'You think *I* had a finger in that pie?'

'Perhaps not at that time. But if Tetting paid you to look the other way, that'd be something you'd both want to keep secret.'

He stared at her without expression. 'I don't do drugs,' he said after a long silence. 'I don't tolerate them on my premises. I've heard rumours, of course — the manor might be in splendid isolation at the north end of the village, but sound carries on the marshes, and people do love to talk. But if you think I'd enter into a sordid deal with Tetting to supply them, then you're even more clueless than I thought.'

* * *

Driving back along the bumpy lane, Rowan felt deflated. He was right about the rumour mill. Yet they could close ranks when they chose to — only one villager had hinted at Tetting's cocaine use, and that was Sal Fabian, who by her own admission was viewed with suspicion — a classic outsider, largely shunned by the core of villagers. Was there more that this outwardly prim, clean-living, conservative community was holding back from the police?

A car was approaching from the direction of Birkenshore and Rowan pulled in to a passing point to give it room. It slowed, and the driver wound down their window. As it drew level, Rowan saw that it was Roy Wicks.

Hell.

She stared at him levelly, and he smirked, wagging a finger at her. He drove on without saying a word, but she knew he'd be on the phone to Weller as soon as he reached the tennis club.

'Bloody hell!' she said aloud.

She had hoped to sneak around to the manor and drop in on Mrs Tetting, but she was in enough trouble already, and anyway the village green was by now heaving with police and press. So she squeezed her car onto the verge at the end of the lane and made straight for DCI Weller.

CHAPTER 38

Back at St Anne Street station, Rowan went to her desk and began typing in a report on her trip to Birkenshore and the phone call that had triggered it. Finch was sitting in front of a screen with another detective, patiently working through hours of dashcam footage.

She was just finishing when her landline rang. It was DCI Warman.

'My office, immediately,' she said.

Once the door was firmly closed, Warman demanded an explanation for her presence in Birkenshore village.

Heart pounding, Rowan related the details of Lukas's call and her interview with Andy Pym.

'Withholding material information in a police investigation is a serious matter, Cassie.'

'I got the intel late last night,' Rowan said. 'That intel was directly related to the Fernleigh inquiry; I wanted to act on it as soon as I could, but I gave DCI Weller all the relevant details of the phone call immediately after I'd spoken to Pym.'

'DCI Weller said you declined to name the source.'

'Sorry, boss — it's too dangerous — if word got out . . .'

'And word does have a habit of doing that in this inquiry, doesn't it?' Warman observed, but she sounded reflective, rather than accusatory. 'All right. If Weller tries to push you on that, refer him to me.'

Rowan nodded, relieved.

'Do you think Mrs Tetting was aware of what was going on?'

How about that? Rowan thought. *Even Warman is finding it hard to let go of Birkenshore.*

'Unclear,' she said. 'She organized the events, from the catering to staging, arranging recordings, music, flowers and place-settings, but Mr Tetting was the "face" of Birken Manor — meeting with the CEOs and PR people on the business side, welcoming the guests — that kind of thing.'

'What's your instinct?'

'Mrs Tetting strikes me as a moral person,' Rowan said. 'She's steeped in the history of the place, and she has a connection to the landscape — she practically lit up, telling me about her parents' vision for the manor.'

'I take it that didn't include hiving off half of it for elaborate weddings?'

'I wouldn't say that — she seems really into that side of the business. But the land is organically farmed, and I gather the marsh and the farmland is teeming with rare birds and stuff.'

'Ah, an eco-warrior.'

Rowan smirked and, seeing Warman bristle, she hastened to explain herself. 'It's hard to see Mrs Tetting as a warrior.' She tilted her head. 'Worrywart's nearer the mark. Although, I do believe she married her husband to try and fulfil her parents' legacy.'

Warman's eyebrows shot up. 'And they say feudalism is dead.'

'Tetting was a hard-headed businessman, as well as a bully and a blusterer,' Rowan went on. 'Mrs Tetting is . . .' She grasped for the right word, wanting to be fair to the woman — 'weak' would be wrong, but she did seem

252

vulnerable. 'Fragile,' she said at last. 'Yet she somehow persuaded her husband to stick to organic farming because she thought it was the right thing to do. And they seem to employ locals, in the main, when I imagine it'd be cheaper to bring in foreigners.'

'So you're saying she wouldn't approve of business yahoos snorting cocaine in the hallowed halls,' Warman said with a rare flash of dry humour.

'I think she'd be in terror of the potential damage that said yahoos might do to the house.'

Warman took a few moments. 'I can see why you would want to approach Pym before DCI Weller's team got to him,' she said at last. 'But I believe it was curiosity about his relationship with Tetting that drove you, rather than any substantive link between Pym and the drugs — I mean your source didn't *actually* mention Mr Pym, did they?'

'Not in so many words,' Rowan muttered, knowing she'd been rumbled.

'Not in so many words,' Warman repeated, sounding for all the world like a lawyer for the prosecution. 'Did it occur to you that if there were any illegal substances on the club premises, you gave Pym ample opportunity to dispose of them?'

Rowan flushed. 'No, boss, it didn't.'

'If you had brought this to me this morning, during or after the briefing — as you should have done — I could have liaised with DCI Weller so that you had your stab at Pym while Weller's team waited in readiness to search the premises. Did that cross your mind?'

Rowan swallowed. 'No, boss,' she admitted.

'No. Because you go at these things like a one-person crusade,' Warman said. 'Worse — you don't trust your colleagues to do their jobs.'

Rowan hung her head; she was right on both counts.

'No doubt you have some justification in making that assumption,' Warman said. 'But you cannot measure all of your colleagues against one sloppy individual.' She was talking about Wicks. Rowan was grateful for that acknowledgement, although it made her feel worse to have been so small-minded about the others.

'Yes, ma'am,' she said, surprised to find that it pained her to have let Warman down. 'I see that — and I'm sorry — really I am.'

Satisfied of her sincerity, Warman nodded. 'Detective work is teamwork, Cassie. If you can't be a team player, then I suggest you think hard about your career in the police.'

Rowan held her breath. Was she going to send her home to think about it? She couldn't bear it if she was taken off the investigation that she herself had instigated.

In the moments that passed, Rowan felt simultaneously hot and cold.

Warman spoke, and for a second her meaning was obscured by the booming in Rowan's ears. But she caught the last of it: '—report in writing.'

'It'll be on your desk in the next ten minutes, ma'am,' Rowan said, unable to quell the tremor in her voice.

'And then get out to Fernleigh. See if there's anything useful you can do there — Mrs Breidon was unavailable yesterday — that would be a good place to start.'

Grateful, shaking, Rowan fumbled with the door handle and practically fell into the corridor.

A few minutes later, having washed her face and soothed herself by taking a few calming breaths, she sat at her computer and completed and emailed her report to Warman. She'd dropped the key to her fleet car in the bottom drawer of her desk and as she reached for it, encountered something soft, yielding, unpleasantly cool. She flashed back to Tetting's body — her fingertips testing the cold flesh of his throat, probing for life — and experienced again the shock of life extinct.

She glanced over to Finch, concerned that she might have cried out, but he was engrossed in his work.

Dragging the hated mask onto the desk, she searched beneath it for the car key and found the printing company's list of retailers who'd ordered boggart masks for Halloween three years ago.

Now that she'd been kicked off Birkenshore, she would have more time to read lists, she thought glumly, glancing again at Finch, still working; stopping and starting, rewinding and running hours of dashcam recordings. It was a wonder he didn't get carsick.

Focusing on her own work, she skimmed the list and saw Gareth Jessop's name. He had ordered a box of fifty masks. She grabbed her coat.

'Off out again?' Finch asked, almost dreamily.

'I'm off to Fernleigh,' she said. 'Want to come?'

'Nah,' he said. 'You're welcome to it.'

Rowan shrugged. 'You'll go blind, binge-watching that stuff.'

'Yeah, well, someone's got to do it.'

Which was true. But she didn't see why it had to be him.

CHAPTER 39

Jessop had wasted no time in making good use of the books Sal had passed on from Birkenshore library. He'd brought two more racks of shelves out of storage, and they were filled end to end, and top to bottom, brightening up what had been a blank section of wall.

He told Rowan over coffee and a digestive biscuit that he'd sold the masks out of his shop.

'I wish I'd never set eyes on the horrible things,' he added with feeling.

'Because of what's happening now, or—'

He glanced around. The only visitors were a mother and toddler. Even so, he lowered his voice and leaned in across the table, his back to them.

'Three years ago,' he said. 'Ten kids — I'd guess eleven-to fourteen-year-olds, boys and girls — steamed through the shop, taking everything they could lay their hands on. In and gone in under a minute, stripped the place like a plague of locusts. All of them were wearing those damned masks.' He shook his head, his shoulders hunched.

'That's when you shut up shop?' Rowan asked.

'No.' He drew the corners of his mouth down. 'I limped on for another four months. The insurance company paid up — I had CCTV of the whole thing — but at the end of the year, they refused to renew. One of the first questions insurance companies ask is have you had insurance declined. Answer yes, and it raises a red flag. I couldn't get affordable insurance anywhere — *no one* would touch this place. That was the end. I felt terrible for Dad. God, he *loved* the shop.' His eyes reddened and he blinked away tears.

'Ridiculous!' he exclaimed with a sudden laugh; it was choked and definitely wet, but there was joy in it, too. He produced a big white hankie from his pocket and wiped his nose. 'Look at it now.' He straightened up, swivelling in his chair and gazing with evident pride on his modest domain, settling finally on the young mother, helping her toddler to choose a book from his impromptu library.

He lowered his voice to a whisper. 'I'm pretty sure Lucy there was one of the gang who steamed the shop. But she was at the front of the queue to volunteer when I made my first steps to set up the hub, and look at her, now.'

Lucy was sitting on a kids' stool, while her daughter snuggled close, reading snippets from each of the books, making big eyes of exaggerated delight or horror, depending on the story.

'Your dad would be proud,' Rowan said, feeling a little choked herself.

She headed out to find Dawson, and they went together to reinterview Mrs Breidon, Craig's mother. It was a mistake, as Rowan had known it would be, and only succeeded in alienating the woman.

By now, it was nearly one o'clock. Rowan was due at Neil's school for the pastoral meeting at two and, promising Dawson she would return later, she hurried back to the parade of shops where she'd parked the car. From a distance, something looked off, but she couldn't tell what.

Three youths were loitering outside the hub; they sauntered off into the garden of one of the derelict houses opposite and disappeared around the back. Two skinny lads and a big one. *Barrel Boy*, she thought.

An SUV drew up alongside her and Rowan stepped away from the kerb with a jolt of alarm, peering in through the driver's window. It was Jim North.

He rolled down the window.

'Do they use smoke signals around here or what?' she asked.

He held up his phone. 'Text. The digital age has even come to the wild west,' he added with a smile that was meant to be disarming. 'You've been avoiding me.'

'I've been busy.'

'Of course,' he said. 'But can you spare five minutes, now?'

'I've got somewhere I need to be.' Something was definitely off about her car. She started walking again.

She heard him call, 'Cassie—' Then the engine shut off and his car door opened and slammed.

She was hurrying now, her eyes on the fleet car. It was too low on its chassis. 'Oh, no,' she murmured. *No, not now . . .*

The tyres had been slashed and it was sitting on the wheel rims. She slapped the flat of her palm to her forehead and swore comprehensively.

North had caught up with her. 'Shit, is that yours?'

'Worse,' she said, digging out her personal mobile. 'It's a job car.'

'Look, if you've got somewhere you need to be, I can give you a lift.'

'No, thanks.' She swiped to the Uber app and her phone buzzed in her hand.

Glancing at the ID, she suppressed a groan of dismay, took a breath, raised a finger to silence North, and slid the icon to 'answer'.

'Mr Singh,' she said. 'How can I help you?'

'Neil was absent from classes today,' he said. 'Can you confirm that he will be at the meeting this afternoon?'

'Sorry, completely my fault,' she said, clicking instantly into protection mode. 'I should have thought to ring you, but it's been a busy day. Neil was feeling a bit under the weather this morning and I suggested he should take a couple of hours.' *Too much information, Cassie. You want a lie to sound convincing, keep it simple.*

'Oh, I'm sorry to hear he's unwell,' Singh said. 'Perhaps we should reschedule?'

'No.' That came out too forcefully, and Rowan made herself repeat more quietly, 'No, that won't be necessary.' Neil's mental state was so unstable she wasn't sure she'd get a second chance at this.

'Well, if you're sure.'

'Absolutely,' Rowan said. 'We'll see you at two.'

She switched back to the Uber app. The nearest driver was ten minutes away. She selected him anyway, then rang the emergency call-out number, gave them the location and status of the car, and told them she'd leave the keys with Gareth Jessop at the community hub.

All of this accomplished, she returned outside to wait. Her Uber was still ten minutes away.

'Offer stands,' North said.

Rowan didn't answer.

'Okay, I'm just going to say it. What I said the other day, the way I cut you off — assumed you were mouthing platitudes — I was out of order.'

'Did you come all this way to tell me that?' Rowan said, with what she hoped was a withering look. 'Or did you just *happen* to be here on your lunch break — again?'

'I had no right to make that assumption,' he ploughed on, ignoring the sarcasm. 'I apologize, and I owe you an honest answer.'

She wanted to hear it. Cop curiosity, a strength and a weakness, made her lean in, and, sensing it, he began.

'I put thousands of miles between me and Fernleigh. But however much distance you create between you and the place that made you, no matter *how* far you go, you carry it with you every step of the way. *That's* why I came back.'

She cocked her head. 'Jackie's been talking.'

It was said as a challenge: she was damned sure he hadn't changed his mind about her after reflecting deeply on their previous conversation. It had to be Jackie.

He considered her and after a few seconds, with the merest lift of one shoulder, he said, 'Jackie said I shouldn't prejudge, that's all. She likes you — and that means something.'

Rowan was intrigued. Was there a romantic connection between Jackie and Jim North? If so, she'd missed it. And Jackie seemed a mismatch to this intense, brooding man. But who was she to judge — it wasn't like her life was packed with romance.

'Jackie needs to learn to keep her mouth—'

'She just told me to reserve judgement, like I'm always telling the kids.,' he interrupted. 'The rest was me.'

Rowan gazed into his face, unsure if she believed him.

'I told you that I'd googled you,' he said. 'But it was just the headlines. I didn't really dive into the detail, so I didn't know about your brother — what happened to him.' He paused, perhaps wondering if he was about to overstep the mark. 'I gather he's struggling?'

Rowan took a breath and let it go. 'Yeah, and I'm not helping.'

'Your parents aren't around?'

She quirked an eyebrow. 'Jackie didn't tell you?'

'Like I said—'

'Joke.' She winced. 'Actually, a bad one.' After what he'd told her, it wasn't fair to deflect him with bad jokes and sarcasm. So she took a moment to gather herself before telling him about the car crash that had killed her parents when Neil was just nine, and a little about her present troubles with her younger brother.

He was a good listener, allowing her to tell the story her way, not asking intrusive questions or offering sympathy. Just quietly hearing her.

When she finished, he seemed to run it through his mind before asking, 'Your older brother's still living in the States?'

She nodded.

'So you brought Neil up.' He gave her an appraising glance. 'You can't be more than, what, twenty-five?'

'Twenty-seven.'

'You were *nineteen* when you basically adopted a nine-year-old?' His appraisal turned to admiration, and Rowan felt her face flush. 'So you've been around for the past eight years, while Alex has been living in New York, jetting around the world, occasionally coming home to spoil him like a rich uncle. I'm guessing Neil looks up to him like a rock star.'

Rowan didn't feel the need to reply — he'd pretty much summed up the situation.

'Sounds like Alex needs to have a word with the kid.'

'He did, a couple of days ago,' Rowan said. 'And Neil seemed so much better — he started to open up, agreed to meet with his teachers — I was really beginning to believe we'd be all right, after all.'

He didn't answer straight away. Once again, Rowan had the sense that he was thinking through different responses before choosing the one he thought best, and she realized that Jim North was a born leader.

'It's natural, when boys reach a certain age, that they want to kick against authority,' he began. 'I've worked with a lot of lads who've had the worst start in life. They can be rebellious, disruptive, aggressive, self-destructive, but they usually come around. Unlike them, Neil has been lucky enough to have had your guidance and support. Till now, he's done okay in school?'

'His grades were okay till recently,' Rowan said. 'He loved sports — he was talking about studying sports science at college — but now . . .' Keeping her worries to herself, ploughing forward like an athlete in a marathon, she could grit her teeth and convince herself that Neil would be fine. He needed discipline, sure — a bit of straightening out — and then he'd get on with his life. But talking about it brought home how bad things were; this problem was huge, and she didn't know how to help. The eight years of responsibility felt like a stone in her chest.

'Look, sticking with the rehab after injuries takes a lot of resilience — this is a setback,' North said. 'But give him time, he'll get his second wind.'

She shook her head, refusing to look at him. 'You don't get it,' she said. 'He got hurt — because of me — because of *my job*.' She felt suddenly angry with herself. 'Maybe it was all a mistake. I fought so hard to keep us together, but maybe that was selfishness — I just didn't want to be alone. I should've let the aunties take him to Scotland; at least he would've been out of harm's way.'

'Hey.' North ducked and looked into her face, forcing eye contact. 'Take it from someone who knows: if fate decides to give you a bloody nose, she'll find you wherever you are.'

Surprised, she brought her head up. 'Are you telling me you believe in fate?'

'No!' He seemed rattled by the suggestion. Then, 'Yeah . . .' Then he raised both hands and bugged his eyes. 'Maybe — a little bit.' He laughed softly at his own confusion. 'The point is you can only do what you can.'

She stiffened, hearing her words quoted back at her. His eyes held an apology, but there was a hint of mischief in them, too.

'It was too late for Ben,' he said, serious, now. 'And I don't pretend to understand your situation, but let's face it — *you* stuck around, I didn't — and I really *should* have done more. Our mother was a mess. But even when I came home on leave, I was too far away — mentally, psychologically. Ben could've been *screaming* for help, I wouldn't have heard.'

She nodded, thinking about her phone conversation with Alex. 'Thanks,' she said at last. 'For coming here — f-for being so . . . open.' Stumbling over her words, suddenly shy of him. 'For telling me about Ben. I appreciate it.'

He opened his arms wide. 'So let me *do* this—'

She checked the app — still ten minutes away. Her panic rising, she refreshed the screen. No change. 'What the f—?'

'Just so you know,' he said with a nod to her stricken car, 'That's the second in two days. Uber Guy might be having second thoughts.'

It was already one fifteen, and she first had to find Neil and then persuade him to come with her to the meeting. 'I can*not* be late for this meeting.'

'So what are we waiting for?' He jerked his head towards his SUV.

'Not an Uber, that's for sure,' she said, cancelling the booking.

CHAPTER 40

Neil was lounging on the sofa, playing a computer game. At least he was dressed, Rowan registered.

'I just had a call from Mr Singh,' she said. 'You weren't in school — again.'

Neil kept his eyes on the screen. 'I said I'd be at the meeting; didn't say I'd be in school all day.'

Rowan felt the rage and frustration of the past year building, but Jim North was waiting in the hallway and she made a supreme effort to remain calm and reasonable. 'Well, it's now one fifty and we have to be there at two, so grab your coat and we'll go.'

'It's like two minutes' drive,' he said.

'We're lucky to have a lift, then, aren't we?'

This got his attention. He turned to question her as North edged past her.

'This is Jim North,' Rowan said. 'He runs a martial-arts club for the Fernleigh kids.'

Neil perked up. 'Cool.'

Rowan left them for a second to check the doors and windows were locked and as she headed downstairs with one of Neil's jackets in her fist, she heard North say, 'Sports injury?'

Neil was wearing a tee shirt and the scar on his right arm was a dull red line from the top of his forearm to just above the elbow.

'Nah,' Neil said. 'I got slashed.'

'How?'

Neil mumbled something she couldn't hear, and Rowan swept into the room. 'Saving my life,' she said, shoving the jacket at her brother.

Startled, he took it, and she snapped off the TV.

North glanced at Rowan, then stared in open appraisal of Neil. 'Well, I know Cassie can fight — so you must be scary, dude!'

Neil flared bright red.

'Had any physio?' North asked, moving to the hall, and Rowan was fascinated to see that, miraculously, her brother seemed compelled to follow him.

Neil slid her a guilty glance from under his lashes as he moved past her towards the front door. 'A bit?'

'That's the trouble with NHS physio provision,' North said, out on the narrow pavement now, clicking the remote to open the SUV doors. 'They cut you off before you're really ready.'

Rowan saw her brother's eyes widen at the prospect of arriving at school in North's flash car.

'Usually, that's exactly when you *think* it's not helping,' North went on, smoothly. 'But that's exactly the time when you're at the tipping point.'

'Tipping point of what?' Rowan asked, since Neil didn't.

'Recovery,' he said, climbing into the car.

Neil scrambled into the front passenger seat, and Rowan was so grateful she didn't even make a dig at his lack of manners.

In the SUV, North rolled back his sleeve. His left forearm had a deep indentation. It was smooth, with rounded edges, like someone had scooped it out with a spoon.

Neil stared openly.

North stuck a thumb into the indentation. 'Muscle's gone,' he said. 'I got hit by shrapnel after an IED blew up the vehicle in front of me.'

'You're a soldier?' Neil asked, now fully in awe.

North started the car and moved off before answering. 'Was. I work in construction, now.'

Neil wasn't interested in construction. 'Does it hurt?' he asked.

'Not anymore. Mostly it's numb. You?'

Neil nodded. He took a breath, stopped. Cradled his right arm in his left, took another breath, and asked the question that Rowan knew had been preying on his mind ever since he was injured. 'How long did it take to — you know . . . ?'

'Do something heroic like lift a fork to feed myself?' North smiled. 'I dunno, mate. Six weeks? Lifting proper weights took a lot longer. I mean, I couldn't manage a one-kilo barbell for six — maybe eight — months. And I lost some coordination.' He flexed his hand and Neil watched, mesmerised.

'You can still fight, though?' he asked.

'Sure. Part of the fun of running the club is I get to fight competitively. And I can climb ladders and scaffolding for my job, swim — all the normal stuff.'

Neil sat back, and Rowan could almost hear the cogs and wheels of his mind grinding.

'It's nearly a year for me,' he said at last.

'Straight cut through muscle and tendon, right?' North asked.

'Yeah.'

'If they reconnected the nerves, you're fine,' North said. 'A knife cut heals better than a jagged tear — or getting a hole blasted in your forearm. But I won't lie — it's a bastard building the strength again.'

'Yeah, but I kind of stopped doing the exercises,' Neil said. 'So it's, like, too late.'

North squinted at him. 'Says who?'

Neil hunched his shoulders up to his ears.

'You worked that gaming console all right,' North observed.

'Well, yeah, but I thought . . .'

North laughed, and Neil stared at him, startled, even offended.

'Man,' North exclaimed, 'You've got to stop *thinking* and start *doing*.'

They were almost at the school, and Rowan half wished he would take another turn around the block — Neil was actually listening.

Instead, North fell silent, pulling into the school car park and scouting for a space.

When he finally spoke, his tone was casual, even off-hand. 'There's an ex-army buddy of mine lives out this way,' he said. 'He's setting up a dojo — ju-jitsu and kickboxing, mainly. If you're interested, I could set up a meet?'

Rowan held her breath.

'Yeah — yes,' Neil said, and Rowan was thrilled to hear carefully controlled excitement in his voice. 'Sure, that'd be cool.'

CHAPTER 41

Sunday evening

The weekend passed quietly. The fact that the Birkenshore inquiry's major incident room was in the new headquarters meant that Rowan was less likely to bump into investigators from DCI Weller's team, and she knew better than to simply show up at their MIR. But that didn't stop her thoughts from drifting to Julius Tetting. The post-mortem would no doubt be complete, although they would be waiting on tox screens and trace evidence analysis.

The police presence on Fernleigh was being maintained, at least for now, and aside from the two tyre-slashings — both police vehicles — the mood was calm. Rowan had passed on her suspicions that Barrel Boy and his sidekicks were responsible. North had identified them from her descriptions, and they had been spoken to. Patrols would keep a close eye out for Barrel Boy, aka Cole Varley, and his pals.

She'd spent a few hours with Neil on Saturday watching a class at the prospective new dojo. At the Fernleigh hub both Dawson and Jessop had told her that good people on the estate felt a little more secure, while the bad elements were keeping under the radar. Barrel Boy had stopped lurking around the hub, too, which was a big bonus and soothed Jessop's nerves wonderfully. And as the police watched from outside, eyes inside the estate were protecting their own community by surveilling it.

On Sunday night, after watching a high-octane shoot-em-up on Netflix, Neil spoke with Alex via Zoom. Forty minutes later, he pounded down the stairs with his tablet in hand.

'He wants to talk to you,' Neil said, leaving the tablet and trotting back up to his room.

While she and Neil were dark-haired like their mother, who had sometimes claimed to have Italian antecedents, Alex was fair. He was lightly tanned, just now, perhaps back from a few days in Bermuda, which he favoured in October.

'Was the meeting grim?' he asked.

'Actually, it was good.'

'Wow!' Alex grinned. 'Neil said pretty much the same and I was worried he'd lapsed into "I'm fine" mode, but coming from you I can almost believe it.'

From the moment she'd taken on the responsibility of bringing up her brother, Rowan had always regarded the authorities as a threat. It was a humbling revelation to realize that the school pastoral team really knew her brother's strengths and wanted to help him achieve his true potential.

'I honestly thought he'd say he wanted to leave,' she began.

'School?'

'School, home, maybe even Liverpool.'

'Jeez, Cassie, I didn't know.'

Rowan bit back her snap reaction that he'd never shown any particular interest. 'Well, now you do,' she said simply.

She'd trodden carefully at the school meeting, not wanting to alienate Neil further, but she'd mentioned that Alex was mainly in the US, so it was just her and Neil, and she worked long hours, shift patterns, and wasn't always there when he needed her.

Neil had stirred at her side, alarmed. 'No . . .' he'd murmured. 'It's not like that.'

Mr Singh had asked how he would characterize it and, to his credit, Neil had been generous and fair about her efforts to support him.

'He told his teachers that he had too much time to brood on things when I was out at work — although he didn't call it brooding,' she said with a small smile. 'He called it thinking.'

'The school suggested group therapy one evening a week and given his interest in sports science, they said they could help him find a volunteer coaching position.'

'What about all the work he needs to catch up on?' Alex asked.

'Apparently, they have after-school study sessions in the sixth form block three times a week.'

Alex spread his hands, eyes wide in amazement. 'Who knew?'

'Yeah, he kept that a closely guarded secret,' Rowan said dryly. 'He's agreed to sign up for two.'

Alex was shaking his head in wonder. 'I've gotta hand it to you, sis — you seem to've pulled off the impossible.'

'Do not jinx it,' she warned, knocking on the coffee table for luck. 'He's still got a long way to go.'

Alex smiled. 'Okay, so what's your news?'

'What news?' Rowan demanded. 'I don't have a life — just work and home.'

'Well, then, I guess it must be news *about* work,' Alex said playfully. 'Neil says you've got a serial killer on the loose.'

'We have a murder — singular.'

'Don't try to feed me the official line — it's all over social media about the voodoo dolls. And I know you've got two: the scally and the lord of the manor.'

'Unconnected, apparently.'

'Ooh! You think they got it wrong.'

'Not in the way you think.'

'No?' He seemed disappointed. 'What about those creepy voodoo dolls?'

'What about them?'

'Weren't the murderees both warned with a life-size effigy of themselves?'

'You really shouldn't get your news from Twitter,' Rowan said. 'Mr Tetting's wife made a scarecrow for their village Halloween bash — the scarecrow was switched for the body.'

'Eugh! I wouldn't want to be the poor sucker who found the body — it's like something out of a movie.'

Rowan blinked away an image of flies lifting in a smoky drift from the back of Tetting's head.

He realized his mistake. 'Oh, God, Cass, was it you?'

'Yes,' she said tightly. 'Now can we change the subject?'

'Sure,' he said, suddenly brisk and business-like. 'Neil tells me he's thinking of taking up martial arts.'

'Yeah,' she said, letting the tension seep away. 'I think it'll be good for him.'

'Well, just make sure he lets his physio know what's involved because—'

'Physio?' she interrupted. 'Keep up, Alex — he dropped out of physio a few months back.'

'I don't mean those half-hour NHS blips,' Alex said. 'I mean the *private* sessions.'

'The *what*?' Her heart jumped — she couldn't afford private physio sessions.

'He didn't tell you.' Alex slumped back in his chair and blew out a long breath. 'I offered to pay for private physio. Get him on-screen, I'll talk to him.'

'No,' Rowan said. Then on an outbreath, 'Give him a bit of space, okay?'

Alex looked ready to argue.

'Look,' she said. 'It's great that you've offered. And I'm sure he'll come around — he's made some real progress these last few days. But that's involved him having to make a lot of compromises — he needs thinking space to adjust. Give him time — he'll talk about it when he's ready.'

CHAPTER 42

Sunday night

Stickman had been playing the same rap song over and over for three solid hours. From nine o'clock to midnight, the dull bass thump of the drums and machine-gun rattle of words pounded against the walls of Marie's flat until they seemed to pulse with it, the unrelenting sound reverberating through her narrow chest till she thought she would go mad. She fled to her bedroom across the inner hallway and turned on the radio, wrapping a pillow around her head, but it went on, conjuring up the rumble of armoured vehicles grinding through the streets of her childhood home.

The song cut off abruptly at just after midnight, and she said a prayer of thanks. Her ears throbbed, so at first she wasn't sure what she heard next. Then it came again, a loud, hard knocking on Stickman's door.

Stickman yelled for whoever it was to eff off, and the awful music started where it had finished. The banging began again, a solemn, solid *thud, thud, thud,* hammering the masonry to the side of Stickman's door — she could swear she heard the bricks being ground to dust by the power of the beating.

Unbidden, a picture formed in her head of the Grim Reaper, cloaked and hooded, all in black.

Trembling, she crept from her bed and peered through the glass of her front door into the concrete hallway, which gave access to two other flats at this corner of the block. She could make out only a looming shadow so dark that it seemed to suck all the light from around it. The shadow raised its fist. It gripped a long pole, and she crouched, covering her ears.

'The Reaper, the Reaper. Oh, dear God, save me — the Reaper!' she whispered.

It pounded on Stickman's door so hard that her own letterbox rattled.

'I'll fucking *burst* you!' Stickman yelled.

She lifted inches off the floor with fright, clamping her hands over her mouth to still her sobs of fear. She knew that if Stickman opened his front door he would have his steel-tipped baseball bat in his bony hand.

A sharp rasp, as Stickman raked the curtain back from his front door. Glass shattered, and Stickman gave a shriek of surprise and pain. A noise, like a stumble — Stickman, staggering back into his flat. Then his front door swung inwards, hitting the interior wall with a crack.

She heard thuds — one, two, three. A groan. Silence.

After that, the most terrible sound of all: the crunch and snap of breaking bones.

CHAPTER 43

Monday, 1 a.m.

It was a bloody mess. Rowan, masked and hooded in Tyvek and wearing protective overshoes, stood just inside the forensic tent at the base of Hartsfern Tower, swallowing hard, trying not to look at what had been done to Stickman. DCI Warman had rung her mobile to say she was on her way, which at least gave Rowan an excuse to stay near the door flap. She was grateful, too, to be out of the competing glare of crime scene arc lamps and media spotlights. The courtyard had been blocked to non-police traffic, but that didn't stop TV news crews from setting up at the perimeter with high-powered LEDs, or directing zoom-lens cameras at the scene. One enterprising crew had even persuaded a household to allow them access to the balcony of their flat in Braunswood Tower, which looked down on the scene, giving them a splendid view of proceedings.

The CSIs, crouching on metal stepping plates, were working with quick efficiency alongside the pathologist. They would process the body as much as possible at the scene, unless the drizzle, which had crept in from the marshes, turned heavier and threatened to wash their evidence away.

Outside the tent, Rowan caught a sudden burst of camera flashes and a moment later, she unzipped the door flap to admit DCI Warman.

'Dear God,' Warman murmured, without emotion.

'This is Thomas Capstick, aka Stickman,' Rowan said, keeping herself under tight rein. 'Main rival to the Lang crew on the estate. The window of his front door is smashed and hanging off its hinges. The flat's been secured and a second team of CSIs is being organized; ETA thirty minutes. I can't raise his immediate neighbour — a Mrs Elliott. The resident across the hallway said they thought she was out visiting a friend.'

'Those facial injuries . . .' Warman said.

Rowan glanced across — a reflex action — and saw again the horrific damage done to Stickman's body. His scalp and left cheek were a mass of blood and bone, and the lower half of his left leg was twisted at right angles to his thigh.

The pathologist, kitted out like the rest, looked up for the first time. 'Judging by the glass beads in his facial tissue, and a round depression fracture to the frontal bone just above the right orbit, he was probably peering through the window when the killer took a hammer to the glazing,' he said.

'I take it he was tipped over the balcony?' Warman asked.

'Very likely,' the pathologist said, not looking up this time.

'That's what — twenty-five metres?'

'Nearer to twenty-seven.' He began palpating the dead man's arms. 'Multiple breaks.'

'From the fall?' Warman asked.

'I can't be sure until I've had a good root round during the PM, but my strictly off-the-record opinion would be *not bloody likely*. This fellow looks like he was pounded and jumped on. You can see the boot marks on his clothing.'

Forty minutes later, Rowan stood with Warman behind a hastily rigged barrier of blue-and-white tape in the communal area on the eighth floor. The pathologist and CSIs were still hard at work below, and a second team of CSIs was processing the flat.

The fire door had already been dusted for prints and retained grey smudges of fingerprint powder. Propped open, it gave onto a narrow concrete hallway with doors to three flats. The CSI's attention was focused on the end flat, which had been occupied by Stickman, and brilliant flashes from the open flat door told them that the forensic photographer was at work. A constable in uniform stood guard at the tape.

'We'll leave the specialists to get on with their work,' Warman said. 'Uniform officers will remain at the scene — both here and below — until the CSIs have cleared it. In light of Mr Capstick's *business*, his flat will need to be guarded until we've had a poke around tomorrow.'

Rowan nodded, blinking the terrible image of Capstick's ruined face from her retinas.

'Go home and get some rest,' Warman said, her tone a little kinder than usual. 'Briefing at seven thirty.'

A common approach path had been roped off with police tape and fencing pins driven into the cracked concrete. Blinded by a brief flurry of camera flashes, Rowan didn't see Jim North, but he tapped her arm as she passed.

She rolled her eyes. 'Have you set up a Google Alert for trouble on the estate, or what?'

'Something like that.' He fell in step with her as she crossed the outer cordon, waiting till they were out of earshot of the press before saying, 'Looks like Stickman got what was coming to him.'

She gave him a hard look. 'Did you see what they did to him?'

'I've a fair idea.'

Keeping her gaze on him, she said, 'Well, you're all heart.'

He shook his head, and in the darkness beyond the rim of blinding light at the crime scene, she couldn't tell if he was smiling or angry.

'I know this guy — knew him, anyway — he's not worth your pity. And if I seem heartless, it's because I'm sick of seeing kids on bikes doing the work of the drug dealers.'

Rowan felt a sudden, white-hot flash of rage. 'Where do you draw the line, Jim — at the dealers, doling out drugs to their under-age mules? What about the suppliers who ship poison into the country like any other commodity? Or the shipping companies, turning a blind eye to importers who bring tonnes of the stuff hidden in tyre wheels and concrete blocks? I mean, if you're gonna condemn the dealers, you should at least spare a thought for what the top-feeders deserve.'

He raised a finger. 'If I had my way—'

Rowan saw a woman approaching uncertainly from North's left. He dropped his hand and turned, following her line of sight.

'Hiya, Jim.' The woman sounded unsure of herself — shy or afraid?

'All right, Joy,' he said, his tone not encouraging.

'Haven't seen you for a bit.'

'You wanna come down the hub,' he said.

'I might do that.' She paused, began to speak, bit her lip, then taking a breath, tried again. 'Marie'd love to see you . . .'

He looked over her head. 'Yeah. Not happening, Joy.'

She bowed her head, an embarrassed smile on her face. 'Well, I asked.'

He watched her leave, and Rowan said, 'Who's Marie?'

North looked down at her, his eyes dead. 'No one,' he said.

CHAPTER 44

Monday morning briefing

Warman addressed the twenty-five personnel present.

'The investigation into surplus deaths on Fernleigh is now officially an inquiry into a *series* of *unlawful* deaths.' She waited for the murmurs to die down before introducing DI Bradley, a raw-boned man in his early thirties with mouse-brown hair and hands like shovels. His small grey eyes, hooded by prominent brows, gave him a permanently pissed-off expression. Bradley would take the lead day to day, and he would have a detective sergeant to assist. The DS was on his way back from a training exercise and would join them by mid-afternoon. DCI Warman was to have oversight as Senior Investigating Officer.

'Craig Breidon was selling drugs for Capstick shortly before he died, but his death has yet to be fully reviewed and will remain a suicide until that review is complete,' Warman went on. 'However, we do now have two confirmed murders of individuals involved in drug supply and dealing on the estate: Damian Novak, who worked for the Lang crew, and Thomas Capstick, alias "Stickman" who led "the Stoners".'

'Gang-related,' a short, fair-haired woman suggested. 'A tussle between Stickman and the Langs?'

'It's possible,' Warman said, pausing to allow other suggestions.

'He fell eight floors,' one new face said, skimming his notes. 'And there's no report of an effigy. Couldn't he have just got wasted and fell?'

Warman gave a brief list of the injuries Stickman had sustained, and then read from the pathologist's preliminary examination. 'Multiple injuries consistent with being struck with a hammer. Boot marks on the dead man's torso and buttocks,' she said. 'Somebody stamped on Thomas Capstick, breaking his legs, arms, ribs, pelvis and spine. Then threw him over the balcony.'

After a shocked silence, she carried on. 'DC Rowan has done excellent work discovering the Novak murder scene, which led to us reclassifying these deaths as murders.'

Rowan's face burned so hot she felt she might self-combust, but she managed a nod of acknowledgement.

'A door-to-door canvass of Hartsfern Tower will begin today,' Warman said.

DI Bradley spoke up. 'I'll put a team on the facing block, as well.' He had a voice to go with his physique and half the room jumped in their seats at his first utterance.

As the meeting broke up, a few of the original team congratulated Rowan and she managed to smile her thanks.

Ian Chan sidled up to her on the stairwell. 'What's up with you? I'd be doing stage bows if old warhorse had paid me a compliment like that.'

'Not everyone likes being the centre of attention, Ian,' she said.

'You wanna get on, get noticed,' he said enigmatically.

'I didn't see you there yesterday,' she said, changing the subject.

'I was helping to process the pedestrian crossing Thursday, remember?' He raised his hands and wiggled his fingers. 'Cross-contamination risk. I've been directing operations from a distance.'

'Cassie!'

Rowan stopped at the turn of the stairs, hearing Jackie Dawson's voice, but Chan carried on down, shouting 'Later, sweetheart!' over his shoulder.

'Hi, Jackie. I didn't see you last night.' Rowan said.

Dawson grimaced. 'I was on crowd control,'

'And I thought I was at the gory end of things,' Rowan said with a smile.

They walked on, but Dawson seemed hesitant to speak until they were outside; even then, she drew Rowan apart from the rest.

'There's someone you should speak to,' she said quietly. 'It's Stickman's neighbour. She won't come into the police station, and she won't talk to anyone but you.'

Rowan had been assigned to help with the canvass at the tower block where Stickman had died, so she didn't feel too guilty about returning to Fernleigh without talking to DI Bradley first.

They knocked at the flat across the hallway from Stickman's and Rowan recognized the occupant as the woman who'd spoken to Jim North at the murder scene. 'Joy, isn't it?' Rowan said.

'That's right.' The woman was plump and sweet-faced, and looked to be in her early fifties. Dawson said she'd wait outside, and Rowan followed Joy through to the sitting room.

'Marie, Detective Rowan's here,' Joy said. 'This is Marie Elliott, Detective.'

Marie must be a similar age to her neighbour, but her face was grey and unmistakably lined with drug addiction, want and fear. Painfully thin, she sat in an armchair that seemed to swamp her.

She reached up and tucked an iron-grey strand of hair behind her ear. The rest was pulled back off her face in a tight ponytail, but fine wisps escaped over her ears and at the crown of her head, and she constantly fussed with it.

'You wanted to speak to me, Marie?' Rowan asked.

The woman stared at her friend's meticulously vacuumed carpet.

'She's been here with me since it happened,' Joy explained. 'Haven't you, luv?' she added, raising her voice as you might to an invalid or deaf person.

Marie blinked as if some awful scene was playing out on the carpet at her feet.

Rowan went to the small dining table tucked against one wall and, raising her eyebrows to ask permission, took a chair and sat opposite Marie.

'Did you hear what happened, Marie?' she asked gently.

Marie's eyes widened momentarily, and her head jerked in an involuntary nod.

'Can you tell me about it?'

The woman's gaze darted to her friend, and Joy smiled encouragement.

'Take your time,' Rowan said.

Slowly, painfully, Marie began. 'Stickman lives in the corner flat,' she began, in a Northern Irish accent. 'I'm right next door, so I hear everything that goes on in there. The people in the flat below must hear something, but they've never let on.' She tilted her head. 'Best not to complain, y'know?'

Rowan nodded.

'Three bloody hours he was playing that rap song. When he shut it off, I thought he was going out — he did that all the time — played that awful row till you think you'll go out of your mind, then *bang!* — there's the door slamming, and off he goes.

'But it was the knock — he heard the knock.' She angled her head as though listening. 'Then it came again. Oh . . .' She covered her ears with her hands. 'Like a summons from hell.

'Stickman started shouting — terrible foul-mouthed profanities — what he wasn't going to do if he opened the door.' She glanced at Rowan confidingly and lowered her voice to a whisper. 'Yon feller has this baseball bat, see. Steel-tipped. I've seen blood on it more than once.' She turned huge, bloodshot eyes on Rowan. 'Don't tell him I told you.'

'No, of course not.' Rowan glanced at Joy. Surely she knew that Stickman was dead? Joy pressed her lips together and shook her head. Marie had been told and had forgotten, she assumed.

'The glass shattered, and I heard him scream.' She gazed up at Joy in wonder. 'Stickman was terrified! I hear two, three, four thuds. Then nothing for — I don't know — a minute? And I'm holding my breath, praying he won't come for me.'

She seemed entirely lost in her nightmare for a few moments, and Rowan gently called her back. 'What then, Marie?'

'He starts kicking him.' She pointed uncertainly in the direction of Stickman's flat, as though she was afraid to say the drug dealer's name. 'Jumping on him, just like the other day. Then he laughs.' She shuddered, raising a trembling hand as if to ward off the sound. 'My heart's beating so bad, I think it's gonna burst out of me.' She clutched at her narrow chest.

'After a little bit, I hear a "*shh-shh-shh*" — he's dragging Stickman's body across the floor.'

'How did you know it was a body?'

'How else d'you think that bastard ended up on the concrete eight floors down?'

'Did you see who did this?' Rowan asked, shocked by the woman's cold pragmatism.

'I seen him, true enough.'

'Can you describe him?'

'I can do better than that — I can name him.'

Rowan waited with quiet attention and Marie muttered something.

'I'm sorry,' Rowan said. 'What did you say?'

'The Grim Reaper, so it was.'

'The . . . ?'

'Aye, it was him right enough. Long black cloak, and that great scythe for reaping the souls. He smote the door with his staff and claimed his blackened soul.'

The Biblical language as much as the wild gleam in her eyes told Rowan that the woman was unhinged.

'Marie—' Rowan began, but Marie raised one thin finger.

'Now don't you look at me like that,' she scolded. 'I'm not *mental* — I know what I saw. And you tell me, if you know so much — who else would have the courage to pound on Stickman's door until he got an answer? Who else would shatter his window and force his way in? Who could make Stickman cry out in fear and pain, but Death Himself?'

To avoid answering the question Rowan said, 'So you came across to Joy?'

'I did *not*. I couldn't move — stayed right where I was till *she* found me.'

'You were in your flat when the police knocked at your door?'

'I was there thirty-odd years — nobody came,' she said angrily. 'Youse lot are years too late. *Years* too late . . .' She seemed to drift off, her eyes lowered again to examine the carpet.

'I've got a key,' Joy explained. 'I come over when the forensics people went. She was on the floor by the front door.' The concerned look on her kindly face said that Marie must have been there all night. 'Brung you here, didn't I, luv?'

Rowan thought back through Marie's rambling narrative. 'This was the *second* time Stickman was attacked?'

Marie's head came up and she stared wildly from Joy to Rowan as if she didn't know who they were.

'You said he was kicking and jumping on him, like he did the other day,' Rowan prompted.

'Not *him*, the *other* one,' Marie shouted. 'You're not *listening*.'

'I'm trying to understand,' Rowan said, softly, 'but I'm confused.'

Marie gave her a scornful look. After taking a few breaths, she began again, summoning her meagre reserves of dignity. 'It was Stickman the other day. And I heard it

283

— that exact same sound — the cracking of bones. Only he done it to himself.'

Rowan was beginning to understand. 'Did you see Stickman doing this?'

'No. He doesn't like to think you're spying on him. But I heard it, all right. It was a warning, and he did not heed.'

As Joy led the way to the front door, Rowan asked if she needed help from social services.

'I'll call her social worker,' Joy said. 'But I think she'll be fine, now.'

A sudden cry from the sitting room made them all turn to the door. Marie appeared, looking anxious and shy.

'I forgot . . . I wanted to ask . . . How's Jim?'

'Jim?' Rowan remembered the brief conversation between Joy and the martial-arts expert the previous night. 'Jim North? What do you know about him?'

'More than he'll admit,' she said with a sly look on her face. 'And a lot more than he'll ever know. You can tell him I said that.'

Rowan furrowed her brow in question.

Marie drew herself to her full height. 'I'm his mother.'

CHAPTER 45

Rowan went looking for DI Bradley but couldn't find him. Knowing she'd pushed her luck as far as she dared in the last few days, she took what she knew to DCI Warman, to avoid accusations of having flouted authority.

'There *was* an effigy,' she burst out as soon as she was through the door.

'I'm sorry?' Surrounded by paperwork, Warman looked exhausted.

'The Stickman — Capstick — he had an effigy.'

Warman set down the pen she'd been using to annotate the documents, and Rowan had a sudden, clear image of her as an academic, or a teacher, marking end-of-term papers.

'Have you spoken to your line manager?' Warman asked severely.

'I can't find DI Bradley, ma'am; he's not on Fernleigh, and he's not in the MIR.'

'Very well. But please begin at the *beginning*, Cassie,' she pleaded with a weary sigh.

Rowan talked her boss through the events of the last two hours, from Jackie's initial approach to Marie Elliott telling her she'd heard Stickman 'kicking and jumping on him, just like the other day.'

'It sounds like your witness has a tenuous grasp of reality,' Warman said.

'She was clear enough that it was Stickman did the kicking and jumping,' Rowan countered. 'She said she heard the crack as he stamped on it.'

'But she doesn't sound very clear about what "it" was that he was stamping on,' Warman chided.

'Maybe, but where's the harm in asking around, seeing if anyone saw an effigy?'

Warman shook her head. 'As far as the effigies are concerned at this point, the residents will tell you whatever you want to hear.'

'A search, then,' Rowan said with rising desperation. 'Wheelie bins, bin sheds, anywhere it might have been hidden.'

Warman pierced her with a look. 'Are you volunteering?'

'If that's what it takes,' Rowan said, jutting her chin out. 'I'll start around Stickman's tower block and spiral out from there — *somebody* must have seen something.'

Warman watched her steadily, tapping the papers in front of her with a forefinger. After an uncomfortable half-minute, she picked up her pen again and made a note on a reporter's notepad.

'All right. The superintendent has allowed us some extra volunteers — I'll allocate two to you.'

'They'll take a lot of stick from the residents, boss,' Rowan said doubtfully. 'I'd rather have a couple of fully trained bobbies.'

Warman shook her head. 'The shooting in town needs every fully trained officer available.'

'And we don't?' Rowan asked. 'A scumbag from Fernleigh stamped to death and chucked twenty-odd metres down from his flat isn't high profile enough, I suppose.'

'Politics and policing,' Warman said implacably. 'They're inextricable — *inescapable* — and the sooner you accept that, the better.'

It wasn't Warman's fault, but Rowan felt fit to explode, and after a moment her boss sighed, adding, 'Take it from someone who knows — it's pointless expending precious energy on things you can't change, Cassie.'

She's right . . . she's right, Rowan thought. *I bloody hate it when she's right.* At last, she lowered her shoulders in a conscious release of tension and exhaled. 'Yes, boss.'

Warman gave a curt nod.

'Couple more things, though,' Rowan said. 'Mrs Elliott reverted to her family name after she divorced. Her married name was North.'

Warman's eyebrows twitched. 'Any relation to the fellow who teaches martial arts on Fernleigh?'

'She's Jim North's mother,' Rowan said.

'Now, that's an interesting coincidence.'

'I thought so, too,' Rowan said. 'I asked him about his mother when he opened up about his brother's overdose, and he implied that she was dead. Plus he blew me off when I asked which gang his brother was involved in, but I just checked with Jackie Dawson, and she says he'd been working for Stickman up to the time of his death.'

'Why was he so evasive?' Warman murmured in a musing tone.

'I'm about to find out,' Rowan said, not wanting to frame it as a request for permission.

But her boss said, 'Good,' and Rowan's heart soared.

'Cassie?'

Rowan was on her way out the door, but she turned back and Warman threw her one of her steely looks. 'Don't be too gentle.'

CHAPTER 46

Rowan threw the binbag she'd just checked over the top of the wheelie bin she'd been searching for the past half-hour.

A yelp of surprise, then, 'Cassie — is that you?'

Rowan peered over the top. Jackie Dawson was immaculately turned out, as usual; cap on straight, the coils of her dark hair neatly twisted into a bun at the nape of her neck.

Rowan was suited up in Tyvek overalls, gloves and overshoes she'd scrounged from Ian Chan. The overalls were smeared and the stink of refuse clung to her. The drizzle hadn't stopped since the early hours, and the overhang at Brackenhill Tower provided minimal shelter.

'Remind me never to volunteer for anything again,' she said. 'I mean ever.'

Climbing over the container, she dropped to the wet concrete and Dawson stepped back with a subdued, 'Oh!'

Rowan reloaded the bags she'd tossed out, then unzipped her overalls and rolled it down, taking care not to smear her clothes with gunk. Stepping out of her overshoes, she saw that Dawson was carrying a travel mug and eyed it jealously.

'Oh!' Dawson exclaimed again. 'This is for you.'

'You are — no exaggeration — the best,' Rowan said, peeling back the gloves, tucking one inside the other to avoid touching the filth clinging to them. 'Problem is, I should have a big biohazard sign stamped on my forehead right now.'

'No worries.' Dawson dipped into her pocket and took out a packet of antibacterial wipes, handing one to Rowan between the tips of one finger and thumb, and Rowan laughed.

'You're a bloody marvel, Jackie Dawson.'

Dawson raised one shoulder, accepting the compliment as a given. 'By the way, Jim North is looking for you.'

'Well, it's about time. Normally I can't walk ten steps without tripping over him, but just when I want him, he becomes the Invisible Man.' Rowan edged away from the dumpster before taking her first sip of coffee. 'Oh, God, that's good . . . I tried his work; he was in a meeting. I rang his mobile — three times — left messages. Rang his office again an hour ago — he's off-site.'

'Well, he's looking for you now.' There was a hint of defensiveness in Dawson's tone and Rowan peered down at her friend.

'Are you and Jim North—?'

'What? No!' The denial was a tad too vehement, and guilty colour crept into the PCSO's face.

Rowan smiled, retrieving her phone and zapping North a text. 'Well, now he knows where to find me.' She took another sip of the sublime drink. 'This is fabulous — what did you put in it?'

'Mum's secret spice recipe,' Dawson said, beaming.

Rowan looked around her. Mid-afternoon, all was quiet, the absentee schoolkids who had been so troublesome the first week having been rounded up and herded into school. She'd worked methodically from block to block with her two special constables, who were currently team-tagging over on Braunswood, the third tower block. *Where to, now?*

She made a decision and took off in the direction she'd come.

'Where are you going?' Dawson asked, catching her up.

'I just remembered — the caretaker on Stickman's block was supposed to get back to me — another one ignoring my calls,' she added with a sly glance at Dawson.

'Speaking of which,' Jackie said primly. 'How's Jim going to know where to find you?'

'He's a big boy. I'm sure he'll find his—' Rowan's eye snagged on something and she stopped abruptly. A photo-copied image of the boggart mask was stuck to a lamppost.

'They started appearing at lunchtime,' Dawson said, frowning.

'Well, the cheeky sods must have done this while I was in the dumpster, cos it wasn't here when I arrived. Brackenhill's Lang territory, isn't it?'

'I guess the whole estate is, now that Stickman's gone,' Dawson said glumly. 'But, yeah — they operate out of this block, and Justin's mum lives here.'

'D'you reckon the community's sending them a message?'

Dawson brightened. 'It's not before time.'

They moved on. At Hartsfern Tower where Stickman had lived and died, every post, pillar, and door on the ground floor was plastered with the image.

'D'you think it's a warning?' Dawson asked.

'To the gangs? "Watch out, you could be next" kind of thing?'

Dawson gave a stiff nod and Rowan cursed softly. 'Like it isn't enough having one vigilante on the loose . . .' She peeled one of the printouts from a door marked RESTRICTED AREA — *Maintenance Staff Only*; the glue was still wet. A dull scraping sound inside held her attention and she tried the door; it was unlocked. A single old-style incandescent light bulb lit the area immediately ahead, but beyond it was a brownish gloom.

'Can I borrow your torch?' Rowan asked.

Dawson produced it in a second, and Rowan handed the cup and photocopied sheet to the PCSO and took a Casco baton from her own trouser pocket. 'Stay here and be ready to call for backup,' she said softly.

She propped open the door with a gallon bottle of disinfectant and called, 'Police — show yourself!'

No response. The scraping sound came again and she turned towards it, clicking on the torchlight. The space opened up. Stacked with boxes, buckets and mops, as well as tubs of graffiti remover and drums of heavy-duty detergent, it had a peculiar smell of chemicals and mould. Shining the beam both ways, Rowan saw that the area to the right ended in a concrete wall; to the left, there was a deeper darkness which she judged to be an extension of the storage space. An odd greyish glimmer flickered in that direction, there one moment, vanished the next, like phantom marsh lights.

Rowan called again. No answer. With a glance over her shoulder to Dawson, she went on, turning left some fifteen feet inside the store. Her foot caught something on the floor, sending it skittering into the darkness and, stomach prickling, Rowan ventured further. Boxes were piled at various heights either side of her, and the lights seemed to be emanating from behind a large stack twenty feet away. She deployed her baton, holding it over her shoulder, tight to her body, ready to strike shoulder, knee, ankle if necessary.

A massive shadow suddenly appeared, monstrously hunched, and she identified herself a third time, yelling as loud as she could. It shrank, and suddenly vanished. Rowan whipped around the end of the narrow corridor of boxes and was suddenly blinded.

'Police!' she roared.

An answering shriek and clatter as the source of the light dropped a brush and shovel.

'Turn that bloody light off!' Rowan shouted.

Fumbling, the hooded man raised his hand to his forehead, and she was blinded a second time, blinking away green splodges from her flooded retinas.

'Stay where you are!' she yelled.

'What the fuck d'you think you're doing?' the man demanded.

'Who *are* you?' she countered. 'Identify yourself.'

'Billy Williams — I work here. More to the point, who are *you*?'

'I *told* you — police.'

He raised a hand and she tensed, but he was only reaching for the hood of his jacket. He pulled it down, revealing headphones. 'Didn't hear you, did I?'

Rowan released a breath in a woosh. 'Well, why the hell are you skulking about in the dark?'

'I'm not skulking, I'm *improvising*,' he argued. 'The lights down this end haven't worked in six months. Can't get the council out to sort it.'

'I've been trying to reach you for hours,' Rowan said, still on the defensive. 'Don't you ever check your phone?'

'Can't get a signal down here.' He eyed her up and down. 'I suppose you've come about the thing have you?'

'The *thing*?'

'Get that light outa me face and point it over there, you'll see.'

Rowan turned the torch beam in the direction he'd pointed and felt a shock from the base of her skull to her heels. An evil red face smiled malevolently down from a clutter of boxes in one corner. She recognized the red trainers Stickman had been wearing as he lay dead on the courtyard of the block. The rest of the effigy was a jumble of clothing and splintered wood. Marie must have heard Stickman pounding the effigy to sawdust: he really had done it to himself.

CHAPTER 47

Rowan had released the special constables from dumpster duty and was standing outside Hartsfern Tower, waiting for a CSI to come and remove the effigy when, true to form, Jim North showed up.

'Now is not a good time, Jim,' she said.

'You're the one who asked to see *me*.'

'Three hours ago, yes. But something's come up since then.'

He glanced past her to the caretaker's store. 'Stickman's effigy?'

'Why would you think that?'

'You've been asking all over about it since this morning. But let's call it a wild guess.' His attitude was so at odds with the way he'd been on Friday night that he might be a different man altogether.

What the hell, she thought. *He doesn't look ready to walk away anytime soon, you might as well ask.* 'I spoke to your mum earlier. You know, Marie — who you said was nobody when I asked about her last night.'

Dawson had been standing by, looking awkward, but now she seemed shocked.

North glanced at the PCSO and Rowan saw a twinge of uncertainty in his face. 'Look, can we take this somewhere else?'

Rowan shrugged. 'You wanted to talk — let's talk. I mean, why would you hide that from me?'

'I didn't *hide* anything. My private life is none of your business.'

'Don't bullshit me, Jim. You failed to mention that your mum and your brother lived next door to Thomas Capstick, aka Stickman, recently deceased — who just *happens* to be Lang's closest rival. *You* were his neighbour as well, at least till you went into the military. That makes it my business.'

'I haven't seen Marie since Ben died, all right?' he said.

'Don't you care that she's been terrorized by that thug for *years*?'

'You don't know the first thing about me or my mother.' His eyes, usually so lively, seemed flat and devoid of emotion, and Rowan felt that she was seeing him clearly for the first time.

'No,' she said. 'I don't suppose I do.'

Dawson watched open-mouthed as he stalked off. 'I can't believe he just left his mum to that wolf,' she said. 'I mean, you wouldn't think it, would you? The way he is with the kids, it's like he's—'

'A different person,' Rowan murmured. Staring after North, she became aware of Dawson wanting to say more. 'What?'

'Why didn't you tell me about his mum?' Dawson asked.

'Because I got to wondering how he always seems to know where I am, plus Warman had a dig at me about how things always seem to get out about the investigation.' She left the rest unsaid.

'You think I—? Ah, come on, Cassie. How could you . . .' She trailed off, biting her lip, and Rowan knew she'd been right.

'I'm not saying you did it for any shady motive — just the opposite — Jim North's been a kind of guardian angel since he started working with the kids, and you've come to trust him — I get that. You're doing a job most of us — including me — would find impossible, and he supports you. You're a part of this community — an important part. But, Jackie — you've got to be a little bit *apart from* it, when it comes to police business, okay? People lie all the time, hide their motives — sometimes for good reasons, sometimes bad. And when you tell people things that should be kept confidential, you don't know who else might get hold of that information and use it against you — against the inquiry.'

Dawson placed the flat of her palm to her forehead. 'I'm such an idiot . . .' She turned her fearful gaze on Rowan. 'Are you gonna report me?'

'No,' Rowan said, and the PCSO's eyes filled with tears of gratitude. 'But no more tip-offs, okay? No more "quiet words" with anyone outside of the investigation.'

Jackie gulped, nodded with such vehemence that tears spilled onto her cheeks.

A plain white CSU van turned into the courtyard at that moment.

'I hope you've got a pack of Kleenex tucked away in one of those pockets, Mary Poppins,' Rowan joked., "Cos you can't be seen bawling your eyes out on duty — you'll *never* live it down.'

With a watery laugh, Jackie magically produced a tissue and turned her back to dab away her tears.

CHAPTER 48

Monday evening debrief

DI Bradley, DCI Warman and Ian Chan stood at the front of the room. Ian's presence meant that they had forensic news, and Rowan offered a prayer to the gods of fate that it was something useful from the effigy. The enhanced team was becoming familiar to her, but she was surprised to see that Jackie Dawson wasn't among them.

After conferring with Warman, Bradley called the meeting to order. 'Most of you will know by now that an effigy of our latest victim, Thomas Capstick, has been found,' he bellowed. 'Cassie?'

Rowan said, 'The block manager, Mr Bill Williams — so good they named him twice — found the mangled effigy at the base of Hartsfern Tower three or four days ago. He can't be exact. He stuck it in his storage cupboard, ready to dump with the rest of the rubbish when the binnies came round — says he "didn't think" to come forward with it. But his estimate tallies with a witness statement from Mrs Elliott, Capstick's next-door neighbour. She heard Capstick pounding something in the communal area on the eighth floor of Hartsfern last Tuesday. From her description, it sounds like it was the effigy.'

'Ian?' Bradley said.

Chan cast an image to the screen. The effigy was a passable match to Thomas 'Stickman' Capstick. It was also extensively boot-marked.

'You're right, Cassie,' Chan said. 'It was Capstick who put the boot in on the effigy. The shoeprints on the dummy match his Nike trainers.'

'So the killer didn't wait seven days then.'

'No,' Chan said. 'If Mrs Elliott's right, it's only five days between the effigy and Capstick's murder.' He waited a moment for the implications of that to sink in before adding, 'The body of this effigy is made from a cheap polycotton mix.'

Mrs Tetting was right about that, Rowan thought.

'The "bones" are constructed from balsa wood,' Chan went on. 'It's lightweight and easy to carve and drill — and the whole thing is stuffed with a bog-standard polyester filling used widely by crafters.'

'Used widely' was not an encouraging term, forensically.

'The caretaker dumped what was left of it in amongst half-chewed boxes, detergent, rat poison, brushes and mops, scrubbing brushes and paint remover. Which has really messed up the trace,' he went on. 'And as if that wasn't enough, apparently he'd discovered rat damage in the store and as he moved a bag of rock salt it split, scattering twenty kilos of the stuff over the floor. He was brushing up when Cassie found him and told him to stop. So what little we do have is contaminated with concrete dust, salt, shredded cardboard and rat faeces — as well as fibres and hairs from Mr Williams's clothing.'

A soft groan went around the assembly.

'*However*, we *did* get fibres from the *inner* layers of clothing, which *might* be useful — once we have a suspect for comparison. And it'll take longer, but we might also get DNA from the stitching. The most significant evidence we collected,' he allowed a theatrical pause while he clicked through to the next image, 'are these flakes of paint. Which are a match to the van that killed Damian Novak.'

A murmur of excitement went up.

'And you've guessed the punchline,' he said, flashing a smile. 'This *unequivocally* links this effigy to the van that killed Damian — *ergo*, the effigies are linked to the murders, and the murders are linked to each other.'

'Finch,' DI Bradley barked, and Rowan saw Finch's shoulders twitch at the volume of the summons. 'Any progress identifying the van?'

'No, boss.'

Bradley turned to Warman. 'Should we be thinking about posting a description?'

Warman looked doubtful. 'We have journalists and podcasters whipping up hysteria as it is,' she said. 'The last thing we need is for an innocent to be targeted just because they happen to drive a white van. My advice would be to hold back for now.'

Bradley gave a reluctant nod and Warman added, 'But I'll ask the Press Office to draft a statement that we're looking for someone who is targeting criminals involved in the supply and sale of drugs on the Fernleigh estate.'

Turning again to Chan she asked, 'Anything from the pathologist on the weapons used?'

'Preliminary only,' Chan said. 'Damage to the bricks around the door are probably caused by a hammer, such as a large claw- or a ball peen hammer. The injuries to Capstick's body are layered: beating, stamping, plus damage from the fall. Yes, he was alive when he fell — barely, but even so . . . Most of the primary injuries were caused by a regular cylindrical object, smooth, with rounded edges—'

'Like a staff?' Rowan asked.

'Yes, that would work,' Chan said. 'Got something in mind?'

'Mrs Elliott said the attacker looked like the Grim Reaper,' Rowan said. 'Long black cloak, hood, and a staff of some kind.'

'It's Gandalf from *Lord of the Rings*!' some comedian exclaimed. 'We've got him bang to rights.'

Rowan barely heard the laughter that provoked. She was picturing the hooded man she'd seen melting into the shadows at Brackenhill Tower the day Lukas Novak had rung, begging for her help.

* * *

Jackie Dawson arrived, buzzing with excitement, just as the debrief was disbanding.

'Where've you been?' Rowan asked. 'You missed all the fun.'

They headed down to the corridor to the MIR and Rowan updated Dawson on the forensic evidence.

'So, now that we've got an effigy, we've a real chance of identifying who's been making them?' Dawson said, only just containing her glee.

'In theory,' Rowan said. 'Why?'

They had reached Rowan's desk. Dawson placed a carrier bag on top of the litter of papers and took out a plastic click-seal bag containing a sample of creamy-white material.

'This is what the Fernleigh Crafters are using to make scarecrows for the primary-school display.'

'It looks like the stuff used in the effigies all right,' Rowan said, tilting the bag to get the best angle under the garish strip lights. 'Where'd you get it?'

'You told us that Mrs Tetting thought the person who's making the effigies uses a cheap polycotton alternative to calico,' Dawson said. 'But when you showed the same images to the Fernleigh Crafters, they didn't even comment on it. So I thought *maybe* that's because it didn't seem out of the ordinary to them.'

'Because they use the same material,' Rowan said. 'Good thinking.'

Dawson's dark eyes sparkled with pleasure. 'And now we've actually got the Stickman effigy, I was thinking Ian could make a direct comparison.'

Rowan's brow furrowed. 'You mean to this?'

Dawson nodded eagerly.

'Uh, there might be a slight problem with that,' Rowan said. 'See, if you lifted the stuff from the crafters' store cupboard, it'd be inadmissible as evidence — obtained without a warrant.'

'Didn't I say why I was late?' Dawson said with a coy smile. 'The crafters were at the hub today, and I thought I'd stick around and help with the tidy up. Got this out of a bin — I asked if anyone minded me taking it — no one did.'

Rowan nudged her. 'Jackie Dawson, you sly fox . . .'

CHAPTER 49

Rowan placed a bottle of Peroni on the table in front of Dawson and took a swig of her own before taking a seat. It had been a while since she'd dropped in at the Baltic Fleet, but it still had the old, relaxed vibe, and she immediately felt at home. She'd gone with the PCSO to show moral support as she made her case for lifting the fabric sample, and, in fairness, DCI Warman had been receptive.

But having logged the evidence with the newly appointed exhibits officer, Dawson seemed all of a jangle, and the finger-tapping habit, which Rowan guessed was a self-calming measure, didn't seem to be working. So she'd invited her for a swift half.

'It's nice of you to do this,' Dawson said. 'I know you've got loads better to do.'

'Nah,' Rowan said. 'You're doing me a favour.' She scratched her nose, oddly embarrassed at being so open about her own predicament. 'It's Neil's first day on the new regime at school. If I go home too early, he'll think I'm checking up on him; if I go too late, he'll think I don't care. A quick bevvy is the perfect time-filler.' They clinked bottles and for the next ten minutes, they chatted about family and TV and kept well clear of work.

Then Rowan saw a familiar tall figure at the bar. 'Bloody hell . . .' She sighed.

Dawson turned just as Rowan began to say, 'Don't turn around.'

A moment later, Jim North was at their side, Dawson all smiles, Rowan less so — wondering disloyally if Dawson had set up the 'chance' meeting.

Inevitably, the conversation got around to the investigation. Rowan wasn't about to share any secrets, and Dawson was heroically on her guard, but he pushed hard, even bringing up the New York 'Guardian Angels'.

'As far as I'm aware, they don't go around whacking people,' Rowan said. 'This killer isn't protecting anyone — he's executing summary justice.'

'He's protecting a whole community,' North came back, with a quick shake of his head.

'How d'you work that one out?'

'He's showing ordinary, decent folks on Fernleigh that the criminals are a minority — and they're not invincible.'

'By killing them?' She stifled a laugh. 'That's kind of extreme, isn't it? I mean, who does that?' She was being sarcastic, but he replied as if she was in earnest.

'My guess — someone who's scared — desperate, even.'

'You're saying a *scared* person forced his way into Thomas Capstick's flat — shattered his bones because he was *desperate*?'

This time, he responded to her flippant tone with a frown.

'Fear is no obstacle if you can control it,' North said. 'Then all you need is clear intent and focus.'

'If that were true, the city-centre pubs and bars would be ankle-high in blood from all the raging drunks making good on their "clear intent" to cripple any poor sod who looks at them sideways.'

'Since when was a drunk *clear* about anything?' North shot back. 'Since when was anyone in a rage *focused*?'

'I'm confused. Now you're saying you think this guy's a psychopath, calmly executing the criminals on the estate?'

He shook his head. 'You don't need to be a psychopath to kill.'

He seemed offended by the suggestion, and Rowan wondered what his role was during his army days.

'So murder is about focus?' she said, deliberately misunderstanding. 'Good to know.'

'I didn't say "murder".' There was an angry rasp in his voice, now, and she noticed Dawson glancing from her to North.

Rowan arched an eyebrow. 'It's hard to see what else you could mean. We aren't in a war zone, Jim.'

'Tell that to the people who live with fear every day on that estate,' he said.

She stared at him. 'This guy psychologically tortures his victims for days before he ever lays a finger on them. And when he abducts them, they know exactly how they're going to die. It's horrible.'

'The likes of Stickman and Lang tore the heart out of what used to be a decent community. Isn't *that* horrible?'

'Of course,' Rowan said. 'And in an ideal world, they would have been locked up for it. But we did away with an eye for an eye in British law some time ago.'

He laughed. '*British law* didn't bring Lang, or Damian — any of them to book, did it? Look around you, Cassie. There *is no law* on Fernleigh.'

'Okay,' she said. 'I'm tired. I'm going home.'

'Wait,' he said. 'I'm sorry. But you've got to admit, whoever's doing this has helped people to stand up to the thugs on their streets.'

She ran her tongue over her teeth before saying, 'Did you ever stop to think that your Ben could be one of this "Guardian Angel's" victims?'

He snapped upright, as if she'd slapped him, and Dawson made a murmur of protest.

'Ben OD'd,' North said through gritted teeth. 'And *he* didn't go around threatening people.'

She stared back at him, coldly and purposefully draining her eyes of emotion, her muscles of tension, her soul of guilt. 'Yeah, well, neither did Craig Breidon. He was trying to get out of the drugs racket. And as I recall, *he* worked for Stickman, just like your Ben.'

He stood, shoving back his stool. The suddenness of the movement, and the loud scraping of wood on tile, drew attention, and, for a second, Rowan experienced a pang of fear, but she forced it down, meeting his eyes.

'Enjoy your drinks,' he said, plucking his beer bottle from the table and carrying it away to a far corner of the bar.

CHAPTER 50

Tuesday morning briefing

Rowan had barely slept. Listening to Jim North advocating for the vigilante who had taken at least two lives had made her re-examine every interaction she'd had with the man since they'd first met.

Could North be angry enough to go after criminals like Capstick and Lang who peddled drugs? Perhaps even men like Tetting, who bought the drugs that had wrecked his community? North was a trained soldier — he might even have experience in urban combat. He had all the right skills, the strength — and the coolness of purpose, the — what did he call it? *The clear intent and focus.*

Rowan was roused from her half-dream by an image on the projector screen. An online news page with photographs of Damian Novak and Thomas Capstick side by side under the headline *LIVERPOOL'S DOPPELGÄNGER MURDERS.*

'A podcast is covering the case under the title, "The Doppelganger Killer",' Warman was saying.

Oh, hell . . .

'Their theory,' Warman went on, 'is that a vigilante killer is handing out justice on the Fernleigh estate, and that "the police" are calling him the Doppelganger Killer. I hardly need to tell you that glorifying these murders could put ideas into the heads of other beleaguered communities. And the last thing we need in Liverpool right now is a spate of copycat killings — it'd be carnage.'

She stopped, casting a steely eye over every person in the room. 'Can anyone shed any light on this doppelganger business?'

Rowan swallowed hard. 'Alan Palmer approached me when the whole voodoo-doll thing blew up a few days ago,' she said, hoping she didn't sound too strangulated.

'Palmer — the psychotherapist?'

Rowan nodded, feeling all eyes on her. 'He said he thought the effigies were a threat, but more like doppel-gangers than voodoo dolls. Apparently voodoo relies on a belief in dark magic to make victims sick — but a doppel-ganger is traditionally seen as an omen of death.'

'Enlightening, if unsolicited,' Warman said with a sniff. 'Well, I don't suppose Mr Palmer would approach the media with his insights.' Her diction was dangerously precise. 'So I would very much like to know how this podcaster got hold of the notion of a doppelganger, and who their police source might be.'

'The only other person I discussed it with was the librar-ian in Birkenshore village.' Rowan spoke into a gathering silence. 'She's a historian and the village's folklorist. I was there to find out about the boggart masks, and I asked for some insight into doppelgangers.'

'Was she helpful?' The words were bland enough, but Warman's tone was like the quiet before a thunderclap.

'She recommended some stories on the subject,' Rowan mumbled.

Warman waited for the sniggers to die down before ask-ing, 'Do you have *any* idea of the potential damage you've done?' She was working herself into a towering rage, and Rowan spoke again before the storm broke.

'With respect, boss, I was exploring possibilities, asking questions. At that point, all we had were the effigies and some excess deaths on Fernleigh — we didn't even confirm that Damian's death was a murder till much later that day. I didn't expect to be quoted out of context, but Ms Fabian is a bit of a mischief-maker. And talking of context, I didn't mention doppelgangers *at all* on Fernleigh.' An uncomfortable thought rose to the top of her mind, and, although she racked her brains, she couldn't recall if she'd said anything to Jackie Dawson.

Warman kept her gaze on Rowan for a few seconds longer. Finally, her brow cleared and she said, 'Where is PCSO Dawson?'

Not for the first time, Rowan had the disturbing notion that the DCI had plucked the thought right out of her head.

She cleared her throat. 'She had something to do on Fernleigh — said it couldn't wait.' It was true that Dawson had texted that she couldn't be at the morning briefing, although Rowan suspected that the reason for her absence was more directly linked to her confrontation with North the night before.

'Pity,' Warman said. 'I wanted her to hear this.'

She nodded to Chan and he explained for the rest that Dawson had brought in a sample of material from the Fernleigh hub after Monday night's debrief. 'It's a visual match to the Stickman effigy,' he said. 'But full mass spec will be delayed — I *might* have it ready for you sometime tomorrow.'

DI Bradley took over. 'Right, I want a list of everyone who uses the community hub, including the names and addresses of the crafting group.'

'I can give you the crafters' details now,' Rowan said. 'Gareth Jessop will have an idea of the rest, although people come and go as they please — it's a fairly informal set up — so he won't necessarily be able to hand over a list of members.'

'Do what you can.' Bradley was about to move on when Rowan spoke again.

'But the crafters aren't viable suspects, surely?'

'Because?'

'According to those who know, the level of crafting in the effigies is basic, well below their standards. Plus, the crafters are all women, and this has to be a man, doesn't it?'

'Does it?'

'Craig Breidon was so drugged up he'd have needed help to walk — and the lifts were out of order the night he died, so that means he must have been helped up ten flights of stairs,' she began. 'Whoever moved Damian Novak had to carry him twenty or thirty metres down a steep embankment to deposit him on the motorway. That takes real strength. And if Lang was one of the victims—'

'That's yet to be established — ditto Breidon,' Bradley interrupted at ninety decibels.

'Okay,' Rowan conceded. 'But we *do* know that Capstick was murdered by the same person who ran down Damian. And witness statements, the severity of his injuries *and* the fact that he was chucked over his balcony all add up to the fact that whoever killed Stickman was wicked-strong and willing to use brute physical force.'

Warman was staring at her, one finely plucked eyebrow raised. 'Do you have someone in mind, Cassie?'

Rowan hesitated. It seemed a betrayal, knowing all that he'd done for the community. But she'd accepted overnight that her empathy with the man had blunted her objectivity and, taking a breath, she said loudly and firmly, 'Jim North.'

She noticed a few wrinkled brows around the room.

'I looked into Marie Elliott — mother of Jim and Ben North,' Rowan explained for those who hadn't kept up to date with developments. 'She and her husband divorced when both boys were under the age of ten and Marie was reported to social services multiple times. Drug use in front of the children; neglect; left abandoned for days without food. It seemed to escalate after Jim enlisted and left the household — Ben was taken into care twice. And Jim admitted that he felt guilty he didn't do more to help his younger brother — also that he came back to make amends for his brother's death.'

'But he seems to have channelled his regret in a positive direction,' Warman said.

Rowan gave a brief shake of her head. 'The way he was talking last night — he seemed to think the killings were a good thing. He was a soldier, he has martial-arts skills, and he manages an entire building site — he must have plenty of access to white vans. Plus the surge in deaths began three years ago, not long after North's return.'

DI Bradley looked ready to interrupt again, but she pushed on. 'Also, the staff Mrs Elliott saw in the attacker's hand could be a "bo" — a fighting stick used in martial arts, which ties in well with the pathologist's prelim findings that Capstick was beaten with a cylindrical object.'

Warman nodded, following her arguments. 'All right. But Capstick had plenty of enemies, including the Langs. And surely anyone who uses the hub would have access to one of these sticks? The volunteers, crafters, the women's groups — who's to say that a woman didn't take one of these sticks and pass it to someone else?'

Rowan couldn't argue with the logic. But there was that niggling feeling — and God help her, it was a feeling, rather than a fact — that the hooded figure she'd seen harrying Lukas Novak had been Jim North.

'Anything else?' Warman said.

Rowan dithered; she had no proof. 'No,' she said reluctantly. 'Nothing concrete.'

'Very well. I suggest you check on the status of any weapons used at the hub — if Mr Jessop is willing to allow it — and report back later.' She switched her attention to encompass the rest of the room, dismissing Rowan. 'Canvassing of Hartsfern Tower continues today — please pick up your task allocations before you leave.'

CHAPTER 51

It was a dull day on the estate — warm, but occasional drenching from scattered showers meant that the teams of canvassers spent the bulk of their time in an uncomfortable combination of damp sweatiness. They had arrived in vans, most of which were parked near the hub and guarded by special constables. Rowan saw Jackie Dawson at a distance a couple of times as she and her colleagues continued the soul-sucking grind from flat to flat with their list of prepared questions. They were shunned by most of the residents, half of whom felt they hadn't done enough, the other half too much in curbing the entrepreneurial activities of Stickman and his crew. A few residents in Braunswood Tower overlooking Hartsfern had smart doorbells, but they either claimed they hadn't been working on the night of Stickman's death, or outright refused to give police access.

At dusk, the temperature dropped suddenly, and the tops of the towers became wreathed in mist. As one of the key inquiry team members, Rowan was due in for the evening debriefing at five, and she made her way to the hub, dispirited and disillusioned. Through the gathering mist, she spied a familiar figure, giving one of the volunteer constables some lip.

Barrel Boy.

'Cole Varley!' she boomed. 'Get yourself home or I'll arrest you.'

The constable blinked in surprise.

'This boy has already been cautioned regarding criminal damage to police vehicles,' Rowan continued at high volume and Barrel Boy stepped away. 'If you see him hanging around here again, lock him up,' she told the volunteer. It was doubtful they would be able to follow through on that threat unless the kid got physical, but the possibility of an arrest was enough to send him back into the shadows.

Moving closer and lowering her voice, Rowan confided, 'That sod's been slashing tyres. Him and a couple of skinny pals — you might want to post a lookout on either side of the vehicles — they're sneaky little bastards.'

He nodded, and his partner moved to the offside to keep an eye out.

The hub was locked up at this hour, and there was no sign of Dawson when Rowan popped into the food co-op next door, so she zapped off a quick text.

Can we talk?

There was no reply by the time she'd reached St Anne Street station, and Dawson wasn't at the evening briefing, either. She asked around after the session, but no one had seen her. Rowan tried her mobile again. No answer.

With a growing unease, she rang Dawson's mother. 'Surely, she's with you?' Mrs Dawson said.

'I've just been at the evening debrief,' Rowan said, trying to keep her tone casual. 'Thought I'd catch her up on that.'

'What do you mean, "catch her up"?' Mrs Dawson said sharply. 'Wasn't she there?'

'Oh, she probably got delayed with the canvass,' Rowan said, hoping to reassure her.

'I suppose the interview might have held her up,' Mrs Dawson said uncertainly. 'She came home for a fifteen-minute break for lunch — hardly enough time to swallow her food, never mind digest it,' she added. 'But she definitely said she would be at the evening briefing — in fact, she said she might be late for dinner. Then she set off for the interview.'

'She did say "interview"?'

'Yes.'

'Not "chat", or "talk to"?'

'I have an excellent memory,' Mrs Dawson snapped. 'And I assure you she said "interview".'

'Okay, sorry . . . Did she seem worried or upset?'

'Oh, no, Jackie isn't a worrier — she has a very sunny disposition.' Mrs Dawson stopped, suddenly understanding the implications of the question. 'Should I be worried?'

'No, of course not. Like I said — she probably got sucked in to do a few extra hours on the canvass,' Rowan said. 'Drop me a line if she gets in touch.'

She tried Jessop's mobile, but it went to answerphone. She left a message then, after a moment's hesitation, rang Jim North and asked him if he'd seen Dawson.

'I've been on site at the building works all day. Why d'you ask?' He sounded concerned.

'She said she was going to interview someone. Would you have any idea who she meant?'

'Sorry, no.'

'She didn't mention a name?'

'I just said — no.' He was instantly prickly again, and she wished she'd spoken to him in person so she could read his face.

'Can you try her number?'

'Wh—' Whatever he was about to say, he swallowed it. 'Uh, all right — hang on.' The line went quiet for a few moments then he said, 'It went to voicemail.'

Rowan hung up and went to see Warman.

'The concept of a line manager seems to have escaped you, Cassie,' Warman said as she poked her head around the door. 'Talk to DI Bradley—'

'It's Jackie Dawson, boss,' she cut in. 'Nobody's seen her since this afternoon. She told her mother she was going to interview someone, hasn't been seen since, and she isn't answering my texts or calls. I'm really worried.'

'Is there something more to this, Cassie?' Warman asked. 'Was she on to something?'

Rowan felt her shoulders slump. If she wanted Warman to take her seriously, she needed to be straight with her, but that meant exposing the fact that Dawson had shared confidential intelligence about the investigation.

'Cassie?'

Rowan blew out a long breath. 'The thing is, boss, I had words with her about being too open about the ongoing investigation.'

'I see.' Warman sounded grim.

'Now I'm worried I was too hard on her, and—'

'Look, if she's taken offence at a little friendly advice—'

'I don't think it's that, ma'am. I think she's gone too much the other way, kept something close she should've shared.'

She pretended not to notice the sardonic look on Warman's face. 'Surely she wouldn't be foolish enough to conduct a private investigation?'

'I don't know,' Rowan said helplessly, 'But it's not like her to be out of contact with her mother and . . .'

Warman didn't comment and in the continuing silence Rowan guessed that she was working through her options. Finally, she lifted the landline phone from the cradle and put in a call, hanging up after a few curt questions.

'Her radio's last location is the food co-op at Fernleigh's shopping parade,' Warman said. 'It's switched off, now.'

'What about her personal mobile — can we ping it?' Rowan asked.

'She might consider that an intrusion of privacy,' Warman said doubtfully. Her hand was still on the phone receiver and her index finger tapped it restlessly. 'I'll get a message out to the canvassers doing the late stint. If she isn't with them, well, then I'll see about locating her mobile phone.'

'Thanks, boss. I'm going to head over to Fernleigh.'

'All right. But report anything suspicious — and be careful.'

Finch was still at his computer. He glanced up when she came in. 'No luck?' He would have heard her conversation with Dawson's mother.

She shook her head, texting her brother to let him know she'd been delayed and to order food in, but he replied seconds later to say he was going to a ju-jitsu session and wouldn't be home till around eight.

Finch was packing up as she ended the call.

'You heading home?' he asked.

'No, Finch,' she said, astonished that she had to say it at all. 'I'm going to look for Jackie. I could use some help, if you're up for it?'

'I'd like to, but . . .'

'A colleague is *missing*, Finch.'

'Not officially,' he said. 'Or we'd've had a shout to muster at Fernleigh.'

'Well, that's cold.'

He flushed. 'Look, if you need someone to coordinate comms at the office later, I—I can come back in.' He faltered, perhaps seeing the disbelief in her expression.

'What's going on with you, Finch?' she demanded. 'You were on the original team. It was *your* intel that brought Craig Breidon into the picture. Why're you sitting in the office shuffling paper, doing shit detail you could have delegated to just about anyone else?'

'It's all about teamwork, isn't it?' he said defensively. 'Working to our strengths.'

'Nah, I'm not buying that,' she said. 'You haven't set foot on Fernleigh since day one.'

His jaw tightened. 'You don't know what it's like.'

'Don't try that with me! You've seen where I grew up — it's not exactly country lanes and vicar's tea parties round our way. You need to decide, mate. What d'you want to be — a detective or office dogsbody?'

Driving to Fernleigh, Rowan fumed. How could Finch opt to sit on his arse squinting at a computer screen rather than use his contacts on the estate — do real police work? Her thoughts strayed to North's pronouncement that the killer on Fernleigh must be afraid, even desperate. She laughed softly. 'You're suspecting everyone, now, Cassie.'

She arrived a bit early for the evening opening of the hub and it was still locked up, and when she checked out the food co-op, the volunteers on duty told her that North had already been in.

'Jackie used her radio in here — d'you know why?' she asked.

'Ugh, that nasty gobshite, Cole Varley, was in causing trouble. One of your lot looking after the bizzie buses come over to move him on.'

Rowan heard a metallic rattling and stepped outside to find Jim North slamming the flat of his hand against the roller shutters of the community hub.

'It's locked, Jim,' she said.

'I can see that,' he said without turning around. 'But Gareth's usually in early to set up. Goes in the back way.'

By now, it was fully dark, and the fog was thickening. Rowan peered through the small gaps in the grating to the shop's interior. 'No lights,' she said. 'Leave it alone.'

He ignored her, disappearing into the fog at the end of the block. She was about to follow when her work mobile rang. It was Warman.

'Jackie isn't with the house-to-house teams,' she said. 'I authorized a ping on her mobile; it's switched off.'

Feeling sick, Rowan said, 'Do we know where it was used last?'

'Best they can do is Speke Boulevard, at three-oh-seven this afternoon.'

'No help at all then.'

'I'm afraid not.'

'I'm going to keep looking,' Rowan said.

'Understood. I've messaged the canvassers to keep an eye out, and to ask if anyone has seen her.'

North came out of the fog. 'Locked up tight.'

Rowan started walking, hardly knowing where, and realized that North was tagging along.

She stopped and faced him. 'What d'you want, Jim?'

'To help.'

'Then clear off and let me do my job.'

'D'you know where you're going? D'you even know which way's up and which is down in this?' By now, the fog was moving in dense swirls and visibility was down to ten yards.

She stared at him. He could probably find his way around the estate with his eyes shut, but he was her chief suspect. And the more she obsessed over the hooded figure who had Lukas Novak so scared, the more she was convinced that it really could have been North.

'Gareth still isn't answering,' he said. 'He should be here by now. And I'm guessing your lot haven't been able to trace Jackie, either.'

'Stay out of this, Jim,' she warned.

'How can I? If anything's happened to Jack—' He choked on her name, then with a small shake of his head, tried again. 'Listen, the Langs are seriously pissed off. All this police activity is cramping their style. Who d'you think it was told Varley to slash your tyres? What if they decided to go after Jackie — Gareth an' all?'

'You got a plan?' she said.

'Gareth's flat. It's in Braunswood.' She frowned up at him, still undecided, and his face seemed to blur in and out of focus in the murk. 'At least it's a place to start,' he added, sounding defensive.

Rowan debated: he was going to stick to her like glue anyway, why not use his knowledge?

'Okay,' she said. 'But you do *not* interfere when we get there.'

316

He didn't answer — he was already moving, and she followed, already regretting her decision.

The roadways were only delineated by the halos of white, shining dimly from the lamps overhead. One in every three seemed to be working, the rest no doubt had been shot out with air rifles by competing drugs gangs, but North found his way with no hesitation, and, a few minutes later, Rowan sensed a massive presence up ahead. Coming closer, she saw pale squares of light struggling to penetrate the gloom. It was one of the tower blocks, but she couldn't have said which. There was no traffic on the road; most people must be doing the sensible thing and keeping indoors. In the silence, Rowan heard a faint clanging, like the sonorous toll of a bell. Its solemn tolling gave her a terrible premonition — something awful had happened to Dawson, she was sure of it.

'You hear that?' North said. Then, 'This way.'

He led her down a set of steps and across a small triangle of wet and slippery grass. The darkness intensified, and she realized he'd taken her into a narrow underpass. She tensed, ready to defend herself.

'Watch out, there's a step immediately you come out,' he said.

The space opened up, and she guessed that they'd come through a shortcut to the courtyard of the two facing tower blocks.

The fog currents spiralled around them and Rowan looked up towards the insistent clanging sound. Was it the fog, or had the bells been muffled? Didn't they only muffle church bells for funerals?

She shivered.

All around her she heard the faint murmur of voices. Doors opening and closing, and over all of it the persistent tolling of the bell.

CHAPTER 52

North had walked a little further into the courtyard for a better line of sight but when Rowan abandoned her survey of the building, he'd disappeared.

'Jim?'

All she saw was grey vapour, the previous day's drizzle fast condensing as freezing fog. A dark shadow blasted out of the greyness — North! His eyes fierce, intense. She scarcely had time to register fear before he hit her, and she was falling.

At the same instant, a clatter and a second, dull *clump*!

She rolled and bounced to her feet, ready to defend herself, but North got up slowly, slapping grit from his clothing.

'You okay?' he said, nodding towards two items on the ground where she'd just been standing — a smashed phone and a leather boot. She dropped her stance, feeling a little foolish: North had saved her.

'I'm fine,' she said, peering into the confusing blur of light and dark caused by the constant eddies of fog and the few intact lamplights. Speaking into her phone, she identified herself by her call sign. 'Falling objects from one of the upper floors on—' she checked the name on the front of the tower — 'Hartsfern. All okay up there?'

The answer came back a second later; it was the newly-assigned detective sergeant. 'Message received. We've finished house-to-house on the upper floors. We're on the third now. Anyone injured?'

'Negative. Need someone to keep an eye on the fallen items — might need CSU to collect.'

'Acknowledge. On way.'

He signed off and was at her side moments later.

Rowan had retreated to the relative safety of the building's overhang and he followed her example as she indicated the fallen items nearby. 'Can you get someone to keep an eye on that and organize a pickup, Sarge?'

'Bloody kids,' he growled. 'You still looking for the missing PCSO?'

She nodded. The clangour continued. 'I'm gonna find out what's making that noise.'

'Okay,' he said. 'Shout if you need assistance.'

She headed up the concrete fire escape, stopping at each landing to listen. The sound got louder on each floor. North was ahead of her; she could hear his footsteps echoing up the stairs.

'North, wait!' she commanded, but he didn't even pause.

He would know the layout of the blocks, so she gave up on listening for the clang of the bell and concentrated on catching up with him.

On the eighth floor, she heard a door slam against the concrete of the stairwell. Seconds later, the splinter of wood. He'd forced his way into one of the flats.

'Bloody hell!'

She sprinted to the landing, deployed her Casco baton and rushed through the shattered door into the flat.

'Police!' she yelled.

No response. The door on the right of the hallway was swinging to. She stopped it with her fingertips, then kicked it hard with her foot before stepping inside. Fog was billowing into the room through the open sliding doors onto the balcony; North was silhouetted against the lights in the courtyard.

'It's Gareth,' he said. 'He's been hanged.'

'Out,' she said. 'This is a crime scene, Jim.'

He ignored her, sidestepping as she reached for him, moving to the small kitchen.

'Jim!'

She followed him, reaching for his arm, but he batted her away easily. In the hall now, he burst open the door to the bedroom, flicking on the light as he went, She was there a second later, blocking the doorway.

'Cassie, don't do this,' he said. She should use the baton, call for backup, but the redness around his eyes made her hesitate. 'Please,' he said. 'If the Langs have got her . . .'

'Okay,' she said, still keeping the baton at the ready. 'I want to help, but this is a crime scene. We *have* to leave.'

'The bathroom,' he said. 'If she's . . .' He folded his arms across his chest and clamped his mouth tight shut.

'All right,' she said. 'I'll check. Do *not* move.'

He stood still while she eased the door open and slid back the shower curtain.

'Empty,' she said.

'The living room — I didn't check.'

'Jeez, Jim!'

'I swear to God, Cass — if she's in there, hurt, and I've just walked out, I'll—'

She backed away. 'I'll take a look. But you've got stay here, in the hall. Understood?'

He gave a jerky nod.

'Say it.'

'Understood — roger wilco — whatever the fuck you wanna hear. Just *do it*, will you?'

She re-entered the room cautiously. The lights were off, and she used the torch on her smartphone to search as she made her way from the threshold to the balcony, clearing each section as she went, aware that someone might be hiding inside, waiting for an opportunity to escape. She couldn't rely on what North had told her; she had to see for herself. Taking a deep breath, she let it go before stepping out and looking over the balcony rail. It was Jessop all right, the clanging was the sound of his boot heel bumping the balcony rail of the flat below.

With a sick, sinking sensation, she recognized the slubby hessian rope from the photographs of Craig Breidon's supposed suicide.

'Poor bastard,' she murmured.

Turning again to the room, she walked past a small, neat bookshelf, crammed with books on the history of the northwest, Liverpool and Lancashire. Sitting on top of the shelves were family pictures: Gareth's parents on their wedding day; his parents beaming proudly outside 'Jessop's Groceries'; Gareth and his dad hauling boxes into the shop. She stalled at an image of Gareth's dad with a fourteen-year-old Jonty in school uniform. It must have been printed on an inkjet, because the colour was slightly faded. What was Gareth's dad doing with a photo of young Jonty?

'You're killing me, Cassie!'

Rowan jumped at the sound of Jim North's voice.

'It's clear,' she called, reaching for her radio and putting in an urgent request for support. The DS said he'd sort it. She ended the communication and when she reached the hallway, North was sitting on his heels with his head in his hands.

As the first police responders made their way up the stairs, North stood. 'It's the Langs,' he said.

'No, Jim, it isn't.'

'It's got to be. You've seen those posters all over the place — they *hate* that the decent people on the estate are fighting back. Who're they gonna blame if not Jackie and Gareth?'

He turned and started striding down the hall.

'Where the hell are you going?' she demanded.

'Lang's mother,' he said. 'I'll get an answer one way or the other.'

Rowan raised her voice. 'Walk through that door, those officers will arrest you. And I'll help them.'

He stopped, glaring down at her like he might do her an injury.

'It's not the Langs,' she said again.

He flung his hands wide. 'Who then?'

'I think it's the Doppelganger.'

'No,' he said. 'No! Why would he target Gareth? He wasn't a criminal — he *helped* people — you're not making sense!'

She closed the baton and pocketed it, held up her hands. 'I know,' she said. 'I can't find any way to square the notion that Gareth would secretly be dealing in drugs. That's not the Gareth I knew. But maybe he was coerced — bullied into facilitating deals, sitting on a drugs stash?' She shrugged, out of ideas, but she saw recognition — a reluctant acceptance — in North's face.

She sucked in air, let it go; she was about to do exactly what she'd counselled Dawson against. 'There's evidence on the body that whoever killed Damian and Stickman was also responsible for Gareth's death,' she said.

His forehead creased.

'Don't ask me for details,' she warned. 'I can't tell you.'

'But it doesn't make *sense*,' he said again, his voice weak with emotion.

'I know, Jim. And there will be time later to try and make sense of it but, right now, Jackie's still missing. Do you want to help me find her?'

'Of course. I'll do anything — except walk away,' he added hastily.

'Okay. Follow me. Do *not* speak.'

She organized two constables who appeared at the flat door to stand guard until the crime scene unit arrived and told them to note her as first on the scene after the body had been discovered by Jim North.

The DS was waiting in the courtyard. He told her that they'd had orders to divert personnel from the canvass to begin a search for Jackie Dawson.

'She was last seen at the food co-op on the shopping arcade,' Rowan said. 'That might be worth a look. The hub's locked up, but—'

'We'll check that as a matter of course,' he said.

'I'm gonna keep looking,' she said, hearing the echo of what she'd said to Warman almost an hour earlier.

He eyed North curiously, but she didn't introduce them, and North followed, obediently silent, until they were out of earshot.

'Where do we start?' he said.

'Who could she have been planning to interview?' she asked.

'I swear, Cassie, *I don't know.*'

'You said that whoever was doing this was scared and desperate. Who does that bring to mind?'

He shook his head. 'Honestly? Half the people who live here.'

'It has to be someone who's hands-on in the community — I can't see a loner or an outsider caring that much.' She hoped North didn't make the connection that she had suspected him for the last few days.

They had reached the edge of the courtyard, and the roadway was a dark blur. 'Which way to the hub?' she asked. 'I want to be there when they open it.'

He turned left. In the distance, sirens wailed, and an eerie light tinted the vapour, flickering blue and red.

'What about the volunteer-helpers?' she said.

'They do what they can, but if it wasn't for Jackie and Gareth always keeping on at them, rallying them and keeping spirits up, I don't think the co-op or the hub would've lasted more than a few months.'

A crime scene van appeared out of the fog and turned into the tower blocks' access road. A second van with police escort continued on towards the hub and they stepped off the road to make way.

'Okay,' Rowan said, walking on. 'Someone who was really badly affected by the likes of Damian and Stickman.'

'Craig Breidon's mum, but she's channelled her energies into education. The Bloor family?' He shrugged, frustrated. 'There's dozens of families here who've lost a child to drug addiction and criminality in one way or another, but most of them are too terrified to even make eye contact.' He faltered. 'What about Jonty Bloor's extended family?'

Rowan began to shake her head, then the photo in Gareth's flat flashed across her retinas. 'Why would Gareth's dad be photographed with Jonty?'

'No idea. His dad was fond of the kid, as I remember, and when Gareth set up the hub, he made sure it was wheel-chair-user friendly. Come to think of it, it was Gareth who set up the JustGiving page for Jonty's new wheelchair when he grew out of the last one.'

Rowan stopped dead. 'Wait a minute. The accident was, what — four years ago?'

'About that.'

'And Jonty's how old, now?'

'Fifteen?'

Her heart was thudding so fast, she could hear it in the tremor of her voice. 'When did Gareth's dad die?'

'I dunno. It was before I came back.'

'Shit.' She dug out her radio and put in a call, asking to be patched through to the CSIs searching Gareth's flat.

'What?' he said.

'I'm an idiot, that's what. The picture on Gareth's book-case of Jonty with his dad is all wrong — Jonty looks about fourteen, and he's standing on his own two feet.'

'That's not possible.'

'Right, on two counts,' Rowan said. 'Gareth's dad was already dead by the time Jonty was fourteen, and Jonty couldn't stand on his own by the age of eleven or twelve.'

He started to ask a question, but she raised her finger to silence him and spoke into the phone. 'Can you look out for boggart masks?'

'We've already found some,' the CSI replied. 'Six of 'em, stuffed in a cupboard in the kitchen.'

She thanked them and ended the call. 'Gareth stocked the masks in his shop,' she explained. 'Told me they were stolen when a gang of kids steamed the place. He hated those masks,' she added, almost to herself.

North nodded. 'I've heard the story. He set up the hub a few months after that.'

'Which means the photo isn't Jonty with Gareth's dad, it's a young *Gareth* with his dad,' Rowan said. 'He and Jonty as teens are the spitting image of each other.'

'You think Gareth and Jonty are half-brothers?'

'If they *are*, Gareth would've definitely had a personal grievance against Damian.'

'Yes, but—'

'When I asked you who would do the horrible things that were done to Stickman, you said, someone who's scared. D'you know anyone more scared than Gareth Jessop?'

He tilted his head, still unconvinced.

'He lost his livelihood, his place in the community — and he felt he'd failed his father. He told me that himself.'

She remembered Jessop at Birkenshore library, wrangling the rolling crate single-handedly. 'And he's stronger than he looks.'

North nodded, hesitant. He seemed to be turning something over in his mind.

'What're you thinking?' Rowan asked.

'I only saw Gareth lose it once,' he said. 'It was the first night Jonty came to the hub — he'd been in rehab for a long while and was a bit tentative getting out and about in his wheelchair. Some of the local scalls had gathered around the arcade, jeering and intimidating the kids. Ben had just died, and I was home on compassionate leave, came to show support, you know.

'When Gareth saw them harassing Jonty, he grabbed a knife and went for them.' He paused, gave his head a brief shake, as if he couldn't believe what he was seeing in his mind's eye. 'I honestly think he would've have killed someone if I hadn't got there first — and he didn't give it up easy.'

'Gareth wasn't *targeted* by the Doppelganger,' she said. 'Gareth *was* the Doppelganger.' She had a sudden misgiving. 'Except—'

'What?' North asked.

'When Gareth went to Birkenshore to pick up books for the hub, he drove a Volvo — but Damian was run down by a van.'

'His dad had one,' North said. 'A dark blue Ford Transit.'

Rowan had thought she was as cold as she could possibly get, but she felt a chill run up her spine, and the back of her neck rose in goosebumps.

'Did Gareth's dad have a lock-up?' she demanded.

He frowned. 'Yeah — he wouldn't leave the van on the estate overnight, so when they restocked the shop, Gareth would follow him in the Volvo, drive his dad back.'

'Where?'

'Over Speke way.'

'Where *exactly*?'

'I'm *thinking*.' He brought his hand up to scratch his brow and his fingers were shaking. 'Shit — I went there once, and I can't—'

'Was it on a housing estate, light industrial—?'

'Shops! Behind a row of shops. Ten lock-ups. Red doors . . . I think they had red doors.'

'Okay,' she said. 'We'll take your car. You can drive us to the general area; it might come back to you as you drive.'

Sprinting, blindly following North who seemed to have the homing instinct of a bird in flight, Rowan called the comms unit, asking them to check the location of a lock-up in Speke owned by Gareth Jessop.

'Or Huw,' North added. 'That was his dad's name.'

North had parked opposite the parade of shops, but they paused only long enough to check that they hadn't found Dawson inside the hub.

They had the address in under ten minutes, but it took another twenty to find the lock-up. Three wrong turns, confusion caused by the fog and new retail and housing developments, which had changed the road layout sending them in circles. But finally they arrived, driving over pot-holed and frost-rent tarmac.

North opened the boot of his SUV and snatched up a torch and a crowbar. Rowan buzzed Warman for permission to break into Gareth Jessop's lock-up, which had been identified — by Finch, as it happened — as the second from the right.

The roll-up door gave with a groan of metal.

The walls either side were lined with shelving — mostly empty — but the back wall housed a cabinet with a locked roller-door. The rest of the space was taken up by a white Ford Transit panel van.

North jemmied the doors. He staggered back, the crowbar dropping from his hand with a clang.

Looking past him, Rowan saw a sleeping bag, the toggle pulled tight at the top. Someone was inside it. She climbed into the van. The top of the sleeping bag was sticky and reeked of blood.

Oh, jeez . . . She gently released the toggle tie, revealing a tangle of sleek black hair. North gave a choked gasp, and Rowan carefully widened the opening and lowered the gathered fabric. It was Dawson.

North shone the torch beam inside, then wildly away, as if he couldn't bear to look at her.

Rowan's heart thudded hard and slow, as if time itself was coming to a halt.

'Focus the beam on her face,' she said.

'What? No!'

'Jim, do it! I think — I think I saw something.'

Wiping his eyes with one hand, he turned the beam on Dawson's stricken face.

Her skin was greyish and she was cold as stone. They watched for two, three seconds. Nothing.

Then . . .

Rowan gasped. 'You see that?'

He took a step closer.

Faintly, mingling with the swirling currents of fog, a thin stream of condensate.

North gasped. 'She's breathing!'

CHAPTER 53

Two days later

DCI Warman stood to address the meeting.

'I've had news from the hospital. Jackie is still in a coma, but the brain swelling has gone down, her vital signs are good, and they are cautiously optimistic.'

A collective sigh of relief went around the room, and Rowan experienced a surge of emotion. She clamped down on it, knowing that some would be looking to her for a reaction.

'Her doctors think the sleeping bag may have saved her — at the temperatures we had on Tuesday night, there was a danger of hypothermia. Well done, Cassie, for finding her so quickly.'

'I had help there, ma'am.'

'Quite right,' Warman said. 'And I want to commend you all for continuing in such a professional manner under such stressful circumstances.'

Her reserves of warmth and praise apparently exhausted, she switched to her usual hawk-like sharpness.

'In the last twenty-four hours, a lot of evidence has been gathered, but we still have a great deal of work to do,' she said. 'Cassie, I understand that Mrs Bloor confirmed your suspicions about Jonty's parentage?'

'Yes, ma'am,' Rowan said. 'It seems she'd had an affair with Jessop's dad. His wife was still alive back then, as was Mrs Bloor's husband. Neither wanted to break up their marriages, so Jonty was passed off as Bloor's son. She says that Huw Jessop helped with expenses — groceries and the like, through the shop — especially after Mr Bloor died, and Gareth carried on for as long as the shop stayed open. She's convinced that Gareth had guessed Jonty was his half-brother — although they never talked about it.'

* * *

Warman called on Ian Chan next. He was seated at the front, and now he stood to face the gathering. 'We've got physical evidence of Damian's murder inside and outside Jessop's van: fibres, traces of tissue and blood. The van paint is a match to the flakes we found on Damian as well. Wheel-width on a trolley cage we found at the community hub match the tracks we found on the motorway embankment. We're checking it for DNA — this could be how he got Damian from his van to the edge of the M62.'

Rowan wondered queasily if it was the same trolley Gareth had brought to move books from Birkenshore library.

'There's no tread on the wheels, so nothing to match in that respect. But we could match soil samples from the wheels and bearings to the embankment, if you need it?'

'You found evidence relating to Thomas Capstick as well as two of the deaths we hadn't finished reviewing,' Warman prompted, clearly unwilling to commit to further expense unless she had to.

'Yep.' Chan clicked quickly through a series of images as he spoke. 'Jessop *did* use one of the martial-arts staffs in the attack on Stickman — we got Capstick's DNA in the wood fibres, as well as traces of concrete from around his doorframe and crud from inside his flat. Jessop had done a clean-up, but we got Stickman's blood in the eyelets and seams of his boots, as well minute traces in the boot treads.'

He switched to a new file, clearly taken inside Jessop's lock-up. 'A search of the locked cabinet in Jessop's lock-up yielded drugs — possibly used to control the victims — also details used in making the mannequins: notebooks containing sketches of clothing, tattoos, earrings and so on. We're currently examining actual jewellery, which might have been taken as trophies from the victims. There's a whole load of photos in the lock-up and on his phone.' He glanced over to Rowan. 'The phone that nearly brained you was his, Cassie. Images on the phone include surveillance pictures of Craig Breidon, Justin Lang, Thomas Capstick and Damian Novak.' He paused. 'And of the murder scenes — but we'll skip those.'

'Questions?' Warman asked.

'Why wasn't Jessop's van flagged in the DVLA search?'

'As I said earlier, it was a DIY job,' Chan said. 'He didn't notify the DVLA about the colour change.'

'But we *knew* the original base coat was blue.'

Finch shifted uncomfortably in his seat. 'We were focused on a white van,' he mumbled.

There were muttered exclamations of disbelief, which Warman cut across. 'It's easy to criticize with the privileged view of hindsight,' she said. 'As I said before, we've all been working under pressure, *and* with limited numbers until the last few days. Anything further?' she added, firmly moving them on.

'We know that Jessop made the effigies and murdered Breidon, Stickman, Lang and Damian,' Rowan said. 'But who killed Jessop?'

'He was hung from his own rope,' someone chirped up. 'That's gotta be personal.'

'As personal as it gets,' Chan agreed. 'We pulled an audio message from Jessop's phone.' He glanced to Warman. 'D'you want the summary or—?'

'Just play it,' Warman said, irritated.

Chan waited while the murmur of conversation swelled and then died away.

It was a confession, a suicide note. All four murders, and the attack on Jackie Dawson. Ending with a sobbing apology and a plea for forgiveness from her mother.

CHAPTER 54

The meeting wrapped up and Rowan returned to her desk in the CID room, where she was still working on a report.

Warman came to find her thirty minutes later, standing in the doorway as if she needed an invitation.

Rowan's heart dropped, and the room seemed to darken. 'Jackie?' she said.

Warman nodded and with a rare smile that brought the light and air back into the room, said, 'She's conscious.'

Rowan raked her fingers through her hair. 'Oh, Jeez, I thought—'

'Oh, no . . . I'm so sorry,' Warman said, stricken. 'I — they say she's doing well.'

A cheer went up from the few people at the desks.

'I came to tell you she wants to talk to you,' Warman said.

Rowan was out of her chair and through the door in a second.

Jim North came out of the lift as she stood waiting to go up to the ward. 'Have you seen her?' she asked.

'They won't let me in. But I thought if I hang around, maybe—'

'She's awake, Jim,' Rowan said.

Tears sprang to his eyes. 'Is she — I mean, will she be—?'

'They think she's going to be fine. Look, why don't you hang around — I'll meet you for coffee after. I can tell you a bit more after I've had a chat with her.'

Dawson was sitting up in bed. She'd been moved from Intensive Care to a high-dependency unit, and she looked a little groggy. The back of her head was dressed and some of her lovely hair had been cut away.

She smiled at Rowan and patted her mother's hand. It must have been a signal, because Mrs Dawson left them with a tactful remark about needing fresh air. She squeezed Rowan's arm as she went past.

Rowan sat and took Dawson's hand.

'Mum told me what you did — you and Jim,' Dawson said. 'I'm sorry I let you down.'

'What d'you mean, you daft bint?' Rowan demanded. 'You practically solved the case. You didn't have to do it by getting your head bashed in, but—'

'Don't,' Dawson said with a weak laugh. 'Mum's already said she hopes it's knocked some sense into me.' She fell silent, frowning. 'I know the DCI will have given you a whole list of questions, but will you humour me for a minute — tell me where we're up to?'

Warman had indeed given her very specific instructions, and Rowan shook her head, smiling. It had taken her months to begin to understand how their boss's mind worked, but Dawson had had the measure of her in fifteen minutes.

'Like I said. Case solved.'

'Gimme a *break*, Cass . . .'

'All right — just keep that heart monitor below ninety.'

She gave Dawson some of the highlights and her friend rested against the pillows and closed her eyes with a sigh. After a few minutes, Rowan thought she'd drifted off.

'I discussed Damian's prison recall with Gareth,' Jackie said out of the silence. 'I didn't have any inside knowledge, or anything. But I was so pissed off with the way the lad was acting up, I said I wouldn't be surprised if he was recalled, and told him I had a good mind to put in a complaint to make sure he was. God, I wish I'd kept my mouth shut.' Tears sprang to her eyes. 'I think I started all this.'

'No, Jackie. No,' Rowan said. 'Gareth Jessop had been heading down this road for a long while — he murdered Craig Breidon a year ago.'

'Oh, is that definite now?'

Rowan nodded. 'We got a match to the rope Gareth used on himself, and there's other evidential stuff.' She didn't mention that Dawson's former friend had taken pictures on the stairwell as Craig died — she wasn't strong enough for that, yet.

Jackie wiped the tears from her face. 'Poor Craig — he tried so hard.'

'Gareth's flat overlooks Stickman's, and we know he was watching the comings and goings — we found photos on his phone and printouts in the lock-up going back nearly four years.'

One of the questions Warman wanted answered was why Dawson had been found at the lock-up. 'Did he abduct you, Jackie?'

'No. I went there to poke about,' she said with a wince of embarrassment. 'But I think he suspected that I was checking up on him. He was in the hub when I took the sample of fabric. He even joked about it, said, "Don't tell me you're taking up crafting — haven't you got enough on your plate?"' She shook her head gently, but even that minute gesture seemed to cause her pain. She gasped and snatched at Rowan's hand and Rowan squeezed back.

'I should've known that would raise a red flag with him. I mean, I told him I'd never turned my hand to anything *remotely* crafty since primary school — what would I want with a piece of cotton used to make the effigies?'

'So, why *were* you at the lock-up that night?' Rowan asked.

Dawson groaned. 'It's so stupid . . . Thing is, I knew the Jessops had a van, but I hadn't seen it on the estate in years, and I kind of assumed he'd got rid of it. It never even occurred to me that the van we were looking for might be *his* van.' She flushed deeply, her creamy-white skin blotching in patches of red. 'This is the *really* stupid part. I knew the Jessops' van was dark, like a *midnight* blue, but Ian said the van we were looking for was *ocean* blue originally, and I pictured a turquoisey blue — Mediterranean seas and all that. So I didn't even . . .'

'Not your fault — we should've had images — I mean, half of these colour names are plain daft, anyway,' Rowan tried to reassure her. 'And anyway, everyone kept saying "white van".'

'Yeah, well, maybe . . .' Dawson pulled a face. 'What made me think again was he looked at me so funny when I took the fabric.'

'You mean, angry? Threatening?'

'Nothing like that.' The notion of Gareth Jessop as a threat seemed to amuse her. 'No, he looked scared — *really* frightened. And for some reason, I started wondering about the van. But I was so mortified I hadn't made the connection before—'

'You thought you'd just go and check.' Rowan sighed, smoothing a finger over her brow. 'Ah, Jackie . . .'

Dawson lowered her eyes. 'I'm going to have to tell them, aren't I?'

'The best explanation of why you were there is the truth, isn't it?'

'Yeah,' Dawson said. 'I suppose.' And they sat without speaking for a few minutes.

'He didn't mean to do it, you know.'

She spoke so softly that Rowan wasn't initially sure of what she'd said. Then she made sense of the words and felt a white-hot flash of anger. 'He didn't mean to bash you over the head and abandon you in a sealed lock-up?'

'Listen — I'm not trying to excuse him.'

Rowan began to speak, but Dawson held up her hand. '*Please*, Cassie. Let me finish.'

Rowan pressed her lips together and waited.

'I realized when I got there that I wouldn't be able to take a look inside without breaking in — I suppose I thought there might be a window or something.' Her mouth twisted. 'Another rookie mistake.'

Rowan began to protest, but Jackie waved away her concern with a fluttering movement of one hand. 'Anyway, I wasn't going to force the lock. So I'm turning my car around to head back out, when he arrived in the Volvo.

'I could see he was panicked, and I would have driven out, but he'd blocked the way. I think *he* thought that I'd seen the van cos he kept saying, "Let me explain". He looked so wild, I freaked out — locked the doors and refused to roll down the windows. I didn't have my radio, so I reached for my mobile phone and . . . I guess he smashed the window. It's all a bit fuzzy after that.'

Rowan nodded. 'We found car-window glass in your hair.'

'I really think he didn't mean to hurt me. But Gareth never knew his own strength. And when he was panicked, he didn't think straight. I think whatever he used to break the window just kept going and . . .' She touched the bandages at the back of her head.

He'd used a hammer to break the glass. Forensic analysis had yielded her blood and hair, as well as traces of Stickman's blood in the wood of the handle. But Rowan wasn't about to tell Dawson that, either.

'You don't need to think about this,' Rowan said. 'You need to concentrate on getting better.'

Dawson answered that with a noncommittal, 'Hm.' Then, 'Have you seen Jim?'

Rowan smiled. 'I think he's been prowling the corridors ever since they brought you in.'

Dawson's lips parted. 'Is he here now?'

'I saw him going down to the café for a cuppa and a bite to eat.'

'D'you think — can you ask him to . . . ?'

'They'll probably have to bar the doors to keep him out now he knows you're awake.' Rowan left her smiling.

North was sitting in Costa's with his back to the wall, a frown on his face, and a sandwich sitting in front of him untouched.

'You take a bite and chew,' Rowan said. 'It's easy, once you get the hang of it.'

He glanced up at her, puzzled.

'You look like you haven't eaten in days,' she said. 'I thought maybe you'd forgotten how.'

'How is she?' he said.

Apparently, he'd forgotten the art of banter, too.

'She's fine,' Rowan said. 'How about I tell you while you eat?'

Over the next five minutes he relaxed a little and even took a few mouthfuls of the sandwich. But when she'd finished giving him all the news that she was allowed to give, he became pensive again and she said, 'What?'

He shoved away the plate and took a swallow of coffee before he answered.

'You said something the other day. About Ben. That he could be another victim.'

'Jim, I'm sorry. I was angry, and I lashed out.'

'So you don't think Jessop—?'

'There's no evidence that Ben's death was anything other than an overdose,' she said.

'You'll tell me if that changes?'

'I will. I promise.'

He nodded. 'A while back, you asked me why I stay.'

Rowan waited.

'We had no choice in Afghanistan,' he said. 'When they told us we had to leave, we had to leave. But they can't kick me off of Fernleigh. I'll stay as long as I can do some good.'

Rowan eyed him askance. 'Does Jackie have anything to do with this?'

He stared at her as though she was dim. 'Jackie's a *big* factor.'

'Does she know?'

He gave a tight shake of his head.

'God.' She sighed. 'You've fought in war zones, but you're too chicken to tell her how you feel?'

'No.' He sounded offended. 'But I thought her and Gareth—'

Rowan laughed. At first it was surprise and annoyance at how stupid that sounded. But then she found she couldn't stop, and at last she had to clap her hand across her mouth to get control of herself.

'Sorry,' she said, wiping away tears. 'I haven't slept in three days, and my mate's been in Intensive Care for two of them — I might be a bit hysterical.' She took a few deep breaths, steadying herself. 'But first of all — Jackie's been batting those big brown eyes at you ever since, well, I'm guessing forever. And second of all — Gareth? Seriously, you blert? Gareth's a — I mean he *was* . . .' She lowered her voice to a whisper. 'A *serial killer.*'

She began to feel that wild laughter bubbling up in her again and stood abruptly, afraid that this time she really wouldn't be able to stop.

'Where are you going?' he asked, startled.

'Doesn't matter where I'm going, mate,' she said. '*You're* going up to that ward to demand to see your girl.'

CHAPTER 55

Monday morning, week three

Rowan was at her desk, still wading through paperwork when a knuckle drum-roll on the door frame caused her to glance up. It was Roy Wicks.

'Thought you'd wanna know — we've arrested Andy Pym for the Tetting murder.'

Rowan gave him a bored look, knowing it would goad him into saying more.

'You were wrong about the drug connection. That row you witnessed was over Tetting's fake campaign to stop the housing development. While he was supposedly campaigning to save the village, he was negotiating behind the scenes to sell out to Turner Homes — trade whole chunks of land.' He seemed to find this funny.

'Pym finds out, storms round to the manor house, calls Tetting a hypocrite in front of his wife and a police officer.' He pointed at Rowan. 'What's Tetting supposed to do? Promise Pym whatever his heart desires, that's what. He tells Pym if he keeps quiet about the development plans, Tetting will pay for a full refurb of the tennis club, add some new

340

facilities — a spa, no less — offer it to his clients as an extra, with a fifty-fifty split between the manor and Pym. He even said he'd put in a good word with the developer, get them to make Pym an offer on a portion of his land. Soft lad must've felt like he'd won the Lottery.'

'So why'd he try for a loan?' Rowan said.

Wicks shrugged. 'Claims he knew Tetting would try to screw him somewhere down the line.' He snorted. 'He was right, like.'

'Can't say it surprises me,' Rowan said, willing him to go on, divulging confidential information about the investigation, hoping that no one would call him out for it. She needed to know.

'The loan company turned Pym down — big surprise — have you seen the kip of his place?' He didn't wait for an answer. 'But he's all fired up, and pissed off, so instead of going for a mooch around the city centre, he bounces into Turner Homes' head office, demanding a meeting with the CEO about selling his land.'

A female clerical worker appeared next to him at the door, but he didn't give way. At last, she said tartly, 'Excuse me,' and squeezed past him.

He jumped as if she'd goosed him "Ey, hands off!' he yelled. 'Inappropriate touching!'

She blushed furiously, flipping him two fingers as she stalked to her desk, and he laughed. For one awful second Rowan thought the interruption had broken the spell — that Wicks was going to walk away, but he hoisted his sagging trousers over his belly and carried on.

'Course, Turner Homes didn't have a clue what he was talking about.' He chuckled. 'I wish I'd seen his face.'

There was always a vicious undertone to Wicks' laughter, and Rowan had to work hard to keep the contempt she felt for him out of her expression.

'He told you all this?'

'Nah, the boss got on to Turner Homes about the development ructions, asking if they'd had threats and that — which is when it all came out. No wonder we couldn't find Pym on the city-centre CCTV — lying toerag was shouting the odds down at Turner's head office.'

Rowan made encouraging sounds.

'So, I'm taking the lead at the interview, and I confront Pym over his shaky alibi. He folds like origami. Says he didn't tell us the truth cos he knew it would look bad. Now his story is he went straight back to his club, parked up at the shore car park, went for a walk "to clear his head".' Wicks paused for effect. 'What's the bet he met Judas Julius on his nature walk?' He shook his head, a faint smile at the corners of his mouth. 'How d'you think that little chat went down?' Then he laughed as if he'd delivered the punchline of a hilarious joke.

Rowan looked at him with a calculatedly confused look on her face. 'It's an interesting story. But is there any physical evidence to go with it?'

His face darkened. 'You know your problem, Cassie? Murder is simple, but you just have to make things complicated.'

'You're probably right, Roy. And I'd love to chat some more, but I've got to write up a report on the four murders we just solved on this "overcomplicated" inquiry.' She tilted her head as if she'd just remembered. 'Oh, sorry, Damian Novak was your case at first, wasn't he? Didn't you write him off as an accident?'

He bared his teeth, but what could he say?

She watched the purple tint spread from his collar to the roots of his hair and continued watching with immense satisfaction as he turned without saying another word and lumbered away.

The clerk peeked at Rowan over the top of her computer screen and whispered, 'Nice one, Cass.'

Rowan waited until she heard the fire door at the far end of the corridor open and shut before googling 'Birkenshore village news'.

The latest Echo headline read:

BIRKENSHORE VILLAGERS CLAIM VICTORY!

News that developers have decided not to go ahead with their plans to extend onto greenbelt land on the banks of the Mersey is being celebrated by villagers in the ancient settlement of Birkenshore. The news follows the shocking murder of Julius Tetting, a popular local businessman and manager of Birken Manor House wedding venue. A thirty-seven-year-old Birkenshore man has been arrested in connection with Mr Tetting's death.

The story was accompanied by photographs of Tetting and the manor house, but other articles featured his widow's response to the news. A BBC TV news team had interviewed her on the steps of the manor. Dignified and quiet as always, she was dressed in black and seemed shy and nervous, but, as she spoke, she pulled back her shoulders and looked straight into the camera lens.

Her statement was short, but resolute.

'I am not, and never have been, interested in striking a deal with property developers on any terms,' she said. 'Birken Manor will remain in my family, as will its historic buildings. I further make a solemn promise that for as long as I have control over the estate, the land surrounding the manor will be preserved for the good of the natural environment and the local community.'

Rowan sat back, musing. Vivienne Tetting had given her the impression from when they'd first met that she would fight to the last to keep the estate intact. So why had she agreed to the sale in the first place? Had Julius coerced her into agreeing to his plans? She'd certainly seemed to wither in his presence — what was it Sal had said? 'So self-effacing she's almost transparent.' Perhaps now that the lady of the manor had only herself to answer to, she'd decided to act according to her conscience.

Rowan felt she had established a rapport with Vivienne Tetting in the short time she'd worked on Birkenshore.

Surely, it wouldn't be taken amiss if she went to offer her condolences and respectfully congratulate her on the success of the village's campaign?

* * *

A wheelbarrow loaded with leaf fall sat to the right of Birken Manor's driveway. It was a brilliant late autumn afternoon, and the sun glinted on the mullioned windows of the house. In the barrow, laid on top of the leaf litter, a heap of rotting chrysanthemum prunings.

There was no sign of Mrs Tetting in the garden, so Rowan made her way up the steps to the front door. It stood slightly ajar, and she eased it open with her fingertips, calling a tentative hello into the echoey shadows of the entrance hall.

She heard a muffled exclamation, then, 'Do come in, Detective Rowan!'

Mrs Tetting, dressed in black, was arranging a huge, lustrous blue vase of red chrysanthemums on the half-landing of the broad oak stairwell; two large woven baskets of flaming orange and vibrant yellow blooms lay at the foot of the stairs, awaiting her attention.

'The last of the season,' she explained. 'One has to gather them before the frost finishes them off.' She added with a sigh, 'Always a sad time of year.'

'Uh, yes,' Rowan said. 'I came to offer my condolences.'

Mrs Tetting bowed her head in acknowledgement.

'You must be delighted by the campaign's success.'

'I am.' She gave Rowan one of her unexpectedly shrewd looks. 'I suppose you're wondering if I betrayed the trust of the village campaigners?'

'Oh, no, Vivienne, I—'

'Why not?' she demanded sharply. 'I should have, if I were you.'

Rowan opened her mouth, closed it and tugged her ear, offering a rueful smile. 'All right. It did occur to me.'

Mrs Tetting shook her head, frowning. 'I assure you, I was completely in the dark about Julius's plans to sell the land,' she said, fussily trimming and primping the flowers as she spoke. 'Oh, this won't do . . .' She gazed severely at the arrangement. 'Would you mind awfully bringing me the trug of yellow flowers?'

The flat-bottomed basket was shaped like a Cambridge punt. Woven from wide, straplike leaves, it had a tall, arched handle and was stacked with enough chrysanths to stock a flower shop. Rowan carried the basket up to the landing and Mrs Tetting immediately seized a spray, burbling while she continued cutting the stems with a pair of shears, which looked somewhere between small hedge-trimmers and large secateurs.

Placing the basket on the floorboards, Rowan found a spot in the corner between the table and the banister.

'I've always been rather torn about chrysanthemums,' Mrs Tetting said. 'I detest the scent, but one forgives them for their vibrant colour at a time of year when fresh garden flowers are so hard to come by.'

The odour was strong, but Rowan's nose prickled with an underlying scent of something sharper.

'In Europe, they're traditionally given at times of mourning,' she went on. Then, with a nervous smile, 'But you're not here to discuss flower arrangements, and I've been evasive.' She picked up another spray of the yellow blooms and trimmed them thoughtfully.

Rowan leaned back against the banister while the lady of the manor composed her thoughts.

'Mr Turner — the developer — approached me after Julius's death, wanting to cement the deal. It was a lot of money, but of course I refused.' Her mouth twisted into a disdainful smile. 'He misunderstood —apologized for the intrusion and suggested that we might speak again after the funeral. I told him I shall never, never sell.' Her hands trembled as she placed the new spray of flowers in amongst the blood-red blooms. 'I have my family heritage as well as my son's inheritance to consider.'

Rowan had the strong impression that she was talking about the Hockenhulls and not the Tettings.

'And what is mere money, compared with this?' She glanced around her.

The musty smell of the chrysanthemums was becoming too much for Rowan, and she snuffed air through her nose. On her first visit to the manor, the predominant smell in the hallway had been beeswax polish and lilies, she remembered. But now, the sharp reek she'd noticed at the foot of the stairs returned with greater force and, suddenly, she knew what it was. Bleach. It rose up from the hallway three metres below them.

The day of Tetting's murder, she'd noticed a metallic tang at the back of her throat when she'd called at the manor house. She'd put it down to the fog at the time, but now she wondered if it had been the copper-pennies taste of blood. The hall had been in darkness, too. Was that to hide a patch of blood where Mr Tetting's body had lain?

Rowan glanced down into the shadows below, then across to Vivienne Tetting's anxious face, to the wickedly sharp shears in her hand, and she knew. They both did.

Mrs Tetting drew herself up, clasping the shears, half-open in her thin, pale hands, the blades uppermost. Rowan still had her back to the banister, trapped between the table, the heavy basket, and Julius's widow.

'Will you listen to what I have to say?' The widow sounded almost plaintive.

'Of course, but you need to put down the shears,' Rowan said.

'I think not,' she said, and Rowan saw again that steely glint under the woman's delicate exterior.

Julius Tetting's widow took a breath and began to speak, slowly and clearly, as if addressing a crowd.

'I discovered Julius's plans for the estate that Monday you first came here,' she said. 'I knew there was something seriously wrong when Andy Pym drove up to the house in such a fury. That wasn't like him. I've known Andy since we

346

were playmates as children, so I was sure he'd talk to me. I went to see him that night. Oh, he tried to deny everything, of course — but he's a terrible liar — by which I mean he could never lie convincingly.' She paused, reflectively. 'I've always rather liked him for that.'

'You like that he's a bad liar?'

'The problem with good liars is you never find out until it's too late to turn back. A few more Andys in this world would make life less hazardous to negotiate,' she added with a wan smile.

Rowan had the feeling the widow was talking about her late husband.

'I told him that I knew he was lying, and he admitted everything.' She let out a long, shuddering breath. 'Julius had been secretly negotiating with Mr Turner to sell a major portion of Birken Manor's land and part of the house to Turner Homes. The Victorian section of the manor house was to be "tastefully converted" to luxury apartments, and an additional parcel of land to the east of the village would be built on. It would effectively enclose the village on three sides with new-build housing.'

Rowan eyed the shears in Mrs Tetting's hands. She might be able to make a grab for them, but the blades were perilously close to the widow's throat, and it would be risky.

'I didn't sleep at all that night.' She gazed intently at Rowan, imploring her understanding. 'And I sought legal advice the very next day. I already knew that I couldn't stop Julius selling the land. It was his — all of it — he'd never seen fit to write me in on the deeds. Richard will inherit everything — that was well established — but what would there be left to inherit? Money? A house hemmed in by an ugly modern development? The land degraded, nature despoiled?'

She gestured wildly and Rowan, caught between the heavy table and the banister, pressed herself to the rail.

'We have nine species of bat on these marshes,' Mrs Tetting went on. 'Nine! Rare birds, too — endangered birds,' she added emphatically, and Rowan had the sense that it was a well-rehearsed argument. 'Skylarks, marsh harriers — oh, and nightjars! Have you ever heard a nightjar? They hunt at dusk and dawn, and their call is the most unearthly sound . . .'

'I get it,' Rowan said. 'And I want to hear what you have to say but please, Vivienne, you need to put the shears down.'

She shook her head. 'No. I want you to understand. I couldn't stop him. There was nothing I could do if he decided to sell the land.' Her face twisted in disgust. 'He was so obsessed with money, so greedy for it, he could never have enough. But there was something I could do. I told him I'd ensure he'd lose on the deal. The events business is entirely in my name — Julius thought that was a clever tax dodge, but for me it was . . .' She seemed to struggle for the right words. 'It represented freedom. A way to assert myself, to be creative, and to provide in my small way to the wealth and well-being of Birkenshore.'

'Did he threaten to take that away? Is that why you killed him?'

The widow looked appalled. 'No! It wasn't like that.'

'All right,' Rowan soothed. 'I'm listening. Help me to understand.'

'I was standing here, arranging flowers, wondering how I might broach the subject with him, and he came bounding in, told me to stop faffing — there was a wedding party due in a few hours. He was going to walk the dogs. He treated me with such casual contempt. I was insulted, but I've become almost inured to that, and I really don't think I would have said anything, even then, except . . .' A momentary pain flickered across her smooth brow.

'Except?' Rowan repeated.

'He told me, grinning like the wolf he was, that he thought he had Turner Homes on the run.' Her eyes were bleak. 'That lie was like a knife in my back. I knew very well that meant he'd got a good deal out of them for the land — my family's land — this village's heritage.'

She was visibly shaking. 'I told him I knew he was a liar, that he had betrayed me, our son, our marriage and everyone who had campaigned for Birkenshore. I would continue to run the business, but I'd take all of the revenue from it, I'd sue him for every penny lost if damaging changes to the beauty and character of Birkenshore affected my business, and I would appeal against any and every planning application.' Her light hazel eyes burned with passion.

'He shrugged, said he wouldn't allow it. He was the sole owner; I'd find it hard to run a business with no premises.'

'I was incensed beyond reason — I told him I'd divorce him, sue for custody, claim recompense for the years of misery I'd suffered as his trophy wife, count every grubby penny he'd earned and claim half his wealth. I'd force him to sell the house — I'd rather that, than see everything my parents fought for destroyed.'

She stopped, breathless, her eyes wide with shock, it seemed, at her own temerity.

'I regretted it as soon as I said it. I was so afraid of what it might mean to me and Richard — that I turned away, began "faffing" with the flowers again. Silly, really, like a child hiding its face, thinking it won't be noticed . . .' She sighed, her narrow shoulders drooping. 'I don't know what I thought . . .'

Her hands had come down a little and the shears were tilted away from her neck.

Now! Grab her! But Rowan hesitated and Mrs Tetting's eyes flew wide.

'Suddenly, he was there! He seized my shoulder, spinning me around. I thought he was going to hit me and I — I brought my hands up to protect myself.' She repeated the action as she flinched at the memory.

'I nicked his face — I didn't mean to, I swear to you by all that is holy. But he staggered and fell backwards over . . . over . . .' She stared past Rowan, tears streaming down her face, reliving the horror of it.

'It was an accident,' Rowan said, and Mrs Tetting stared at the shears as if she couldn't recall how they got there.

Rowan closed her hand over the woman's, gently easing the blades from her grip and finally, Mrs Tetting yielded, sagging against her for support.

EPILOGUE

'Congratulations on closing your case,' Palmer said, raising his glass of wine.

Rowan clinked it with the neck of her beer bottle. They were sitting in a bar in Old Hall Street on his invitation.

'Did you get a commendation this time?'

'Actually, yes.'

'Even more cause to celebrate.' He paused. 'How is your colleague?'

Rowan smiled. 'Jackie's doing well; they're sending her home tomorrow.'

'Good,' he said, then, tilting his head. 'And how are you?'

She stopped, mid-sip, and shot him a quizzical look. 'Me? I'm fine — why wouldn't I be?'

'You've been coping with a depressed child, and you had a couple of brushes with death yourself in the course of this investigation, Cassie.'

She finished taking her swallow of beer before answering. 'I'm good. Thanks.'

'I saw that Mrs Tetting wasn't to face any charges relating to her husband's death.'

Rowan nodded. 'The inquest won't be heard till after Christmas, but if nothing new comes up in that time, I'd say she was in the clear.' Online newsfeeds had been speculating on the possibility of Mrs Tetting facing charges for the past ten days, with headlines ranging from the salacious to the sentimental, mostly at the polar opposites of Julius Tetting as a drug-dealing monster and Vivienne Tetting the delicate English rose, terribly wronged by her debauched husband.

The post-mortem results had been widely reported and discussed, so she didn't mind adding, 'There were no signs of struggle on Tetting's body — just a small nick on his cheek and a single blow to the back of his head, consistent with a fall.'

Mrs Tetting had been questioned exhaustively and had never wavered from the story she'd told Rowan that sunny autumn morning: her husband had rushed at her in a rage, and, startled, she'd brought her hands up, inadvertently cutting his face. She'd moved the body out of the house in a wheelbarrow. The evidence the CSIs had found at the scene corroborated her story, too, and the idea that the waifish Mrs Tetting might have heaved a thirteen-stone man over the staircase banister in anger had been dismissed as ludicrous. The CPS concurred with the police view: no jury would convict Vivienne on that evidence.

'All of the sympathy seems to be with Mrs Tetting,' Palmer observed.

'She's become a local hero,' Rowan agreed.

'Justifiably?' Palmer asked with his usual incisiveness.

'She says her husband wasn't violent,' Rowan said. 'But that doesn't mean he wasn't abusive — and she was afraid of him — I'm sure of that.' She considered for a few moments. 'I think she told me the truth. And honestly, Alan? I believe Vivienne Tetting will do a lot more good in her little corner of the planet than Julius would ever have done.'

Palmer looked comically askance at her. 'But the Birkenshore murder wasn't officially your case, was it?'

She chuckled. 'No, that was just me sticking my nose in, as usual.' She picked at the label of the bottle for a few moments. 'I wouldn't have thought it of Jessop,' she said.

'I mean, I've heard since that he did have a temper, but it sounds like in those instances he overreacted — the way frightened people do. But what he did to Damian and the others was so calculated — the effigies, the way he killed them — and the masks . . .'

'What's bothering you about that?'

'Well, masks are worn as disguise — obviously,' she said. 'So why would Jessop make the effigies so recognizable?'

'He wanted his victims to know they'd been targeted.'

'He wanted them to be scared, like he was scared,' she said. 'I get that — but if that's the case, why bother with the masks at all?'

Palmer frowned. 'Only Jessop could answer that — and I'm not certain that even he could have rationalized it for you.' He replaced the glass on the table and rotated it by the stem. 'There might be a clue in the mask he chose, though.'

She shot him a sceptical glance. 'A red-faced demon?'

He dipped his head. 'Classically, we think of masks as providing anonymity: the elaborate masks of the Venetian Festival; stocking masks of bank robbers; Romeo disguising himself so that he could meet with Juliet; more recently, the Guy Fawkes mask has been used by "Anonymous" activists for the dual purpose of both showing joint identity and preserving anonymity.'

'The joint identity of our victims being that they're drug-dealing criminals . . .' Rowan thought back to her conversation with the Birkenshore librarian. 'Birkenshore's folklorist told me that the boggart was a mischief-maker — a malign spirit.'

'And the mask manifests this quite vividly — it's hideous,' Palmer agreed. 'Even terrifying.'

Rowan shuddered, remembering her encounter with the effigy in the fog.

'In a sense, the mask symbolized the power of the mischief-makers to strike fear into the ordinary people living on Fernleigh,' Palmer went on. 'But strip off the mask, and you can see that the faces beneath are ordinary, human. Vulnerable, even.'

'Sending a message that they can be beaten,' Rowan murmured. Jim North had said something similar. She tried to square this calculated and subversive attack on the criminal bullies with Gareth Jessop's kindly, bumbling persona. After a moment, she sat back.

'Why are you smiling?' Palmer asked.

'*The Double*,' she said. 'Remember that chat we had?'

He nodded. 'Dostoevsky's doppelganger story.'

'I've just remembered; you told me that Golyadkin, the man who haunted himself in the story, wasn't a bad man — he was well-meaning but inept — apt to make blunders. It kind of sums up Gareth.'

Palmer didn't comment, but she saw a sadness settling on his shoulders and in the fine lines around his eyes.

'So, now you've put my mind at ease, how's it going with you?' Rowan asked, watching him as she took another swallow.

He smiled. 'Better.' For the next ten minutes, he talked about his daughter, the unsupervised visits his ex-wife had gradually been allowing, and the softening of her anger towards him.

'You deserve it,' Rowan said, when a comfortable silence fell between them at last.

He glanced up, surprised. 'Deserve what?'

'Happiness,' she said.

THE END

ACKNOWLEDGEMENTS

My thanks to all the team at Joffe Books who gave Detective Constable Cassie Rowan such a brilliant start in life, especially to Emma Grundy Haigh who was so enthusiastic in support of Rowan's first major case. Publishing Director Kate Lyall Grant has overseen Detective Rowan's second outing, and neither Cassie nor I could have hoped for a smoother transition. I am grateful for Kate's keen eye for detail, as well as her understanding of Cassie Rowan's world and the contrasts and conflicts she faces. Thanks, too, to Daniel Sellers, whose response to my brief summation of the story idea prompted a change of season, which gave me the opportunity to explore the dark and downright creepy aspects of a series of murders committed in the approach to Halloween.

THE JOFFE BOOKS STORY

We began in 2014 when Jasper agreed to publish his mum's much-rejected romance novel and it became a bestseller.

Since then we've grown into the largest independent publisher in the UK. We're extremely proud to publish some of the very best writers in the world, including Joy Ellis, Faith Martin, Caro Ramsay, Helen Forrester, Simon Brett and Robert Goddard. Everyone at Joffe Books loves reading and we never forget that it all begins with the magic of an author telling a story.

We are proud to publish talented first-time authors, as well as established writers whose books we love introducing to a new generation of readers.

We have been shortlisted for Independent Publisher of the Year at the British Book Awards three times, in 2020, 2021 and 2022, and for the Diversity and Inclusivity Award at the Independent Publishing Awards in 2022.

We built this company with your help, and we love to hear from you, so please email us about absolutely anything bookish at: feedback@joffebooks.com.

If you want to receive free books every Friday and hear about all our new releases, join our mailing list: www.joffebooks.com/contact.

And when you tell your friends about us, just remember: it's pronounced Joffe as in coffee or toffee!

ALSO BY MARGARET MURPHY

DETECTIVE CASSIE ROWAN SERIES
Book 1: BEFORE HE KILLS AGAIN
Book 2: THE SCARECROW KILLER

CLARA PASCAL SERIES
Book 1: DARKNESS FALLS
Book 2: WEAVING SHADOWS

DETECTIVE JEFF RICKMAN SERIES
Book 1: SEE HER BURN
Book 2: SEE HER DIE
Book 3: DON'T SCREAM

STANDALONE NOVELS
DEAR MUM
HER HUSBAND'S KILLER
THE LOST BOY
DYING EMBERS
THE DARKEST HOURS